Also available from Alyson Books by
Julie K. Trevelyan and Scott Brassart

*The Ghost of Carmen Miranda and
Other Spooky Gay and Lesbian Tales*

Wilma loves Betty

and Other Hilarious
Gay and Lesbian Parodies

**EDITED BY JULIE K. TREVELYAN
AND SCOTT BRASSART**

los angeles | new york

© 1999 BY ALYSON PUBLICATIONS. AUTHORS RETAIN RIGHTS TO THEIR INDIVIDUAL PIECES OF WORK. ALL RIGHTS RESERVED.

MANUFACTURED IN THE UNITED STATES OF AMERICA.
COVER DESIGN BY CHRISTOPHER HARRITY.

THIS TRADE PAPERBACK ORIGINAL IS PUBLISHED BY ALYSON PUBLICATIONS, P.O. BOX 4371, LOS ANGELES, CALIFORNIA 90078-4371.
DISTRIBUTION IN THE UNITED KINGDOM BY TURNAROUND PUBLISHER SERVICES LTD., UNIT 3 OLYMPIA TRADING ESTATE, COBURG ROAD, WOOD GREEN, LONDON N22 6TZ ENGLAND.

FIRST EDITION: AUGUST 1999

99 00 01 02 03 **a** 10 9 8 7 6 5 4 3 2 1

ISBN 1-55583-499-X

LIBRARY OF CONGRESS CATALOGING-IN-PUBLICATION DATA
WILMA LOVES BETTY AND OTHER HILARIOUS GAY AND LESBIAN PARODIES / [EDITED BY JULIE K. TREVELYAN AND SCOTT BRASSART].—1ST ED.
ISBN 1-55583-499-X
1. HOMOSEXUALITY—HUMOR. 2. GAY WIT AND HUMOR. I. TREVELYAN, JULIE K. II. BRASSART, SCOTT.
PN6231.H57W55 1999
817'.54080353—DC21   99-10499 CIP

CREDITS
COVER ILLUSTRATION BY JULIANNA PARR.
"CUMIN THE BARBARIAN" BY M.S. HUNTER WAS PREVIOUSLY PUBLISHED IN *MANSCAPE 2* (FIRSTHAND LTD., FALL 1986).
"JE T'AIME, BATMAN, JE T'ADORE" BY KELLY MCQUAIN WAS PREVIOUSLY PUBLISHED IN *BEST GAY EROTICA 1997* (CLEIS PRESS, 1997).
"ROBUST RAPTURE AND POTENT PLEASURES" BY ELLEN ORLEANS IS REPRINTED FROM *THE BUTCHES OF MADISON COUNTY.* "WHO CARES IF IT'S A CHOICE?" IS REPRINTED FROM *WHO CARES IF IT'S A CHOICE?* "CRUISING" AND "A MID-AFTERNOON'S DREAM" ARE REPRINTED FROM *STILL CAN'T KEEP A STRAIGHT FACE.* ALL PUBLISHED BY LAUGH LINES PRESS, P.O. BOX 259, BALA CYNWYD, PA, 19004, (610) 668-4252, E-MAIL ROZWARREN@AOL.COM.
EXCERPTS FROM "UNCLE FRED'S EX-STRAIGHT MINISTRY" BY JACK PANTALEO WERE PREVIOUSLY PUBLISHED IN *SECOND STONE,* SEPTEMBER/OCTOBER 1994 (UNDER THE TITLE "UNCLE FRED'S MINISTRY").
"THE LORD MAY BARF," "A BOY'S OWN LIMP WRIST," "TAILS OF THE CITY," AND "RUBYFRUIT DISCOMFORT" BY THE SAINT WERE PREVIOUSLY PUBLISHED IN *MANIFEST,* JANUARY 1984.

Contents

Introduction

When I showed my friend Dan Cullinane the initial draft of this introduction, he said, "*Wilma Loves Betty* is a very funny book. You need to begin the introduction with something humorous. Otherwise, readers will either be disappointed or skip straight to the first parody." Normally, I ignore my critics. But since Dan is the director of marketing at Alyson Books, the publisher of this volume, I'll take his advice and start with a joke. (This was originally told to me by a man whose job is making balloon animals for small children.) Q: Where does dragon milk come from? A: Short-legged cows. Get it?

Now, on to the important stuff.

A parodist looks at something as it exists—art, culture, a personality—and then twists it to suit his or her expressive needs. The result is often funny, sometimes poignant, and frequently offensive. Which is why so many individuals throughout the ages have raised a ruckus whenever they or their work have been parodied.

The issue of whether the First Amendment's guarantee of free speech protects the right to parody has come before our nation's

Supreme Court on countless occasions. But only relatively recently, in 1994, did the court issue a definitive opinion. In 1989 rap artist Luther Campbell of 2 Live Crew wrote a parody of Roy Orbison and William Dees's classic rock ballad, *Pretty Woman*. Orbison croons about a pretty woman "walking down the street" that he'd "like to meet." 2 Live Crew, however, sings about a "bald-headed woman" with a "teeny-weeny Afro."

Not surprisingly, a lawsuit ensued between Acuff-Rose Music, copyright holder to the original music and lyrics, and Campbell. The Supreme Court eventually ruled that Campbell's version was a constitutionally protected parody "substituting predictable lyrics with shocking ones" to show "how bland and banal the Orbison" version is. The court further stated, "Aesthetic judgments as to whether the parody is tasteful or offensive do not even belong on the graph." (Do you hear that potential litigators? Parody is constitutionally protected. So nyah, nyah, nyah.)

Thus, the genesis for this book. For too many years gays and lesbians have been the subject of parody, so much so that the parody—the swishy faggot, the masculine dyke—has become the reality. Or at least the perception of reality for much of the world. As an example, when John Lennon and Elvis Presley died, I didn't much care. I didn't care because Lennon was a greasy-haired weirdo with a bizarre, screeching wife, and Presley was a fat guy with big hair and bad clothes. Lennon and Presley had become parodies—of themselves—and the parodies had become the reality. For me, anyway. In much the same way, a lisping Peter Lorre in *The Maltese Falcon* and a tuxedoed Marlene Dietrich in *Morocco* (or their equivalent in any number of television shows, movies, books, magazine articles, and tasteless jokes) became the world's collective vision of homosexual men and women.

My illustrious coeditor, Julie Trevelyan, and I decided it was time for us queers to fight back, to skewer a few sacred cows of our own. The 43 pieces in this collection are the side-splitting result. Contributors have lambasted television and movies, literature both high and low, religion, people, events, style, and culture.

The subject of many of the parodies we've chosen to include is obvious. The title story, "Wilma Loves Betty," for instance, rips the television cartoon, *The Flintstones*. The subject of others, such as Raymond Luczak's dead-on stylistic parody of Ernest Hemingway, titled "A Rodeo Romance," is less obvious. And some pieces, like Ellen Orleans' "A Mid-Afternoon's Dream," combine subjects—in this instance, Ricki Lake and Othello.

We were not surprised to find that writers were as willing to lambaste gay subjects as straight subjects. The Saint rips icons of queer literature in a series of faux stories. Bonnie Morris laughs at all things lesbian and musical in "The Lost Women's Music Festival Diaries." And Jeff Black lampoons writer-activist Larry Kramer. We were also not surprised to see writers, time and again, taking the "almost gay" and pushing it over the edge. Chandler, for instance, comes out. As does Xena, Warrior Princess. Not to mention Agents Mulder and Scully. And is anyone really shocked to learn that Dorian Gray was really a sleazy, self-obsessed gay-porn star nicknamed "Beelzebubblebutt"?

Julie and I hope you enjoy reading the parodies in this volume as much as we enjoyed collecting them. We would, however, like to say that the two parodies of editors we've included, "I'm Somebody; Whom Are You?" by Susie Day, and "Rejection Letter From Bedsheet Books" by Shelly Rafferty, are completely accurate—except in relation to us. We're not like that at all.

Scott Brassart
Julie K. Trevelyan
Los Angeles, August 1999

Wilma Loves Betty

by Shari J. Berman

The theme song plays, accompanied by the usual scenes—
with a few added shots of Wilma and Betty looking meaning-
fully at one another. "...When you're with the Flintstones,
have a yabba-dabba-doo time, a dabba-doo time, you'll have a
GAY old time. (short musical interlude) You'll have a GAY
old time."

Betty and Wilma meet outside in the morning in front of the
Flintmobile.

BETTY: Good morning, Wilma.
WILMA: Hi, Betty!
BAMM BAMM: Bamm, Bamm.
WILMA: Hi, Bamm Bamm. Let me see that bat. Hmm, it's a
bit large. OK, Betty, we have to drop the kids off and then we'll
have that all-important time at the mall to shop.
BETTY: Not to mention that all-important time after the mall
to... tee hee hee.

WILMA: Tee hee hee.
PEBBLES: Goo...

Wilma and Betty at the mall. In a far, dark corner is a store with two humping dinosaurs called SexToySaurUs. Wilma and Betty enter and examine the assorted prehistoric gadgets. Wilma crooks a finger suggestively and calls Betty to the dildos on the back wall.

WILMA: What do you think of this one, Betty? The Rock Hard 2000? It has 2000 bees buzzing in the attached sack to give the vibration of a lifetime.
BETTY: Hmm, what if the sack breaks?
WILMA: Ouch. Tee hee hee.
BETTY: Tee hee hee. I don't know, Wilma, some of these look awfully inflexible to me.
WILMA: Well, it's thousands of years until they invent soft plastic. I don't think I can wait that long.

Wilma looks longingly into Betty's eyes and bats her animated eyelashes.

BETTY: Me, either.
WILMA: How about this one? The Worm Turn 50. "Fifty anxious worms twisting under wrapped hypoallergenic leaves. Wash after use. Feed worm food weekly through the small replaceable cork."

Betty nods her agreement and they head for the "Ten Toys or Less" counter.

SNOOTY CLERK WITH BAD SINUSES: Will that be all for madam today?

WILMA: I think so.

SNOOTY CLERK WITH BAD SINUSES: Would you like supercharge batteries with that?

He points to small whirling animals that grab for worms, making them dance and release bio-energy.

WILMA: Yes, please.

SNOOTY CLERK WITH BAD SINUSES: And how would you like to pay for this?

Betty snuggles up to her, rubbing her amply exposed thigh against Wilma's. Wilma proffers her credit card dramatically.

WILMA and BETTY (in unison): Charge it! Tee hee hee.

BETTY: What will Fred say when he sees the bill from Sex-ToySaurUs?

WILMA: Oh, Betty, they're much more discreet than that these days.

Wilma holds up the charge slip and shows it to Betty. It says "Amusement Services."

WILMA: I'll just tell Freddie I was having his bowling ball cleaned. Tee hee hee.

BETTY: Tee hee hee.

In the Flintmobile.

BETTY: You know, Wilma, I've been thinking. These leaves look pretty dry. I think we should stop at Woolmammoth's and get some lube.

Wilma jerks the car over to the far lane and pulls up in front of the dime store.

BETTY: I'll run in and get it.
WILMA: Great. Oh, Betty, remember to get the Generock brand. We're boycotting Jonstone and Jonstone. Remember? They didn't sponsor Ellen Degranitus's coming-out episode.
BETTY: Thanks, Wilma. That almost slipped my mind.

Back at home. Betty sidles up to Wilma.

BETTY: Oh, Wilma, I've missed you, so.
WILMA: Betty, darling.

Betty gently takes Wilma's bun down. She nuzzles her neck and whispers breathily.

BETTY: Oh, Wilma, I hope Bill and Joe have drawn us anatomically correct this week.
WILMA: They must have, because... oooh, the throbbing. I want you, Betty, I want you now. Take me!

Betty unfastens the furry frock from around Wilma's neck and pulls it down to expose her dainty breasts. She takes Wilma's nipples between her teeth. Wilma moans.

BETTY: Ah, Wilma, the pebbles you've kept hidden. Is it the chill in the air from having no glass in these carved out windows, or do I... (she clears her throat) do something for you?
WILMA: Betty, Betty, sweet Betty.

Wilma works her hands up under Betty's dress and assists her in completely disrobing.

WILMA: Say it, Betty. Utter those words you've avoided all these years on prime time and then cable."

Dramatic pause.

BETTY: Go down on me, Wilma. Now!

The mounds of Wilma's orange hair, bound in a prehistoric bun for decades and now loosened bob up and down between Betty's legs.

Cut to: Betty wears the new dildo in a harness.

BETTY: How much of this lube should I put on it? Is this enough?
WILMA: Yeah, a dab'll do! Tee, hee, hee.
BETTY: Tee, hee, hee.

Wilma and Betty lie naked in one another's arms.

BETTY: Oh, Wilma, would you look at the time! I don't know where the day goes.
WILMA: I'm so happy the boys are going to pick up the kids from day care and take them to Craggy Cheese for pizza tonight.
BETTY: It gives us a few more minutes together.

Betty squeezes Wilma affectionately.

WILMA: Betty?
BETTY: Yeah?
WILMA: The boys spend so much time together.... You don't think...?
BETTY: You mean?

Wilma wiggles her eyebrows suggestively.

BETTY: Do you think?
WILMA: Oh, Betty. Tee hee hee.
BETTY: Tee hee hee.

"...When you're with the Flintstones, have a yabba-dabba-doo time, a dabba-doo time, you'll have a GAY old time. (short musical interlude) You'll have a GAY old time."

BETTY: (bleating orgasmically) "W-i-i-ilma!"

Je T'aime, Batman, Je T'adore

by Kelly McQuain

>:Rob00062

I can't hide the truth anymore. I love Batman—his furrowed brow, his chiseled jaw, his Bat emblem emblazoned atop pectorals hard as marble. I love his sculpted stomach, his running-back thighs and gymnast calves, the impressive bump of the safety cup sewn into his shorts.

These feelings grow as wild as I do—in the past year I've shot up a good six inches—the *Gotham Gazette* now dubbing me the "Teen Wonder" instead of "Boy Wonder." Why is life so confusing? I long for simpler days, when fighting the Joker, Penguin, and Riddler was enough, when each fisted blow produced an explosive *BAM!* or *POW!* I could almost see.

Yesterday, Alfred caught me preening in the mirror, trying to master a hustler's roguish come-on. He pretended to be dusting, but I could feel his eyes undressing me. Alfred's old, has only five hairs on his head, but still I got a chubber simply from being desired by a man. But I have standards. I want a superhero.

>:Rob00063

Last night in the Bat Cave, as I sat typing this computer journal, Bruce crept up so quietly I was nearly discovered. Damn his Bela Lugosi moves! I hit the exit key just as his gloved hand clamped down on my shoulder. Whirling around, I experienced familiar breathlessness upon seeing the width of his shoulders, his tapered waist. "Just finishing my French homework!" I lied, glad my mask was on so he couldn't see my eyes.

"Good," Bruce said, adjusting his cowl. "Let's patrol before it gets late. Tomorrow's a school day."

"Sure." (I wished he hadn't reminded me. At school, everyone teases me for being his ward, calling me "pretty boy" and "millionaire jailbait." I can't fight back, can't flaunt my Bat-training. Even my French teacher arches an eyebrow, his slimy mind imagining naughty scenarios Bruce puts me through each night. If only it were true!)

As Bruce revved the Batmobile, I flung my yellow cape around my shoulders. Over the past months the hem line has crept up my calves, reminding me of the frilly shoulder piece the ringmaster wore back in my circus days. My red tunic feels snug as well, and my green shorts never more skimpy. But I like how these old clothes show off the muscles thickening my boyish limbs. The only drawback is the difficulty in concealing the Bat Boners that pop up with increasing frequency, so I've taken to wearing my utility belt low on my hips, like a gunslinger's holster, like I'm ready to shoot.

Hidden hydraulics rumbled as the faux cave wall raised before us. I leapt over the Batmobile's fin, sliding into shotgun. Bruce shot me a look that said, "Ever hear of a door?" He pressed the turbos, and in a roar of flame we rocketed toward Gotham City.

Dark woods flashed by. I tried not to stare as Bruce's powerful hand gripped the gearshift. We turned off the old logging road onto the Gotham Expressway, and the familiar peaks and spires of the city loomed before us.

"Stay alert, chum," Bruce said, patting my knee.

I bit my lip. Suddenly the Bat Signal cut a golden swath through the sky. Skidding through a maze of streets, Bruce pulled up beside Police Headquarters—completely disregarding a conspicuous fire hydrant. It thrilled me how easily he took the law into his hands.

Commissioner Gordon greeted us in his office. "Working out a bit?" he asked, seizing me in a neck hold and rubbing my head.

"You'll wreck my mousse!" I cried.

The Commissioner laughed, his fingers tweaking the nape of my neck before he let go. He directed Bruce's gaze toward what appeared, to the untrained eye, an ordinary piece of mail. "From the Joker," Gordon announced. "That madcap menace broke out of Arkham Asylum again. Sent me this birthday card."

"Your birthday?" asked Bruce. "I didn't know. Robin usually keeps better track of such things." He shot me a wicked glance.

"That's just it," said the Commissioner, lighting his pipe. "My birthday was months ago."

Bruce picked up the card with a pair of Bat Tweezers. "Obviously that crazed psychopath is taunting us with clues to whatever crime he's hatching."

"Well, duh," I said.

"Don't give me any lip," Bruce glared. He studied the card. I slunk up beside him, breathing deep his intoxicating perspiration, resting my head against his hard shoulder.

"Robin. Do you mind?"

"Sorry," I said, lifting my head. I concentrated on the card.

In the Joker's messy handwriting an inscription read, *Sorry—no present! But you'll soon have a GRAND time OPENING your front page to discover what I have in STORE!* As Bruce read aloud, the madman's usual trademark—a Joker from a deck of playing cards—fell onto the desktop.

Bruce rubbed his chin. "A card within a card. Anything else?"

"Well," said Gordon. "I had the lab boys look it over. It's a Hallmark."

I cracked my knuckles, imagining the Joker's jaw. "At least he cares to send the best."

Bruce frowned. "A Hallmark. That, combined with the Joker's peculiar emphasis on the words *grand* and *opening,* can only mean one thing. He's going to rob the Hallmark card store at the brand new Gotham Shopping Plaza."

"A brilliant deduction!" cried the Commissioner. "Should I send a patrol car to check it out?"

"No," said Bruce. "The Joker's slippery—he's already struck once today; he'll let us stew awhile before hitting again."

"Your insight astounds me," croaked Gordon.

Bruce's chest swelled at the compliment. He shook hands with the Commissioner and ordered me to gather the evidence. From my utility belt I extracted a Bat Baggy. It pained me to recall the countless hours I had spent stenciling bats onto endless, ordinary Ziploc bags.

Outside in the Batmobile I asked, "Why do villains insist on sending us clues? Don't they know we'll figure them out?"

"Ah," said Bruce. "You have much to learn. Criminal minds are compelled to throw such crumbs. Sometimes I think they want to be found out, to be punished, to feel the rock-hard fist of the law pounding their flesh."

"Holy Freud," I muttered.

Bruce pushed the pedal to the floor; the Bat Speedometer

shot up several notches as we ricocheted through Crime Alley. My partner's enthusiasm fired my own, hot tremors emanating from the epicenter of my crotch. I fanned myself with my cape.

The Batmobile skidded to a halt as Bruce spotted a purse snatcher. In one savage motion he pitched himself onto the hoodlum. He was hard on crime. I loved it.

I began to rise, but froze when I noticed my Bat Chubber had created an embarrassing pup tent in my shorts. While Bruce delivered the old one-two, I pulled my aching python free. He whirled to kick the lawbreaker in the abdomen. My prick thrashed with a life of its own! As the dark knight delivered the final blow, I shot a huge wad beneath the dashboard.

Maybe Bruce would think it was…chewing gum.

I watched my partner loom over the criminal, cast in a light I had never before noticed. Always a still-waters type, he seldom showed emotion—not even Catwoman wagging her tail could get a rise out of him. This pent-up fury spent on a common hoodlum, this primal release—what did it mean? Was it a crumb he threw my way, a desperate clue I was meant to decipher?

I stuffed my limp pee-pee back in my shorts.

Bruce glanced my way. "Don't just sit there," he panted. "Throw me the Bat Cuffs."

>:Rob00064

I can't believe what I'm reduced to.

Yesterday, coming from the shower, I saw Alfred gathering our uniforms to throw in the Bat Washer, so I filched Bruce's cape and took it to my room. Shutting the door, I dropped my towel and admired myself in the armoire's mirror. I ran my hands over my nipples, down my chest, toward my crotch. How could someone not want this virgin skin, these limbs plump with young muscle? Pretty boy. Pretty bird. If Bruce had any sense, he'd lock me in a cage so only he could ravish me. Doesn't he notice the Riddler salivating as he takes me hostage, the Joker catching his breath as I bend to retrieve my Batarang? No. He's as blind as the proverbial bat.

Naked on my bed, I whipped the blue cape in the air. As it parachuted over me, I imagined Bruce's dark eyes and muscled torso swooping down—a vampire mad with blood lust. His finned gloves gouged me, his belt buckle ground my pelvis. My costume ripped as his fingers gripped my ass and his Bat Cock pierced my Bat Hole. I wanted him to need me like he needed Gotham's criminals—locked in a battle not of good or evil, but of desires rampant in us both. I wanted to be more than just the boy behind the mask.

Pulling out, Bruce whacked my face with his billy club of flesh until I cried, "Excessive force!"

"'Eat my fat worm, little bird!" he grunted. "Chew that Bat Boner!"

I did, and I liked it.

Suddenly Bruce's seed pelted the back of my throat like a hail of bullets. I gripped my own cock, a thousand Batsignals exploding as I came. Tears eddied in the eyes of my mask as Bruce nuzzled my cheek, grateful....

"Excuse me, Master Dick," said Alfred, barging in and cutting short my reverie. I bolted up, covered my crotch. "Have you seen—Excuse me, but why is Master Bruce's cape in here?" He averted his eyes from my compromising position.

"It's not what you think! I was cold! I needed a blanket!"

"'The lady doth protest too much,'" replied Alfred, shutting the door.

>:Rob00065

I paused outside of Bruce's study. Desire warmed me at the sight of my partner relaxing in his favorite chair, reading the newspaper—handsome in his smoking jacket, a silk cravat knotted at his throat. From a vial in my pocket I poured several colorless, odorless drops of liquid into the snifter of brandy I had brought for him—a concoction derived from the Bat Computer's catalog of Poison Ivy's Spanish fly recipes.

Bruce looked up as I entered the room. "Alfred thought you might enjoy a drink," I lied.

He folded his paper in half. Our fingertips brushed as he took the glass. "Thank you," he said grimly.

My pulse quickened as the brandy wetted his lips. Before he could take a full sip, the Bat Phone rang. Bruce rose, crossed to his desk, switched on the speakerphone. Commissioner Gordon's voice rattled the air: "The Joker's swiped a wrecking crane from the site of the new convention center!"

"Holy demolition," I said unenthusiastically.

Bruce's voice sank to the dramatic register of the Batman. "That's lowbrow even for him; there must be a greater scheme!" I stared at the glass in his hand, willing Bruce to take that first swallow. "Robin and I will head to the plaza to see if that madman strikes there as expected."

Hanging up, Bruce flashed the crisp stretch of pearly whites that passed for his smile. He dumped his drink in a houseplant, then flung the empty snifter into the fireplace. I wanted to scream!

"Ready for a little action, old chum?" he asked.

Anytime, anyplace, I nearly confessed.

Bruce pressed a secret button, and a bookcase slid aside to reveal the entrance to the Bat Cave. He leapt through the gloomy portal. Sliding down the Bat Pole after him made me yearn all the more. It felt bittersweet having my legs wrapped around something long and hard, but cold, just like Bruce.

On the way to Gotham Plaza I broached a delicate subject. "I think it's time I received an allowance." I wanted to update my costume with a new mask or a rakish scarf—anything to get Bruce to notice me.

His eyes narrowed, becoming more angular than usual. "You don't need an allowance," he said coldly.

"Everybody else—"

"*Everybody else* hasn't devoted their lives to battling crime," he intoned.

"It's not fair!" My voice broke like the waves in Gotham Harbor. "I know crime doesn't pay, but crime *fighting* should be worth something!"

Bruce's arm shot out, seizing my collar. "Look, mister," he growled," we've got a job to do! Financial compensation is not our motivation." He shook me like a rag doll, producing a strange stirring in my utility belt.

"At least give me a cut of the Bat Merchandising," I pleaded.

"I will not tolerate insubordination!" His spittle stung my cheeks with each word. "If you're going to behave like a child, you should wait in the car." He shoved me against my seat.

Pulling into the plaza parking lot, Bruce cut the engine and we coasted to a stop. A van, marked Clown Catering, was parked near the employee entrance. Bruce leapt out and raced toward the mall. I pressed the button for the Bat Wet Bar and snuck a cocktail as Bruce launched a Bat Rope to the roof, then scaled the building. His cape caught the wind, lifting from his shoulders. I sighed at the movement of his back, the tremor of muscle and tendon as he pulled himself over the rooftop and disappeared.

Sipping my drink, I scanned the deserted parking lot. Banners announcing grand opening sales fluttered in the breeze. Suddenly a terrific crash came from the back of the mall near the card store. Cinder blocks crumbled as a section of the wall gave way. The Joker's heinous laughter pierced the air. Through the dust came a menacing wrecking crane, driven by none other than the Clown Prince of Crime!

"Holy wanton destruction of private property!" I cried as Bruce leapt from the ruined facade. The Joker whirled the crane's iron ball through the air, shattering the wall above Bruce's head. With inhuman agility the caped crusader dodged the debris. The wrecking crane turned, thundered toward the Batmobile, the iron ball swinging back as the Joker aimed my way. I dropped my cocktail and launched a Bat Rope to the mall roof, leaping clear as the Joker smashed the Batmobile to smithereens. He whirled toward Bruce once more. "You might have a lot of balls, Batman," he taunted, "but mine's bigger!"

Bruce double-flipped into the air as the ball crashed toward him. Avoiding the blow, he grabbed onto the cable as it swung back around.

"Curses!" screamed the Joker, locking the crane controls in a head-on collision with the crumbling plaza wall. He leapt toward his getaway van.

Bruce glanced up. "Quick, Robin, throw me your Bat Rope!" The wrecking crane volleyed toward destruction.

"Maybe this is a good time to reconsider that allowance," I said woozily. Being cruel turned me on.

"The rope, Robin! The rope!"

"Is that in my job description? Do I even have a job description?"

"I'M NOT KIDDING!"

"All right, all right." I threw him my rope, and he began climbing up. "But you're probably violating child labor laws."

Bruce vaulted the building's cornice, grabbed me, and shoved me down. Blood surged toward my groin at such manhandling. "Punish me if you must," I said, hoping he'd beat my ass with his utility belt.

From below, the Joker's laughter echoed in our ears as he escaped.

"You rotten whelp!" screamed Bruce.

He shook me by the scruff of my neck. I loved it.

A terrific jolt shook us apart as the crane plowed into the plaza. The roof crumbled like cardboard; I plummeted toward doom like a wounded bird. Would Bruce clutch my lifeless body to his? Would he shed a tear? At the last second, his gloved hand seized my wrist. I dangled for life—the closest to climax I got all night.

Bruce pulled me up, held me close. Sniffing, he asked, "Have you been drinking?"

>:Rob00066

Bruce punishes me by patrolling alone—still mad that we had to bus it home. No sign of the Joker, so Bruce busies himself poring over the birthday card, searching for more clues. I go mad from neglect, frittering away hours on the Soloflex, using the Batcomputer to hack in and change my French grade. This evening I shaved my legs, deciding that if I'm going to wear those damn shorts I have to do something about this embarrassing bikini line. Dark curly hairs have begun to trickle down my inner thighs. If I'm to win Bruce over, I have to look hot.

In desperation, I sought Alfred's advice. "You've known Bruce longer than I have," I said as we cleared the dinner table. "What's the bug up his Bat Butt?"

The butler fixed me with a knowing wink. "His idiosyncrasies are getting to you, are they?" He smiled. "It's true, he's always been rather complex. Take him at any level of social intercourse: He's a man possessed of fearful strengths and endearing weaknesses; a careful strategist but impetuous risk-taker; a gregarious host yet reticent with his feelings; a bon vivant but a street brawler; a nonconformist yet a supporter of moral absolutes; an appreciator of both abstract and realistic art...."

"You're saying he's schizoid?"

"Not exactly. What were Walt Whitman's words of wisdom?" Alfred's British accent cut through the tongue twister with laser precision. "Ah, yes. 'I am vast, I contain multitudes.'"

>:Rob00067

Today while Bruce was at the Wayne Foundation, I peeked in his desk and came across an application for Andover. He's planning to ship me to boarding school! A small notebook was filled with forgeries of my signature. I cried over an ad I found addressed to the *Gotham Gazette*: *SWM seeks subordinate younger WM partner for nite-time activities....*

I mustn't lose him! I used to spend nights worrying—what if he were shot or crippled? Or sprayed with acid and disfigured like Two-Face? What if he got testicular cancer—a real possibility the way he keeps his balls knotted up. Would I still love him? Of course.

I've seen other boys develop crushes on mentor figures—coaches, teachers, Catholic priests—but our relationship penetrates deeper. If Bruce has taught me anything, it's the courage to face our darkest parts. But ever since his parents died, Bruce has locked everything up! There was no comforting stranger for him like there was for me. I must show him the way out. Now, before he sends me away.

>:Rob00068

The Bat Cave is very quiet. I study Bruce's shoulders as he hunches over his crime-analysis equipment. His head does not turn, but he knows I am here. There's still a chance.

Unfastening my cape, I throw it on the Bat Trampoline. The prospect of our joined flesh sends shivers through my body. What will happen after we touch? Will Bruce still send me away? Will he be jealous and obsessed, tortured by the memory of our union—an empty shell, drifting from one sidekick to the next, looking for the silky texture of my skin in their inadequate flesh? I pull off my gloves and kick off my shoes.

"Fascinating," Bruce says, still not turning. "The Bat Spectrograph has isolated seven different microfilaments on the card sent to the Commissioner."

I remove my tunic and drop it on the floor, catching a glimpse of myself in the polished instruments above Bruce's shoulder. Will you be regretful, maudlin—nights spent in endless self-flagellation, days spent reciting countless Hail Marys?

"Five of them are used in textile production around Gotham City."

I remove my shorts and stand naked, growing hard, waiting. I must confess my love. Say it fast, blurt it out so we can pretend we didn't hear it if the words are too painful.

"Another matches the Commissioner's wool sweater."

Finally, I remove my mask. "I love you," I whisper.

Bruce freezes. He does not turn, he does not speak.

I am doomed.

>:Rob00069

Bruce, unable to fathom the Joker's next move, has given me the cold shoulder for days. He was studying plans for a new Batmobile when I tried to engage in small talk. "So, the Joker knocked over a card store—"

"Quiet, Robin—Wait! That's it! The Joker knocked over a store of cards. And tomorrow, the Gotham Museum will display a rare collection of playing cards by Aubrey Beardsley. The other night's crime was a metaphor of his real scheme. Good work, chum."

Redeemed, I accompanied Bruce into town on the Bat Cycle. Unfortunately, I had to ride in the little sidecar. "Holy humiliation!" I fumed, but after a while, the hypnotic vibrations of the motor lulled me into the usual sexual thoughts. My thighs tensed as yet another Bat Boner popped up, my shorts stretched so tight I could make out each engorged vein.

At the museum, Bruce leapt off the Bat Cycle, whisked a Bat Rope into the air, and scaled the building. In my condition, I could barely scale fish. Still, I drew my cape around to disguise my chubber, then clambered up. Looking down, I noticed my green slipper tarnished by feces from an uncurbed dog. Faint brown footprints trailed up the side of the museum. "Holy shit!" I yelled.

Bruce flashed an icy glare. "Don't swear, Robin. It reflects poorly on our image." He made his way across the rooftop, dropping through a skylight in the east wing. I lingered, scraping my shoe.

Suddenly, a dark figure pounced from the shadows, knocking me against the wall of an access stair. Dazed, I looked up to find the Joker grinning more hideously than usual. "Ah! The Boy Wonder—*oops!*—Teen Blunder. Say, is that a Batarang in your pocket or are you happy to see me?"

My face blushed as red as my tunic.

The Joker grabbed my throat in an iron grip. "Your partner may stop my henchmen below, but you're my ticket out of here! One move and I'll break your neck!" Being insane gave him the strength of ten.

He pulled me to him, slipped his hand down the back of my shorts. "I know your desires," he whispered, "the fierce longing to tangle with Batman." He pressed a chalky finger against my ass. "But you'll never occupy his attention like I do." He ground his fist into me. "You're just not bad enough." I strained against him, thinking of Bruce. There was a wildness in the madman's probing that curled my toes.

"Ahh, my little finger puppet," cooed the Joker, slipping a digit inside me. "It's a shame I must destroy you." Any protest stuck in my throat as my Bat Boner tore at my shorts.

Suddenly Bruce burst through the access door, unconscious hoodlums slung over each arm. "Holy full house!" I cried as he threw them in a heap on the rooftop.

"Let the boy go," he scowled. Maybe Bruce did care, after all.

"One step closer and I snap his neck," warned the Joker.

"All right, take it easy," replied Bruce. He lowered his arms and his cape slid down his shoulders. Our foppish foe dragged me toward the roof's edge. "Let me get rid of Robin," the Joker prissed. "He's just baggage! It's you and I who are meant for each other." He plunged another finger in me, nearly driving me mad.

"Whoa, nelly!" I cried. I could tell the Joker was trying to distract Bruce so he could hurl a lethal round of razor-edged playing cards, but I wasn't about to free his hand. I clamped my ass cheeks harder.

His fingers floundered inside of me like a trout caught in a net. "Face it," he leered at my partner, "You don't give a damn about the kid's plight." He squeezed my throat tighter with his other arm. Oxygen deprivation intensified my rush. "So pathetic, it reminds me of a poem," chortled the Joker, clearing his throat.

"There once was a boy who was sobbin'
Cause his dick was so hard it was throbbin'
He felt sad to be slighted
For his Love, unrequited,
Wouldn't bugger the hell out of Robin!"

Suddenly Bruce's hand flashed in a streak of midnight blue. Light glinted off whirling metal as his Batarang coursed through the air, cracking hard against the Joker's elbow.

"Ack!" the clown cried, "My funny bone!" With his hand still tangled in my shorts, it was easy to wallop the Joker's face until there was nothing left but bruises and battered flesh. Bruce watched but said nothing. Perhaps it was just the sight of my ridiculous, mangled shorts, but his scowl softened, seemed to give in.

While Bruce secured the criminals for the police, I headed back to the Bat Cycle, happy to find a rusty nail had punctured the side car's front tire. Fate had dealt a hand in my favor. We left the side car behind when we rode home. I sat behind Bruce, my arms circling his waist, my weary head resting between his shoulder blades. With my ear pressed against his back, I heard the tumble of his inner workings unlocking like a safe. His cape whipped the air, surrounding me like a dark flower. I inhaled his sturdy scent, reached down and released my straining boner, resting it against the soft cloth of Bruce's shorts. As Gotham fell behind us, I worked my shaft snugly beneath his utility belt and rocked against him like a baby. If he noticed, he did not say anything. Once or twice a light sound escaped his lips—a murmur of pleasure? We turned onto the logging road, each bump offering new levels of sensation. The friction built to a fever pitch. The woods whizzed by. The cave entrance loomed before us. And like all good heroes, I came just in the nick of time.

Dedicated to Bob Kane and Donald Barthelme.

Petunia Farnsworth, First Lieutenant and Proud

by Susie Day

Hi. I'm a former lesbian. I got this way from seeing a full-page ad in *The New York Times* about how I could experience God's healing and forgiveness by giving up my homosexual ways. I said, "Thank you, ex-gay ministries!"

See, I'd already spent several self-debasing years as a lesbian activist, trying to get gays accepted into the military. I also organized demonstrations for the right of queers to be legally married. You know: March-March-March; Chant-Chant-Chant: "We're Not Cads And We're Not Slatterns; We Just Want To Register Our Silver Patterns!" That sort of thing. But deep down, I was miserable—a sure sign that homosexuality is not in God's Plan.

From time to time, some of us lesbians would get together and talk about our troubled, women-identified relationships. We'd say things like, "My lover's so overbearing, I might as well be with a *man*." Then we'd go back to the misguided "here-'n-queer" fray. But politically, we made no progress, and there was constant infighting—*more* signs that our "lifestyle" is not what our Creator intended. My soul was weary. In fact, I was probably already "postgay" by the time I saw that ad.

I opened the *Times*, took one look at that pert and pretty "Anne Paulk," all tastefully groomed and plucked, with a huge diamond wedding ring you could really scar up somebody's face with, and I thought: "I know you! You're really Hermione Entwhistle! The girl who ran off with my first lover, then stole all my credit cards! I'm gonna kill you, bitch."

But, under her photo, I read that Hermione had become a lesbian because some boy molested her when she was four. "How tragic," I thought. "But then, that's lesbianism, isn't it?" I wished something unspeakable like that had happened to me; it would explain a lot. But if Hermione was renouncing her lesbianism, why didn't she mention her thievery?

Then I remembered that Senate majority leader Trent Lott had equated homosexuality with kleptomania. It dawned on me, as an organizer, how much more difficult it must be to "come out" as kleptomaniacal than as queer. The torment of starting a movement, for instance. Getting a permit for your first-ever Klepto Pride March.

Persuading thousands of silent, shifty-eyed people in grey, unmemorable clothing to march furtively down Fifth Avenue, maybe holding up their enlarged mug shots as Pride signs. The heartbreak of having your reviewing stand stolen by klepto wanna-bes. Compassion filled my being. If Hermione could give up her twin scourges, I, too, could get a grip!

So I took that ad home and told my overbearing lover of nine years that there was a God! That He had created a God-sized hole in my heart, and that I needed to plug it. Her reaction was to blaspheme. She said, "Jesusfuckingchrist, Petunia, doesn't God think there are worse things in the world than homosexuality? What about racism? Sexism? The wholesale slaughter of unarmed civilians? What about when an HMO surgeon drops his Rolex into your intestines, and then sews you up without even noticing?"

When I answered, it was with God's words: "Silly Mavis. You worship adversity and exalt victims over ordinary working people. That's not only idolatrous, it's a vestige of '70s lesbianism. Besides, those things couldn't matter as much as homosexuality. Do you see the ex-gay ministries taking out full-page ads in the *Times* about stopping racism, sexism, and the wholesale slaughter of unarmed civilians?"

Mavis admitted that I had her there. Then God told me to finish her off. "You are *so* overbearing," I sniffed, "I might as well be with a *man*." Then I walked out the door and I bought a one-way ticket on the God-train to Heterosexualityville. Population: most people!

Ever since, my life has been full of divine healing and forgiveness! After all those joyless years of marching and chanting, I have finally accomplished the two main goals I was struggling for as a lesbian. Thanks to God, I joined the Army! Then I got legally married! (Of course, I had to marry a man, but you can't have everything.) I feel so healed! So forgiven!

And can you keep a secret? The Army has asked me to use my expertise in organizing gay marches and chants to teach specialized torture techniques at the School of the Americas.

The God-perks just keep coming! My husband Rocko and I had no problem getting a mortgage for our beautiful brownstone in a neighborhood where people wouldn't *think* of spraypainting antigay slogans on our stoop. That's a such relief. Because if they did, Rocko would probably lash out at me about my past. He's a tad overbearing.

But when my hubby gets me down, I find support from others like me in the ex-gay ministries. Women who used to be lesbians. We get together and repent of our former lives. We talk about how healed and forgiven we are. Then we have sex.

Hey, look. I'm a "former lesbian," remember? I never said I was a heterosexual.

The Dildo of Dorian Gay

by Patrick Cather

Artie is the creator of beautiful—shall we say—"things."
Since the Jeff Stryker business, he had all the work he could
possibly handle (and I do mean handle). A dildo modeled after
one's own genitalia had become de rigueur in certain A-list circles. It seems that every gay man of any consequence—actors,
models, circuit party climbers, U.S. senators—wanted one of
Artie's lifelike, but in the case of the senators not necessarily
life-size, models of their dick. Customized dildos. Plastic
pricks. Polyurethane peters.

To be sure, there are those who have found ugly meanings in
Artie's productions, but the less said about those Peckersniffs
the better. There is no such thing as a moral or immoral dildo.
Dildos are either well-made or badly made. That is all.

* * *

The studio was filled with the rich odors of ladslove and purple lilac. Henry Lord, as was his custom, layabout in the corner

smoking even though second-hand smoke was now considered rather gauche. Artie Basil, whose studio it was, told him so, but Henry was filthy rich and vulgar enough to ignore any comments for which he didn't care.

On a small pedestal in the center of Artie's studio was a full-length dildo, modeled after the actual organ of a young man of extraordinary endowment. As Artie looked at and stroked the comely form so skillfully rendered by his hands, a smile of pleasure passed across his face—as if in remembrance of things past. But that's another story completely.

"Simply scandalous. It's your best work yet, Artie. The best thingy you've ever done. Makes me want to get fucked right here and right now. Why don't you call and have a telegraph boy sent around?"

"That is so retro. There are no telegraph boys anymore, Miss Henrietta. Quit living in the past, will you? Have you no... remorse code?"

"I...I wish I'd said that."

"Don't worry. You will."

"You should have an opening. Become an exhibitionist—in a manner of speaking. The A-listers have already begun to talk about your work you know."

"How scandalous."

"Nonsense. The only thing worse than being talked about is not being talked about."

"So they say. Those of them that talk, at least."

"The obvious question must now be asked and answered. Whose bounteous cock is that?"

"I don't know that I wish to tell you that, Miss Henry. I'll only tell if...if...you...find some way to force it out of me!"

"Come! Come! You must!" ordered Henry, taking matters into his own hands.

"All right. Anyway, you're already acquainted with Lord Bunbury, the old auntie he runs around with. The young man's name is Dorian Gay. His penis is named Pat Robertson."

"You're joking. How apt. How *recherché*. How juvenile. Do boys still name their tallywackers?"

"They do when their fortune is between their thighs."

"Did you say something about *Fortune and Men's Eyes?*"

"No, turn up your hearing aid, dearie."

"Huh?"

"Never mind; you've had worse things up your ears. Anyway, Miss Henry, this is my last dildo. What with your rank and wealth, and with my talent and with friend Dorian's...endowment...we shall all suffer for what the gods have given us. Suffer terribly."

"Oooh, suffering. Is leather involved? Chain mail? A daisy chain? After all, what's a daisy chain among friends?"

"You're hopeless, Henrietta. And you don't know the meaning of the word 'friendship'."

"Nonsense," Henry said. "I choose my friends for their beauty, my acquaintances for their good character, and my enemies for their intellect. Or something like that, *n'est-ce pas?* And speaking of friends, just how did you meet this young man?"

"At seminary. How else does one meet anybody these days? We began our work that night. I felt as if I was shaping my own soul. Some strange force seemed to be guiding my hands."

"Strange force, my ass! That was horniness!"

"Do tell. At any rate, Dorian taught me—how can I put this?— the harmony of body and soul."

"To one like myself who is so world weary, that sounds awfully like a euphemism for the love that dare not speak its name. Do you? Love him, I mean."

"Oh fuck you and the epigram you wrote in on! Anyway, Dorian does treat me wretchedly at times. Plucks my soul from some butchified bouquet to wear like a green carnation upon his coat—just a bit of foppish decoration to charm his vanity."

"Vanity! Vanity! All is vanity!"

"Vanity! Vanity! Thy name is woman!"

"Well, I'd rather not get into that. Besides genius outlasts beauty and virility. You'll have the last laugh on your young friend."

"Oh? You think so, do you?" said the sculptor ominously. As if on cue, the doorbell rang. "Speaking of my young friend, I suspect he's at my door. Are you tempted to meet him?"

"The only way to be rid of a temptation is to yield to it."

"Yes. And I'm sure when you do you'll want to fly away with him to Hawaii and change his name to Dorian Lord."

"Oh for God's sake, Miss Thing. Don't be such a soap opera queen."

Artie opened the door, allowing the hunky young dandy to enter.

"You have something for me?" he asked.

"Yes, it's ready," said Basil, with some degree of largesse. "By the way, have you met my friend, Henry Lord, West Hollywood's biggest porno movie producer? He has his fingers in nearly everything. Or should I say in nearly every thingy?"

"I haven't had the pleasure," gushed Dorian with an outstretched hand as he walked toward Henry.

"It's my pleasure, I assure you," Henry declared as he caught Dorian's anticipating hand and deftly guided it toward his own aroused crotch.

They fondled each other while Artie smirked and fidgeted in high dudgeon.

"The gods have been good to you, Mr. Gay. But whatever the gods give they can quickly snatch away. Especially snatch.

Look at Jim Bakker and Jimmy Swaggart."

"I'd rather not."

"Snatch? Or Bakker and Swaggart?

"Quite. I am glad I met you, Mr. Lord. I wonder if I shall always be glad?"

"'Always.' Such a terrible expression don't you think? Almost as bad as those scary three little words."

"I love you?"

"Long-term relationship."

Artie interrupted. "Enough of this chat line chit-chat. Dorian, what do you think of the dildo?"

Dorian walked to the pedestal and picked up the sensuous model of his erect organ.

"It's beautiful, Artie. You've outdone yourself. Is my dick really that cute? I never thought so. Otherwise I'd have named it Ralph Reed."

"Now don't fall in lust with a model of your own cock, Miss Narcissus. In time, you may come to hate my representation. The real thingy will grow old and ugly, wrinkled and soft, while this dildo will stay forever young, and as erect and hardened as it is right now. That's when you'll need those touchy-feely thoughts."

"Well who fucked you and made you the whore of Babylon? Why can't it be the other way around? Why can't my dick stay hard and virile forever while this plastic tool grows old and impotent? Why? Tell me! For that I would give…anything!"

"Anything?" asked Henry, incredulously—even though he had heard it all before. "Really. Don't be so…uh…hard-on…yourself!"

"Anything. Money, my ass, a ton of crystal meth, all my Streisand CDs. Anything. I'd even sell my very soul."

"You go, girl!"

"Why can't I be forever young? Forever hung?"

"Hmm. Sounds like a good movie title to me," said Henry as he continued to fondle Dorian's privates.

Then, after Dorian dismissed his army buddies—Private Teleny and, more importantly, Private Earnest—the three new friends had a three-way. What else could they do? Their intertwined destinies were already written in the stars. Indeed! Each of them—unbeknownst to the others—had called the Psychic Friends Hotline that very day and had listened, for the first time, to an old eight-track tape of the song *Deja Vu*—again.

Later that evening, Henry reflected upon this new friendship. "I'll have a great influence over this young man. There is nothing I cannot do with him. He could be made a boy titan or a boy toy. Whatever."

Henry much preferred the latter option.

Years passed and, after much water-based lubricant over the dental dam, Henry and Dorian were at a supposedly chi-chi party. In actuality, however, it was a tawdry he/she affair—all ostrich feathers, Cupids, and cornucopia, and attended by petty, pretty people who knew the price of everything and the value of nothing (in other words, bar owners). The affair was given by a famous drag queen who was so dowdy that she reminded one of a badly bound hymnal. Or was that Tammy Faye Bakker? Whatever.

Over smart cocktails, Dorian, now an infamous porno star, and Henry, as wicked as ever, discussed the biz and, due to the ageless star's recent predilection for water sports, the whiz.

"To get back one's youth one has merely to repeat one's youthful follies," said Henry.

"Like wetting the bed?"

"I'll ignore that because of my feelings for you."

"In love, we begin by deceiving ourselves yet end up by deceiving others."

"Odd. I don't feel that."

"Well," Dorian took his friend's hand, "feel this. This represents all the sins you never had the courage to commit."

After an evening full of such drunken aphorisms and feelings up, the party came to an end.

"Au reservoir, Dorian. You've really made a place for yourself on the…map…of my heart."

"Au reservoir yourself."

Later that evening, Dorian answered a knock at the door of his smart town house. He was expecting the latest in a long series of call boys. Instead, he found Artie Basil on his threshold.

"Dorian! Old friend…." Artie was out of breath and quite upset. Quite.

"Well you bitch! *Old* indeed! Am I not as beautiful and as virile as when you first began toying with me in your studio years ago?"

"Yes, you are. And I can't believe it's just from aloe and vitamin E. Even so, you've turned evil. Why is it that a man like Lord Bunbury leaves the back room of the club whenever you enter? Why is it that so many A-list men will not invite you into their houses? I know you were once known to steal silverware in your hustling days, but there's much more to your reputation than that now. Why do even such throwback clones as the circuit party regulars tend to avoid you of late? You and your beauty? Why has everyone taken to calling you 'Beelzebubblebutt' behind your back? Answer me!"

"Beelzebubblebutt? Hmm, I can't possibly say, but I rather like it," he said as he patted himself gently on the backside. "Beelzebubblebutt. Imagine that. But enough of these silly word games. So, you want answers? I'll give you answers. You deserve that, at least, since you're largely responsible. I'll show you the very center of my being." With that, Dorian grabbed Artie and pulled him upstairs to what had once been known as the "Leather Room," but was now referred to as the "Whiz Bang Room."

After entering, Dorian pushed his former mentor toward what appeared to be a piece of sculpture on a pedestal, all covered by a heavy cloth.

"Ecce homo!" demanded Dorian as he pulled the cover off.

"Ai-e-ee!" screamed Artie. He was confronted by a very life-like model of a diseased, aged, badly shaped, syphilitic penis.

"This is the real picture of Dorian Gay! This represents my soul!" screamed Dorian. (It should be noted here that the diseased penis model, while possibly symbolic, might be construed by some to be a stereotype and, therefore, it must be understood that such a model does not represent the souls of *all* gay men.)

"That is not my work!" shouted Artie as he reached over to pick up and look beneath the infectious model.

But it was too late. Those who go beneath the surface do so at their own peril. Under the dildo was a knife, which Dorian quickly grabbed and plunged into Artie's gut. There was no longer any doubt. The dildo was constantly changing. The age lines were growing deeper, more cruel. Dorian faced the dildo as he faced the truth at last. With resignation he plunged the knife into his own heart.

An hour later—gay men always being tardy—the call boy rang the bell. Finding the door still open from Artie's earlier arrival, he let himself into the house. The young man immediately noticed an eerie luminescence coming from the dark at the top of the stairs.

"Oh wow! Glow-in-the-dark drugs! Just like the old days at

Boy Scout camp!" With only the slightest trepidation, he rushed upstairs and opened the backlit door all the way. There, on the bloodied floor, was the knife, Artie's body, and the body of an ugly, diseased old troll.

"Fuck!" screamed the call boy. But no one could hear.

So he forced himself to be calm. "Well, at least there aren't any fats or fems." That's when he saw the dildo—vibrant, life-like, beautiful, just as it had been on the day it was first admired by Dorian.

"Jeez. It's better than Stryker's."

He picked it up and promptly forgot about the nonfem, nonfat bodies on the floor as he retraced his steps downstairs. Then he proceeded to pleasure himself on the thick, creamy carpet of the parlor as he fantasized about his younger days at Boy Scout camp.

"Come into my parlor indeed!"

The next morning, after a good night's satisfied sleep, he again got off with the dildo of Dorian Gay, after which he ripped off the silverware, a VCR, and lots of tacky gold jewelry. Then, call boys being the fickle creatures they are, he left the building to go to a tea dance. Or maybe a tearoom. I forget which.

It wasn't until the Naked Male Maid service arrived the next day that the bodies were reported to the constabulary. And, of course, the naked male maid wanted an extra fee for that, not to mention the messes upstairs and in the parlor, but this is neither the time nor the place to get into a long-term labor relations problem.

A man's destiny, they say, is written in the stars. All he'll ever be is recorded there. And once written it can never be changed. Only one question remains: who does the writing?

Perhaps Dorian's people should have paid the writers more, the fluffers less. Who could know? It was all Wonderbread and Ecstasy to them anyway. To him, too. Who could know? After joining West Hollywood's life in the fast lane, Dorian had come to love himself more than anyone else, had come to think his dick was the standard by which all others should be...measured. Sad. Erect unto the end, he found out the hard way that each man kills the thing—or the thingy—he loves.

A Mid-Afternoon's Dream

by Ellen Orleans

RICKI: Welcome, everyone, to "Elizabethan Theater Week" here on *Ricki Lake*. Today's very special topic is "My Best Friend Told Me My Wife Is Cheating on Me and Now I Want to Kill Her." Let's bring our first guest on stage. Othello, come on out.

Othello comes on stage.

RICKI: Othello, you're a general, you're a hero, you have a beautiful wife—yet moments before you called the show last week you were in your bedroom, about to murder your wife. *What* is up?
OTHELLO: Ricki, my wife is a lying, impudent strumpet.
RICKI: And you were about to kill her for it.
OTHELLO: Yes, but as I approached her in our chambers, knife in hand, I chanced to look at the television—
RICKI: What an anachronism, huh?
OTHELLO: Truly. Nonetheless, I glanced at the screen and

read, "Are you a violent and jealous Shakespearean character? Call us and maybe you can be on *Ricki Lake*."

RICKI: And here you are. So, tell us, General, what makes you believe that Desdemona is cheating on you?

OTHELLO: Iago told me. And Iago is an honest man.

RICKI: An honest man? Let's see for ourselves. Iago, would you join us?

Iago comes on stage. Audience both applauds and hisses.

RICKI: Iago, isn't it true that Othello passed you over for a promotion in favor of Cassio? Aren't you getting back at him for that snub?

IAGO: I certainly am not, you foul wench!

Further audience hisses.

RICKI: Ooh, do we have a tad of unprocessed anger here? Oh! An audience member wants to speak.

AUDIENCE MEMBER: Yes, Ricki. I'm BillieRae from SLAM—that's Socialist Lesbians Allied against Men. And once again, all I see on stage are men. Men dominating the issue. Men speaking for—

RICKI: I take it you'd like to hear from Desdemona herself. Audience, shall we bring her out?

Enthusiastic applause. Desdemona walks on stage. Hoots, hollers, and wolf whistles erupt.

RICKI: Desdemona. Iago says you did it. Othello believes you did it. *Did* you do it?

DESDEMONA: Forsooth, Ricki, no!

AUDIENCE MEMBER: Desdemona, baby, you are welcome to *do it* in my bed anytime.

OTHELLO and IAGO (nearly leaping off the stage): You profane dog!

RICKI: Gentlemen, let's restrain ourselves. We have another question from the audience. Go ahead, sir.

AUDIENCE MEMBER: Othello, as one brother to another, why'd you marry a white chick? Open your eyes! There are gorgeous sisters out there, man!

RICKI: Now, now, sir. You're not actually suggesting that we have a serious discussion of a socially relevant topic such as interracial marriage, are you? Remember, everyone, keep your comments sensationalistic and shallow. After all, this *is* daytime TV.

Rabid audience applause.

RICKI: So, Othello, tell us. Beyond Iago's word, what evidence do you have that Desdemona is cheating on you?

OTHELLO: I trust Iago. He is like a brother. I need no other proof.

IAGO: Truly, I am loyal to my master Othello. I cannot let Desdemona cuckold him.

RICKI: We have a caller. Go ahead.

CALLER: Yeah. Hey, Othello. For a general, you ain't too bright. Iago is after your girl, man, and if he can't have her, he'd rather see her dead.

IAGO: A lie! An outrageous lie! I have no desire for Desdemona, only for....

RICKI: Only what, Iago?

IAGO: I...I....

RICKI: Hold it right there, Iago, because I want to introduce

James, a licensed therapist and volunteer with PFLAG.

James enters.

JAMES: Iago, clearly you are attracted to Othello and cannot control your jealousy in regard to him and Desdemona.
OTHELLO: What? You wretched cur!
JAMES: Now, Othello, honey—you have *got* to come to terms with your homosexuality.
IAGO (head in hands, breaks down and cries): Alack! I can bear it no longer. I love you, Othello!
OTHELLO (reaching out, hugging Iago): My brother! My soul! Oh, that you had told me years ago!

Sincere and touching applause from the audience.

IAGO (rising): My cursed soul be damned, I shall never again deny my love for you!
JAMES: Iago, homosexuality is nothing to be ashamed of. Many of history's great men have been gay: Alexander the Great, William Shakespeare....
IAGO (puzzled): Who's he?

Music swells in the background.

RICKI: Oops, looks like we're out of time.
DESDEMONA: Wait, Ricki! Can I get BillieRae's phone number?
RICKI: Of course. Thanks to all our guests, and be sure to join us tomorrow for "My Mother Stole My Biker Boyfriend." Good-bye, everyone!

A Rodeo Romance
(à la Ernest Hemingway)

by Raymond Luczak

It was Friday night at the Dude-A-Rude. The bar was very quiet. It was not even 5 o'clock. Nicky Adams stared out the window on Christopher Street. It was raining. It was raining so hard only the umbrellas moved. The beer tasted so good in his throat.

The front door opened. Out of the summer rain came a cowboy in a clean, white, well-lighted rhinestone outfit. He shone like a pearl against black velvet. His white boots were perfect as his teeth. He walked up to the bar and nodded his hat at the bartender.

Nicky knew the bartender well. They had an affair once years ago. He thought about the type of sex the bartender might practice now. It was hard to tell.

The cowboy took a gulp. The gulp nearly thundered in Nicky's ears. He remembered summers past in Michigan when he made love to his father's groom. It was a beautiful stable, and it had everything a valet could possibly want. Time was such a cruel enemy.

Nicky approached the cowboy. "Hi?"

"Hi." The cowboy's eyes shone like emeralds.

"Your first time here?"

The cowboy's eyes flashed like fire. "Yes, it's my first time here," he said. "How about you?"

"It's my first time here," he said. "What do you think of it here?"

"It's raining. Let's go."

All night they made love that only stallions could. It was mad, filled with a trembling fear of more pain.

It was now Saturday morning. They made love for one more furious time in the foyer. It was beautiful, far too beautiful to be put into words. They were both happy. It was something like love.

They prowled together the streets of the Village, checking out their sideburns in reflection. Their hair were perfect. They did not say much to each other. There was no need to. They were both happy. It was not until 3 o'clock that afternoon when Nicky asked, "What's your name?"

"Name's Buddy," he said. "What's yours?"

"Nicky," he said.

They shook hands. Their handshakes were strong and steady as only two Marlboro Men could give. Their palms turned moist from the knowledge they possessed of each other. The knowledge could not be had anywhere else.

"Let's fuck," Nicky said.

"Sure thing," Buddy said.

The night turned cold. Windows everywhere were covered with mist in the lower panes. The skies held the promise of a good rain. Nicky lay there, snuffing out another cigarette in the ashtray next to his bed. "Buddy?" he called out to the bathroom.

Buddy was shaving his dimpled chin. He was shaving very closely. He was shaving so that he could wake up with an un-shaven face. "What?"

"Buddy," he said. There was something unsettling in that name. "Where do you come from?"

"I come from all over," he said. He shook lather off his razor strap. He shook it gracefully over the edge of the sink. Nicky thought, violence has its own beauty. "How about you?" Buddy asked.

"I come from Michigan," said Nicky.

He stepped forward to touch Buddy's profile. It was chiseled as in stone. "You are beautiful," he said. "I love you."

"I don't know what you mean." Buddy peered closer to the mirror. "Damn!" There were a few hairs on one side of his jaw. They were less than one sixteenth of an inch high. They were an eyesore.

"I love you," Nicky said. He thought of Papa's favorite groom. He had a beautiful chest. His chest were a pair of meadows. His nipples were like the pacifiers he once suckled as a little boy. He missed being out in the woods with the groom. "Have you heard those words before?" he asked.

"Maybe," Buddy said. "They don't mean a thing, do they?"

Nicky sat on the edge of the bed, listening to Buddy flick more lather off his razor strap. He thought of those summer nights when the groom whipped him before fucking him. He was so young then. He was waiting to be mercifully whipped now.

Nicky stood up and walked to the bathroom. He put a hand on Buddy's arm. "Please whip me," he said.

"Come on now," he said. "This ain't no time for games." Buddy fixed his hat back on his perfectly moussed head and left.

Nicky stayed awake all that night wondering if Buddy was right. Rain pounded his windows as he finally fell asleep.

Nancy Drew and George Fayne

by Michael Dubson Sage

Like adolescent versions of Charlie's Angels, they zoomed around the country for 60 years, eternally 18, solving mystery after mystery, never a hair out of place. Adventure and excitement could always be found in the company of Nancy Drew and her partners in crime solving, Bess Marvin and George Fayne. But what was never revealed in those escapade-ridden pages is that George Fayne was a hard and true closeted lesbian.

How stupid did they think we were? The name alone was a dead giveaway. How many heterosexual girls described as tall, slender, and athletic with short dark hair are going to take a boy's name? Why not just come out and call her a dyke and be done with it!

The horror of it all was that Nancy, who was a whiz at recovering lost jewels, finding missing persons, and capturing criminals, knew all along. She let George come along with her for their adventures as long as George was willing to slip into obligatory heterosexuality when required—donning a dress, dancing with a boy, not drooling. And George, tragic figure that she was, went along with it—denying herself, her needs, her identity.

So that no one would suspect anything, Nancy rounded out her threesome with Bess Marvin. Bess was typical, hysterical, heterosexual pudding. Screaming, frightened, and drowning her insecurities in second and third helpings of cake and ice cream, Bess made it clear to all observers that these were just three straight girls out for a good time.

Nancy Drew was a shameless hypocrite. Operating from a number of comfortable positions of patriarchal power, Nancy's insistence on George staying in the closet was disgraceful. Nancy herself was a gorgeous blonde with a face and figure to die for. She was keen, intelligent, adventurous—a feminist ahead of her time. Leading her troupe, she refused to be discouraged as she asked questions and demanded answers. But behind her was her omniloving father, criminal lawyer Carson Drew, whose power supplemented and reinforced her own. While he encouraged his brilliant, beautiful progeny to do her own thing, she knew if she went too far, like having an openly lesbian sidekick, Carson would withdraw his economic and emotional support, and she would have to go to college or get a job. She also had Ned Nickerson, a dumb heterosexual hunk, to Ken-doll it whenever Nancy needed a presentable escort. He even had a buddy for George.

And why did George Fayne put up with this? Because George drew her love from Nancy. She loved Nancy's ability to look at a footprint in the mud and know who stole the antique table. She loved Nancy's courage as Nancy laughed and tore up yet another threatening letter before zooming off for another adventure in her roadster. She loved Nancy's high sense of right and wrong, as Nancy would risk health, life, sanity, and shiny convertible to return a missing tea service to a sweet little old lady who never did any harm to anybody. And she loved the way Nancy's skirts would swirl around her thighs and come to a gentle caressing rest against her calves. George loved Nancy so much, not only did she willingly play second fiddle to this sexy, aggressive feminist, she stayed tightly in the closet to do so.

Nancy used George's closeted, desperate love for her own selfish ends. When Nancy was tied up in the basement of a haunted house, traipsing into dark mansions, or crawling through fog-shrouded nights, George Fayne—not Carson Drew or Ned Nickerson—was there. When they went looking for mad killers on decaying ships way out in the middle of the ocean, George was there. Why? Because George loved the moments when Nancy's hand would touch her as she pulled her into a secret room. Because she loved the sweet smell of Nancy's cologne as the wind of a dark and stormy night whipped it about. Because she loved the pearly caress of Nancy's light, lilting voice when, tied up in the tower room, she screamed for help.

George risked life and limb through book after book for six decades to be with the woman she loved. She did it because she hoped that Nancy would realize that Ned was just a jock with a handsome face, and that sooner or later, Nancy would turn to her in one of their tense, mystery-racked moments and say to this slender, dark-haired, athletic womyn, "George, I really like you, more than anyone else, and I want you to sit on my face."

Posing Strap Pirates

by Michael Van Duzer

"Posing Strap Pirates" is a parody of a type of novel that, thankfully, no longer exists. In the days before Stonewall and gay rights these stories were written and circulated through a vast nocturnal underground. Writers sat at typewriters clutching their thesauruses (or other important writing instruments) and cast their heroes in schlocky rip-offs of Hollywood "B" films. Flowery, overblown language and unsubtle innuendo were the hallmarks of these novels, and sometimes they served as the only sexual outlet for men with secret lives.

Cast:

NARRATOR: The soothing voice of our collective unconscious.

TOYE BUCK: Our All-American Hero—handsome, virile, and a little dense.

MISS MARZIPAN: A classic mother figure—plain, caring, and sexually frustrated.

RAKE MATELOT: The name says it all—rugged and reeking of raw sensuality.

SABRE: Rake's right-hand man—jealous, vindictive, and a great dancer.

BILGE: Crusty mariner type—almost incomprehensible.

BEAU IDEAL: The world's greatest boyfriend—cute, loyal, and experienced.

Scene One:

The deck of a frigate traveling through the Spanish Main. The narrator sits at a piano and plays "We Sail the Ocean Blue" from *HMS Pinafore*. Toye Buck enters and stands at the railing, gazing at the horizon. He is dressed in a vaguely 18th century outfit.

NARRATOR: A merciless daystar blazed low in the cloudless sky over the good ship *Billy Budd*. The manly but sun-sensitive crew sought relief from the afternoon swelter with a below-deck siesta. Alone on the foredeck or, perhaps, the poop deck.

Toye glances at the Narrator and then quickly changes places.

NARRATOR: Toye Buck drank in the sun's dazzling rays with the desperation of a derelict downing demon rum. At 23, he was in the full flower of his manhood. Every molecule of his broad-shouldered being overflowed with irrepressible strength and the vitality of youth. Sometimes it seemed that the sheer energy of his rampant life force might burst through its confines (chord) to flood the world (chord).

TOYE: Ah, the Caribbean. A treacherous sea, known for its…treacherousness.

NARRATOR: All right, so the kid's not a poet. But picture, for a moment, the poetry in motion of this dazzling young Adonis.

In days gone by, he and the other boys of his hometown would often strip off their clothes and gambol in the lazy waters of the lake under a blushing Louisiana sky. Sometimes impromptu wrestling matches would erupt, but Toye Buck was always the winner. Even with the larger boys, his enthusiasm and incredibly developed musculature easily won the day.

MISS MARZIPAN (offstage) Toye. Toye Buck.

NARRATOR (Playing Debussy's Arabesque #1): Ah, the familiar voice of Miss Marzipan, Toye Buck's faithful nursemaid and boon companion. At the advanced age of 35 she has yet to feel the salacious hand of a man on her person.

Miss Marzipan enters, dressed in a demure gown, and joins Toye at the railing. She carries a hat with a feather.

MISS MARZIPAN: I might have known I would find you out here. Exposing yourself to the cruel sun without even the protection of your chapeau.

NARRATOR: Toye sighed deeply (Toye does so) for, though he was uncommonly fond of the woman who had raised him since the death of his mother, he sometimes felt so smothered by her feminine concerns it seemed as if the next good-intentioned blandishment might detonate him like a keg of powder.

TOYE: You know I despise that hat. I won't wear it! I tell you, I won't!

NARRATOR: Miss Marzipan smiled seraphically at her strapping but willful charge and gave in without further fuss. Experience had taught her that Toye usually got his way.

MISS MARZIPAN: I declare, your new bride will have her hands full with you, Toye Buck.

TOYE: You speak as if I were already engaged. I am not engaged yet. And I don't know that I ever will be.

MISS MARZIPAN: You know how your father, the wealthy Louisiana sugar plantation owner, has long had his heart set on marrying you to Toinette, the virginal daughter of a close school chum who owns a sugar plantation and rum distillery on the island of Martinique. This marriage would not only provide a highly suitable match within your social station, but would have the added advantage of combining your fathers' plantations, creating a virtual monopoly on sugar in this part of the world. This is the reason we have been packed onto this uncomfortable frigate during the hottest month of the year and are sailing as quickly as the trade winds will carry us through the Spanish Main, to our destination of Martinique.

NARRATOR: Now that's what I call exposition! (Toye and Miss Marzipan look over at him. He covers his embarrassment by striking a chord and saying.) Sail sighted off the starboard bow.

TOYE: Yes, I know all that. But I'm far too busy to concern myself with marriage.

NARRATOR: This was sad, but true. Females meant nothing to Toye Buck. In fact, they meant less than nothing. He was ignorant of the wanton thoughts he provoked as he propelled his handsome frame through town. He knew nothing of the young girls who imagined gazing into his laughing, green eyes and running their hands through his curly locks; or the teenage nymphs who spent hours dreaming about feeding off his sweet and succulent lips. He'd never guess that, behind her kindly smile, Widow LeBeau longed to tear off his shirt, expose the tender, white flesh beneath, and run her tongue across the velvety expanse of his manly, well-formed chest. He could scarcely imagine that Brother Pierre, safe in daydreams, often fantasized doling out an exquisite punishment to his prize pupil: placing a helpless Toye across his lap and carefully caning his quivering, melon-shaped buttocks. And he would never comprehend those shameless hussies who gladly would have ripped the formfitting breeches from his well-muscled legs, to run their hands along his sizzling shanks; trembling and salivating as they approached the very center of his manhood....

The Narrator has become very involved in his story and suddenly breaks off, realizing that Miss Marzipan and Toye are staring at him curiously. He mops his brow and pulls himself together.

NARRATOR: Pardon me. I'm afraid I...I got a little carried away. (chord) Ship approaching, sailing to windward.
TOYE: What an ominous looking frigate. It glides through the waves as quickly and quietly as a jungle panther. I see no colors. From whence does she hail?
MISS MARZIPAN: They're raising a flag. It seems—oh, *mon dieu!* The Jolly Roger!
NARRATOR: Pirates! We are boarded.

There is the sound of a tremendous fight offstage. Miss Marzipan grabs hold of Toye.

MISS MARZIPAN: Say your prayers, Toye, for nothing can save us now. We are mere fodder to these pillaging villains. If we survive the battle, I will offer myself to these depraved renegades in the hope that they spare your life.

Blackout. The noise eventually dies down and the Narrator plays a doleful series of chords.

NARRATOR: The battle ended almost before it had begun. The crew of the *Billy Budd,* lithe and rock-hard as they were, had no

chance against the marauding crew of the "Cutlass Supreme"—
cutthroats known throughout the Spanish Main for their cunning, their brute strength, and their skill with a blade. There
were also persistent rumors that this crew indulged in a vice so
illicit it could only be whispered in public houses and bordel-
los of the islands.

Scene Two:

Aboard the "Cutlass Supreme. A few minutes later. Rake
Matelot, the pirate captain, is surveying the end of the battle.
Sabre, his trusty henchman, is cooling him with a large pea-
cock fan.

RAKE: A damnably disappointing fight these fops put up
today. It galls me even to have been wounded in this pitiful fray.
(calling off) What ho, me hearties! Is the ship secure?
VOICE (offstage): Aye, sir.
RAKE: Set her aflame and bring any prisoners to me. (to
Sabre) Get away from me with that, Sabre. Always fussing
about me. Worse than my granny. What have we here?

Bilge enters with Miss Marzipan and Toye as prisoners. Bilge
has a stuffed parrot on his shoulder. Although all of Bilge's
lines will be written in standard English, they are delivered in
such a gruff "pirate" accent that they are 80% unintelligible. No
one acknowledges this.

BILGE: Here be the prisoners, Cap'n. A scurvy lot, by gum.
RAKE: Thank you, Bilge. Welcome to the "Cutlass Supreme."
(He crosses to Toye and raises his face.) Hmm. Not bad. Not
bad at all.

MISS MARZIPAN: Oh, sir, don't harm him. He is only a *pauvre garcon.*

RAKE: A what?

BILGE: A boy, Cap'n.

MISS MARZIPAN: Ah, *monsieur*, you speak French?

RAKE: A boy? That's where you're wrong. He is so much more than a boy.

NARRATOR: Toye gazed helplessly into the eyes of the broad-shouldered captain. Those dark orbs turned to molten lava as they caressed Toye from head to foot. Suddenly his huge, piratical hands began pawing at Toye like an anxious mongoose. Toye felt every sinew in his virile, young body ablaze with an extraordinary fever. As if sleepwalking, he pulled fiercely away from the hot-blooded corsair.

TOYE: Unhand me, you black-hearted knave!

RAKE: Ah, a spirit to match those piercing green eyes. You will make a most interesting diversion. What's your name, boy?

TOYE: My name is Toye Buck, if that's of any interest to a creature like yourself.

RAKE: I find anything about you begins to interest me deeply. I am Rake Matelot (chord), the scourge of the Spanish Main. I am your captain, your captor, and the man who will tame your wild, wayward spirit, Toye Buck.

TOYE: You flatter yourself, Rake Matelot.

RAKE: Before I've done with you, you will beg for me. I will teach you the ways of seamen below-decks, in the steamy darkness of the bunks. You are unformed now, a mere chrysalis. Within a month I will have the pleasure of watching your beautiful, young body quivering with heady arousal.

SABRE (annoyed): Captain, we have another prisoner.

RAKE: Quite right. I had forgotten. You are catnip to a man, Toye Buck. You go straight to the head and make me forget meself. (to Miss Marzipan) Who are you?

MISS MARZIPAN: I am Miss Euphoria Marzipan. The guardian of that child you are manhandling. To spare him, I am prepared to sacrifice myself to your degenerate lusts. I will be your pirate bride.

RAKE: I'm really not the marrying kind.

MISS MARZIPAN(throwing herself on him): Be gentle with me. My maiden's treasure is unsullied.

RAKE (trying to pull away): Madame….

MISS MARZIPAN: My honor is yours for the taking. Take it. Take it now!

Rake succeeds in pushing her away. Bilge and Sabre grab hold of her.

RAKE: Madame, your honor is sacred on this ship. Profligate though we may be, we are not keen for your variety of sport. I can see no profit or pleasure we can reap by your presence. Run out the plank, boys. We'll see how far this lady walks.

BILGE: Shiver me timbers, matey.

Bilge and Sabre set out the plank.

MISS MARZIPAN: No, sir, *s'il vous plait*. Don't separate me from my boy. I'm extremely useful. I can clean. I navigate by the night stars. I make a terrific étouffee.

They blindfold Miss Marzipan.

SABRE: She's ready, sir. Shall I prepare the boy?
RAKE: The boy stays.

TOYE: I regret to find that you are nothing more than a cowardly brigand of the sea.

RAKE: You dare to call me a coward?

TOYE: Aye, and more. Only a coward and a scoundrel would take advantage of a defenseless woman.

RAKE: Quite the contrary, through my largesse this woman goes to her grave intact.

MISS MARZIPAN: Damn!

TOYE: But still to her grave. An unmarked stretch of ocean in a vast sea. A cruel fate for one whose only crime was to love me.

RAKE: The law of the sea is cruel. It is survival of the fittest. The strong over the weak; the weak over the innocent; and the innocent over us all. For that is the terrible, terrible strength of an innocent like yourself.

TOYE: I beg you, is there nothing I can say, nothing I can do, to spare her life?

RAKE: Hmm. There might be something....

TOYE: Name it.

RAKE: A kiss from you, Toye Buck, might inspire mercy.

TOYE: You shameless villain. Must you ever wallow in degenerate desires?

RAKE: Your presence leaves me little recourse. Besides, you can't know the sweet exhilaration of a man's kiss, or you wouldn't spurn it so freely.

TOYE: A kiss?

MISS MARZIPAN: No, Toye. Don't even think of it. You cannot humor a voluptuary's will.

TOYE: What choice have I? I cannot let you die. One kiss, Rake Matelot?

RAKE: One kiss, Toye Buck.

TOYE: Very well. Then come and pillage my pride.

MISS MARZIPAN: Ah, horror. *Quelle catastrophe!*

NARRATOR: The brawny pirate pulled Toye into his arms with the eagerness of a Viking decimating a village. Toye felt the raw strength and power in the hands that enveloped him and, yet, he felt strangely comforted and protected. Rake was so huge, so powerful, so dark, so sinister. Their mouths met in a blazing conflagration that seared Toye's lips and sent lightning bolts of fire through his anxious loins. He felt the pressure of Rake's turgid power like a gleaming cutlass pressed against him, and he lost all will to struggle. Finally when it seemed that Toye would never breathe again and warm darkness might envelope him forever, the randy buccaneer pulled away. Toye opened his eyes to life (chord), but what kind of life was this?

Toye stands dazed and confused.

RAKE: Now you'll see, Toye Buck, that I am a man of my word. Bilge, put the woman afloat with a week's rations.

BILGE: She'll be caught amidships, indeed.

RAKE (licking finger and holding it up): With these trade winds she should make land in two days.

Bilge drags Miss Marzipan off.

MISS MARZIPAN: Toye, *mon petite*, don't despair. I shall not rest until I have rescued you. I will set you free, I swear it.

Rake crosses to Toye and takes his arm. Toye pulls away violently.

TOYE (hysterically): Get away from me! What more do you want? My blood? My life? Take it. Take it all.

He bursts into tears. Rake watches him a moment, then turns to Sabre.

RAKE: Take him to my cabin and prepare him for an evening of bliss.

Toye wails loudly.

SABRE: No, Captain, he's not one of us. Put him on the boat with the female before it's too late. He brings trouble in his wake.
RAKE: Nonsense. You're blathering like a jealous schoolgirl.
SABRE: I smell danger on the boy.
RAKE: Then bathe him.
SABRE: Cap'n, he don't belong here.
RAKE: I decide who sails my ship.
SABRE: But, sir—
RAKE: Who is master here?
SABRE: I can't—
RAKE: Belay that! Take him below and have him bathed and scented. I will visit him this evening. Is that understood, Mr. Sabre?
SABRE: Yes, sir.
RAKE: Good. Then do it.

Rake leaves. Sabre takes the overwrought Toye to the Captain's cabin.

NARRATOR: And so a reluctant Sabre escorted Toye Buck to the Captain's cabin. Where, even in his present torpor, Toye found himself dazzled by this plethora of piratical plunder pilfered from the powerful. This was no ordinary outlaw's motley accumulation of loot. The pieces that filled Rake Matelot's

cabin were beautiful and quite, quite rare. They had been chosen by someone with artistic sense and exquisite taste. Toye
had the impression the decor had been curated, like a museum.
He found himself wondering, not for the first time, about the
type of man who had captured him.

Scene Three:

Rake's cabin. Toye is looking around in wonder at the tawdry
splendor that surrounds him. Sabre and Bilge carry in a large
tin wash tub.

BILGE: They'll sail to windward, by gum.
SABRE: Aye, Bilge. Thank you.
BILGE: Yar young man. Wouldn't mind a bit of a tickle me-
self....
SABRE: Belay that, Bilge!
BILGE: Shiver me timbers, sir. A little of what you fancy does
you good.
SABRE: We'll leave the bathing to the cabin boy. Fetch Beau
for me.
BILGE: Aye aye, sir.

Bilge exits.

SABRE: You seem to have made quite an impression on the
captain.
TOYE: Believe me, it is entirely unintentional.
SABRE: I don't believe you. I don't trust you and I don't like
the cut of your jib. You may captivate him for the moment, but
you can never hold the heart of Rake Matelot.
TOYE: Never fear. I want no part of his anatomy.

SABRE: You lie. Like the mealy-mouthed wretch you are. Remember that he is a tar—a creature of the salt and foam. A coxswain of the highest order and as tied to this ship as any barnacle. You are merely booty.

TOYE: I am not a trophy for any seagoing scoundrel.

SABRE: Oh, but you are, Toye Buck. And a pretty plum at that. But it's not enough. He'll weigh anchor and cut you adrift when he tires of you.

TOYE: I don't understand you.

SABRE: I think you do. We're talking about love.

TOYE: Love?

SABRE: A passion you landlubbers only aspire to. But I am a sailor, and when I love, I love with the fathomless depths of the sea. And when I hate (he pulls out a dagger), I get even.

Chord. Sabre pulls Toye into an arm lock and holds the knife against his throat. Beau Ideal, carrying a box of bath salts and a towel, enters and stands in the doorway unseen.

TOYE: What do you want from me?

SABRE: I wonder how Rake would like you if we were to mar that pretty cheek of yours.

NARRATOR: Toye felt the sharp edge of Sabre's steel on his throat and he knew, for the first time in his life, the icy chill of fear. The men onboard the "Cutlass Supreme" were a new breed to him—desperate (chord), impulsive (chord), and enigmatic. (chord) They were capable of anything.

BEAU: Sabre!

NARRATOR (playing a triumphant chord): The new voice hit Toye like the sting of a whip. But there was something in the tone that inspired confidence. A masculine authority that would brook no dissension.

BEAU: I wonder what Rake Matelot would say if he could see you now.

SABRE: I was just entertaining the lad while we waited for you, Beau. Nothing worth bothering the Cap'n about.

BEAU: Then, perhaps, you'll clear out while I get to my job. Rake Matelot won't be kept waiting. Bring that in, Bilge.

Bilge enters with a pail of water, which he pours into the tub.

SABRE: You mind what I've said, boy. I'll be watching you.

BEAU: And I'll be watching you, Mr. Sabre.

SABRE: I won't be threatened by a common cabin boy.

BEAU: I may be a cabin boy, but you know very well that I am anything but common.

SABRE: I know that onboard you are the lowliest minion of the ship.

BEAU: And you are as base a villain as ever sailed under the Jolly Roger.

SABRE: Dirty little lackey.

BEAU: Heinous giant villain.

SABRE: Menial.

BEAU: Scoundrel.

SABRE: Slave.

BEAU: Brute.

SABRE: Knave.

BEAU: Cad.

SABRE: (slight pause) Menial.

BEAU: You're repeating yourself. Let's end this now. We both know I have the larger…vocabulary.

SABRE: And I have the strength to best you in hand-to-hand. Let's wrestle!

They tear off their shirts and perform a badly choreographed fight sequence. Bilge and Toye are a good audience. There is much huffing and puffing and straining but little actual danger. One should watch some of the old AMG film loops to get the idea. They stop fighting as suddenly as they began and shake hands. Bilge finds a sign that says "Beau Ideal vs. Sabre" and holds it up in front of them as they point to their names and wave at the audience. Sabre and Bilge exit.

TOYE: You were most gallant, coming to my defense.
BEAU: I confess, I take pleasure in getting the best of Sabre.
TOYE: My name is….
BEAU: I know. You are Toye Buck, scion of a wealthy Louisiana sugar plantation. News travels fast onboard.
TOYE: And who am I to thank for my deliverance?
BEAU: I beg your pardon. I have lived around rough men so long, I have forgotten my manners. My name is Beau Ideal. (triumphant chord) But we mustn't waste more time. You'd best get undressed and into the bath, Toye Buck. Rake Matelot is anxious to visit you.

During the following Toye undresses, though actual nudity is only suggested, not shown. He and Beau make significant eye contact several times.

NARRATOR: Toye stripped off his clothes while surreptitiously studying the cabin boy. He hadn't wanted a bath earlier, but something made him want one now. He secretly reveled in displaying his supple naked body and innocently wondered what Beau would think of his fleshly charms. He could see that Beau shone like a brilliant diamond through the surrounding gloom. His gentle hands, compassionate smile, and graceful movements belied the fact that, like all men onboard, he was taut, lithe, and muscular. Only his awesomely broad shoulders broadcast the fact that this young man was a force to be reckoned with. Toye wondered if he might have found a friend.

TOYE: (stepping into the tub) The water's warm.

BEAU: I had it heated for you. Settle in and let's get you (Beau rips off his sleeves) squeaky clean.

Toye settles himself in the tub. The Narrator obligingly blows soap bubbles. Beau scrubs Toye with a bath mitt.

TOYE: I seem to have made an enemy in that Sabre fellow.

BEAU: He's merely jealous.

TOYE: Of what?

BEAU: Your blazing youth, your guileless innocence, your peerless beauty, and most of all, your power over Rake Matelot. You are a Ganymede.

TOYE: A what?

BEAU: Not what, who. Ganymede was the cupbearer of the gods. A dazzlingly beautiful boy who became the paramour of Zeus, king of the gods.

TOYE: I don't understand. Is Rake Matelot…? I mean, I've seen those silly fops in New Orleans with their brilliantly colored scarves and their high-pitched voices. He is nothing like that.

BEAU: Not all men who love men are like those fops, as you call them. (The Narrator plays "A Time for Us" under the speech.) From the beginning of time kings and wise men and, yes, even soldiers have known a love that surpasses the common inclination for women. Alexander and Hephastion, Socrates and Alcibiades, Hadrian and Antinous are only a few in this proud lineage. The love of a man for a man is more overpowering than any love for a woman. If Romeo and Juliet could love each other to distraction, imagine the tale of woe of Romeo and Benvolio. Think of the compelling magnetism in their initial attraction. The ferocious power of their joining and, finally, the blissful peace that follows the ultimate moment of sharing.

TOYE: You talk as if you know.

BEAU: I do, Toye Buck.

TOYE: You mean…you too?

Beau nods slowly.

NARRATOR: Toye could scarcely believe his ears. His new found friend was one of them. The man who even now was running his strong, talented hands over Toye's firmly muscled stomach and hard, chiseled thighs was unnatural—a lover of men. Somehow that didn't seem so abhorrent any longer. "After all," Toye mused, "Is there really anything so wrong in that? Isn't love the emotion that separates us from the animals? Why should that love be confined to only the historically safe coupling of man and woman?"

A sign appears reading THE AUTHOR'S PLEA FOR TOLERANCE. Beau redoubles his scrubbing efforts.

NARRATOR: Beau Ideal was obviously a man of character, breeding, and boundless sophistication, while Toye Buck was as callow and sexless as a newt. Passion lay dormant in him, waiting to be stirred, to be aroused, to go roaring through his lithe and sensuous body like whitewater rapids. He had yet to meet the person whose unbridled hunger would bring him the rapture of erotic awakening. The glowing ember was alive within him waiting to burst forth in fantastic flames at a touch—but the touch had not come. (Tremulous chord. Beau and Toye look down into the bath.) Or had it? (They quickly look away.) "Damn it all!" thought Toye "Why did Nature have to build man so that his innermost thoughts were always clearly revealed by looking in the right places?"

BEAU: Oh, Toye Buck, how I envy the lucky person who'll finally win your love.

TOYE: Beau, can you tell me—

BEAU: Hush, there's not time. Rake Matelot will be here any minute. Step out of the bath and let me dry you.

Toye does so. Beau pats him dry.

TOYE: What does Rake Matelot want of me?

BEAU: I think you already know.

TOYE: To be his Ganymede? What kind of men are these?

BEAU: They are animals, pure and simple. I daresay you have never known the sort of people that live on this frigate, the men who sleep in these flea-bitten bunks. When the days are lean, they fast and pray for better, but when there is a kill they slash and claw at it, sinking their fangs into the feast and filling their greedy bellies. Rake Matelot is their king, their sovereign—the monarch who tosses an occasional crumb to them.

TOYE: As he'll toss me to them when he's through.

Chord. Rake appears in the doorway.

RAKE: I don't know when I've seen a prettier picture.

BEAU (wrapping the towel around Toye): I'm sorry, sir, he's not dressed yet.

Sabre follows Rake in with a tray of food.

RAKE: No reason to stand on formality here. I prefer him in his natural state. You've done well, Beau. Leave us. You too, Sabre.

SABRE: But, Captain—

RAKE: We'll be fine.

SABRE: But I must—

RAKE: Set down the tray and leave.

Sabre does so very unhappily. He and Beau exit.

RAKE: Come, boy, let's eat. You must be famished. (He sits down and starts to fill a plate.) Join me.

TOYE: I'm not hungry.

RAKE: Are you going to be petulant over that harridan we put over the side? She'll make land. I promise. (He holds up a bowl) Have you ever tried this? It's a recipe from some far-off islands.

TOYE: What is it?

RAKE: It's poi, Toye. Try it.

TOYE: No, thank you.

RAKE: What about a slice of this cool, sweet melon? (He bites into it.) Mmm. It's juicy. Sure you wouldn't like a bite?

TOYE: No, thank you.

RAKE: You don't know what you're missing. (Toye turns away.) Mmm. Mmm. You must try some of this. I insist. Just one little bite. (He has come very close to Toye and is holding the fruit in front of him. His tone loses all playfulness.) Try it.

Toye takes a bite. He turns his head away when he chews, but Rake turns it back.

RAKE: We wouldn't want you to faint with hunger.

TOYE: I assure you that I'm quite able…. (He stops because Rake is laughing.) What is it?

RAKE: I'm afraid you'll have to learn to eat more dainty-like. You got a little dribble of juice running down onto….

Rake suddenly leans forward and licks the juice off of Toye's chest with an audible slurp. Toye recoils.

TOYE: What are you doing?

RAKE: Don't it feel good, Toye?

TOYE: I…I think…

RAKE: I can make you feel even better. There are things men do in the dark, things that are sweeter than the juice of any fruit. Let me teach you. Don't be coy, Toye. Let me show you the secret ways of the sea.

NARRATOR: Toye Buck was rooted to the spot as he stared into the eyes of his captor, those reckless black eyes that blazed with the light of deviant sexuality. He noticed Rake's broad shoulders, the way his animal muscles played beneath his skimpy cotton shirt and suddenly felt powerless in his presence. For the first time he felt a victim of this savage new world in which, up to this moment, he had been no more than a spectator, a mere—

RAKE: (to Narrator) Can we get through one interesting scene without your purple prose?

NARRATOR: I beg your pardon.

RAKE: This audience is looking for a little action.

NARRATOR: Excuse me for trying to add some style and elegance to your sordid story.

RAKE: They're tired of your potboiler narration. They want sex.

NARRATOR: And must we pander to the lowest denominator? What's wrong with engaging them intellectually? The mind is the most potent sexual organ.

RAKE: Naked boys rutting, that's their style.

NARRATOR: I refuse to believe that everyone is so shallow. (To Toye) What do you think?

TOYE: Well, you do tend to slow things down a little.

NARRATOR: *Et tu*, Toye Buck. After all the flattering description I've lavished on you. Go ahead, then. Give them what they want. Don't pay any attention to me. From now on, I'm mute.

Rake grabs Toye and kisses him roughly. Toye starts to respond and then runs away. Rake reaches for him and ends up with only the towel for his efforts.

RAKE: Love me, Toye Buck. I am in agony.

TOYE: I am sorry for you, Rake Matelot. But I cannot love you.

RAKE: You're a beautiful boy, Toye. I look at you now, unhusked, your naked glory exposed to the world, and I realize the truth. You are one of those breathtaking Lotharios whose awesome beauty drives a weak man to suicide and a strong man to madness. (They execute a complicated and ridiculous series of crosses.) I want you, Toye Buck. Like I've never wanted anyone or anything before. Not for just this hour, or this week, but forever.

TOYE: You have all the advantages, Rake Matelot. You have brute strength and the power of your position. You can force me, if that's what you want. But it's only my body you'll enjoy. My spirit you can never possess.

RAKE: Damn, but I want it all. I want you to come smiling, with your manly arms open wide, and invite me to your bed.

TOYE: Your dream is futile, Rake Matelot, for no man has ever touched me and no man ever will. I swear it.

RAKE: I've never said these words before, but I want to share my life with you. Stay with me. Let me love you. Let me be good to you.

Rake kneels and puts him arms around Toye's waist.

TOYE: You ask the impossible.
RAKE: You are hard, boy. I will leave you your precious honor tonight; secure in the knowledge that no other man has ever had you and content to wait for that day when you will surrender yourself to me. That day of breathtaking joy, Toye.
TOYE: You hope in vain, Rake Matelot, for that day will never come.

There is a long pause. Toye and Rake look over to the Narrator.

RAKE: (finally) That's your cue.
NARRATOR: Oh, so now you need me? Did you find that your precious "action" wasn't enough? I suppose you expect me to forget your insults and jump back in.
RAKE: It's your line.
NARRATOR: I suppose an apology would be too much to expect.
RAKE: Would you just read your damn lines?
NARRATOR: I will. But I want you to know, this isn't to accommodate you. It's the audience I'm thinking about. But even as Toye bravely faced the unapologetically sensual gaze of his would-be ravisher, he was struck by a blinding realization. A knowledge that someday, somehow a man would take the full range of pleasure from him, and he would be helpless to defend his body, his dignity, or his innocence.

Vita Victorious

by Joanne Ashwell

The following is from a recently discovered bundle of letters written by Victoria "Vita" Sackville-West to Violet Trefusis. Sorbonne literature professors refuse to divulge the exact location of their find; a highly reliable source, however, has confided that a bidet in the Paris Ritz was used as a file cabinet by Ms. Trefusis. As with so many of her English expatriates, she viewed bidets—indeed all indoor plumbing—as appalling examples of French decadence.

* * *

My dearest Violet,

Thanks awfully for yours of 14th November. Am bereft to learn you were injured. Surely that Parisian chiropractor will soon be able to realign your vertebrae? Perhaps our 11 November rendezvous in Flanders Fields was a bit too strenuous for my little poppet. Laundress was overheard complaining to Cook that my trousers were permanently grass-stained. But what a jolly Armistice Day tribute to our fallen English lads.

Home to find Harold flushed and fatigued. The new French exchange student is a most enthusiastic learner, à la grecque. Harold truly shines as Pygmalion to Pierre's Galatea. Today Harold went up to London with young Pierre to enjoy something by Sophocles, whom they both adore. I'm rather relishing their absence and am contentedly puffing on one of Harold's pipes whilst sporting his jaunty old Balliol boater. Feel ever so manly, in the understated Oxford way, of course.

Radclyffe just rang me up. She and Una have regretfully canceled their pilgrimage to Lesbos upon advice of their ever-so-grim barrister. They will join you next Friday at Natalie's Rue Jacob salon. Darling Violet, do *not* venture into Nat's "Temple d'Amitié"—too friendly by half!

Virginia and Leonard Woolf remain entombed in their dreary Monk's House. V.W. has begun compiling notes, photos, paintings, and memorabilia with the intention of completing in a decade or two a "fantasy" of my life and illustrious ancestors. I have strongly suggested that she title her work *Mars,* but she wants *Orlando* as its title. May I confess that V.'s hero-worship becomes a bit of a bore? I desire her love, not her reverence. Why cannot she see that? Posted the following couplets to her at Rodmel; these will, I hope, shock her out of celibacy:

"V.W., All Passion Spent"

"Dearest Creature, I fear our love is hexed.
In a word, my darling, you are undersexed.

"I therefore busy myself, and Gardeners too,
Clipping *all* the rosebuds at Knole and at Kew.

"Virginia, beloved, I am ever so vexed;
Leonard never told me you are undersexed."

Yes, I realize the couplets are crude. One might almost say they're essentially American in their vulgarity. The Blooms-bury critics will chide me, but I know a little secret about Vir-ginia—smut turns her on.

Sweet, tender Violet, please do recover quickly. We must meet in a fortnight at that splendid English Military Cemetery just east of Calais. I shall crush your delicate petals against my uniform till the khaki turns purple from your fragrant and co-pious essences.

Mon dieu, one's loins are beginning to throb. I shall over-come my urgent needs by cultivating several acres of ancient Sackville soil. Do so wish you could join me whilst I plow the moist, musky furrows.

Bloody hell! An ember from my pipe has fallen and burned a hold in the ermine rug. I'd best obtain some water.

In haste,
Vita

P.S. Please pack your cunning little Red Cross nurse's uni-form for our Calais Memorial.

Ballad of the Lonesome Cowboy

by Rik Isensee

I once met a handsome dude,
Who swept me off my feet—
His eyes as blue as cornflowers,
Hair the color of wheat.

He told me I was mighty fine,
Then clutched me to his chest—
Kissed me with his burning lips,
More times than I can guess.

My sister Gwen she cautioned me,
That a man will break your heart—
She said that it's far better
To quit before you start!

But I knew I was his treasure,
Not just momentary lust—

I never could believe that he
Would leave me in the dust.

He swore that he'd be true to me,
I was his only love—
Arm in arm we'd walk along,
The stars ablaze above.

I thought I was in heaven
As we set upon life's road—
But then my boyfriend found
Another man to take his load!

My mother she admonished me
That what I done was sin.
She said the sweet Lord Jesus
Would never let me in—

When my boyfriend left me,
I could see that she was right—
So now I've turned away from sin,
To walk the path of light.

Still, I wish that he was holding me
Within his loving arms—
I wish that he was telling me
The bounty of my charms.

Take heed, my friend, the next time
You're flattered by some stud—
The truth, my sister told to me, is
"Men will fuck mud."

"Who Cares If It's A Choice? Snappy Answers to 101 Nosy, Intrusive, and Highly Personal Questions About Lesbians and Gay Men"

by Ellen Orleans

Where did the word "lesbian" come from?

Roughly translated from the Greek, lesbian means "lover of wet sex."

Are lesbians and gays born that way?

No, we are conceived that way. Consider it an act of divine intervention.

Does just one homosexual experience make you lesbian or gay?

Absolutely. In fact, if you've even had so much as a homosexual thought, you're automatically lesbian or gay. So if you have had any homosexual experiences, as dull or nonstimulating as they might have been, turn yourself in to your nearest gay or lesbian center and register immediately. Your gay I.D. will be sent to you within 10 working days. Questions? Call 1-800-I'M QUEER.

Are most gay men militant homosexuals? Or is that a stereotype?

It's a stereotype, albeit a refreshing one. At the 1996 NGLTF conference, gay men voted 3 to 1 to revise the official national gay male stereotype from "sissified pansy" to "militant homosexual." The official dyke stereotype is still unratified; it's a toss-up between "political activist do-gooder" and "chic trendsetter." Lesbians have yet to reach consensus on the issue.

In a male-couple relationship, who takes out the garbage? And who does the cooking, the laundry, and the yard work?

Into traditional gender roles, are we? OK, it *is* a legitimate question, and honestly, one whose answer I wasn't sure of myself. So I asked my friends Steve and Mike. They divulged that, in most gay male couples, the decision of who takes out the trash, cleans the toilets, etc., is settled by wrestling in the nude. I had suspected this was the case, but it was good to have my suspicions confirmed.

Why don't lesbians wear makeup?

Because by the time we finish changing the oil, splitting a cord of firewood, repainting the backyard shed, and cleaning the cat box, then *finally* get out to the store to pick some up, the drag queens have bought the place out.

Do lesbians have more fun in restaurants than straight people? Or is that just my imagination?

It's true. Lesbians have more fun than straights because they nibble off each others' plates and eat artichokes suggestively. Also, most lesbians play footsie under the table. Lesbian parents out with their kids, however, have the same amount of fun as straight people out with their kids.

Why do lesbians want to look like men?

We like to tease straight women.

At a party, a gay man walked up to an attractive lesbian and commented, "You're gorgeous. Too bad you're not a man." She threw her drink in his face. Was that remark a social faux pas?

Yes. The correct comment would have been, "You're gorgeous. Too bad I'm not a lesbian."

A friend told me she was bisexual. I said, "So that means you can only date other bisexuals, right?" She gave me a funny look. Can you explain?

The reason she gave you that funny look is that bisexual dating rituals are terribly complex. But—in oversimplified terms—bisexual women date in a specific cycle: January, straight men; February, bisexual women; March, bisexual men; April, lesbians. The cycle starts over again in May. The bisexual male's cycle is a mirror image of the female cycle, with a 45° difference.

If lesbians like to use dildos, why don't they like penises?

After sex, dildos go back in the drawer.

How long do gay and lesbian couples relationships last?

Forever. Even after a couple breaks up, the relationship goes on and on. Lesbian Thanksgiving dinners prove this fact as they tend to be a conglomeration of ex-lovers, teenage sweethearts, and former girlfriends all choosing carefully who they sit next to.

I've heard that a disproportionate number of gays and lesbians have homosexual siblings. Does this mean that homosexuality is genetic?

No, it means it's contagious.

Why do lesbians have a thing for cats?

We like surrounding ourselves with peaceful, intelligent, and independent beings, who, unlike straight people, aren't always asking us dumb questions about our sexuality.

Are gay people innately funnier than straights?

We'd like to think so.

Can you be seduced into being gay?

Is that an offer?

Cinderella's Prince

by Michael Dubson Sage

Once upon a time, in a kingdom far, far way, there lived a handsome Crown Prince whose sizable libido roamed in the direction of hot pecs, tight buns, and bulging baskets. Yes, the Crown Prince was a happy, horny Size Queen.

To the people of the kingdom, however, he was a handsome, charming, heterosexual, available heir to the throne. The mention of his name, or the sight of him passing in his carriage, or even a mere rumor that he might make an appearance, sent female hearts fluttering. The Prime Minister, the Prince, and the Palace Press office, better known as the Town Crier, did all in their power to reinforce the Prince's hetero image.

Privately, though, the Prince preferred to spend his time with stable boys, the gardener, and various footmen. He developed, in certain circles, a secret reputation for being a hot bottom with an affinity for rough trade. And he had a sunburn on the soles of his feet to prove it.

The unenlightened King eventually grew concerned with the Prince's failure to display interest in any of the kingdom's gentrified ladies; he suspected a princely affinity for serving wenches. More than once, while meandering the grounds of the Royal Gaudy Palace, the King happened across the Prince's silk breeches, usually torn at the crotch. Littering ordinances aside, the King firmly believed this was no way and no place for a person of royal blood to disrobe.

The King devoutly believed the Prince to be a God's-gift-to-women kind of guy, and had no problem with the idea of his beloved progeny boffing (female) servants. But the King desperately wanted his son to marry a proper princess and produce grandchildren—grandchildren not born outside of wedlock by a member of the laboring class.

One night at supper, when the Prince was smiling frequently and saying little, the King issued an ultimatum. If the Crown Prince did not produce a blushing, soon-to-be-impregnated bride within the year, he would be cut off. Gone would be the throne, the money, and the power. And, the Prince thought with horror, the services of the stable boys.

The Prince was flummoxed. He didn't want to lose any of his pleasures, but the idea of heterosexual marriage distressed him deeply.

Meanwhile, to speed the marrying process, the King arranged for a Grand Ball to be held in the Prince's honor, decreeing by order of law that all eligible young maidens in the kingdom attend.

And attend they did. The golddiggers arranged themselves in lacy, low-cut finery and overwhelming perfumes. Not only did they fail to realize how exploitative this was—parading themselves before a man in the hope he might select one of them to become his royal, blushing betrothed—they failed to notice that the Prince was bored silly. He tried his best to smile politely, to not yawn, and to act interested in the things the young women had to say. But mostly he hoped the regular winks he kept getting from one of the footmen signaled fun in the moonlight once the boring ball bounced to a close.

The young prince was in the process of meeting two sisters, Anastasia and Drizzella, the ugliest, most awkward, most unpleasant women in attendance—a duo with desperation and snippy entitlement scribbled all over them—when SHE walked in.

It was the glitter of her gown that first caught his eye. It was the same glitter he'd seen in the full moon sky after he'd just been righteously reamed at the annual Radical Faeries' Celebration.

Fairy dust.

Who could have designed such a gown? The Prince sensed a man after his own heart, and hopefully other organs as well. The Prince pranced toward the gown, his eyes shining, his smile growing.

She called herself Cinderella. She was there by benefit of her fairy godmother, whom the Prince quickly placed as a Drag Queen of long standing. The Prince resolved to learn more about the dress so he could drop in at the tailor's the following morn.

As the Prince and the dress…err, Cinderella…danced across the floor in a shimmer, she told him her life story. She told him about the house of horrors she lived in, how her stepmother and stepsister abused her, ridiculed her, and laughed at her. She told him how she cooked all the meals, tended the barnyard animals, and took care of everyone's personal needs day after day.

"Why don't you leave?" he asked.

She smiled blankly and shrugged. "I don't know. I believe in my dreams, and my fantasy life will do until the real thing comes along," she said. "I really don't mind having to do all the work and going without things while my stepsisters have everything."

Cinderella, the Prince thought as he waltzed her across the dance floor, was a bit of a simp. Naive, gullible, and dumb. She made Sandra Dee look like Sandra Bernhard. As he pondered this, a brilliant, wonderful idea formed in his brain: he would marry Cinderella. It would shut the King up, he would retain his throne, and his nights of pleasure could continue indefinitely. He would rescue Cinderella from her house of hate, and, because she was a such a cluck, she would accept almost any excuse for him not wanting to consummate their marriage.

At the stroke of 12, however, Cinderella fled—not wanting the Prince to see her in rags—losing a slipper en route.

The Prince was crestfallen. He knew not her last name or address, so his beautiful plan was lost. The King, of course, misinterpreted his son's reaction as unrequited love. He was thrilled to see his son so miserable, and even more thrilled to send his son, accompanied by the Grade Duke, into the kingdom to find the foot that fit the shoe.

Cinderella was soon located, the couple was married, and everyone lived Happily Ever After. The Prince kept his lineage, his fortune, and his nights with the stable boys. Cinderella got away from her family and developed a taste for stable boys herself. And within a year, the Royal Couple presented the king with his much desired grandson (sired by a stable boy, of course).

Death in Delaware

by Barry Becker

I looked forward to Memorial Day weekend as if I had never been on vacation before. I thought when I left my high pressured position as Chief Medical Examiner for the Commonwealth of Virginia that I had chosen a less stressful path. Now, after only six months on the job as Chief Medical Examiner for the State of Delaware, I realized my tragic mistake.

I had assumed in a state so tiny its motto was "Small Wonder, Big Deal," that the job would be a piece of cake compared to the unimaginably obtuse, bloody murders and serial killings I dealt with in Virginia. I had visions of sunning at the beach and sailing the Chesapeake Bay, interrupted by one or two autopsies a week. I hadn't counted on so many bloated, disgusting bodies washing ashore to stink up my lab.

Already burned out, I planned a long weekend with my beloved niece Liz in Rehoboth Beach. I hadn't seen her in months, and was concerned about her, as I knew she was devastated that Carmine, her lover of three years, had recently dumped her. I thought a weekend away would do us both good, and I chose a growing lesbian/gay resort in the hope that it would be just the ticket to distract her from thinking about Carmine.

When I arrived at the high-rise hotel overlooking the boardwalk and the Atlantic it was nearly dinner time. I went to the bustling front desk where a muscular and handsome but harried looking man greeted me, "Yes, ma'am, checking in?"

"Dr. Gaye Scalpeletta," I said. "Presidential Suite."

Tapping rapidly on his computer keys, he said "Yes, ma'am, you're all set. Your niece has already checked in. Do enjoy your stay with us." A bagman whisked my luggage away.

"Oh, Aunt Gaye, thank you for all this," gushed Liz when I entered the living room of the gorgeous two-bedroom, two-bath suite. She ran and gave me a big hug, then with a sweep of her arm said, "Just look at this view! It's divine!"

"It's so good to see you," I said. "Oh, you've already started with the champagne."

Looking sheepish she said, "I'm sorry, it just looked so good. Let's take it out on the balcony and finish it off, then head to dinner. I've already made reservations."

"That sounds lovely. I've had a long day, and I'm really hungry." We sat and talked, enjoying each other's company as the perfect light of dusk softened the ocean waves and made them glow against the cloudless sky. Seagulls squawked and small biplanes buzzed over the ocean trailing long, colorful banners waving with ads trying to lure vacationers into local restaurants.

Liz had chosen a marvelous restaurant known for its imaginative cuisine, festive atmosphere and personal service. She looked depressed, and I was concerned about her drinking.

"Hi, my name is Cindy, and I'll be at your service tonight," said a velvet voice that appeared at our table seemingly out of nowhere. "May I get you something to drink before dinner?" she asked with her eyes glued to Liz.

"Two martinis, dry with a twist" Liz said, staring back.

"Oh, that sounds perfect," I said. "I haven't had a martini in ages."

"Oh, did you want one, too? Better make that three, then."

Before I could register my shock and displeasure, there was a commotion around us as a table of four was being seated. The party was loud and rude, and as one of the portly diners stood on his tip toes to get by, a scar-faced man two tables away sneered, "Well, hi Mayor, how've you been? Haven't seen you in awhile."

"I'm just fine, thanks." He smiled nervously.

The mayor sat down with his party, and when our eyes met I thought I was looking into the soul of Satan himself. My skin turned clammy, and when he apologized for all the commotion I could only nod and mouth, "That's OK."

I turned my attention back to the menu, which lived up to its reputation. "This just all sounds too wonderful," I sighed. "Where will I begin?"

Cindy reappeared just as an exquisite plate went by with one of the most splendidly arrayed presentations of food I had ever seen. Nodding at it and inhaling its wonderful fragrance, Liz asked, "What's that?"

"The wild mushroom, radicchio, and smoked mozzarella lasagna," Cindy cooed. "It's to die for."

Liz didn't miss a beat. "Well, I must have that, then."

I ordered a smoked trout appetizer with a rosemary duck entree. As good as it smelled, I knew the lasagna would be no match for the many variations I made. Being a second generation Italian, I could whip up the most delectable and creative dishes this side of Florence.

We sipped our martinis as Cindy slipped back to the table

and announced, "I'm sorry, we're all out of the lasagna."

Then she leaned between us and whispered, "Actually there was quite a ruckus in the kitchen between the sous chef and one of the waiters. The whole tray of lasagna was thrown out the window. What a shame. We only got the one serving out of it. May I recommend another dish?"

"Just bring me whatever you would eat," Liz said, staring into her eyes.

This was certainly not a good way to start a relaxing vacation. The food was wonderful, but there was so much bad energy in the air. We finished our meals and headed back to the hotel. I went right to bed, but Liz had found a second wind and wanted to go out. We agreed to have breakfast together at 8:30.

I had a fitful night. I didn't hear Liz come in until after two, and I kept hearing voices and moaning and giggling most of the night, but I couldn't tell where the sounds were coming from.

When I got up the next morning, Liz was already gone. I thought she was out for an early morning jog, but she never returned, so I went to have breakfast alone. When I got to the splendid little seaside cafe downstairs, Liz was already there, and Cindy was with her. How nice that they ran into each other, I thought. Liz beamed and said "Aunt Gaye, there you are. I was beginning to think you were never coming down. Look who I found having breakfast here. I asked her to join us, is that OK?"

"Why yes, of course," I said. I sat and ordered, ready to put a fresh start on this vacation when a police officer walked up and said, "Excuse me, are you Dr. Scalpeletta?"

After I'd affirmed that I was, he said, "I'm Detective Boil. Our medical examiner is on vacation this weekend, and we had a mysterious death here last night I hoped you could help us with."

"I am on vacation as well, detective," I said curtly. Typical

small town cops, I thought derisively. Paunchy, balding, po
ester Marine rejects with gun fetishes who couldn't make it
the real world. "But how may I help?"

"Seems a perfectly healthy guy went out for dinner last nigh
at one of our overpriced, fancy shmancy restaurants, had some
exotic mushroom lasagna, got violently sick, and died on his
way to the hospital."

My heart froze in my chest. "What restaurant are you talking
about?" His answer confirmed my worst fears. My God, what
if Liz had eaten that lasagna? Was this really the cause of
death? It was too early to tell. One thing I did know, this death
wasn't going to put a damper on my vacation. Luckily I had
asked all my employees for numbers where they could be
reached in case of emergency. I called my assistant at his weekend getaway and told him to pick up the body, take it back to
Dover, and autopsy it immediately.

Detective Boil and I headed to the restaurant where police
were dusting for prints.

The sous chef, Bubba LaBar, was our first suspect; he had
just been hired a few weeks earlier, and I detected immediately
how much he resented working with a female chef. He was
probably trying to set her up, undermine her sterling reputation.
I knew men like this from my legal and medical world, and I
doubted the restaurant scene was any different.

We found him in the kitchen and flashed our badges at him.

"Walk this through for us quickly," I said, thinking of the
beach time I was missing. "There's a suspicion that the mushrooms used in your signature lasagna were poisonous. Where
did they come from?

"Same vendor we always use, have used apparently for years."

"And who signed for them when they were delivered?"

"I did. I signed for most of our deliveries yesterday."

"Anything out of the ordinary yesterday? Anyone in the kitchen who shouldn't have been, any guests? Different delivery guy?"

"No, nothing out of the ordinary I know of."

"And just what happened with the lasagna that it was never served last night?"

He fidgeted, a bead of sweat running down his forehead. "It was overdone. I was very upset with it. I didn't want to serve it. That's all."

I glanced at my watch. "I need to get going before all the beach umbrellas are rented," I whispered to Boil.

"OK. We're through for now. Just don't be leaving town," he warned Bubba. "We may need to ask you some more questions as the investigation continues."

As we walked away, Boil said, "It doesn't add up, Doc. Why would he slip poison mushrooms in that dish? Even if he wanted to ruin the chef's reputation, he would be taking the whole restaurant down with him, and where would that leave him?"

"I think he lied to us about the lasagna," I said. "What's that about?"

"He's hiding something, that's for sure. But that's not the worst of it. The stiff we ID'd is a top aide of the Governor's. This is going to go very high profile. Be ready for it."

I spent the afternoon on the beach with the latest mystery from my favorite author, Patsy Wheatfield, but I was too distracted to read. I looked out to sea and saw a dozen playful dolphins leaping out of the water. This is what I needed: getting absorbed in nature, letting the rhythm of the sea rejuvenate me, soaking up the sun. No more dead bodies. I fell into a deep sleep under my beach umbrella and woke up refreshed.

That night, I took Liz and Cindy to a restaurant I'd heard served the best sushi on the East Coast. We ordered pots of

sake, and round after round of the most delectable sushi. Cindy was a delight, and Liz was the perkiest I had seen her since the breakup.

Suffering from too much sake the next morning, I set out for the beach to sleep it off. The dolphins returned, but this time they had a large plaything with them, a beach ball. How tacky; if I had wanted to be entertained at Sea World I would have gone there, I thought to myself in disgust.

I closed my eyes and was on the verge of a deep sleep when I heard the lifeguard's shrill whistle, and I jolted awake as the mobs on the beach went screaming and running toward the boardwalk. And then I saw it. It wasn't a beach ball at all, but a body, a rather battered and bloated one, now washing on shore. I grabbed a pair of fresh latex gloves from my beach bag and ran to the body.

He came in face up, or I guess I should say "back down" because there wasn't much of his face left to call "face up." I carefully poked around his body, and found what appeared to be a small entrance wound in the back of what remained of his head. I slowly pushed my finger in, feeling for a bullet.

"Call for an ambulance and get a stretcher over here," I yelled to a hunky lifeguard. Just then, my pager went off, but my finger was stuck in the wound and I couldn't reach it.

The lifeguard returned to see if he could be of any assistance. I didn't want him to know of my predicament, so I asked him to carefully check the man's pants for a wallet so we could ID him. Pulling out his driver's license, he said, "Says here his name is Michel LaBar. My God, this is Bubba!"

My heart sank. Finally working my finger free, I realized how badly I had destroyed the trail of evidence. It had been years since I was the first one on the scene, and I had done everything wrong. I got my crime scene kit out of my beach bag and waited for a few waves to obliterate our tracks in the sand all around the body. I took the requisite pictures and felt sure no one would be able to detect how badly the scene had been compromised.

"Yo, Doc, you won't believe this one," Boil began when I finally returned his call. "I'm at county hospital with another stiff who apparently had some poison sushi last night. Died right after he left the restaurant."

"Good God, what's going on here?" I demanded. "Bubba just washed ashore like Jersey trash, and he may have been shot."

I couldn't believe how quickly this vacation was unraveling. "Put that body in the fridge at the county coroner's. I'll drive it back to Dover later and do the autopsy myself. In the meantime, I think it's time we called in FTD," I barked to Boil.

"You want to send flowers to the families?" he sneered.

God, I hate working with these small town police. "The FTD is the FBI's Food Terrorism Division," I snapped. "These murders seem to be centered around food, and somehow we need to get a profile on this killer or there will be a lot more bodies showing up. There are an awful lot of restaurants in this town.

"And Boil. Any news on the fingerprints yet?"

"They all match employees, except for one. We're running an FBI search on that right now. Maybe we'll be lucky."

"Fine. Get the sushi place dusted, too."

"Yeah, I do know how to do my job. A step ahead of you," Boil snarled.

Washington, D.C., is a short drive away, and by midday the FBI's food terrorist profiler, Juanita Oats, was in town.

"I would say, based on what little we know so far, that we're dealing with someone who knows a lot about food. Poison mushrooms and poison puffer fish from Japan, if they are indeed the culprits as we suspect, are almost unheard of.

"We could be dealing with a woman, one who hates men. In both cases the sous chefs were men who had replaced women, and the crimes were set up to implicate them. Keep your eyes open for any angry women in town.

"Then again, it could be an anorexic. Someone who hates food so much they want other people to suffer with them. Keep your eyes open for very thin people in town. The killer may still be among us."

I was confused. I had never seen Juanita so out of sorts. What was this crap she was pushing? But before I could say anything, she continued.

"Or it could be someone who flunked out of culinary school and is now trying to get back the only way he knows how. Strike at the heart. Strike terror in the restaurant world. Could be a recently fired waitress, chef, busboy, food delivery person, line cook. Detective, check out all the culinary schools on the East Coast, get lists of everyone who failed or left, have your men track them down. Also, call all the restaurants in Delaware, compile a list of anyone who's been fired in the food industry in the past two months, get their whereabouts. Get it done now."

I hadn't smoked in years, but after that performance I bought a pack of unfiltered Camels and headed back to my room. I intended to smoke the whole pack. I fumbled with my keys at the door and heard some scurrying around inside, and thought I heard doors slamming. When I finally got the door open, Liz was sitting on the sofa out of breath, looking guilty, and there were a pair of panties under the coffee table. How odd, I thought; Liz always told me she didn't wear any.

"What are you doing in here?" I snapped. "It's too beautiful a day to be sitting inside. You should be out enjoying the beach and this weather. And what's that smell in here?"

"Hello to you, too, Aunt Gaye. I just came in to take a nap. What are you doing here?"

"I need to relax. It's been a stressful day."

I went out on the balcony. As soon as my back was turned I heard Liz's bedroom door open, then the hall door slam shut, and she was gone. She sure was acting strange. I lit my first cigarette and inhaled deeply. As I blew the smoke through my nose, I saw Liz and Cindy emerge from the hotel's front door below. How nice that they ran into each other again, I thought.

I took another drag. I was getting kicked in the ass with dizziness as the smoke seeped into my lungs. What am I doing, I thought as I tossed the still-burning cigarette off the balcony and went inside to raid my minibar instead.

As I drank those little amber bottles of scotch, I looked at the deluxe basket of toiletries in the bathroom. A facial and a nice bubble bath is just the ticket, I thought, so I turned the water on hot and poured the bath oil into the churning water. I piled a thick towel around my head like a turban and coated my face with a thick green mask of clay which promised to make my skin clean and healthy. God, if anyone saw me now! The sandalwood scent of the bath oil filled the room, and I opened the door so I could listen to the ocean while I soaked.

But it wasn't the ocean I heard. It was a wail of sirens from fire trucks and people screaming on the boardwalk. A wall of smoke rose from below, and I quickly shut the door to keep out the acrid fumes. As the fire alarm went off in the hall outside my room, Liz barged in screaming, "We have to get out, Aunt Gaye! The building's on fire!"

I was a naked version of Tallulah Bankhead, slathered with drying clay. I threw a towel around me and grabbed my suitcase, as there was no time to get dressed. With the press converging on the town, and with my sorry history of harassment from them, I was sure there would be a photographer outside the hotel. I expected to see my picture on page one of the newspaper over a caption reading, "Murderer Runs Amok While Medical Examiner Soaks."

Emerging at last on the boardwalk, we ran into Boil who just shook his head and smiled when he saw my sorry state.

"What a scene in there," he yelled over the noise. "Seems the couple in 211 were grilling salmon steaks on their balcony when their can of lighter fluid exploded. Not much left of them. Room's toasted, too. They look worse than their charcoal briquettes. Can't figure out how it happened, though. We found a cigarette butt on the balcony, which we think caused the explosion. Trouble is, neither of them smoke. Looks like a Camel. We'll have to run a check on everyone in the joint, see what they're smoking. Man, what a way to go."

I couldn't believe I was hearing this. Was I responsible for these deaths? Did I fry these people because of my carelessness? Me, surrounded by the horrors and carnage of death every day, responsible for such a scene? I felt weak in the knees, and then wondered if I'd left those cigarettes in the room.

Once the smoke cleared, we all headed back inside. My nerves were so shot I just wanted an IV-drip of Scotch.

"Liz, honey, the thought of going out to dinner again scares me to death. What are you up to? I think I just want to drink my dinner tonight."

"Well, Cindy and I were going to go out to a bar, too, but it's almost all men, so I..."

"Liz, I can't believe I'm hearing you talk this way," I cut her off angrily. "I don't care how many men there are, whether this is a men's bar or not. Have I ever told you that when I was in law school how that old boys' network excluded me from everything? In medical school it was worse. A society and a

culture that is predominantly men-centered has kept me shack-
led and on the outside my entire professional life. I will not be
intimidated by a men's bar. That's where we'll go."

"But Aunt—"

"NO BUTS! I will not be stopped!"

Liz scowled. I had another scotch and a hot soothing shower.

We walked to the bar, and I could see from a block away that
it was packed. "Don't let all these men bother you, Liz," I
yelled into her ear as we ducked in the door. "You have as much
right as they do to be here."

Her reply was lost in the pounding beat of the music. Once
inside, it finally dawned on me what Liz had been trying to tell
me. This was a gay bar, packed with sweaty, shirtless men.

The crew-cut bartender with the dimpled smile spotted me
from across the room, so I headed over to order a drink. "Hey,
aren't you the woman I saw on the news tonight? Man, I almost
didn't recognize you without all that stuff on your face. I bet
you could sure use a drink."

I had forgotten the blur of TV cameras when we emerged
from the burning hotel. I didn't even want to know what he saw
on the news, or what the papers would bring. I grimaced at the
thought and yelled, "Scotch, in the largest glass you can find."

"You're the one looking into all these murders?" he asked
when he came back with my drink.

"Yes, unfortunately I am. But right now I am so over people
dying at every restaurant I eat at that tonight I thought I would
just drink my dinner. I can't deal with one more body dropping."

Just then there was a piercing scream from the next room and
the music stopped suddenly. Someone yelled "Is there a doctor
in the house?"

"I am!" I slurred, and a path opened up for me as the men
yielded. I found a young man desperately gasping for air, strug-

gling wide-eyed for oxygen. He fell on the floor, thrashed about, went into a wild convulsion and stopped.

"Does he have any medical problems?" I asked a friend.

"None that I know of."

"Drugs?"

"Never touched 'em."

"What did he eat today?"

"Nothing from this town. We're afraid of eating here, with people dying in restaurants. We only had food we brought from home."

I was examining the now-still body as I talked. "What did he have here?"

"Only a seltzer. That's his glass."

I opened my purse and took out a fresh pair of latex gloves and an evidence bag, and carefully placed the glass inside.

"Your friend is dead," I said, and as I looked up I saw the mayor and his entourage working their way through the crowd and out the back door. How strange I thought...not only that they were here, but that they left so secretively.

Just then my pager went off. "Doc, I know it's late," Boil began when I returned his call, "but can you come down to the police station? There's been another murder, and we got a hit on the prints that I think you'll find interesting as well."

"Sure, detective, but we have another body here, too. Young man just dropped dead at a bar. Can you have him picked up and put with the others? I'll drive them all to Dover tomorrow."

I arrived at the station a few minutes later, and Boil motioned me into a room. "It was bad enough with the governor's aide, but this last body we found is the daughter of one of the wealthiest families in southern Delaware," he said. He looked exhausted. "The mayor will be here any minute. He wants to talk to you, to see what we can come up with."

I cringed at the thought of being in the same room with that creep again, but when the door opened and a beefy, tanned handsome man walked in I was taken aback. Before I could stop my mouth I blurted "And who the hell are you?"

"Well," he said laughing, "I see what I heard about you is true. I'm Mayor Fife. I wish we were meeting under better circumstances, Doctor. I've been wanting to meet you for a very long time. I'm a big fan of yours."

"But I'm confused," I stuttered. "When I was at dinner the other night there was another man who was being called Mayor, and I just assumed he was the mayor here."

"No, I can assure you I'm the Mayor, though right now I wouldn't mind someone else having the job for awhile."

At that moment, the door opened again and Juanita walked in. "Hi, Gaye," she said. "I know you weren't expecting to see me, but we have some new developments you need to know about."

I sat dumbstruck as she told me prints found at both restaurants were from the same perpetrator. "What's more interesting, though, is that the prints are a match for a case from the FBI finger file. The perp went on trial for a string of burglaries and murders in Northern Jersey about seven years ago, but was acquitted on a mistrial. Odd thing is, the current governor of Jersey was his defense attorney. Here's his file. Bart Stone."

I opened the file and turned ashen, all life draining out of me. "This is the man I saw in the restaurant the other night...and again just an hour ago at the last death scene. He's the one I thought was the mayor!"

We were all stumped for a second, then I said, "We need to smoke him out. Normally when I get in this kind of predicament I have the press plant a story of misinformation, and somehow it always drives the criminal mad and they make a mistake. But since you don't have any daily papers here, we could have a pretty high body count by the time the *Sea Breeze* is published on Wednesday. Detective, I think we need all your men on the street spreading misinformation, assuring business leaders that there has been a major breakthrough and we're closing in on the killer."

"But Gaye, that's the truth," said the mayor.

"Oh, yeah, right," I mumbled. "Well, maybe this will force his hand anyhow, and we can wrap this thing up."

Juanita spoke up. "This sounds very dangerous for you, Gaye. I don't know that we need to endanger your life so recklessly."

"I can take care of myself, Juanita. I've survived worse, you know. Boil, get your men on the street as soon as businesses open in the morning. This is a small town, and small-town gossip will have this circulated by 9:00 A.M. I'll load the bodies up in the car in the morning and go to Dover."

With that, we left. It was 2:00 A.M., and I was beat. When I got back to the room Liz had left a note for me "Hope you're OK. See you in the morning."

I had a nightcap, followed by a restless sleep. I somehow missed the alarm clock and didn't wake until 8:30. When I opened the blinds to the balcony, I was surprised to see a biplane heading down the beach already with a colorful banner flapping behind it. This one read "Cape Fey, New Jersey—a safe place to vacation!" My God, how tasteless. I couldn't believe anyone would capitalize on all this carnage. What was this world coming to?

As the plane flew past at window level, a shot rang out and ricocheted off the railing. It took a second bullet shattering the plate glass door behind me to let it sink in that I was being shot at from that damn plane! I lunged into my room and ripped open my luggage to inspect my arsenal: a .357 Colt, .380 semiautomatic, .38 Smith and Wesson, and my trusty old .45. I glanced out the window quickly to see the plane heading north, arcing around for a second pass as I grabbed my shotgun from the closet.

I heard Liz moaning loudly in her room, and tears welled up in my eyes. I knew she must have been hit, but I had no time to attend to her. As the plane flew past again I knelt behind the chunky wood patio furniture and pulled the gun up to my eye. There, caught in the site, was one of the men I had seen twice with the "mayor." He began spraying my suite with bullets again, shattering glass, shredding furniture. I lined him up in the cross hairs and blew that son of a bitch's head off. The plane teetered and the pilot flew it out of range. Once again the air was filled with the annoying screams of people on the board-walk out for their morning stroll and from the dozens of people with ocean-view rooms in the hotel. I would certainly never be allowed back here again.

I ran back inside and heard Liz yelling even louder. I knew her wounds would probably be fatal, so I braced myself for a bloody scene as I threw open her door. She was thrashing about on the bed, naked, wild with sweat, her knees bent up with wild gyrations going on under the covers. My God, I thought, she's in convulsions, and if the wounds aren't fatal she'll probably be paralyzed for life. "Oh Liz," I screamed at the top of my lungs, "I'm so sorry," and she suddenly bolted upright and screamed just as loud.

"AAAGGGGGHHHH, Aunt Gaye, what the hell are you doing in here?" She blushed crimson as Cindy's head popped out from under the covers.

"Oh my God, Liz, I am so sorry. I thought you'd been shot. Someone's trying to kill me! The place has been destroyed. Didn't you hear all the gunfire?"

"Why, no, Aunt Gaye, can't say that I did," she said furiously. "I was kinda busy."

"Well, get dressed," I ordered. "We're getting out of here."

I drove to the morgue to pick up the bodies. I hadn't counted on transporting death during my vacation, so I had driven my Jeep. Counting the strangled body discovered that morning, I was now taking four cadavers with me, two of them so stiff with rigor mortis we had no option but to take off the canvas roof and stand them upright in the backseat. Somehow we squeezed in the other two as well, but it wasn't pretty. As I got out to Route 1, I finally saw the impact of these killings. Traffic heading out of town was a solid, sitting parking lot. As it was now pushing noon, the sun was high in the sky and the stench from these baking bodies was overpowering. I could put my removable siren and light on the roof, I thought, but the roof wasn't up. So, I held it up in the air with my left hand as I headed onto the shoulder and flew past the sitting traffic.

When we finally arrived in Dover, I called in to the front desk and had someone sent out to retrieve the bodies. Inside I greeted my staff and gave them the quick details of the grisly work ahead of us. I got my green scrubs and booties on, and the four bodies were wheeled into the room. External measurements were taken and data recorded for each body.

Then, scalpel in hand, I began with the bar death. I carefully cut a large Y incision from his shoulders and down across his stomach. "Cyanide!" my staff all yelled in unison as his organs were exposed. Although only a small percentage of people can detect the odor of such a poison, I was blessed with an entire staff capable of it.

"Good job," I congratulated them. "Next!" I yelled.

"Ah, doctor, aren't we going to finish the autopsy?"

"Oh, right. You weigh his brains and finish up here, Matt. I'll start on sushi."

I opened up the next man with another large Y incision,

pulled back his skin, and lifted out his stomach. I placed it on the cutting board and emptied its contents into a glass beaker. "Mary, send this up to the lab right away and check for the presence of poison puffer fish. Then finish up here."

On to the wealthy girl. The pupil of Courtney's left eye was dilated, indicating a possible blow to the head. I found multiple skull fractures. With my scalpel, I made a bone-deep incision across the top of her head at the hairline, from ear to ear, and pulled the skin down over her face. I revved up the Stryker saw and noisily cut her skull open. God, I loved my job!

When we were finished, I called Boil and Oats with the details. All murdered in a different way—gunshot, various poisons, blunt trauma, suffocation. This is what had made this profiling so difficult. Usually a serial killer uses the same method of killing from one victim to the next, but not here. We were dealing with a truly mad man.

"I've got a hunch," I told Juanita once Boil was off the line. "On my way back I'm going to take the ferry over to Cape Fey and snoop around a little."

"Be careful, Gaye. These are dangerous men," she warned. "They'll be looking for you."

When I arrived in the picturesque Victorian town, I drove to town hall. The cheery receptionist lost her smile when I said, "You know, this morning I saw a banner flying over Rehoboth inviting people to come here for a safe vacation. I am so insulted! Did the town sanction that banner? Who paid for it?"

"Why, ma'am, I don't know, but I agree with you." Then I looked up on the far wall of the office and stood petrified, my hands trembling. "Ma'am, are you OK?" she asked tenderly.

"Who is that in the picture on that wall?" I asked shakily.

"Why, that's Mayor Stone, ma'am. He's been our mayor for the last two years now." Leaning over, she whispered "If you ask me, he bought the election, though. There were so many election irregularities, and I never did understand why the governor was down here all the time campaigning for him."

"Do you know where the mayor is now?" I inquired.

"He's on vacation in Tahiti," she replied, and anticipating my next question said, "And no, he didn't leave a number."

I found a pay phone in the park across the street. "Juanita, you'll never believe this. Stone is the mayor of Cape Fey, New Jersey. His staff here believes he's on vacation in Tahiti."

"Gaye, get out of there. We found his car and his hideout here. Empty. We were narrowing in on him, but probably your blowing his friend out of the sky this morning spooked him. We have reason to believe he's on the next ferry home. From what we found, he should be considered armed and extremely dangerous."

"What the hell is going on, Oats?"

"From what we've discovered, the governor's been channeling big bucks to Stone to lure vacationers to Cape Fey. The town's been killed with everyone going to Atlantic City. He's been using that money to destroy Rehoboth Beach, because its been growing as Cape Fey's heading into the toilet. Plus, he has some old unexplained score to settle with the governor here. Hence, the dead aide. But there are a lot of loose ends involving payoffs we just haven't unraveled, Gaye. It's a mystery, you know? Leave. Now. We believe the pilot flew back there this morning. You could be in grave danger."

I got on the next ferry back. My body was fighting that awful tension of raw nerves and total exhaustion, not knowing whether to keep pumping adrenaline or shut down. I got coffee in the small snack shop and stood alone on the top deck in the windy cold. The Jersey-bound ferry approached, and I wondered if Stone was on it. I was really angry that he had ruined my vacation, and wondered whether Liz would ever forgive me. My mind was racing when I felt the barrel of steel in my back.

"Enjoying the view, Doctor?" the sinister voice asked. I didn't need to see Stone's sidekick's face. I recognized his voice from the restaurant. "I hope so, because it will be your last memory."

He cocked the gun, and I heard the unmistakable thwap of a silencer, but I felt nothing. Instead, he collapsed dead behind me. An FBI marksmen emerged from undercover. "Sorry for the close call, Doc," he said, gun in hand.

As the northbound ferry drew closer, I could see that Stone had taken over the pilot's wheel, and he was heading straight at us. Gunfire raked our deck, screaming passengers flew in all directions. Navy Seal teams clamored on board the other ship and state police helicopter gunships swept in—all returning fire. I pulled out my Colt .45 and took aim into the Captain's quarters. As I shot, Stone erupted in blood. Before anyone could get to him, though, he dove overboard. Despite a massive search involving hundreds of people, his body was never found.

Safely back on shore I ran to Liz, who I found sitting with Cindy on the beach eating caramel corn. "Oh, Liz, why does this always happen to us? When will we ever have a quiet vacation together?" But the only response I heard was the piercing screams of hundreds of people on the boardwalk when they saw that I was back.

On the Rod

by Trebor Healey

"Blow, baby, blow," I yelled into the maw of orgasmic bliss as the angel-headed Marco bobbed up and down on my sad ghostly-hungry shaft—long after beers drank too swiftly in sultry afternoon of San Francisco July when the boys take their shirts off and temptation is around every bend and I couldn't help myself, and into his little overpriced studio with beads hanging in the doorway and needles full of crystal meth atop the stereo and an old half-empty bottle of red wine echoing the joys of nights spent long before this too-bright afternoon—when, I'd later learn, Marco'd been fucking Cody and Alvah and all the gang before I even got here. But it's a long, long story and I'm so tired and impotent now, I'd have to go all the way back to that forlorn summer of groping bodhisattvas and the white, milky sunbursts of Marco, Marco—it was San Francisco in the summer of 1989 and there wasn't a boy I couldn't make, and did make them all until the final foggy days of August humping their way through the Golden Gate and I was sad and Cody and Alvah gone and Marco too, gone, gone—and me with a stubborn case of clap to boot.

And Marco, Marco—angelic-choired, song-singing orgasms of sweating summer nights in Oakland hills and Alvah going on about Cavafy and Rumi and all the other long-dead, buggering poets of antiquity and beyond. Cody said right out: "I'd as soon suck your cock than read your damn poetry, Alvah!"

And Alvah pulling off his belt and letting it fall heavy out of his pants—he wears no underwear, old Jew of the desert, sackcloth and ashes in his baggy pants, uncuffed and unpleated. It's in the first stars of evening in the Berkeley backyard and Cody falls to his knees, genuflecting and paying homage to the sad religion of a desert people that predated our own and sent us on this long sad journey of unredemption and fear of an angry God out to prove we're nothing but a bunch of deadbeat winos, sloppy with our sacrifice. And he must be appeased.

Cody'd gotten to turning Alvah around now and putting it in him with a groan and so I went inside to find Marco, who'd fallen into a tea stupor watching *Jeopardy* on the TV and muttering sutras or koans—I couldn't tell which, but it was holy, as all his ruined words are.

And not two days later, Marco'd nearly overdosed on crystal and so was gathered up by his mother and father in sad, dusty, mauve Oldsmobile driven all the way down from Sacramento on a lonely Sunday wherein no one went to mass and traffic snarled in hated, heated lack of love—and Christ would have been disappointed even and was probably a tired Mexican field hand gathering strawberries or kiwis unbeknownst to all the lost wanderers on the American going-nowhere highway of it all.

He'd said he'd be back in a week, calling out to me from the loud, noisome corridor of S.F. General, above the din of crying mothers, their babies shot in drive-bys, and old folks choking on their own phlegm and harried doctors Christlike trying to love their neighbor—and giving up sometimes even—as green lines ran straight across cardiac machines, echoing the sad end of us all in white corridors and mopped tiles of disinfectant-stinking floors ripe for death and decay.

So, a week gone, I went looking for Marco, who'd sent me a sad little postcard of Old Town Sacramento, with pictures of broken brick wino alleys refurbished into the horror of a sub-urban tourist mall. I came stumbling off the tired mule train of the underground MUNI dying its slow death at a dollar-a-ride—"Hey bud!" I yelled, as it stalled for the eighth time, "what's this, a subway worse than Mexico City?"

"And you can get off then!" he snapped, and turning to glare me down I recognized him as a sax man from the little club on 3rd Street and apologized profusely, like confession and "Bless me father, for I have sinned. A poor sinner, I know not what I do...." I hopped out then and there and tripped up the steps to Market Street, busy with suited, booby-prize, lost American working man and woman rushing madness and the Gabrielic shouts of bike messengers warning them all of impending dis-aster and imminent destruction.

I wanted Marco and to make sweet love to his bejeweled, flower-decked, bodhisattva sphincter that opens for me like a lotus flower and sings sutras while I ride the old hobo rails deep into his groaning rectum, sad and forlorn with loss of another turd that very day.

Last night I'd nearly given up the ghost, drinking wine with Cody, ambling our way down Folsom Street, missing my sweet 19-year-old boyman who I told everyone I met was a saint for sure, an angel sent from the lonely nowhere of Central Valley California where the railroads died and gave birth to a mes-sianic hobo boy, name of Marco. And bartenders yelping at me to get out and carry on my crazy lovelorn rantings somewhere else, which I did until waking up on the floor in a pool of my own vomit and not a small number of men's wads in the back room of some bear bar where I was later told I sucked off the whole house and all in a half hour's time, accomplishing some of the finest blow jobs many of these men had ever known. All for the missing of Marco.

And the other nights with my dear Marco gone were the same, seeing mirages on street corners and in dance clubs of the golden locks and smile of my boy child, my very own Antinous, who'd been the sweet boy lover of the Emperor Hadrian in the honey-colored ancient world, forever smothered in the old greasy olive oil of time. And I'm one sad Roman emperor with no empire but an old bottle of Port and a limp cock weaving my way down Howard Street looking for an all-night market to get me a refill of this here nectar that brings before me visions of Marco and deep dreamings—even while I walk—of Marco, Marco, golden favorite of Caesar and dead all these long years in the Nile. And it can't be he's gone. And I get to fearing the whereabouts and condition of my guardian angel lost satyr born 2,500 years too late for our destined acropoliptic love-fucking comeblasts in the dawn of civilization.

But it's all premature and Marco returns on schedule, his head hung low with a big bag on his back at the Greyhound station, and I run to him and hug him hard in my arms, witnessing his sad visage because he's disappointed the folks and before then they didn't even know he was gay and knocked out on a dozen different drugs, living in the Haight-Ashbury and making his money doing massage and selling speed.

"And it's OK Marco," I say. "I still haven't come out to my mother. But she'd send me money anyway I think. And it's not important. What's important is we get back to my hotel room down on 6th Street and I drive this train into your empty

Wyoming of droughted ranchlands and cattle skulls staring at the highway—and you'll forget, you'll forget Marco, you'll forget the pain and your parents both."

Marco nods his head and is soon shooting speed in an alleyway while I run to the corner for a bottle, and then me and Marco are arguing with the guy at the desk because this fleabag residential hotel has a big NO GUESTS IN THE ROOMS sign in the lobby. And I want to tell him that this fine bodhi boy emanation of the very Buddha himself who loves all beings endlessly and without preference is a different story altogether from a guest and will in fact reign blessings of flowers and rainbow light on this very nowhere sad hell of a hotel, but I'm drunk and in my own way sort of closeted so I jabber a few pleas and fall silent. And I'm unself-confident now, especially on 6th Street where you need to be a transvestite or a violent son of the devil to get any respect and I'm certainly not either. I'm just another broken-down wino.

But Marco persists: "Oh come on dude, be a bro."

And the manager finally agrees, throwing his hands up. "Go ahead, do whatever you want, the world's a sty and I can't stop it from falling apart before my eyes. I don't care anymore. I'll give you 20 minutes!"

And I find relief and a crazy kind of satori with Marco as we get stiff and sinfully hungry and I think I see the host as he comes—he's arrived too soon for the Millennium and my heart's not ready yet—and he's weeping now and I give him a drink and more speed and he calms down, burdened by the demands of buddhahood and the certainty of being a reincarnation of Avalokiteshvara, the Buddha of Compassion. And it's hard on young Marco, just a boy from Sacramento become the one under whose very footsteps lotus flowers bloom, falling asleep in the arms of a horny old wino.

I rouse him and we head out. "Not 20 minutes!" I yelp to the man at the desk. Off to the Stud to dance and drink a beer or two, and forget, but before we get there we see a fight and a drag queen is left lying in the gutter, her forehead bloodied and her cheap wig a crown of thorns. The tough guys have run off and Marco, my dear St. Francis of Faggotdom, rushes and I think I see his wings briefly, but I was drunk and can't be sure. But I know he's an angel—I'm sure of that. And Marco, he helps her to her tottering high-heeled feet and she's a mess and probably was before they jumped her, but now a real mess and so we know we have to take her somewhere but the 20 minutes are up and they'll never let us back in the hotel and even though I said a transvestite gets respect that doesn't mean they let them in hotels, especially if they haven't paid for a room and they aren't local. And this girl we've got looks the Castro type. She's no Tenderloin tart, but a well-bred college-educated young man on his own delusory road of fame, mimicking Judy Garland or Patsy Cline. And I'm muttering as I gather up her heels and scattered costume jewelry: "Why are so few of the great jazz singers inspirers of drag queens? Where is Bessie Smith and Billie Holiday, singing their plaintive broken-hearted nowhere and nobody and left-again-by-another-lousy-man blues? And where are they?" I ask Marco.

And he snaps, shaking with adrenaline and the last of the speed. "Why don't you do drag as one of them if you're so obsessed with it, Sal?"

And I'm taken aback and hurt at upsetting Marco and I get to weeping through my wine and falling on my knees in the drag queen's blood and smeared makeup on the sidewalk and begging Marco to forgive me and Marco storming away with the drag queen, flagging a cab, and gone. Gone.

I figure Marco will take the drag queen back to his pad and

like Mother Teresa herself in old dusty Calcutta where the funeral pyres burn on the Ganges, he'll put her back together again, bandage her wounds. And me, I'll go find Cody to get my mind off Marco.

And sure enough I find him not an hour later in the back of My Place on his knees sucking a big bear cock expertly, his tongue moving like how he'd perfected moving cars around the parking lots in Manhattan where he worked the summer I met him and we first fucked each other. I order a beer and wait and soon enough Cody's back on his feet, leaving the man shuddering still with pleasure, and he's hitting me on the back and saying: "Sal, Sal, why'd you run off like that the other night?"

And I can't even remember the other night or running off or anything, but Cody's always seeing things in his own epic way so I explain I must have left on account of Marco which leads him to logically ask me just where Marco is and why not here and I say, "Drop it, Cody, he's mad and ran off with a drag queen."

And Cody, undiminishably enthusiastic and cheerful, crazy comeshot of a crazed bodhisattva, pulls me off the barstool and says, "We're going out to get supremely laid!"

And I huff and tell him *'I don't wanna'* and Cody can't be appeased and off we go to more bars and sex clubs and I land a 20-year-old Latino boy at the Detour who plows me until I see Matthew, Mark and John in their lost Mediterranean madness of centuries past and he's uncut and it brings to mind Marco, sad little messiah, Christlike and written of by them all.

The young Chicano boy grunts loudly as cherubs fly furiously around my own genitals, inspiring me to spill my sad drops of heaven on the empty, unloved pavement. He disengages himself from me and sighs the breath of a lost angel, attempting but failing to climb his way home. Disheveled, I thank the young Aztec prince and wonder about the lovely floating gardens of Lake Tenochtitlán he must dream of ere he rests each night, and I go on my way. And having lost Cody whom I left in the bar pissing on a troll in the bathroom, I go back in to find him and now he's arguing with some redneck-looking nelly queen in a baseball cap, plaid shirt and construction boots, who looks like he might have worked lookout on Sourdough Mountain with me and Japhy last summer but there isn't a speck of dust on his new America-promising-cleanliness-forever-and-no-pain boots. Cody reached out to pull his hair but the queen had none under her cap—her pate was wholly shaved. And she hissed and spit at Cody and he slapped her face, turned and stormed out, me on his heels.

"I've got to find Marco," was all I could say.

And Cody ranting and raving into Market Street about how he can't find anyone to lay and these Castro clones will be the death of him. And now the police are flashing their lights after Cody, as he runs along the median toward Castro Street, screaming and carrying on like a madman. I lurk back in the shadows of the Detour's black doorway, hoping I won't have to bail him out again at 850 Bryant where they know him too well now he's been here in San Francisco six months. Cody darts and dodges and loses himself in the crowd on the sidewalk running down Castro Street and the cops give up and leave him alone. I'll never catch up with him now and besides I need Marco.

So I head across town to the Haight-Ashbury to his old yellow apartment building, the shade of old dark urine left too long in the pot and the sad fate of all nectars and liquids, including dear Marco's come that splashed against the back of my throat not even so much as a broken-down quarter of a day ago, all of those strong young wiggly sperm beastly dead.

He's not home it turns out—I can tell by the light and the

buzzer goes unanswered. I head across town to maybe catch up with Cody but go this time by way of Buena Vista Park that looks out on the whole bay, down to San Bruno Mountain and all the way up to the Marin Headlands beyond the Bridge which crouch like a great Chinese Dragon. And then the sea beyond which folds in all the lights and makes of the great San Francisco peninsula a lost prick deep in the asshole of time unending. A long sorry fuck that leaves the world spent. And the universe is casual sex as it is here at Buena Vista. The big bang perchance was an orgasm without love and so we sad mortals wander in search of that which the universe is not premised on. The universe is premised on wine and a fast fuck in the toilet.

I find a lean cowboy type who jacks off in my face and as my cock explodes in my pants I imagine the cowboy come to be my Marco's and whiningly demand in prayerful stations of the cross, begging for mercy and forgiveness, that the universe not be about meaningless sex and venereal disease but about Marco and love and Billie Holiday being treated right by her man.

I wake at dawn scruffing in some bushes on the slopes of this very same Buena Vista, dried come flaking off the grizzled beard of my unshaven chin. There's no telling who followed the cowboy but I think I remember a young Indian boy who whispered to me that he was the entire continent of North America, it's distilled essence, come to me like a phantom angel of 100 years ago to deliver the seed of understanding, to shoot it against the back of my throat and so leave me to swallow the truth, the truth—and become from thence on the lonely bard storyteller of stiff cock and colonic laundering in the long forgotten washerwoman blues laundromat of the emptied warehouse of the unremembered heaven and the celestial Buddha realms rife with boyhood.

But just now I've got to find Marco I mutter, drifting back down the hill to the Haight having unknowingly abandoned my last night's search for Cody which brought me by way of this brush-strewn promontory and nob of devastated earth and volcanic sorrow, Buena Vista.

He wasn't home then and not for days afterward. Never home when I called and I drank more and more and wondered and wandered, thinking of no one but him.

And then one afternoon, strolling down Haight Street like a couple of dandies—it's Marco and the drag queen, all dolled-up like boulevardiers or cheap, thrift-store Oscar Wildes. They've got on floppy hats and long coats, wild-colored scarves adorning their Adam's-appled necks.

"Marco, Marco," I called, "I've been missing you something terrible!"

But he cut me off. "You need a 12-step program Sal, get out of our way," and he brushed me aside, the clone drag queen's nose so high I could see straight up her nostrils into the heavenly firmament itself. I stood slack-jawed as they hurried off, wondering why I'd messed things up with my talk about Billie Holiday and maybe I've gone and cursed everything with her sad, man-done-left-me dirges flickering about the halo of Marco. *Give him what he wants,* Marco'd probably figured. He's just another young stud on the make, I conclude, not an angel at all—a trick, and the universe is a cheap fuck anyway. I'll just duck into this here bar and get myself royally soused.

And the next time I went by Marco's apartment, there was a man changing the name on the doorbell. And though I asked him, "What, has Marco gone and gotten married and changed his name?" I knew Marco'd left.

The man only moved the toothpick around in his mouth and said, "I'm only the manager, I don't know folks' business. The whole world's goin' to hell. If I were you, I'd check there for your friend."

I hoped my Antinous hadn't thrown himself into the bay for love of me. A sudden regret he's had I imagined, strung out on speed, young Marco realizing my love for him and his for me and he's gone and thrown himself in the drink unable to wait out the drug's haunting voice. But I think better of it, Antinous and the rest. I was no Roman Emperor and besides Marco didn't love me anymore. I was a damn fool wino in need of my mother's money and he was just another speed freak with a sweet body and golden locks.

I found Cody a few blocks away on Hippie Hill scoring some tea. He called to me from out of the bushes when he saw me ambling forlorn along the opposite sidewalk.

"Sal, yo Sal, we've got a plan to turn this whole park into Big Sur! We want you to be the old Chinese hermit living up on Bung-Ho mountain in the mist, dripping down poems on the people like leaves and feathers on the fog."

I crossed the street, my head turned plaintively toward the pavement. "Cody, Cody, I can't be anybody on account of Marco's gone and vanished."

"Oh, Sal, forget about him. He's gone to New York with that drag queen who has illusions of making it big as RuPaul or Noël Coward or some such. Forget Marco."

I was stunned, and me having thought he'd thrown himself in the drink for poor broken me.

"Will you take me out there after him, Cody?"

But he just laughed and said, "No chance Sal, I got me a nice little club kid with a big weenie. I ain't going nowhere for a while." He laughed and inhaled a bong hit, neither of us knowing then he'd be picked up for possession that very night to disappear into the county jail for another six-month gig, club kid or no.

"I gotta go, Cody."

"Ah, come on, Sal, we got big plans here," his voice rang out, diminishing in the wind as I walked back across the bright sunny street that was holding the premonition of a chill. And I turned to see a wall of fog spilling over the Golden Gate in the distance, thinking I'm nothing but a forlorn homosexual plying his hungry, sorry trade, wondering about Marco and hearing church bells and Latin verses from the mass as I imagined him lurching his pelvis up as he did so many times to shoot the hot white host and bless me with his madness and his young golden-locked promise of holding me all that night long. And he was gone, and not a jumper from the bridge, though I would be yet I moped. And I called out into the dying day, "Go in peace," like a lonely priest or half-baked St. Francis in love with the little bird boys, though Marco was more like my St. Michael who'd pitchforked me into a mean depression that would require a lot of drink and Western Unions from Mom to resurface from. And so I said goodbye to Marco, the white fog spilling as I wished him peace, a wall of my golden boy's jism drowning me in the reverie of our short lost summer—and life's a sad, mean trick by an impotent card shark laughing at our premature ejaculations who's colored a boy's seed the same color as ice and snow and fog and keeps on saying 'Got Milk?' and laughing. And Cody's got it and I don't and I realize I love Cody and he me, but we'll never admit it and besides there's a whole new army of cute boys spilling into the city like that fog bank every day and we both want a taste of it.

But Cody's in jail now anyway because I'm telling you all this long after it's all over. But I thought of Cody then as I shuffled down Page Street, and the relationship we never had, and the endless string of boys we'd shared and chased after like a long freight train bound for the West and its endless bounty.

And the train's impending whistle takes me back to Marco, gone and never come back. I thought of my lost boy, grabbed a bottle and headed to the old Greyhound station to search out Alvah who'd gone off to Mexico City to argue literature with old Bull in dusty cantinas and crazy racket of Mexican street vendors crying "un peso, un peso, un peso!" on the old ancient, muddied, earth-sinking zocalo, dilapidated remnant of once great temples to the sun and moon, stained with the blood of a thousand broken hearts.

I thought perhaps I'd find a new angel down at the Greyhound station just growing wings from his acne-ed shoulder blades, tight-skinned in anticipation of flight and newfound gayboy fame and wonder. But San Francisco is always Marco's and I couldn't bear the beauty of any more of them. So I hopped the first bus south to LA, too tired to ride the rails, and full of despair besides, weeping for Marco who I'd lost and Cody who I'd never have and dreaming about Bull and Alvah who will call me a damn fool and buy me a drink and babble me batty into the infernal Mexican night where the stars will wink back at me, because they know where I am, and even if the universe is a cheap fuck, it's horny all the time and makes me feel loved and wanted, and it will listen to me beyond the night and into the dawn—me, the lonely bard storyteller of stiff cock and colonic laundering in the long forgotten washerwoman blues laundromat of the emptied warehouse of the unremembered heaven and the celestial Buddha realms rife with boyhood's blissful being.

Paul's Letters to the Lesbians

by Caitlin E. Glasson

THE FIRST LETTER OF PAUL TO THE LESBIANS

¹ Paul, an apostle of Christ Jesus by command of God our Saviour and of Christ Jesus our hope.

² To those who reside in that island known as Lesbos, Grace to you and peace from God our Father and the Lord Jesus Christ.

³ I am eager to preach the gospel among you, who are in that island. I appeal to you, sisters, that there be no dissension among you, that you come before the Lord in unity.

⁴ It has been reported that you are lying one with the other in ways unwholesome and abominable in the sight of the Lord.

⁵ This you must forsake, this unnatural relation, one woman with another, this passionate forbearance of the natural and good company of men, for it is God's decree that those who should live in this way should deserve to die.

⁶ We know that the judgment of God rightly falls upon those who should practice this vile, hateful, insolent, faithless thing, that you are preparing yourself ill for the day when

His righteous wrath will be revealed.

7 For He will give tribulation and distress, woe and dismay to those who follow not His law, but choose instead the path of wickedness and evil.

8 Some among you may cry that this seems unjust, that God has no right nor reason to inflict His wrath upon you that do only as seems to you natural and good.

9 But know you that God cares not for the beliefs of man or woman in what is or is not sin;

10 But that His law applies equally to all, and more so yet to those who believe it applies not to them.

11 Even then as I have written to the Romans, "Let not sin therefore reign in your mortal bodies, to make you obey their passions."

12 Though your mortal body speak to you, saying, "Yea, lie even with your ex-girlfriend just one more time," as you love God, endure, deny, refuse.

13 Some even among you have been reported to engage in practices yet more vile, wherein a woman might experience pleasure in relations with another person;

14 Know you, then, that this too is an abomination in the eyes of God. This practice, this abomination, this cunnilingus, this must be ended, lest ye fall even further from grace.

15 But should it come to pass that in your counsels you decide to forgo the ways of God, and behave in ways which are an abomination in His sight;

16 Should, then, these things come to pass, and you women shall lie with one another, yea, even in the marital bed, possibly even in groups larger than two;

17 Then know you that I, Paul, apostle of God…would really like to watch.

THE SECOND LETTER OF PAUL TO THE LESBIANS

1 Fine, then, be that way.

Cruising

by Ellen Orleans

Are stylishly lipsticked, brave-new-hair lesbians challenging your queer world? Do you feel about as relevant as moldy soy cheese? Do you find yourself asking: With the queer world changing so quickly, what's a left-leaning, work-boot–wearing dyke politico supposed to do?

Why, escape to the high seas, that's what!

"An Olivia cruise?" you reply in utter disbelief. "Why, those cruises are symptomatic of the whole problem!"

No, not an Olivia cruise, an *Oblivia* cruise. You see, at Oblivia Cruise Lines, we flounder between our craving for personal pampering and our longing for political purpose. Sound confusing? Well, we are!

Is an Oblivia cruise is right for you? Find out as we present our no-obligation slide show of your Oblivia vacation. So let's dim the lights and start the show. Pop! (Damn—there's goes the projector bulb again. Wait, here's another.) Focus!

Before boarding our luxury vessel, you'll check in with our "Welcome to Oblivia" staff members. (Don't confuse us with the other line—look for the wobbly card table and dented cash box—that's us!) These women will confirm that you've paid your sliding scale fee of $5,000 (more if you can, less if you can't). Remember, up to $300 can be paid in work exchange. All paid up? Then get your hand stamped, grab your bags, and climb aboard!

As we set sail, look to the dock where our on-land staff wishes us bon voyage, waving political action leaflets in their hands. Yes, it's time—sort of—to let go of your social consciousness. Whether it's government tampering with organic foods, violence in the schools, or yet more antigay legislation, forget it all while indulging in the opulence of our fabulous cruise ship.

Time to select your sleeping quarters! We offer three levels of comfort, designed to accommodate a variety of needs and guilt levels. You may recall that in many parts of the world, families of 12 sleep in a single room. But don't let *that* bother you as you choose between upper deck berths (queen size beds, private baths, and port windows) and middle deck group housing (bunk beds and shared baths). Of course, if you're feeling particularly globally aware, the bottom deck is available for camping. Be careful pounding in those tent stakes!

The captain is sounding the dinner bell! Don't forget to bring a vegetarian casserole, nonalcoholic beverage, or fresh-baked loaf of bread with you. Yes, the first night aboard *is* a potluck. (We may be running a luxury cruise line, but we're still dykes.)

But don't worry, the next 12 meals feature lavish arrays of fresh fruit and vegetables, gourmet cheeses, lobster, oysters, and various other shellfish (we're only kind-of/sort-of vegetarians). And you can always count on lots of sweet and gooey desserts. Of course, after dinner you'll have to do a clean-up shift. (You put in for work exchange, remember?) Those not volunteering in the kitchen are treated to an after-dinner lecture on world hunger.

During the day, you can play shuffleboard or volleyball, or swim in our Olympic-sized pool, just like on the other line. Or you can participate in something the other line doesn't offer: Oblivia's unique mind-enriching discussions on the devastation of Caribbean coral reefs and North American old-growth forests. Just the thing to perk up your afternoon. And for you intellectual types, check out our tea-time debates; last year's match-up of Camille Paglia and Sonia Johnson was quite the crowd-pleaser.

Or perhaps you'd enjoy just lying under that blue Caribbean sky, drinking cold beer as a warm breeze wafts over you. No problem. Just remember to sign the circulating petitions!

What's that you're saying? Want to stop in the tropics to snap photos and buy trinkets? Hey, *we* don't exploit indigenous cultures with blatant U.S. capitalistic imperialism. (That must be the *other* line.) However, we do visit the island of Carmelupé, where every Oblivia passenger puts in a half day of work in the employee-owned weaving and glass-blowing co-op.

Oh, come on, it's not that bad. Besides, at the end of the day you receive a 5% discount on...Hey, wait! Where are you going? The slide show isn't over yet! Don't leave!

Damn. Another pack of snooty lesbians lost to that other cruise line. Where *are* their priorities?

Uncle Fred's Ex-Straight Ministry: A Play in One Unnatural Act

by Jack Pantaleo

Cast:

FRED TURNER (UNCLE FRED): A middle-aged minister with a Southern accent.

HANK: A guilt-ridden man seeking "deliverance" from his sinful, heterosexual lifestyle.

Setting:

Uncle Fred's cozy living room. Center stage are two comfortable chairs flanking a floor-length, lace-skirted table. Lace curtains cover the windows, and the rest of the furniture is overpopulated with doilies. If Norman Rockwell had had a very nellie grandfather, this would have been his living room.

Uncle Fred is seated, reading his Bible, when there is a loud knock at the door.

UNCLE FRED: Come right in, my boy! Come right in! I'm Fred Turner. Most of the guys here just call me Uncle Fred.

HANK: It's nice to meet you. I've read all your books. I can't tell you how much they've helped me. I just hope I have the courage to go through with this.

UNCLE FRED: My boy, my boy, you've got nothing to worry about. If you made it this far, you're more than halfway home. Now let's sit a spell and see what's going on here.

They sit. Hank begins to fidget.

UNCLE FRED: So tell me, Hank, how are you feeling at this very moment? You can be honest with me.

HANK: Well, actually, I'm not doing very well. I guess I'm pretty nervous.

UNCLE FRED: Nervous? About what?

HANK: About this whole thing. Do you really think I can change? What I mean is, do you really think God can change someone like me?

UNCLE FRED: Of that you can be assured. There is nothing God cannot do. No one is too far gone for our Lord and Savior, Jesus Christ, the Almighty One. Those testimonies in my books are eyewitness accounts of the healing, transforming, restorative powers of our Lord and Savior Jesus Christ, the Almighty One who was, who is, and who will come again. Alleluia! Oh, praise be to God. Hank, it's no accident you're here. It's no accident you've been sent to Uncle Fred's Ex-Straight Ministries International to be cured of your heterosexuality. Yes, heterosexuality *can* be cured!

HANK: All my life I've wanted to be free of the bondage of heterosexuality. Uncle Fred, I've waited for this day for a very long time.

UNCLE FRED: My boy, your wait is over. Let's get started right now. Let's begin with your childhood. When do you first recall being attracted to members of the opposite sex?

HANK: It really started at a very young age. My first memory is from when I was about four or five years old. It was summer, and our neighbors had a teenage daughter. She had long, beautiful, flowing red hair and a reddish, freckled face. Well, one day this particular summer, I happened to be looking out my bedroom window, and I saw her in her bedroom.

Hank pauses, recalling the moment.

HANK: She changed her clothes in front of my very eyes. I'm quite certain that my heart skipped a beat when she took off her training bra. I've felt ashamed of myself ever since.

UNCLE FRED: What a traumatic thing to happen at such an impressionable age. Did you tell your parents?

HANK: No! I was too ashamed. I had gay parents like every normal person. And they were very loving and all, but....

UNCLE FRED: Are you sure they were loving? If they were so loving, how did you turn out to be straight? Think about it, my boy. Before I get through, I'll be able to point out just how unloving your parents really were. But let me take a stab in the dark. You probably did *not* have passive, same-sex parents, did you?

HANK: (sheepishly) Well, no. I didn't want to mention this before, but one of my parents was actually…how can I put it delicately? I'll just say it. He was…assertive.

UNCLE FRED: I knew it! I just knew it. The same patterns repeat themselves over and over again in the broken men who come to me. To act in an assertive way around a young boy is nothing short of child abuse. That's what it is all right, child abuse, plain and simple. Oh, my boy, the trauma, the trauma. But that's why I'm here. That's why Uncle Fred's Ex-Straight

Ministries International is here. I'm here to help men like you leave the sinful, wanton heterosexual lifestyle. I'm here to combat the unrestrained immorality that has overtaken this country—may God's hand spare this nation! Why, just the other day, some California judge gave custody of a child to a heterosexual couple! Can you believe it? Son, I say, son, that just turns my stomach. But let us continue. Now, tell me about your first heterosexual encounter.

HANK: Do I really have to?

UNCLE FRED: (fiendishly delighted) Oh, yes, my boy. Oh, yes. But first let me turn on the tape recorder.

Uncle Fred pulls a minirecorder from under the table.

UNCLE FRED: I wouldn't want to miss a single detail. Not a one.

He clicks on the recorder.

HANK: OK, here goes. I was a senior in high school at the time. I was able to resist Satan until then.

UNCLE FRED: Splendid! That's a big point in your favor.

Uncle Fred leans over and pats Hank's knee, and a bit of thigh as well.

UNCLE FRED: You're going to be just fine, my boy, just fine.

HANK: It happened after the senior Christmas dance. Cindy and I were walking home and we passed by the Wilson's vacant barn. I don't quite know how it all began, but we decided to check out the barn. We sat on this pile of hay and talked—just talked—until—well—I don't know. I reached over and held her hand. Uncle Fred, it was so soft. She squeezed back, and then it happened. We ended up having heterosexual…intermingling.

UNCLE FRED: No!

HANK: Yes. And worst of all, I liked it.

UNCLE FRED: No! Didn't you know it was wrong?

HANK: Of course I knew it was wrong, but by that time Satan had invaded my heart. (He swoons with heterosexual lust) All I could think about were her two oval-shaped breasts, and her wide, ruby-red lips. All I could think about…

UNCLE FRED: OK, OK, I get the point, boy. Take it easy. I just had lunch.

HANK: Sorry. Since that time, I've had other encounters. But only in the back rooms and alleys people of my kind frequent. My undoing was six months ago when an undercover female cop lured me into one of the city bathrooms. The moment I touched her breasts, she arrested me. I've spent the last six months in prison. That's where I heard about your ex-straight ministry. Why, I had never even heard of such a thing. It was something I had been praying for all my life. Ever since I heard about you, I've been trying to change on my own. On a good day I can actually lisp. And just last week a friend told me that he actually noticed a slight swish when I walk. I've seen every Bette Davis movie 101 times, trying to copy her mannerisms.

UNCLE FRED: Any luck?

HANK: Not really. I try for Bette Davis, but—but all that comes out is—is Fred MacMurray.

Hank is near tears.

UNCLE FRED: Oh, I *am* sorry. Fred MacMurray was just another one of Hollywood's unrepentant heterosexuals. That town is crawling with 'em. In fact, all over this country heterosexuals are getting straight rights laws passed. Sorry to digress, my boy. It's just that after all the work I've done, it grieves my heart to know this country is beginning to accept a lifestyle that Holy Scripture clearly condemns. Let us turn to Holy Scripture this very moment and see for ourselves what God says about this unnatural lifestyle.

Uncle Fred opens his Bible.

UNCLE FRED: Here in the 99h Book of Romans, Chapter 1, Verse 1, it says, "Thou shalt not lieth with a member of a sex which is opposite to thine own. To thine own, and thine own *only* be ye true. To do otherwise is contrary to the nature which I, your Maker and God, have ordained from the beginning of time. Besides that, it's disgusting." And turning to 13th Corinthians, St. Paul says in Chapter 13, verse 13, "Heterosexuals make me want to puke. Heterosexuality is unnatural. Childbirth is nothing but the fruit of sinful men and women being unfruitful in a fruitful sort of way. During childbirth, flesh teareth and blood gets all over the place. How unnatural. How icky." Please note, Hank, that this is the only place in Holy Scripture where St. Paul uses the word "icky." That's significant, as icky was translated from the ancient Greek phrase *ickthos pukethos wretch*. But let me continue with Verse 14. It says: "I, your Maker and God, proclaimeth that childbirth is an abomination, punishable by 2 A.M. feedings and changing dirty diapers. The fruit of thy womb shall lead to thy doom!"

Uncle Fred closes his Bible and pounds it with his fist for emphasis.

UNCLE FRED: Did You Hear Those Words, my boy?

HANK: Yes, Uncle Fred.

UNCLE FRED: Doesn't it strike terror into your heart to know that you still desire such licentious activity?

HANK: I'm sickened. I know how very unnatural it is.

UNCLE FRED: Not only is it unnatural, but heterosexuals will stop at nothing to trap young people into following the straight lifestyle. As a matter of fact, that's the reason straight people have so many children. They can't recruit, so they have to reproduce. (He pauses to calm himself) Now, let me check in with you, my boy. How are you doing?

HANK: I feel so relieved to be here with you. You're so smart, Uncle Fred. You know everything.

UNCLE FRED: Not true, my boy. Why, I'm faced with challenges daily.

HANK: Is that true, Uncle Fred? What would you say is your greatest challenge as a gay theologian?

UNCLE FRED: My greatest challenge…(thinks carefully) is trying to figure out if God is fabulous, or simply divine! Now, my boy, enough about me. What do *you* think about me? (He laughs heartily) That's just a joke, son. Just a joke. Seriously, Hank, let's get back to you. Are you strong enough to take the first step in our ex-straight program?

HANK: Uncle Fred, I couldn't be more ready.

UNCLE FRED: I'm proud of you, Hank. Here's where it all starts. Beginning tonight, you'll sleep with a pair of Liberace's sequined boxers under your pillow.

HANK: Will that make me gay?

UNCLE FRED: Not by itself, but pretty damn close. And tomorrow, you'll carry a pin with you at all times. That way, whenever you feel even the slightest attraction to the opposite sex, you can prick yourself to bring you out of Satan's spell. Now, you've had a hard day and I want you to get a good night's rest, but before I let you go I want to say a prayer for you. It's time to speak that prayer of healing to our Lord and Savior Jesus Christ, the Almighty One.

Uncle Fred stands behind Hank and places his hands on top of Hank's head.

UNCLE FRED: Hocus pocus, dominocus, being gay will be your primary focus!

Uncle Fred lifts his hands, and Hank shakes his head as if just waking up.

UNCLE FRED: Well, my boy, is it working?

Hank stands, cocks his hip, and speaks like Bette Davis (or with any other campy voice).

HANK: What a dump! Let's get out of this rat hole and go shopping.

Hank removes a pair of white gloves from the table top and puts them on.

UNCLE FRED: Fabulous! Fabulous! It's another victory of our Lord and Savior Jesus Christ, the Almighty One. Alleluia! Alleluia!
HANK: Let's not dawdle, Fred dahling. I'm just dying for a new pair of pumps to match the outfit I'll be wearing tomorrow.
UNCLE FRED: There's a cute little shop down the street that has just the thing you're looking for. But before we go, let's tell the girls you've been healed.

HANK: Do lets! Free at last! Free at last! Thank God Almighty,
I'm free at last!

Uncle Fred and Hank gayly exit, arm in arm.

Renegades of the Coral Sauna

by Felicia Von Botchinova

22.1.1 JOURNAL OF NONERVA

I am Nonerva, the historian. I have dutifully recorded the tale of our Unity, beginning with our perilous escape from Earth to today, the 20th anniversary of our landing and settlement on our adopted home planet, Maternas. My grapefruits swell with pride that my texts are studied by each and every woman in our Unity. Yet, it is with heavy cantaloupes that I must renounce my sanitized chronicle of our history. In doing so, I join my sisters—Pesta, Laurel, Venus, and many others—who, for years, have met secretly at the Coral Sauna strategizing how to combat the menace that has plagued us. Now is the time for us to openly expose the GEM. And I must reveal the unofficial chapters of our saga...

It began in 2199.2.22, when Mother gathered all of her 6,000 lesbian descendants together, and we made the decision to leave earth and its inferior male leadership for a new world. Mother chose MG, a young colony coordinator, to direct our exodus. And our Inner Circle, the first generation born, quickly assented after seeing MG's tart figure and her two drifting green orbs winking at us from the lumiscreen.

MG was constructed of blade-straight tension. Wearing only black and white for command imagery, she was in constant motion as she oversaw every aspect of the operation. No, she tittered when someone suggested painting the dull gray interior of our spaceship, the Amelia. Never, she sniggered to anyone else wearing black and white clothing. Impossible, she chortled to pleas to bring personal mementos along. Two thousand of us stayed behind because they simply could not leave their cats. Even Mother considered remaining on Earth until my sister, Venus, spoke with her.

"You have to come with us, Mother. You're the only one who MG even considers taking counsel from."

"Phosh," Mother retorted in her usual offhanded manner. "Don't you girls know how to handle things? Besides, I'm not going without my vibrator."

Venus smuggled it aboard, and we finally departed from Earth.

Though MG had ordered all of us to dress alike in synsock clothing, the pressures of space travel impelled us to rebel. We held contraband dress parties in the lower storage cubile just to feel the excitement of leather, cotton and anything else against our skin. Even so, these small happinesses soon disintegrated before our very eyes.

MG was everywhere; leading raids on our quarters, confiscating all the powdered beer, and placing the disruptive elements of our Unity under sedation. Then she went too far. She stormed Venus' cubile in an attempt to seize her collection of erotic film computer chips. Venus knew of MG's solemn pledge to Mother: not to let anything interfere with her capability to lead us. Also aware that MG thought her vow to mean celibacy, Venus fondled the strap of her synsock suit, exposing a lustrous piece of her smooth bust where the chips were hidden.

"Come and get them yourself, MG."

MG turned a deep coral red and shot back in her most authoritarian tone, "How would you like to be stuffed in a decomposition tube?"

Despite Venus' hot giggles, MG lunged at the mammarian hiding place and promptly became disoriented by the soft, swelling response around her hands. Most of the chips scampered down Venus' wiggling stomach. Clutching the few left in her grasp, our stoic leader raced down the corridor and threw them into the nearest ejection tube. Venus retaliated by snapping naughty photos of her friends on an old sled MG had secretly brought onboard, then tossing the wooden keepsake out into space. Mortified that so many stood behind, on top, and underneath Venus, MG took revenge by forcing the rest of us to eat dehydrated tofu kabobs for a week.

In no time, half of our Unity were barfing out the crystal windows of the Amelia, causing the ship to tilt off course. The reeking heaves floated aimlessly out into space, allowing pursuing earthlings to trace us. And, in our command module, the viewscreen revealed four tiny blips closing in on the Amelia.

The Inner Circle advised distracting the earthlings by shooting holographic images of supermodels into their viewfinders. We would then gain enough time to drive into hyperspace. MG decided instead to explode an old hydrogen bomb she had picked up at a third-world garage sale.

"Great Geezerass," Mother protested. "Do you girls know what you're doing?"

MG tranquilized Mother and placed her back in her cubile. The bomb was detonated, and the Amelia was blown into an optical tertiary star system. Having run out of spectrographic garbage bags, we were forced to land on a prehistoric geological orbus—our new home.

Many of the women started to call our leader GEM, the green-eyed monster. Worried, I tried to discuss MG's uncompromising behavior with the Inner Circle. But they were too involved with the settlement of our new planet. When I approached Mother, she was preoccupied with her Whoofie—a fury, indigenous animal that MG had given her as a landing gift.

"Phosh," Mother cast off my concern. "Don't you girls know how to handle things?"

Finally, I confided my fears to Pesta, our psychological expert, and she agreed to start sessions with MG as soon as possible.

1.9.24 PERSONAL JOURNAL OF PESTA—MATERNAS PSYCHOLO-GIST, DMD, LLM, LLLM, M&M, AND ELECTROLYCIST

I started counseling MG after completion of the first colony on Maternas. She had recently been banned from the festival games for deducting points from a nude gymnastics routine. Our entire Unity watched in dismay as MG stalked out of the coral-hued stadium, still insisting that the winner's nipples had illegally straddled the balance beam.

MG was in an acutely foul mood when she came in to my clinic. She complained about shortages of black and white power attire, the impropriety of everyone who wore pea-green contact lenses at her last birthday party, and the lurid conversation of her advisory board, the Inner Circle.

"All they want to talk about is sex, sex, sex. Pesta, I know they have their earthly needs, but…."

"MG," I inquired delicately. "What makes you feel good?"

I observed a resplendent vapor covering her eyes as her voice became increasingly rapturous. "Nothing beats the feeling when hydroponic coordinates are correctly calibrated to scan a taut fractal nebulae. When you probe a tantalizing shift in stroking pressure, it yields like a steamy vessel traveling on a lithe, orbital wave. The intensity increases the diametric humidity, sweeping through geo-heat like a particle storm, and transforms into rapidly shifting metabolic flames. Then, if you lock into a directional beam that propels the biocongruities into complete fusion, full thrust can be achieved. Optimal parafriction causes an explosive core release of unbridled electrons, entirely draining the physical mass."

Suddenly, I understood the immensity of what she had been grappling with.

"What does it mean?" she asked me acutely.

"MG, why don't we try another technique?" I suggested sculpting; the arts offering a luminous release from pressures. After several attempts which resembled old wooden sleds, her only finished creation was a likeness of two women, each carrying armfuls of gigantic melons, which she named "Sultry bipedian conveyors."

"What does it mean?" MG asked even more acutely than before.

"Try again," I gently coaxed her.

Many months later, she finally formed something that moved her: two identifiable feminine figures; one kissing the other on the forehead.

That's when I decided to join my sisters at the Coral Sauna.

2214.2.12 JOURNAL OF LT. LAUREL N. HARDY, SSA

Upon making an emergency landing, my earth expeditionary crew was met by a group of women who identified their planet as Maternas. Gazing upon a multitude of bulbous bodies, I realized that they were of the Unity which had fled Earth some 15 years ago. I was elated that the rumors of their escape were true and was tempted to avail myself of their ripe hospitality. But being a closeted lesbian in the Earth Expeditionary Space Force, I kept my identity to myself.

After being given wrist beacons to monitor our whereabouts, my crew and I were confined to a specified area until the Unity could repair our damaged craft. Glad to be on gravitational ground after several months in space, I strolled down to the beautiful coral shores and gazed out over the luminous sky. Enthralled by the possibilities offered by this luscious planet, I stood deep in thought when one of my crew members walked up to my side.

"Laurel," he started. "Listen, you know how I feel about you." He moved closer, obviously having forgotten the painful groin kicks received from my boot throughout our journey.

"Coulter," I warned, moving a step backward. "Don't even try it."

All at once, we were both flung to the ground. Dazed from the energy charge that had hit us, I looked up to see a green-eyed woman standing before me.

"I came to save you," she proclaimed triumphantly.

I glanced at Coulter, who was out cold, then pulled myself angrily off the ground. "Listen, I traveled 15 billion light-years alone with these Neanderthals. You don't think I know how to handle myself?"

"I…" she stuttered. "I…"

"I was in the warning position for dyke-wanna-go, a self-defense art. He was the one who was going to be hurt," I declared.

"Dyke-wanna-…?" Her whole expression changed and she extended the hospitality of Maternas to me. It was an offer I could not refuse. So I packed an extra jumpsuit and my syn-guitar module, and went with her.

I told her my name, but she insisted on calling me "Rosebud." Maternas seemed such a coral paradise that I gave her the liberty.

"All of you live here without any strife?" I asked, amazed.

"Once in a coral moon, someone makes a...mistake. And there's another colony on the other side of the whoofie tracks, but we don't talk about them much." She quickly changed the subject. "You're welcome to stay with me for a few days. Then I have to take my annual isolation holiday."

"What's that?" I asked curiously.

"Since I'm the dominant female here, all menstrual cycles are calibrated to mine. Most of the time it works out fine because of our two suns, three and a half moons and an orbiting whoofie. But once a year all Hell breaks loose if anyone's around me. An uncontrollable energy wave is formed, causing earthquakes, torrential storms, and general bloating across the continent."

She noticed my syn-guitar module and asked me to play. Rather than conventional music, I created a swirl of overtones projecting the bass through spheric amps surrounding the listener. I saw her gyrate through a dent in a grotesque sculpture standing at the center of the house. Her reflection intensified as her gaze caressed my forehead, drifted to my chin, darted to my toes, then lingered again on my forehead.

Aroused, I slammed my hands into the syn-strings, producing an earsplitting crash. When I looked over, I saw eyes filled with tears, cheeks streaking with tears, tears forming a puddle at the edge of my boots. MG sat holding a piece of sculpture that had cracked off because of my loud syn-frequencies; a piece of one figure's forehead.

"Oh, GEM, I didn't mean to do that," I apologized, realizing it must have some significance in her life.

Her head sprung up defensively. "Why did you call me GEM?"

"I overheard a few women call you that. I thought it was your name."

MG immediately called security and threw me out of her house. So I stayed with Pesta and Farina in the colony of Cymbele. And it was there that I learned of the Coral Sauna.

15.1.16 JOURNAL OF NONERVA

Pesta and Farina welcomed Laurel hardily into their home after the incident with MG. The earthwoman had breasts like Mother's, before they had turned from kiwi to grapefruits to cantaloupes to.... She was pleasant and wished to learn everything about our planet.

"What form of government do you have?" she asked.

"Very little," Farina answered. "The GEM refuses to give up any power."

We told Laurel of how we were to build a democracy after settlement on Maternas and how it was thwarted by the rule of the GEM. We confided in her our great clandestine movement that met in a remote volcanic lava sauna, hidden by the mountains from MG's surveillance. Laurel accompanied us that night to the Coral Sauna, where hordes of women discarded their wrist beacons at the door, threw off their colorful attire to don black and white, and discussed rebellion. Venus immediately noticed Laurel's sapphotic stride and welcomed her with a luscious embrace.

After a few glasses of mineral water mixed with coral moonshine, the topic turned to the fate of Laurel's crew members. It was agreed that if they survived and made it back to Earth, the space corps would return and designate Maternas as a colony, thus destroying the Unity. The only answer was to dispose of the intruders. The group gazed hesitatingly at Laurel, who was busy entertaining some women in the lava bubble bath. She smiled brightly and called over to us.

"I'm staying!"

Venus flashed a shrewd grin around our group. "I knew it. I can spot one a light-year away."

The next day, the Inner Circle took our recommendations to MG, only to be told that the crisis had been resolved. MG had not only blown up the earth vessel and our beloved spaceship Amelia, she had blasted the orbiting whoofie. Outraged, the renegades of the Coral Sauna called all members together to vote on immediate overthrow of our tyrant. Amidst a tidal wave of mutinous palaver, Pesta and I spoke in favor of a more humane solution for the GEM. If Mother released her from her vow of celibacy, perhaps a democracy could be installed without the anticipated bloodshed. A show of hands gave us one last chance to remedy our situation peacefully, and we accompanied MG to Mother's whoofie ranch.

After hearing our tale, Mother leapt off her chaise with a astonished look on her face. "Great Geezerass! My dear deluded MG, it's been 15 years. Are you telling me you haven't had sex all this time?"

"But what about my vow?"

"Phosh! I never asked you to give up—"

"There are dangers," MG insisted.

"There will always be dangers, and the others must learn to deal with them. The Unity is clamoring for a democracy. And you need some time on your back, or your front, or…Don't you girls know how to handle this?"

Pesta stepped in. "MG, what do you think of Lt. Hardy?"

"I find her configuration of mass, radius, and density to be within optimal parameters."

Pesta sighed, and we arranged a meeting between the two, hoping that Laurel found some attraction in MG. They met on the luminous coral shoreline of our colony.

"I guess you've heard I'm staying on," Laurel started.

"Yes. I had to read it in the lumiscreen gossip column," MG mumbled acutely. Summoning all her courage, she stepped forward and kissed the earthwoman on the forehead. Laurel moved to embrace her, but she retreated backwards. "I want you to understand what I did to your crew members."

Laurel drew a frustrated breadth. "Listen, I said I'd stay. What's your problem? Everybody on the planet wanted those dregs zapped out into space. But you didn't have to blow up the Amelia and the whoofie to get the job done. What are you, some kind of control freak? And what's this kiss on the forehead routine? I want to be ravished!"

"I've never ravished. I thought we would be joined," MG said, her eyes fleeing from Laurel.

"After one kiss on the forehead? What do you think I am, some kind of earth bumpkin? You should take a few lessons from Venus."

"You were with Venus?" MG asked intricately baffled.

"I don't ravish and tell."

"Rosebud," MG pleaded. "You're the first."

"You're the dominant female on this planet and you're telling me you've never had sex?" Laurel exclaimed, even more intricately baffled than MG.

"I gave my word—or I mean I thought I gave my—I'm not quite sure now. Maybe if I check my records." She ran into her house and flipped through 15 years of privately taped conversations. "I'm sure it's here somewhere."

Laurel stalked into the room after her. "MG, you can sit here all day fiddling with your instruments or you can ravish me right now."

"Just a minute. I know I pledged something to—"

"That's it! I'm going to the club."

MG looked up suspiciously from the viewscreen. "What club?"

"The Coral Sauna. Everyone knows about it. Except you." Laurel arrogantly smacked her lips.

"I've been searching for that renegade hangout for years."

"It's easy to find. It's the unmarked door in back of the shopping strip behind the whoofie tracks." Laurel threw her wrist beacon on the floor. "Let me know when you're ready to ravish. Oh, and get some color in your wardrobe." With that, she marched out of MG's life.

20.1.1 TOP SECRET, CONFIDENTIAL JOURNAL OF NONERVA— CODE CORAL—BLABBERMOUTH PROHIBITIVE ACCESS

Our first democratic elections on Maternas were greeted with oohs, infectious giggles, and ecstatic shrieks. The end of MG's unitary command revitalized our lives with new buoyancy, and the lumiscreen broadcast an endless flow of theories as to the sudden change in government. Nevertheless, the Inner Circle decided that the true details of the GEM's departure were not to be disclosed to the public. Therefore, I write these notes only within the isolation of my privacy shields.

Shortly after Laurel had left MG's house, Farina, Venus, and I arrived. We looked on with formidable consternation as MG realized that no evidence of a celibacy demand from Mother existed.

"Even if it did exist," whispered Venus, "who would be that dim-witted to…."

Farina silenced her with an acute jab. Slowly, MG's eyeballs seared into her forehead. Her melons turned inside out. Her mind dilated, compressed, then ruptured in vivid coral colors. We quickly helped the dazed woman into a restraining pod and escorted her to Pesta's clinic.

MG spent six weeks in a sweaty delirium. After she finally dried off, Pesta started to gently counsel her. With a puissant nudge from the Inner Circle, prompted by certain election campaigns under way, Pesta suggested a long sabbatical, and MG agreed.

Familiar with only one way to release her repressed energy, MG procured an exercise hovercraft and pedaled up to a safe orbiting distance. Since then, all transmissions have been rejected, save weekly sessions with Pesta, and ever more frequent requests, under an alias, for computer film chips. Pesta has even expressed some optimism about a recent requisition for MG's first pair of coral eyeglasses.

Sometimes, when the wind embraces our voluptuous mountains, pale coral clouds part over the coral seas. And from the crystalline coastline of GEM point, one can see a faint, blade-straight gleam crossing the horizon. At this reflective time, a mystifying echo from far above can be heard as MG pedals past.

"Rosebud. Rosebud."

Perhaps one day its meaning will not be beyond our comprehension...or hers. With every rotation of our beloved home, our Unity holds such a seed of hope in our berries, peaches, and watermelons. Then MG may return to us. And she too will experience the wonders of a lava pool franchise, Laurel's torrid new band, and the coral radiance of Maternas—a world surely meant for lesbians.

6,240 and Counting

by Jeff Black

If the state of today's theater doesn't scare the shit out of you, we're in real trouble. If it doesn't rouse you to anger, fury, rage, and action, gay men and the art form we love best may have no more to look forward to than the blue-haired Jersey matrons who kvetch their ways through Wednesday matinees.

I am writing this as Larry Kramer, and I am speaking for myself, and my views are not to be attributed to anyone else—because who else could match them in insight, influence, and power? My views are more important and certainly more on-target than anyone else's views might be.

Our continued existence as gay men with a God-given right to have orchestra seats on the aisle is at stake. Many of us are already flocking to the video stores instead of to opening nights at the Shubert or the Walter Kerr. Unless we do something about this, theater as we know it is going to die.

One by one, play by play, musical by musical, good theater is being killed.

Yet you do nothing. And I'm tired of it. AND MOST OF ALL, I'M TIRED OF YOU.

Before I tell you what you must do, let me tell you why I'm on this crusade. There is a short reason and a long reason. I'll begin with the long.

The friends I can bear to listen to encouraged me to do it. My therapist said it would be good for me too. My doctors agreed. None thought I could continue as I was, at white heat.

Even my dentist hinted it was time. (The bastard's afraid that if I don't change, if not the tone than the subject of my writing, someone will finally bash my teeth in and ruin his overpriced work. I HELPED SEND HIS FUCKING BRAT TO STAN-FORD LAW, and he tells me—ME?—what to do?)

But I did it anyway. I decided to shift gears. To enter a more mellow realm. I decided to become the most important theater critic in the country.

Not because they said to. I'm doing it because as I've long known, as I've long told you even though nobody seems to listen (ARE YOU AWAKE YET?), the world needs Larry Kramer to keep it in line. The world needs Larry Kramer to kick it in its ass. To tell it what to think and do and feel. That is what I'm doing now. Pay attention, asshole.

That's the long reason. The short reason I am doing this can be summed up in four words, four words that infuriate me, send me around the bend: ANDREW FUCKING LLOYD WEBBER.

Theater is slowly but surely being killed. By *Phantom*. By *Sunset*. Especially by *Cats*, which has done more to hurt this country than any stage production since *Our American Cousin*. ("Other than that, Mrs. Lincoln, how did you like the show?")

What the fuck is going on here, and what the fuck are you doing about it?

As of this writing, *Cats*, by Andrew Fucking Lloyd Webber,

has now been performed at New York's Winter Garden Theater 6,240 times. And there is no end in sight. THIS IS A CRISIS. Are you too stupid or blind to see that?

Are you furious yet? You should be. Have you seen *Cats* yourself? Have you seen *Evita*? Movie or on stage? Pick your poison and prepare to die. Because you're at risk. You're a target. For, as Italian chemist and writer Primo Levi wrote, "Anyone who has been tortured remains tortured." And we have been tortured 6,240 times by *Cats* alone. 6,240 times by Andrew Fucking Lloyd Webber.

CATS AND ITS ILK WILL BE THE DEATH OF THEATER. AND OF YOU. YOU'VE BEEN WARNED AND YOU'D BETTER LISTEN.

Andrew Fucking Lloyd Webber wants theater to die. And you right along with it. And gay men of influence simply hold their tongues. Their silence hastens our demise. (Does it surprise anyone that *Cats* was originally produced by, among others, that I-have-megabucks-and-I-don't-give-a-shit, David Geffen?)

I watched performance number 6,240 of *Cats* last night. I deliberately exposed myself to the danger. To the contagion. To see if anything had changed. To see if Andrew Fucking Lloyd Webber had loosened his grip on theater's collective testicles.

Nothing, nothing had changed. Nothing at all.

Here is a list of 16 performances of *Cats* I have seen over the years:

#34
#107
#452
#891
#917
#1,000

#1,099

#1,336

#2,550

#2,862

#3,421

#3,989

#4,141

#4,594

#5,617

#6,240

Why have I attended this hateful spectacle so many times? I'm famous. I get invited places. I get comped. Besides, most of the performances have been fund-raisers for a cause I've been involved with over the last several years. Maybe you've heard of it. But that's another story.

The important point here is that, because I have been exposed so many times to the repugnant work of Andrew Fucking Lloyd Webber, I am at high-risk. So are you. If you're not too stupid to understand that fact.

Are you mad yet? Why not? You ought to be.

BUT ENOUGH ABOUT YOU. LET'S TALK ABOUT ME.

Let me remind you of my amazing credentials.

Have you heard of *Faggots*? Published by Random House? In 1978? That's mine. I wrote it. *Faggots*. Genius! I assume you love it. Because I'm telling you that you should. And because I named it after you. Critics hated it. In America at least. I'm proud of that too. I'm proud that gay critics hated it most. It cut too close to the self-absorbed, pretty-boy bone. They said it was "antisex." They said it had a "the wages of sin is death" theme. Who's laughing now, boys? Will the last one to leave the room please turn out the lights?

They understood *Faggots* in Europe. Especially in France.

They saw it for what it was. Not as a pathetic cry for help. Not as a therapy exercise gone terribly wrong. But as a work of genius. I WAS CALLED A GENIUS BY THE VERY PEOPLE WHO INVENTED THE GUILLOTINE!

Even before *Faggots* I was on the genius map. *Women In Love*? Academy Award nomination for best adapted screenplay? The nude wrestling match in front of the fire? Genius! D. H. Lawrence should thank me. Probably would if he weren't long dead. Would D. H. Lawrence want to wrestle nude with me? Would you want to watch?

I first thought of that nude wrestling scene when I was 12 years old. I kept thinking of it almost every day until I was 19. The Kleenex I went through! I still think of it just before I go to sleep some nights. It eases the tension, if it's anyone's business, which it's not. Many critics said it was an adolescent fantasy come true. But it got me my seat at the Dorothy Chandler Pavilion, didn't it?

Have you ever been nominated for anything, you lazy, untalented slug? Have you ever been close to anything named Oscar that wasn't a hot dog?

The Normal Heart and *The Destiny of Me*. They're mine too. Groundbreaking plays. Genius! *The Normal Heart* has starred Brad Davis and then Joel Grey and then Richard Dreyfuss and then Tom Hulce and then Martin Sheen. What have you done lately that's broken ground? What have you done lately but broken wind?

Barbra Streisand is turning *The Normal Heart* into a major motion picture. Or she's supposed to be. She's taking her fucking sweet time about it. And now that she's boinking Marcus Welby's has-been sweetmeat, she's become more maddeningly self-important than ever. What a waste of her time.

DOESN'T SHE UNDERSTAND HOW IMPORTANT I AM?

When she finally gets off her ass long enough to produce *The Normal Heart*—look out Dorothy Chandler, I'm coming back!—Barbra and I will record a duet of the movie's love theme. I've written the song myself. Friends who've heard it don't think Barbra will warm to a love song called "You Incompetent Fuck." But what do they know? What does anyone but me know? BARBRA, DO YOU HEAR ME?

Barbra is a friend of Andrew Fucking Lloyd Webber. She records his songs. I tell her she is a collaborator. But I don't press too hard. She's on the verge of giving me her home phone number. And I do want that seat at the Pavilion!

The bottom line is this: I do have the right to pass judgment on theater. I do have the right to hate Andrew Fucking Lloyd Webber. I do have the right to tell you what to do.

But I can't do it here. It'll have to wait until my next column. My fucking editor has limited the space I can take and he says I've already taken all the inches I possibly can. Like I should be given limits.

Let me leave you with this:

What have you done to stop Andrew Fucking Lloyd Webber? What have you done to close *Cats*? Have you thrown out your Betty Buckley CDs?

What have you done to stop Andrew Fucking Lloyd Webber? Did you think casting Faye Dunaway in *Sunset* was going to be enough? Didn't Andrew Fucking Lloyd Webber have the last laugh on that?

What have you done to stop Andrew Fucking Lloyd Webber? Have you stormed Times Square demanding a revival of *Starlight Express* with Christopher Reeve? Or *Evita* with Penny Marshall? Or *Phantom* with Don Knotts? Or *Jesus Christ Superstar* with Jackie Mason? That ought to put a stick in his spokes.

WHAT HAVE YOU DONE? WHAT HAVE YOU DONE?
WHAT HAVE YOU DONE?

Don't you ask yourself the Important Questions? Why am I so
fucking stupid? Why am I not listening to Larry Kramer? Why
am I not doing what Larry says? Why can't I be a genius too?

Does theater really deserve to die? What are you doing to
save it? Unless you do something—you will forgive me—theater and by extension you deserve to die. Unless you do something, you prove daily that this is what you want, too.

I can't believe that in your heart of hearts you feel this way.
I can't believe you want theater to die.

DO YOU?

The Butches of
Madison County

by Ellen Orleans

What follows is one the two obligatory sex scenes from my book, The Butches of Madison County. *However, unlike gay male books where the hot stuff starts on page two,* Butches *is more typical of lesbian romance novels: You have to read through 20 chapters before you get to the sex.*

So, let me fill you in on what's happened so far: As the book opens, Billie Bold is leaving behind her tastefully remodeled farmhouse in Northampton to visit friends of her youth, a butch/femme couple living in—of all places—Madison County, Iowa. Once Billie arrives in Madison County, however, she gets lost and has to ask for directions from a beautiful but lonely farmwife, Patsy Plain (who bears a striking resemblance to Meryl Streep). Patsy is quite taken with Billie, and before we know it, they are having coffee, then dinner and, as we now join them, they are dancing together in Patsy's kitchen.

Oh, did I mention that Patsy's husband, Pete, is out of town for the week?

* * *

The next song was peppier, and as Billie spun and dipped Patsy, they both broke into giggles. "Are all lesbians as wonderful as you, Billie?" Patsy asked as the song ended.

"No one is as wonderful as I am," laughed Billie, "except you."

The song *Your Cheatin' Heart* followed. Billie hoped that Patsy wouldn't get thrown off by the lyrics, but Patsy, who was off on a cloud of bliss, only looked up dreamily and asked, "Where did you get this CD? I know it's not mine."

"It's mine," Billie said. "I brought it in from the truck. Thought I'd surprise you."

"And what other surprises do you have for me?"

"Oh, I think it's your turn to show me a surprise," Billie whispered.

"I think you're right," Patsy whispered back. And she led Billie Bold up the stairs.

a little later...

"Oh, yes! Yes! Yessss!" Patsy screamed in full-bodied delight.

"Patsy, Patsy," Billie soothed, "I'm glad you like how I look with my shirt unbuttoned, but perhaps you should pace yourself."

Patsy stretched across the formerly uneventful bed she had shared with Pete for over 20 years. Now, with candles lit and her husband's things stuffed in the closet, the bedroom felt cleansed. In fact, it had taken on a whole new essence—a place where human cravings belonged, where womanly ecstasy could thrive.

Pulling off Patsy's sweatshirt, Billie purred in deep arousal as she took in the curves of Patsy's tank-topped torso. Patsy smiled, aware of the feelings she was stirring in Billie. Then she could wait no longer. She leaned over and kissed Billie on the mouth. Overwhelmed by the unanticipated pleasure of the kiss, Patsy sank into the freshly laundered sheets.

But Billie held onto her and soon tongues and teeth, nipples and lips were engaged in a passion play of tasting and teasing. Billie had never experienced anyone like Patsy before: so fresh and innocent to Sapphic joys, yet so self-assured and willing to partake in lesbian ways.

As they continued to cavort, with a motion both swift and agile, Patsy flipped Billie over. As surprised as she was to find herself on her back, Billie was still more shocked to discover she liked it. Body on top of body, they moved now, in a horizontal dance of fierce pleasure. Thighs pressing, breasts firming, and that ache, that wonderful ache, spreading throughout.

Soon they could not stand the barrier of clothing and in a fine percussion symphony, zippers were unzipped, snaps unsnapped, and Velcro ripped, followed by an unfastening of buttons, both brass and plastic, until not only their clothes, but the very outer trappings of their souls lay in a heap at the foot of the bed.

"Wait, wait," Patsy cried. And for one terrible moment Billie was afraid that they'd gone too fast and Patsy would curl up in a tight ball of heterosexual denial or, worse, monogamous guilt.

"Birth control," Patsy gasped. "We need birth control."

Billie laughed. "It doesn't work that way."

Patsy blushed. "Oh, right. Would you believe, Pete still uses rubbers? As backup. Even though he's had a vasectomy. Even though we only have sex twice a year. And it's nothing like this."

"I can imagine," Billie said. "Although, frankly, I'd rather not."

Patsy laughed and pounced on top of her with a playful growl. They tickled and wrestled, then shifted into a more fervent motion.

"I feel powerful with you, Billie Bold," Patsy said, her voice low and seething with sex. "We are nature—primal, moving by instinct. We're like two lions, fierce and mighty."

"Lions, huh?" Billie said. "Gives a new twist to the phrase 'lesbian pride.' Or should I say, 'I am woman. Hear me roar?'"

Patsy groaned. "You're bad, Billie. Billie Bold is Billie Bad."

"No, I'm good. Billie Bold is very good."

And to prove her point, Billie moistened her index finger in Patsy's mouth and slid it down Patsy's body—between her breasts, over her stomach, and finally between her legs. As she moved her cupped hand over Patsy's hard bud of pleasure, they both drew in sharp ragged breaths, their hearts beating with lust and desire.

"Oh," Patsy rasped. "Oh." Her body was a quaking valley ready to split, a tidal wave rolling toward shore, a potent geyser about to explode. Billie, caught in the powerful tempest of Patsy's desire, grew ripe, raw, and ready.

"Now," Billie screamed to the goddess, the universe, and several unnamed asteroid belts. "Oh, yes—now!" And as one, they came in an immensely powerful, deeply spiritual, and perfectly synchronized simultaneous orgasm.

"Wow," Patsy said a few minutes later as their entwined bodies, minds, and spirits slowly floated apart, "Is lesbian lovemaking always like that?"

"Usually it's not so understated," Billie said sleepily. "But let's cut ourselves some slack. After all, this is our first time together."

Pulling Billie close and then the sheet over both of them, Patsy yawned and fell into a blissful slumber.

Juan With the Kin

by Dean Backus

"Fiddle-dee-dee!" screamed Crimson O'Hara in a fury. "The Yankees are in Georgia! Do you know what this means?"

Rat Butler regarded his young companion with mild amusement. Crimson was not quite beautiful, but few men noticed this fact when caught in his spell as thoroughly as Rat was now. The sky turned a gentle early evening pink, then a blushing rose, then an incandescent orange, followed by a blazing red. Yes, Atlanta was definitely on fire. "No, my darling. What does it mean?"

Crimson ignored him and paced the formerly imposing porch of Farrah (even in 1860 a clichéd—but beautiful—home with pillars, porches, staircases, slaves, and ever so much more; it was named for a Woman Artist of the Future glimpsed only in hallucinatory visions by the town's ancient negress seer, who spoke only two words on the subject: "Body Paint." Once wedding-cake white, the porch now grayed like a Confederate uniform from the ash falling from above. Crimson's boots sounded a firm *click click clack* as he strode back and forth. His black hair fell across his dark eyebrows. His emerald-green eyes glittered with emotion. His 46-inch chest heaved, and a sob seemed to rise up from deep in the pit of his 28-inch waist. A 17-year-old was not meant to suffer so. "It means," he wailed, "I can't get a mint julep!"

Rat laughed—a hearty laugh that boomed from deep within his Yankee-stitched silk shirt, causing a tiny split to occur in the Confederate breeches that tightly embraced his masculine thighs and buttocks as firmly and lovingly as a Georgia peach embraced her pit. Crimson noticed the ash was settling about Rat's chestnut curls and mustache, making him seem more mature and distinguished than his 22 years. "Oh, you are a brute," snapped Crimson, "I shall never love you. Never, never, never! Laughing at me at a time like this! When we're completely out of liquor and mint leaves and glassware, and the whole city's burning down! Where will we go to buy supplies? I'll have to sell myself for spare cash like that terrible dyed-hair woman with the four-story hotel!"

Rat rose, chest hair curling forth from the slit of his shirt, flexing his arms to push himself out of the rocking chair. He crossed the porch and, from behind, enfolded his young lover into the masculine sanctuary of his ham hock–thick arms. "My darling, you are such a child. Our city, undone, is stripped of its pride, its glory, its protection. The South is slowly sinking to its knees…"

"More, more," Crimson begged. He loved stories that began like this.

"…and you could be found at any time as a deceiver of the Confederate army, and hanged as a traitor. Doesn't that scare you at all?"

"Why, Rat, you know perfectly well I was discharged by the army. I just whipped down my mother's old drapes and turned them into a dress, marched into the recruiting office in my Aunt

Spankmepat's best bonnet, and told them there must have been a mistake since, in this instance, Crimson was obviously a girl's name. I even got a compliment from one of the lieutenants on how nice my gown was."

"How do I know that's all you got from the lieutenant?" Rat growled.

Honestly, Rat could turn from being sweet as pecan pie to sour as grandpa's whiskey. Crimson considered tactics and decided to be coy. "Honeylamb, I'm sure I haven't the slightest idea what you're talking about."

"You do too know." Rat whipped Crimson around and examined him, letting his Swanee-dark eyes bore into Crimson's...uh...green ones. "You've been sighing after that cotton-headed blonde nothing Cash Lee Milkes for months now. You think I don't see it? Me, the guy who stood by you after your two previous boyfriends died under oh-so-mysterious circumstances."

"They weren't! They weren't!"

"Boyfriends? Or circumstances?"

"No, mysterious! They just...had bad luck, that's all. Poor Karl, dying of those infections he got after the doctors tried to leech the bruises off his...um...butter churn."

"You *had* to try to give him that blow job in the back of a wagon on a dirt road, didn't you?"

"Well, Rat, I do declare. I seem to recall that *you* never complained the first time you took me down under the bridge south of Farrah and I dressed up as South Carolina so you could play Sherman's Invasion?"

"Go on."

"Oh, and then poor Hank, getting shot while trying to shoplift me some of those pretty white sheets from the mercantile downtown so we could fuck in the countryside under a magnolia tree without me getting grass stains on my tushy. But that was *not* my fault."

How petulant Crimson looked now, under the deep scarlet sky wherein a smoky moon rose like a sow's butt in slop. Rat felt a familiar stirring deep (or perhaps not so deep) within his loins. Had it been just an hour before that he had rutted so freely on the parlor floor with this wondrous boy? The two of them, naked, pouring sweet Southern syrup down each other's chest and stomach and licking it off until... *My, my,* thought Rat, *the South is rising again.*

Crimson knew what Rat was thinking; he could sense it in his mind, intuit it in his heart, feel it pressed against his thigh. Already Rat had pulled off Crimson's tie, his shirt. Already the gold buttons on Rat's coat were undone, the silk shirt gently opened—chest hair as soft as a Magnolia flower. Their nipples touched, then their lips. A swirling vortex of passion overtook them, sucking them down into something too big, too powerful, too dark to resist.

"Mr. Crimson! Mr. Rat!"

With matching groans of pleasure spiked with pain, the lovers pulled apart. Inside their trousers, their erections fell like Rebel flags, and their balls turned Yankee-uniform blue. Around the corner of the house came Hammy, the woman before whom all of Atlanta bowed—in the hope that she'd one day lift up her red silk petticoat. She was as black as Aunt Spankmepat's coffee, and as kind and noble as The Most Condescending Compliment You Can Think Of. "Mr. Crimson! I've got us a way to get out of Atlanta!"

"You do?" Crimson was stunned. He'd thought that darkies were only good for washing, cleaning, ironing, cooking, picking cotton, farming, threshing, gardening, hauling, serving, raising white folks' children and barns, and acting as Heavy

Handed Symbolism. Was it possible that they were, in fact, smarter than he was? (In all truth, a pile of flapjacks was smarter than Crimson.) "How, Hammy, how?"

"Like this!" Hammy gestured with a flourish, and out of the shadows stepped the strangest looking man Crimson had ever seen. He didn't seem black, nor did he seem white, nor did his eyes do that adorable little piquant thing he'd seen in picture books of Asia. Crimson tried to remember what a well-bred gentleman said when introduced to someone new. "What are you?" he finally asked.

"Mexicanos," the man said, smiling broadly. The stranger stepped further into the light, and Crimson absorbed his bronze skin and white teeth, his open-necked white shirt and tight—very tight—black pants. Crimson felt an exhale of hot breath on the back of his neck and a "Hot damn!" from Rat.

"Juan has a wagon," Hammy explained, running in and out of the house with the china, the linens, the dry goods, the family photos, the silverware, the drapes, and some pregnant woman they'd stuck upstairs whose name no one could remember, "and kin hiding a block away. They'll put us inside the wagon and act as camouflage in case we get stopped by soldiers. If we get moving now we should be in Texas by the time the war's over."

"Do they have mint juleps in Texas?" Crimson asked carefully. He liked to keep his priorities in order.

"Tequila," Juan said, smiling even more broadly than before. "Margaritas. I drink you into the bed, no?" He dropped a wink at Rat and Crimson; both stiffened—everywhere.

"Out here, we say 'under the table,'" Rat corrected.

Hammy shrugged. "You say tomato, he say tomatah."

"You say biscuit, I say tostada," Juan pitched in. "Ready?"

"I didn't even know Texas was a state yet," Crimson commented as they all clambered into the wagon. Behind them, Atlanta belched sparks and flames into the night sky.

"It will be by the time we're there," said Rat cheerfully. "It'll be fun. We'll be out where the deer and the antelope play."

"Who's going to play the deer, and who's going to play the antelope?" Crimson asked. Heavens, here he was a nice white boy—admittedly, one who liked to sleep with men—on a buckboard with a darkie and some sort of Indian man, heading off to God-knew-where as if they were all...well...social equals or something! Next thing you knew, they'd be forming a coalition and opening a co-op.

The wagon slowed to a halt. A group of small, brown children exploded from a clump of shrubbery, followed by a black-haired woman wearing a shawl that, Crimson noted, appeared to be handwoven. He'd have to ask for the pattern. They headed toward the outskirts of town and the bridge. Crimson hopped out of the wagon for a moment to survey the devastation that lay behind him. It was so thorough, so horrifying, so staggering in its enormity and awfulness that it reminded him of Cash Lee's 16th birthday party, where he and Cash Lee had been caught in the stables, naked from the waist up, pretending to be centaurs. He'd spent the rest of the party being introduced as "the boy who thinks he's a mare." He'd shown them, though. He was a stallion now! No, a racehorse, a thoroughbred. He whinnied with pleasure at the thought.

Rat moved in behind Crimson and enfolded him into his ham hock arms once more. "Lovely, isn't it darling?"

"Not quite. I can't hear the screaming anymore."

"You'll hear some again soon enough. Those kids are going to be ravenous by the time we get out of Georgia. Aren't you hungry?"

"God, no! After this afternoon, with the syrup and the honey and the molasses and the…oh help me, Rat, what was that other sticky stuff I squirted on you?"

"I couldn't see, my love. Your head was in the way. Nice consistency, though."

"Well, anyway, I feel like I'll never be hungry again. We'll just have to find other things to use from now on. Out with the cowboys, can you imagine! I wonder if Juan would like to join us. Maybe we can convince him to leave his family behind for one night, and we'll go on ahead claiming we're 'scouting territory' or some such nonsense. We can cover him in some sort of…oh, I don't know…fruit preserves, and we'll lick it off slowly, by the light of a campfire. Fiddle-dee-dee! How does that sound?"

Rat's tongue lovingly patrolled Crimson's ear. "Frankly, my dear, I don't give a jam."

Xena: The Lost Episodes, Number 1

by A. L. Store

Nighttime. The Southern (oops, Northern) Cross shines brightly above Xena and her trusty pal Gabrielle. Gabrielle trips. She
bumps into Xena. Xena jumps away, alarmed.

XENA: (blushing) Sorry!
GABRIELLE: What? I tripped, not you. (disgruntled) I didn't
mean to touch you or anything.
XENA: (composing herself) Oh, I, er, er…I was just thinking
about the good old days with Hercules. You know, just loving
him forever.
GABRIELLE: Gotcha. I know all about that with Perdicus and all.
XENA: You know, I'm sorry he died. Usually five seconds is
plenty of time for me to stop a murderer like Callisto with my
chakram. But you know that Callisto. She's so…quick.
GABRIELLE: You two have a strange relationship.
XENA: Had. (smiling) Had. (she looks down)
GABRIELLE: Oh, I meant to ask you. Have you ever, you
know, been with a…?

A blinding flash of red light startles the two women. Xena jumps quickly to protect Gabrielle from the apparent danger.

GABRIELLE: By the gods, what is it?

Xena pulls out her sword as a woman dressed in red, white, and blue appears, spinning through the air. The mysterious woman lands in a graceful clump on the forest floor. She looks confused.

WOMAN: Where am I?
GABRIELLE: You're in the Thracian forest, a day's walk north of Mount Olympus and two days west of Delphi. It seems like—
XENA: Gabrielle. Quiet. (looks at the woman) Who are you?
WOMAN: My name is Diana.
GABRIELLE: *The* Diana? You mean you're *the* Diana? Xena, do you know *the* Diana?
XENA: I knew Diana, and this is no Diana. (pauses) I'm Xena. This is Gabrielle.
GABRIELLE: Xena's a warrior princess, you know.
WOMAN: (to Xena) Great outfit.
XENA: Thanks. Now who are you really?

The woman straightens herself up, fixes her hair, and looks around.

WOMAN: I don't assume you two have heard of Wonder Woman?
GABRIELLE: *The* Wonder Woman? Uh, no, I haven't.
XENA: (slowly) Gabrielle.
GABRIELLE: Xena?
WONDER WOMAN: There's something really strange going on between you two.

Xena gives Wonder Woman a threatening look.

XENA: We'll have to take you to Delphi. Perhaps the oracle can tell you how you got here and how to return home. We're on our way there now.

GABRIELLE: It's a two-day walk, you know. And we can't all ride Argo.

At the sound of her name, Argo whinnies without moving her nostrils. Wonder Woman looks perplexed.

XENA: An old war horse trick.

WONDER WOMAN: Oh. Well, take me to Delphi if you can. We don't need your horse, though. We can just take my jet. It's so much faster.

GABRIELLE: Your what?

WONDER WOMAN: Jesus, where am I?

GABRIELLE: Who?

WONDER WOMAN: (pointing at Xena) You look like you're in charge. Just trust me. (She looks around for a few minutes, then pulls Xena aside) Umm, I can't seem to find my jet. I guess we'll have to walk after all. Do you have anything to eat? I'm hungry.

XENA: Gabrielle and I were about to get some dinner. We should camp here tonight, it's safe. I'll have to catch another rabbit, though, so there will be enough.

WONDER WOMAN: You didn't bring enough food with you?

GABRIELLE: (puzzled) From where?

WONDER WOMAN: Never mind. I'm forgetting where I am. Sure, Xena, rabbit would be great.

XENA: I'll be back as soon as I can,

Xena disappears into the darkness in search of food.

GABRIELLE: Wonder Woman...is that your name? Uh, do you want me to tell you a story while Xena is hunting?

WONDER WOMAN: (eyeing Xena suspiciously) Maybe I'll tell you one, Gabrielle.

GABRIELLE: You'll tell me a story?

WONDER WOMAN: Yep...how long have you known Xena?

GABRIELLE: Two years, six months, three days, four hours and, uh, 32 minutes. She rescued me from Draco.

WONDER WOMAN: Who?

GABRIELLE: Draco. He's a warlord and he came to my village, I'm from Potedeia, that's not too far from here, and I was engaged to marry this guy Perdicus—

WONDER WOMAN: I know, I know...back to Xena. What do you think of her? Does she treat you well?

GABRIELLE: She's just the greatest. I do the stupidest things like waking the Titans or letting some cute Bacchae bite me or eating drugged nut bread, and she always rescues me and never gets mad and, well, I just wish she would tell me more about herself and her past. She's so distant, but she's so...(she smiles dreamily, then, catches herself) so much like Perdicus. He was so wonderful. I'd do anything to get him back.

WONDER WOMAN: (smiling) Really?

GABRIELLE: (brow furrowed with worry) Sure. He taught me what love was all about.

Wonder Woman pulls a golden lasso from her belt and quickly snares Gabrielle around the waist. Gabrielle screams, Wonder Woman covers her mouth.

WONDER WOMAN: Shh! This is important!

GABRIELLE: Get off me! Don't hurt me! Xena! (Gabrielle is suddenly quiet and pensive) You know, Wonder Woman, Xena has the greatest lips. Sometimes when she's talking I find myself just staring at them, and when I married Perdicus and she kissed me, her lips just brushed against mine, and I felt like my world was crumbling. It was the most intense feeling in the world. And the way she looked at me, I didn't know what to do. And when she says my name. You know, real deep and gravelly—"Gabbrrieellle"—it just sends shivers down my spine. I just want to hold her. But you know, she loves Marcus the most. She doesn't need a lowly bard like me. She couldn't, I guess.

They hear footsteps in the woods. Wonder Woman quickly removes the lasso from Gabrielle's waist.

GABRIELLE: (joyously) Xena! (quieter) I mean, uh, Xena. You get dinner?
XENA: Sure did. Are you OK? (to Wonder Woman) Did Gabrielle keep you entertained?
WONDER WOMAN: Very much so.

The three women gather around the fire to cook dinner.

WONDER WOMAN: So, Xena, why are you headed to Delphi?
XENA: We're meeting up with an old friend of mine, Oedipus. He's worried about Thrace and needs counseling. I haven't seen him for years.
WONDER WOMAN: (laughs) I've heard of him. Tough luck, eh?
XENA: What? Where did you come from?
WONDER WOMAN: That's a long story...um, you'll have to

excuse me for just a minute. I have to, well, go to the bathroom.

GABRIELLE: The what?

WONDER WOMAN: The…er, I'll be right back. Oh, Xena, could you hold this for me? (Wonder Woman tosses the golden lasso to Xena)

XENA: Sure, what is it?

WONDER WOMAN: Just a rope. (She smiles at Gabrielle and disappears behind a nearby clump of trees)

XENA: (fingering the lasso) Wonder what you do with this? (She laughs and throws it over her own head. It settles across her shoulders) Not as good as a chakram by any means.

GABRIELLE: Nope.

XENA: (dazzled) You know, Gabrielle, you look so beautiful in the firelight. You have such beautiful hair and the most beautiful skin. (Xena reaches out and runs her fingers across Gabrielle's cheek) When you married Perdicus, it broke my heart. I tried not to let it show. Gabrielle, don't you see?

GABRIELLE: (shocked) See what? I don't understand. I thought you gave Perdicus and I your blessing. You don't need me…

XENA: (interrupting) But I do! Callisto knew. She told me she was going to kill my soul and then she set out to kill *you*! She knows you're my soul. All the warlords and the gods know you're my weakness. Why do you think they're always capturing you and using you as a pawn to get me?

GABRIELLE: Xena….

XENA: At night when you sleep I dare myself to lie beside you, to kiss your shoulders, your neck, your lips. I actually liked it when we got thrown in the well, because you had to touch me. I find myself thanking Bacchus for making you bite me. And, when we bathe together, it's torture to watch you, to not touch you. Oh, Gabrielle, I'm sorry if I haven't let you know me.

Wonder Woman reappears.

WONDER WOMAN: Thanks for holding my lasso. I don't like to leave it unattended. It shouldn't get in the wrong hands. (She pauses, then gently removes the lasso from Xena's neck) Should it?
XENA: (shakes herself as if dispersing a magic spell) I guess not.
GABRIELLE: (looking bewildered) What's it do?
WONDER WOMAN: (coyly) I think there is a reason I'm here after all.
XENA: You're making me nervous.
GABRIELLE: (to Xena) No, you're making *me* nervous.
XENA: Gabrielle....

Wonder Woman throws the lasso in a large loop across the fire onto the unsuspecting shoulders of both Xena and Gabrielle.

WONDER WOMAN: (under her breath) That should do the trick.
GABRIELLE: (breathless) Xena, I want you to know...
XENA: No, Gabrielle, I want you to know...
GABRIELLE: No, me first...
XENA: No, me...no, you, my love.

Gabrielle leans slowly towards Xena and kisses her gently on the mouth.

GABRIELLE: I love you.

The two are lost in a deep and passionate kiss, their first.

XENA: I love you. I always have. I always will.
WONDER WOMAN: (looks at the camera, smiling) Somebody had to do it!

Chandler Comes Out

by Jeffrey M. Hannan

Rachel and Monica's apartment. Rachel is in the kitchen pouring a glass of white wine. Although Rachel and Ross rekindled their small-screen romance last week—for the fifth time this season—there is new tension, brought about by the hiring of a hot, brown-haired stud to work alongside Rachel in Bloomingdale's buying department. There is no word yet on which way the stud's pendulum swings.

Phoebe sits quietly at the kitchen table gluing butterfly appliqués onto a denim jacket.

Monica, minimum-wage *bon vivant* now working at a Jamaican theme restaurant, sits reading personal ads in *The Manhattanite*, a trendy weekly newspaper. Monica hasn't yet realized that her relationship with a millionaire software developer is on the skids. Consequently, she has taken to roaming from scene to scene whimpering, "I just know he's going to marry me! It's only a matter of time."

MONICA: (reading aloud) Valentine's Day. You—tall, beautiful redhead, waiting alone for bus on 7th Avenue. Me—guy on motorcycle. You waved. My light turned green. Call me. Am getting dizzy driving circles around the block trying to find you.

RACHEL: Oh…how sweet.

PHOEBE: (gets up from the table and skitters over to the sofa) Oh, is that the personals? Lemme, lemme, I love the personals! (She yanks the paper away and reads.) Cross-dressing pinafored sissykins seeks other goody two-shoes for gentle play with horse whips and restraining devices. Weekdays only.

MONICA: Not those! (She yanks the paper back.) I'm reading the Crossed Signals. You know, where two people meet by chance but for some reason they don't connect, or time escapes them, or…

RACHEL: Or they're so completely and instantly in love they can't speak!

PHOEBE: Hullo…you mean, they're too stupid to speak. Or maybe they're dumb, in which case they really can't speak. (disturbed all of a sudden) Oh, my.

MONICA: What?

PHOEBE: What happens if I meet the man of my dreams, except he's mute and I blow him off because I think he's rude, even though he's totally gorgeous, and the truth is it's not that he's rude but he literally can't say anything. And here I've insulted him and will probably never get to know what's probably a completely fantastic, groovy guy.

RACHEL: Umm, let's go back to that horsewhipping thing.

Cut to opening credits—happy music, smiling faces, swimming in dirty public fountains.

Chandler and Joey's apartment. Joey sits in one of a pair of matching leather recliners watching TV. In last week's episode, he and Phoebe joined a 24-hour gym in the West Village. (In real life, Joey was given an ultimatum by the show's executive producers after he took off his shirt and the flab rolled over his belt and into commercial airtime.)

Chandler—who has been pinching at Joey's love handles a bit too often lately, leading many to wonder what those two actually do on their matching recliners besides watching *Baywatch*—hasn't had a date all season. In fact, he's barely had a story line. Until now. He opens a kitchen cupboard. Empty. He opens another. Only a box of Wheaties. He panics.

CHANDLER: Joey! Did you eat my last Top Ramen?
JOEY: (pats his gut) No way!
CHANDLER: (ranting mildly) Top Ramen, Top Ramen, I need my Top Ramen, I must have Top Ramen, I am hungry for Top Ramen....
JOEY: Chill out, man. Go downstairs and get some.
CHANDLER: No way! I am not paying premium for my Top Ramen! That place gouges you on everything—from Fig Tarts to Pop Newtons.
JOEY: Don't you mean Pop-Tarts and Fig Newtons?

Canned laughter.

CHANDLER: Whatever.
JOEY: You know, I coulda sworn they were advertising Top Ramen at three for a buck.
CHANDLER: Three for a dollar? Three Top Ramen, assorted flavors, assorted spices, curly cutey swirling Top Ramen noodles with a seasoning packet, only three for a dollar?

Chandler exits the apartment in a flash.

Downstairs at the Corner Market. A sign reads "Top Ramen, 3 for $1." Chandler arrives, trips his way over to the disheveled soup aisle.

CHANDLER: Top Ramen! Top Ramen! Three for a buck! Top Ramen...

There is a gaping hole on the shelf where the Top Ramen used to be.

CHANDLER: Oh, my God! It's like, gone! It's all gone!

He attacks the shelves, looking for one last Ramen, which, as fate would have it, he spies hidden behind some dried Lipton soup mix. His eyes light up. *Slow Motion*—Chandler reaches to grab the lone Ramen. Assorted instant soup mixes fly from the shelf, including the Ramen, which sails through the air, spinning deliciously. Chandler's eyes become wide with challenge: he dives to catch it in midair but misses. The Ramen lands with an audible crunch. Chandler reaches for the injured package, but is beaten to his prize by the heel of a man's shoe. Crunch!

CHANDLER: You...You...You smashed my Top Ramen!

Bryce, handsome with brown hair and a hot body, notices Chandler sprawled on the floor.

BRYCE: Maybe you should go with canned soup next time.

More canned laughter. Chandler seethes.

CHANDLER: You are an inane, careless ass, and you should watch where the hell you're going!

Bryce smiles.

BRYCE: Relax, friend. I doubt it was the last Ramen in Manhattan. There's another store across the street. They've probably got tons of it.
CHANDLER: Not for 33 and a third cents, plus tax. Friend.
BRYCE: Oh. Well, sorry. And by the way, I'm not.
CHANDLER: Not what?
BRYCE: An inane, careless ass.
CHANDLER: What, you *meant* to step on my Ramen?

A mysterious young woman, pretty, with styled hair and perky tits like Rachel and Monica, approaches from a neighboring aisle.

YOUNG WOMAN: Bryce? I found it!

She holds up and shakes a small box containing nonaspirin pain reliever.

BRYCE: Great! (turns to Chandler) Look, I'm really sorry. If you want—
CHANDLER: You mean to tell me you smashed my Ramen for buffered pain reliever? Don't you know that aspirin is in aisle number two, with scrubbing sponges and personal hygiene products?
BRYCE: Look, I'm sorry. I just moved to the city and I've never been in this store before! I'm sorry!

Bryce and the mystery woman leave.

CHANDLER: OK, fine! Go ahead and go! Just…leave me…stranded…alone…with no Top Ramen.

Rachel and Monica's apartment, one hour later. Rachel is on the sofa reading *W*. Phoebe is still gluing appliqués to her denim jacket. A few pairs of jeans are now stacked on the table as well. Monica crosses the living room into the kitchen, transfixed by the personal ads in her trendy newspaper.

MONICA: This is nothing but…people for sale. Tons and tons of people!
RACHEL: I know, it's incredible.
MONICA: Tell me, what exactly is a DBJM ISO S/MHF?
PHOEBE: Divorced black Jewish man in search of…well, this is tricky. Is it S slash M space HF, or S slash MHF?
MONICA: No space, just a slash.
PHOEBE: In that case…Divorced black Jewish man in search of a single or married Hispanic female.

Canned laughter. Lots of it.

RACHEL: Wow, you're good!
PHOEBE: I used to sell personals in a previous life.

More canned laughter.

RACHEL: No kidding?

PHOEBE: Well, not a real previous life—in this life. Before I did what I do now.

RACHEL: Which is?

PHOEBE: Don't you have fashion photographs to look at? You know, emaciated women in evening gowns made by apparel slaves?

Cautious canned laughter.

MONICA: Hey, Phoebes, what would it mean if there was a space?

PHOEBE: Remember the one about riding crops and handcuffs?

MONICA: Ick.

PHOEBE: You asked.

The front door opens, no knock. Joey enters.

JOEY: Is Chandler here?

MONICA: (in a poor imitation of a Caribbean accent) No way, mon. Haven't seen him all morning.

JOEY: Shoot. He went to the corner market an hour ago and he's not back yet.

PHOEBE: And the problem is…?

JOEY: The problem is, it doesn't take an hour to go to a store that's maybe 50 paces away from the front door of our building.

MONICA: Maybe there's a long line.

RACHEL: Maybe they didn't have what he wanted.

PHOEBE: Maybe he forgot where he was going.

JOEY: We're talking Chandler, here!

PHOEBE: Oh, that's right. I'm confusing him with you.

MONICA: (inspired) Maybe he got a crossed signal!

JOEY: Hey…don't be saying things like that about Chandler. He may not be in the altogether, if you know what I mean (points to his head), but he's a good man.

MONICA: Or maybe their signals didn't cross. Maybe he actually connected!

PHOEBE: So, Joey, tell us. What kind of initials have you dated?

Mild canned laughter.

JOEY: 'Scuse me?

RACHEL: You know, initials.

MONICA: (In her Caribbean dialect) Yah, mon, like a cocoa-brown SWF, 20-something.

JOEY: Oh, I get it. Yeah, yeah. (to Monica) Hey, what's wrong with your voice?

MONICA: (as if it were an accomplishment) It's for my new job at the Jamaican Jerk House.

JOEY: Love it. Mean it. Not. Anyway, I once dated a... (uses his fingers to "count" the letters) T—F—H—D—W with H—somethin' somethin' somethin'.

RACHEL: Which translates how?

PHOEBE: (befuddled) Don't look at me.

JOEY: A two-fisted heavy-drinking woman with handcuffs in the glove box and five on the floor.

MONICA: What was she, a lady of GLOW?

Canned laughter.

JOEY: Nah, my cousin Frankie's sister, Magdalena.

PHOEBE: Hullo...that still makes her your cousin, which, last time I checked, was illegal, not to mention highly abnormal, unless you're from the deep, deep South, where they don't have televisions to tell them what's normal.

JOEY: It wasn't a real date! We just went bowling together a few times. I never even kissed her.

PHOEBE: She's probably still standing on the front porch of that row house in the Bronx, her lips puckered up, waiting for your tongue to... (beat) I've got to get away from this glue! The fumes...

Chandler enters nonchalantly, also without knocking.

JOEY: Chandler, buddy, what happened?

CHANDLER: Um...nothing? Everything? Venus collided with Mars? I don't know! Tell me!

JOEY: (worried) Venus collided with Mars? You mean the planets?

PHOEBE: Oh, my God! Where will all the women and men come from now?

CHANDLER: (swatting at both Joey and Phoebe with his hands) Get away from me, you ignoramuses. They didn't have any Top Ramen, so I had to go up the street.

JOEY: Oh?

CHANDLER: Oh!

JOEY: Oh, yeah?

CHANDLER: Yeah!

JOEY: (beaten) Well, in that case sorry, bud. But hey, where's it at?

Joey makes stupid hand signals, possibly but not probably suggesting Top Ramen.

CHANDLER: You mean, the...

Chandler responds with similar gestures.

CHANDLER: On the stove!

JOEY: Enough for two?
CHANDLER: You know it!

Joey and Chandler exit, an arm wrapped around each other's shoulder.

PHOEBE: And you thought the personals made no sense.

The buying office at Bloomingdale's. Rachel and Bryce, the handsome stud hired in last week's episode (and Chandler's stepper-onner of Top Ramen), are analyzing large fabric swatches.

RACHEL: (holding one up) What do you think? Too Southern California?
BRYCE: Too Florida.
RACHEL: Like there's a difference?
BRYCE: Look at the cut, it's retiree city.
RACHEL: And there are no retirees in Palm Springs?
BRYCE: We're buying young women's, Rachel. That's totally *Golden Girls.*

Canned laughter—again.

RACHEL: What about this one?
BRYCE: A little too *Partridge Family.*
RACHEL: Yeah, it does kind of resemble that ugly bus.

They laugh, accompanied by nostalgic canned laughter. Rachel rummages through more swatches, holds yet another ugly one against her chest.

RACHEL: Um...Bryce?

BRYCE: Yeah, Rachel?

RACHEL: I need to get something off my chest.

BRYCE: I'll say. That's the worst one so far.

RACHEL: No, I...I mean about yesterday, when I accidentally grabbed your butt in the storage room. I am *so* embarrassed by that. I hope it doesn't impact our professional relationship.

BRYCE: Don't worry about it, it's completely forgotten.

RACHEL: It really was an accident. I would never intentionally grab your butt. Well, I mean not never never, but not... What I'm saying is, you have a really great butt.

BRYCE: Thank you.

RACHEL: (frustrated) But that's not what I'm saying! You see...I have Ross.

BRYCE: Who probably wouldn't be thrilled to know you go around squeezing other guys' butts.

RACHEL: I swear, I thought it was a stack of fall fabric samples. I would never do anything to jeopardize my relationship with Ross.

BRYCE: I'm sure you wouldn't. Listen, Rachel, it's no big deal. It was an accident, it doesn't matter. Besides, (beat) I'm gay.

RACHEL: Y-you are?

BRYCE: Relieved?

RACHEL: I...I don't know.

Ross knocks on the door frame and enters the room.

ROSS: Hi, there, worker bees.

RACHEL: (startled) Ross, sweetheart! Hi!

ROSS: How's my honey?

RACHEL: Sweet on you, sugar pie. (beat) Ross, this is Bryce, the new assistant buyer I told you about last night. Bryce, this is my boyfriend, Ross—who I was mentioning a minute ago.

BRYCE: The pleasure's mine.

ROSS: Don't be so sure.

Suspicious canned laughter.

ROSS: You ready for lunch, honey doll?

RACHEL: Sure, sweetie bear. Let me grab my purse.

ROSS: I'll go find Chandler.

RACHEL: You brought Chandler? Great! There'll be four of us.

BRYCE: Who's Chandler?

ROSS: He's our resident clown. (looks around) He was with me a minute ago. I hope I don't have to go pry him out of the mannequin room again.

Canned laughter.

RACHEL: (flinging purse over her shoulder) I'm ready.

BRYCE: (securing his fanny pack) Me, too.

Before Ross has a chance to go looking for him, Chandler enters excitedly.

CHANDLER: Whoa-ho, guess who got lost in the lingerie department!

ROSS: Glad you found your way out.

BRYCE: (coyly) Likewise.

CHANDLER: (recognizing him) You. You again.

RACHEL: You know each other?

CHANDLER: This man is a Philistine!

ROSS: No. Actually this unnaturally handsome duoped is your lunch date.

RACHEL: Well, no, not exactly his...

CHANDLER: My what?

BRYCE: This is perfect...Chandler, was it? I owe you one anyway, after smashing your Ramen the other day.

ROSS: What Ramen?

RACHEL: You're the Top Ramen guy?

ROSS: *What* Ramen?

RACHEL: I'll tell you later.

BRYCE: Yes, I was the stupid, careless ass who smashed Chandler's lunch in the Westside Market on Saturday.

CHANDLER: *Inane,* careless ass.

RACHEL: Fine, fine, whatever. Let's go.

CHANDLER: I'm not going if he is.

ROSS: Grow up, Chandler.

BRYCE: That's OK, Ross. I'll stay here. You guys go have a good time.

RACHEL: (to Bryce) We can't leave you here. (to Ross) We can't leave him here. (to Chandler) It's only his second week and he doesn't know anyone.

ROSS: (whining) I'm hungry.

CHANDLER: Oh, all right. He can come. (pointing at Bryce) But keep your feet to yourself!

BRYCE: I'll try.

Ross and Rachel sit at a four-top table in a nice Manhattan restaurant. Lunch is obviously over. Bryce and Chandler stand together, beside the table, ready to go.

CHANDLER: Thanks again for lunch, Ross. That was a treat.

BRYCE: Yes. It was really kind of you.

ROSS: Don't mention it.

RACHEL: So you boys are off to work?

CHANDLER: No pay, no play! (to Bryce) Let's go, big guy.
ALL: See ya! Bye!

Chandler and Bryce exit.

ROSS: Well, that was an awfully nice lunch.
RACHEL: The two boys sure hit it off well.
ROSS: Yeah, they did, didn't they. You know, if I didn't know better, I'd be tempted to say that Bryce and Chandler had a thing for each other.
RACHEL: Oh, Ross. (beat) Oh, Ross!

The women's apartment, one week later. Phoebe is at the table working on her denim appliqués, now and then taking a sniff of glue. She now has a huge stack of denim clothing beside her. Monica and Rachel are in the kitchen chopping vegetables. Ross is on the sofa reading the newest edition of *The Manhattanite*. Joey enters abruptly, without knocking. He carries a basketball in one hand and a note in the other.

JOEY: (waving note) Can you believe Chandler? He blew off our game so he could go clothes shopping with his new friend—(said with disgust) Bryce. Did he mention where they were going?
MONICA: No, he didn't. Sorry, sweetie.
JOEY: Well, I'll find him. And when I do, he'd better have bought me something.

Joey storms out.

ROSS: Hey, listen to this one. (reading) BiWM ISO daddy. Hairy male or butch les w/strap-on will do.

RACHEL: You don't need to read those, sweetie.

ROSS: What's a BiWM? It sounds like a kinky convertible.

Canned laughter.

MONICA: It means bisexual white male.

PHOEBE: Very good!

RACHEL: (cautiously) Mon?

MONICA: (shrugs) I've been working the slow shift at the Jerk House.

ROSS: Hey, here's a good one. It's a Crossed Signal. (reading) Saturday, Westside Market. I smashed your Ramen, you stole my heart. Three days later we shared a cab. Wanted to kiss you but I chickened out. Call me. Bryce.

RACHEL: Oh…My…God!

ROSS: Now, honey, relax. Maybe it's a different Bryce.

RACHEL: What, there was a Ramen stomping festival for men named Bryce in the Westside Market last Saturday? How could it not be our Bryce?

MONICA: Would somebody clue me in, please?

RACHEL: Chandler met a boy in the market the other day. The other boy stepped on Chandler's Top Ramen. The boy, it turns out, is Bryce, the new guy at work. Bryce and Chandler had lunch with Ross and me and left together.

ROSS: In the same cab.

PHOEBE: So now Bryce has fallen head over heels for Chandler. But Chandler, like always, doesn't know it. Poor Chandler is always the last to get clued in to things—well, except for Joey, who is really always the last to get clued in. Meanwhile, Phoebe—that would be me—is left explaining everything to everyone else because I tend to provide comic relief *and* insight to every situation. All at the same time. Not entirely unlike the idiot savant who appears in many of Shakespeare's plays. (sniffs glue) Mmm, this stuff is addictive.

Later that night. Bryce's apartment, the epitome of contemporary, multiethnic, queer domesticity—all that's missing is the same-sex partner and a small pet. Bryce crosses into the kitchen as Chandler, carrying a shopping bag decorated with Antonio Sabato Jr.'s torso, enters.

BRYCE: So, are you pleased with your purchases?
CHANDLER: Absolutely! A new silk shirt and a striking tie to go with it. (He holds them up together—a lavender silk shirt and a purple tie covered with small pink triangles) It's a very festive pattern on the tie, don't you think?
BRYCE: Absolutely.
CHANDLER: But speaking of money, what do I owe you for the taxis? It was, what, ten, 12 bucks each?
BRYCE: Ten bucks, but don't worry about it.
CHANDLER: No, no, my friend. Let's keep this even-Steven.

Chandler pulls a $10 bill from his wallet and crosses into the kitchen to hand it to Bryce. Once in the kitchen, he notices an artistic black-and-white photograph of a male nude hanging on the wall.

CHANDLER: Oh wow, you're into Greek art?
BRYCE: Uh, it's not exactly Greek, Chandler. It's a Bruce Weber.
CHANDLER: Why, it all but resonates with the form and line of antiquity.
BRYCE: It's hot, huh?
CHANDLER: Hot?

BRYCE: (grinning) Yeah, hot. You like it don't you?

CHANDLER: Well, certainly—who couldn't appreciate the rounded lines of the shoulders and buttocks…the subtle shadows on the arms and thighs… (getting warm) the slightly arching back… (beat) I have to go.

BRYCE: Cut it out, Chandler. We're going to have dinner and watch *Baywatch* together, as agreed. Let's be adult about this.

CHANDLER: I am being adult! This highly heterosexual adult male does not watch *Baywatch* with men who don't ogle Pamela Lee.

BRYCE: Like you really ogle Pamela Lee.

CHANDLER: Of course I do! Joey and I exclusively ogle the babes on *Baywatch*!

BRYCE: You and Joey, eh?

Bryce grabs Chandler around the waist and yanks him close so that the two men are face to face.

CHANDLER: Now don't get rough here!

BRYCE: All I ever hear about is Joey. What's the story between you two, anyway?

CHANDLER: (squirming) Just let go of me, you, you—presumptive ass!

BRYCE: Joey never holds you like this, does he?

CHANDLER: Of course not. It's obscene.

BRYCE: It's what you've been wanting for a long time. Admit it.

CHANDLER: Hogwash! Let go, you big bollocks. You're suffocating me.

Chandler struggles to free himself—sort of.

BRYCE: If that's what you want….

Bryce lets go.

CHANDLER: I...I didn't mean completely.

Audible gasps from the audience.

BRYCE: No? (wrapping his arms around Chandler's waist) You mean you like it?
CHANDLER: It's kind of tight, but... Do you work out? You must. Hmm. Great arms... Well...other than the precariousness closeness of the two bodies, it's...it's...
BRYCE: (gently) You can say it.
CHANDLER: Not bad.
BRYCE: So you like it?
CHANDLER: To a degree. We're still just friends, of course.
BRYCE: Of course.
CHANDLER: And there's nothing else between us?
BRYCE: (looks down and sees what's between them) Not exactly. (beat) Is that a degree in your pocket, or are you just *really* happy to be here?
CHANDLER: OK, I lied! It's the boys in red bathing suits I like! It's the boys! The boys! Oh, kiss me!

Bryce leans forward and kisses Chandler on the lips. The audience shrieks and howls. After an extended, wet kiss, Bryce pulls his head back and loosens his grip on the petrified yet enamored and utterly transformed Chandler.

Later that night, Bryce's bed. On the night stand is a tube of lube and several torn condom packs. Chandler rests his head on Bryce's requisitely muscled shoulder.

BRYCE: You OK?

CHANDLER: More than OK. I'm stunned. I had no idea what I've been missing all these years.

BRYCE: It kind of puts your world in perspective, doesn't it?

CHANDLER: It really does. But....

Chandler becomes contemplative.

BRYCE: What's the matter?

CHANDLER: It's silly.

BRYCE: (delicately touching the tip of Chandler's nose) Come on...

CHANDLER: Nothing's the matter, honestly. It's just...does this mean Joey and I have to buy you a recliner for our living room?

BRYCE: I don't know. Ask him.

Camera pulls back and reveals Joey, sound asleep beside them.

JOEY: (groggy) Mph...mmm...recliner...*Baywatch*...Hasselhoff. Mmm.

BRYCE and CHANDLER: Nah. Let him sleep.

Pushed Out of Heaven

by Caril Behr

(And pure thou wert created),we enjoy
In eminence, and obstacle find none
Of membrane, joint, or limb, exclusive bars.
Easier than air with air, if spirits embrace,
Total they mix, union of pure with pure
Desiring; nor restrained conveyance need
As flesh to mix with flesh or soul with soul.
—*Paradise Lost,* Book 8 (lines 623–629), by John Milton

It was no accident. The young angel was pushed out of heaven for reasons of jealousy and spite. He was a softly beautiful creature who inspired admiration and sought attention with a flirtatiousness which made him a favorite in some quarters. While his admirers indulged his foppishness, his enemies gathered in rancorous gloom.

In truth he was not clever enough to do them any harm, but they'd convinced themselves that he was a parvenu, an upstart who would discredit their divinity. The Immaculate One had seen the conflict developing and done nothing. Possibly there was more pressing business to attend to on another planet, or maybe young Gaybriel simply had it coming. Pride is, after all, a deadly sin, and heaven is as full of random misfortune as anywhere on earth.

So it happened in the rosy glow of a summer's dawn. A number of embittered saints pulled Gaybriel off his cloud and pitched him earthward. It was no hardship floating through the stratosphere. In fact, all manner of curious sensations penetrated his ethereal body, causing him to laugh and weep by turns as he contemplated the vastness of the nonheavenly environment.

On approach to earth, the view was stupendous thanks to the helping hand of The Immaculate One, who manipulated prevailing winds so that he was swept across oceans, mountain ranges, and deserts before hovering over London in the United Kingdom. There, a ridge of high pressure kept him motionless. He was able to observe, from an invisible height, the ways of the people below, who seemed to be every bit as petty and erratic as his heavenly colleagues. Meanwhile in the great beyond, his presence was neither missed nor mourned. Other crises had eclipsed his swift departure, and the entire community was in an uproar over a misplaced harp.

The Immaculate One did not abandon Gaybriel without some preparation. His nakedness was clothed in flattering garments which hugged his comely form. His ears and nipples were pierced with gold and loose change appeared in his pockets. He was made aware of a wallet distended with notes, the denominations of which were explained to him. Then his wings were severed, rendering him flightless. He descended onto the pavement just outside Tottenham Court Road Tube Station on an airless Friday afternoon in late July, and thought that he'd landed in hell.

After some hours of aimless wandering, he began to get feelings of déjà vu, and by the time the summer sky had turned the color of ink, his feet, which seemed to know the way, had taken him to a club near Charing Cross. Once inside he stared in wonderment at the gyrating bodies. He swayed his hips to the hypnotic rhythm. Someone winked at him. He winked back, and thus began a roller-coaster ride of casual encounters. He found out about back rooms and cottages and condoms, which were completely alien to him.

"Where I've just come from, we would interpenetrate ourselves entirely. Our vapors used to coalesce completely. Our conjunctions were not so painstakingly genital."

"Bloody hell, where've you been?"

"Heaven."

"Really? Whatcha doing here then?"

"I was forcibly ejected. I don't know what for. Maybe I was contaminated with the burden of sin."

"Look mate, maybe you'd better speak to a priest or something. Let's forget it for now, shall we? Ta'ra then."

It was in a bar in Soho that he met silver-haired Barry, who responded to his naïveté with fatherly patience. Barry took him home and explained many things, among them the necessity for safe sex.

"Oh," said Gaybriel, "we never had problems like this in heaven."

"Living in a fantasy world is all very well, but it won't do to take risks with your health or the health of others."

Gaybriel only half understood. He was not made of flesh and blood despite appearances, but he and Barry were fond of each other, and so he moved in. It happened by default more than by design, because he had nowhere else to go. He had spent the warm summer evenings sleeping in St. James's Park, but Au-

gust came and went, and by the end of September he was beginning to merge vapors with the damp night air. The Immaculate One would have intervened, but Barry came along instead
and that was altogether more convenient.

They lived together through the autumn, over the winter, and
into the following spring, during which time Gaybriel became
domesticated under Barry's tutelage. He kept the flat spotless.
He learned to cook gourmet meals. He was a considerate companion and a faithful lover, but neither of them was happy.

On reflection it became clear that they had absolutely nothing in common. Once the newness had rubbed off their relationship, a dull despair set in. They never argued. They were
both too polite for that, but they chipped away at each other
with throwaway remarks and small gestures. A pall hung over
the flat. Barry's skin turned almost as gray as his hair, and the
most irksome thing was that he'd met another man whom he
wanted to bring home, but couldn't because Gaybriel was always there. For his part, Gaybriel remained as beautiful to look
at as ever, only now he had a stilted aura about him, a bit like a
shop dummy.

The day arrived when Barry couldn't stand it any more and
said so.

"Look old chap, we can't carry on like this. It stands to reason
I won't throw you into the street, but you must make plans to
move on. Why don't you start by moving into the spare room and
going out more at night? You need to meet people your own age."

Gaybriel was more relieved than hurt. Nevertheless, he took
his time getting going. Out on the scene this time round, he was
more self-conscious about his ignorance than before. Luckily
he managed to make friends who were charmed by his innocence and kept him afloat. He moved out of Barry's flat into a
mixed house in South London.

Spring turned to summer. He was out drinking with his buddies in an Old Compton Street pub when he saw the boy of his dreams. It was love at first sight.

"Do you know him?"

"Yeah, we were at art school together. He's a she."

"What's that?"

"Jesus, where have you been all your life? She's a woman, a lesbian, a dyke! Can't you see she's cruising up the chick with the green hair?"

"What does that mean?" Gaybriel looked perplexed.

"What do you think it means? She wants to take her to bed."

"But I want to take him to bed."

"Well, you can't, and anyway, she's not a he. Didn't you hear the first time?"

"I heard, but I still don't know what it means."

Gaybriel's companion explained in crude detail the anatomical variations of gendered human existence.

"I don't care if she's different, I still want to ask her out."

"Forget it, you'd have to change your sex first."

"Why?"

"Because she likes girls, dummy. She wouldn't be remotely interested in you."

That night Gaybriel called upon The Immaculate One for the first time since his plunge to earth.

"I want to be a woman," he said. "Please help me, this is really important."

"It would mean giving up your divinity," Gaybriel was told. "You'd be made of flesh and blood. You'll feel cold, hunger, and pain. You'll bleed."

"I'll go for it," Gaybriel insisted. "I'm in love."

"You'll be on your own," said The Immaculate One.

"I've always been on my own. I've always been at odds with

everything around me. Let's face it, I'm not normal. I'll never be normal, but I could be happy."

And so Gaybriel became Gaybriella. She courted Eva, who returned her affections, and they moved in together on their second date. Thereafter they became inseparable, and Gaybriella found out what it was to love a woman. She learned to put up with period pains and premenstrual tension, with jealousy and infidelity and bouts of lesbian bed death. They stayed together and grew old together, growing more alike with the passing years.

Gaybriella never regretted her decision. She became a stalwart human being, energetic, resourceful, and quietly long suffering. After all, what else is there to do once you've been pushed out of heaven?

Tails of the City, by Heritage Twinklefluff

by The Saint

The A-Gays were hard at work putting on their tuxedos. "Let's go! Let's go!" cried Michael Mouse. "If we don't rush, however shall we get to Placido's expensive opening?"

The others agreed and finished putting on their best clothes, which they had rented from the most fashionable tailor in San Francisco. They began hurrying out the door to the Opera House.

"My God, Cory, what are you *doing*!" Michael said, aghast.

"I'm picking a pimple!" Cory explained.

"A-Gays do not have pimples! Get back into our terribly chic apartment and stay there. You can't go to Placido's opening!"

Cory begged and begged, but they were adamant. He consoled himself by masturbating to a terribly chic Joan Sutherland album.

When the others got to the Opera House, they had some terribly chic snacks at the Terribly Chic Snack Bar. "Did you see the terribly chic buns on that counterman!" Binky said.

"A-Gays don't fraternize with countermen!" Michael said

furiously. "How many times must I tell you this? Come away at once. People like that are never interviewed in the right magazines!"

"But—"

"How can we get anywhere with people like you?" Michael exclaimed, spotting the Opera Director talking to a terribly smart woman in a terribly smart white gown. "Oh, goodie, two at once!" Michael said, advancing.

The Opera Director weighed 400 pounds and was said to indulge in unnatural practices with computers. Michael wasn't positive who the woman might be, but he had an idea.

"How do you do? I'm Michael Mouse of the A-Gays," he introduced himself.

"Do I *know* you?" the woman asked.

"No, but I know you!"

"Was Maria callous?" the Opera Director asked.

"You're the woman who sponsored this cocktail party, aren't you?"

"Do I *know* you?" the woman asked.

Michael hesitated, then pressed on. "I'm such a fan of opera. I have four copies of Donna Summer's greatest hits from *Tosca!*"

"*Dona* who?" asked the Opera Director.

"The quail tail on these little crackers is quite delicious!" Michael said. "Was it your idea?"

"Do I *know* him?" the woman asked the Opera Director.

"I'm Michael. From the A-Gays. That organization of bright young men about town who think opera is so important for making a person feel good. Don't you? I can't say how much better I feel after a good death scene."

"What's Leontyne's price?" asked the fat man.

"We're an offshoot of Twinkies Anonymous!"

They stared at him.

"I'm a friend of Derek Maillard's. He used to be a member of our group, although we had to let go when he refused not to be over 27."

"Was Marilyn horny?" the Opera Director asked.

"*Why* do you keep talking to us?" the woman said, frowning. She and the Opera Director walked away.

Michael rushed over to his friends. "You'll never guess who I just talked to!" he said.

"Guess who's coming to San Francisco?" Michael shrieked.

"Who?" Cory asked, simultaneously reading *Gentleman's Quarterly* and Andy Warhol's *Interview*.

"The Queen!"

"Which one?"

"The Queen of England, the richest woman in the world, that's who!"

Cory practically fell on his face. "Oh, my God, we must race down to greet her ship when she docks."

"Cory, Cory, Cory, whatever am I going to do with you! The Queen of England doesn't dock! Do you think she'd ever stoop to anything so *vulgar*!"

"I'm sorry."

"I should hope so! Oh, if only we could get on board the Britannia. We could do something really super special for the Queen. If I could get to meet her, just once, it would be to die!"

"Yeah, maybe we could even meet Prince Philip!"

"We mustn't ask the impossible, Cory!"

"Do you think we can get on board?"

"I'll put in a request. After all, it's very vital that people think well of gays, and who better than we A-Gays to carry that banner."

"Why us?" Cory said, confused.

"Oh, Cory, Cory, Cory! Who else is going to make sparkling conversation about Bette Midler's latest album or Sigourney's divorce? It's up to us to carry the dignity and reputation of homosexuals so the Queen and people like that will like us and find us terribly amusing, just as they always have! Where would we be now if we didn't twinkle like we do?"

"Oh, I'm so excited I may soil my latest fashions!"

"Come, Cory, we must make plans!"

And plan they did. They secreted themselves as busboys—what a clever disguise!—with the catering service that was to serve dinner to Her Majesty on board the royal yacht that night.

"Do you see her?" Michael asked Cory as they sneaked up on deck.

"I see a dumpy-looking woman in a decidedly lower-class frock, standing over by the rail."

"That's her!" Michael screamed, trying hard not to point. "Let's introduce ourselves."

They rushed over and curtseyed. "Ma'am, we're from the A-Gays," Michael said, showing her the official proclamation signed by all ten of the group. "On behalf of the smart set of gay San Francisco, we'd like to welcome you to America!"

"Do I *know* you?" the woman asked, eyeing them, her hand ready to swing her purse if need be.

"We're very chic and know all the right crowd," Michael said.

"What do you want from me?"

"Nothing but to bask."

"Do you give autographs?" Cory asked.

"Shame on you!" Michael said. "Excuse him, Ma'am. He's rather new to all this. All we'd really like to do is give a memento of your visit here. May we?"

"Well, what is it?"

"I've been authorized to kiss your royal rump as a slight token of what you mean to all of us."

"Do I *know* you?" the woman asked.

"If you would kindly bend over and touch your shoes, we will proceed with the ceremony," Michael said.

"Blimey, I don't know as I want to!"

"Oh, please, Ma'am! Pretty please!...For us?"

She tossed her cigarette overboard. "Oh, lord, all right!"

She bent and he kissed.

The woman stood upright just as someone called to her. "Hey, Molly, get your bleedin' ass in here! The loo's clogged up!"

The woman stopped to wave as she disappeared below deck. "Thanks, blokes!" she called to Michael and Cory. "You made my day!"

"That wasn't the queen's royal rump we kissed, Michael!" Cory said.

Michael froze in horror. "You're right for once, Cory. But we have our reputation to maintain." He paused. "Now who's to know it wasn't royal if we tell them it was!"

"You mean *lie*?"

"Even though it wasn't really the queen's arse, it was a lovely ceremony anyway!" Michael said, transfixed. "So it isn't a lie, Cory. Don't you see that somebody, *somebody's* got to preserve the standards in this world!"

Rubyfruit Discomfort, by Rita Mae Blunt

by The Saint

"How are you today, my tall, half-black son?" inquired Hortensia eloquently.

Goliath was illegitimate, but he didn't realize it, although his mother was white. "I'm fine," answered the muscular 16-year-old, who had just finished reading all of Proust in one afternoon. "Why do you talk so funny, Mother?"

"Because people have to know what elegant types we really are, Goliath," retorted his still-beautiful, nearly lesbian, liberated parent, tossing her copy of Thucydides on the ornate, expensive sofa in her luxurious Southern mansion in 1918.

"I want to be a boxer, Ma. I never liked Proust."

"I know, my colossus of a child. But I wouldn't want anybody to think I have a stupid jock offspring."

"I just want to knock guys' teeth out and then fuck their women, Ma!"

"I know, my gladiator of a son, yet people would get upset if they knew the truth."

"Where's Banana Split and Blue Rhonda?" Goliath worried, looking around.

"Here we are!" said the effervescent young prostitutes, romping into the salon. "I just gave the best head I've ever given anybody!" intoned Blue Rhonda.

"Got any dope?" queried Banana Split. "I'm oppressed and therefore it's OK for me to destroy my brain and body every chance I get!"

"Here's some!" replied Hortensia smilingly. "It's all men's fault—for everything—and so it's all right if you're a junkie and an exploiter of men's sex drives." She took the stash out of a credenza and passed it around.

"Hey, let's have a four-way," snickered Goliath, eyeing the others.

"Will you lick my rubyfruit?" questioned Banana Split.

"Like a fly in an outhouse!" Goliath lustily responded, grabbing Banana's legs and splitting them.

"I don't like that simile about outhouses!" objected Hortensia strenuously. "You make sex seem dirty, Goliath. But it's beautiful. Beautiful!"

"Aw, Ma!"

"I don't care what you do between Banana Split's legs, but I do insist that you speak about it like a modern gentleman—with correctness, Political Correctness. Say it! Say it!"

Goliath got down on his knees and examined Banana Split's rubyfruit. "It's all red, Ma!"

"It's full of beautiful juices! Gleaming, cascading lanes of luscious love. Say it!"

"I've got crabs, so watch out!" Banana Split effervesced.

"I've got a hair stuck in the back of my throat," Goliath choked, coming up for air.

"Tell Banana Split how beautiful she is down there! Tell

her!" Hortensia screamed, beating her son by a man who wasn't her husband on his broad, brawny back.

"Aw, Ma!"

"Tell her, or you can't have any more!"

"Gosh, Ma, I can't put my tongue in here and talk at the same time!"

"Oh, these men; they're so unfeeling and crude," Hortensia lamented. "Not like us Southern belles or women tennis players."

"A little to the left!" Banana Split squealed.

"Do it with good manners, my son!"

Goliath set to work again, trying not to slurp.

Hortensia watched and sighed resignedly. "I think the world needs a little poetry." She took Blue Rhonda's hand, noting the way her drugged eyes rolled up into her head. "These are my people," she said aloud. "One day maybe I'll write a book about them and fill it with good writing and honest feelings about female genitalia and even throw in a horror movie about chopping up women and possibly even an expose of an ex-lover in the sports world, and then I'll be famous, and I'll write arrogant prefaces telling the fuckheads to write their *own* books if they don't like my uplifting, well-crafted ones!"

A Boy's Own Limp Wrist, by Edmund Wimp

by The Saint

Percival was different from other boys. He was rich and spoiled and nobody liked him one bit because he was a snot. He had his own set of all the world's opera records and was majoring in Mandarin Chinese at Endover-End Academy, the exclusive, high-tuition boys' school for ambitious aesthetes.

"Do you think I should transfer to Choate?" Percival, his maculate, mascaraed eyes trained on his future career, asked.

"Isn't that a young pig or something?" asked Neville, his one companion, a dwarfish, brain-damaged boy of exquisite Pre-Raphaelite beauty.

"That's *shoat!*" Percival snapped. "Don't you know anything? How will you ever get anywhere? Like I intend to!"

"Where do you want to go? Don't leave me!" cried Neville.

"I'm going to conquer Literary New York one day." Percival's eyes twinkled like gnats at twilight. "I shall get Susan Sontag to write a blurb for me! Even Michel Foucault!"

"Is that what you really want, Percival?" Neville said, hurt that his friend should even think about leaving him.

"I shall be the reincarnation of Ronald Firbank," Percival exclaimed, his bony-wristed arms flopping about.

"Who?"

"You're hopeless, Neville! It's quite obvious Susan Sontag or Foucault will never write a blurb for *you!*"

"But I love you, Percival!"

"I know, I know. And I wish you to know that I'm ever so grateful that you have allowed me to hump your young behind, dwarfish though it be, for these last three years."

"Take me with you!" Neville cried

"Not possible!" Percival said, trying to keep his osseous wrists from hitting his head as he waved them in the air. "I desire some travels in America—alone."

"But where will you go?"

"Wherever fate, and great ambition, take me. I shall write superficially, but with enormously noticeable style, about a great many subjects. I shall win prizes and make heterosexuals feel comfortable knowing that sissies are still sissies. If only...." Here Percival stopped.

"If only what?"

"If only I don't put out an eye with my limp wrists before I'm 40," Percival said, almost despairing. "It is indeed expected that a boy of my talent and background should have a limp wrist—but to have *two* may strike some potential patrons as an affectation. Alas, my wrists might even actually *strike* someone and do damage! Whatever am I to do?"

"You could tape your arms to your sides," Neville said.

"How will I write then? How will I use my quill?"

"You could learn to type with a stylus taped to your forehead."

Percival mused on the suggestion. "You know, that's not a bad idea. Such a shame that you are so short, Neville. I could have used you in New York."

"I've tried to please you, Percival! I've given you every-thing—helped with your homework, taught you every sexual technique I could think of!"

"I know, I know. Don't think I'm unappreciative, you little clod! I shall make use of the information. I have decided I shall first make my name with a three-volume sex manual, using everything you've taught me. Thank you."

"Won't I get credit, too?" Neville wondered.

"Don't be absurd! Do you want my readers to think I got my ideas about sex from a brain-damaged dwarf? I'm afraid there's no place in Literary New York for dwarves, Neville. Only Big-gies! If I'm to succeed, and, by God, I mean to, I have no choice but to leave you—and your behind—behind. Do you imagine I'd ever get a Guggenheim if people thought you were my lover?"

"But I'm devoted to you, Percival!"

"Listen, you little fool, I'm leaving and that's all there is to it! Good-bye and don't follow me!" He set off, taking great strides.

"Oh, wait!" Neville called, his stunted little legs trying des-perately to keep up with Percival's long, ambitious ones.

"Get back, you cretinous creep!" Percival shouted, kicking dirt into his former lover's overheated, oleaginous face.

Neville could not see and fell forward onto the ground, sobbing. He sat up and began to pick bits of muck from his moist eyes.

Percival did not even look back, for he was busy thinking. "First, I shall tape one wrist to my side, thus keeping my state of 'limpirity,' as I shall call it, within manageable limits. Then I shall interview three persons in four cities and make vast gen-eralizations about what it all means. Since it will of necessity be shallow, I shall call it Art. Next I shall devise a style so im-

penetrable that even Sontag and Foucault won't know what I
mean and will give me anything to be able to stop reading—
even a blurb! Ultimately all of Literary New York—editors,
critics, writers—with their BA's in Mandarin Chinese and marketing techniques—won't be able to tell what in the world I'm
saying, and, thus properly intimidated, they'll have to embrace
me as a peer! Finally, at long last, I shall triumph as the first
socially acceptable, nonthreatening sodomite in history, whereupon I shall become wealthy and famous and the subject of vicious satires by the likes of the Nevilles I've had to step on to
get where I am!"

The Gluck Clique

by The Saint

They sat around the table in the back of the tiny bookshop, all of them with bony bodies and prominent Adam's apples and high foreheads. These were the Gluck clique.

"Let's be writers!" they cried. No, they didn't cry; they mumbled. "How shall we go about it?" asked the teacher, Gluck. Gluck had no hair, but he was hung with an IQ that would choke a porn star.

"Let's tell a story," somebody, a newcomer, suggested.

All the heads—with egg on their brows (Get it?)—turned as one, disdain dribbling from their eyeballs like existential come from an old bathhouse. (I don't know what it means either.) "Tell a *story*?" they snorted. "In a *novel*?" they gagged. "How mundane! How quaint!"

Gluck smiled. He had trained them well. "Indeed, no stories in this room. If I ever catch anyone telling a story, I'll excommunicate him faster than Lassie can eat a postage stamp from Schopenhauer's last letter." (Beats me.) Gluck waved his hand. "Somebody read what he's working on."

Several hands went up.

Gluck nodded at the chosen one.

The writer-reader stood, wiping sweat from his glasses, trembling, afraid he would be understood. He began: "Polly want a pomorphous." He looked around. "Pompadour, prescient, writhing penises!"

"I love it!" Gluck clucked. "Words starting with *p*. It's fantastic. It combines the cerebral and the pornographic—a major breakthrough. But it's not enough. Sit down!"

There was a hush. They knew what was coming. They had seen it happen many times before.

Gluck rose from his chair. His eyes bulged. He put on his pince-nez. He cleared his throat, which was phlegmy. "I, Gluck, will now read from my new work."

Applause. Ecstasy.

"It is called *Kculg*," which you of course realize is—?"

Their eyes twisted from one to the next; their throats went dry. They hung their heads. No one knew.

"It's Gluck spelled backwards, you dumb clucks!" Gluck clucked. He lifted his manuscript, which was festooned with scraps torn from old poems of his, lines lifted from camp movies as well as old philosophy course notes, to say nothing of the Encyclopedia Britannica. "I, Gluck, was in love with Jack's cock," he began.

Oohs, aahs.

"Jack's velvety cylinder reminded me of quintessential questions of right and wrong, morality and amorality, insincerity and incomprehensibility." Gluck stopped reading. He grabbed his ballpoint pen and began scribbling on his manuscript before their very eyes. "I think of a play." He wrote: "GLUCK: I am writing a play about Jack's cock. Now I am writing a sentence about writing about Jack's cock." He was inspired and kept writing: "And now I am writing a sentence about writing a sentence about writing a sentence. SENTENCE...ENCE SENT!"

The group was overcome by admiration; they fell off their chairs, mouths agape.

(It makes me want to write this sentence even as I write this.)

JACK'S PENIS: Why?

ME AS GLUCK: Because I just thought of it. I thought I'd throw it in.

READER: What does this have to do with anything?

ME AS GLUCK: Oh, don't be so banal! It has to do with my telling a story and you enjoying it because you can't follow it. Now you're afraid you're dumb, aren't you? Ha!

READER: What?

GLUCK: Now you're getting into it?

READER: I am?

JACK'S PENIS: Hey, what about me?

GLUCK: Who are you?

JACK'S PENIS: I thought Gluck's book was about me?

GLUCK: Oh, was it? I forgot. I'm so brilliant I often forget what I'm talking about.

More oohs and aahs. A student fainted. (Author's Note: actually the guy fell asleep.) Sheer electricity of Karmic intelligence was in the air—an unbearable concatenation of super-rational forces and poetic overachievement. (Take that in your vocabulary kisser, you losers!)

"Shall I go on?" Gluck wondered.

"It's so exquisite," one of the Gluck clique said.

"So out there, so multidimensional," said another.

"So fine."

"So modern."

"So postmodern.

"So post-postmodern."

"I'd love to deconstruct it."

"So literary, in the best sense," someone sighed.

"Yes, yes, yes!" Gluck beamed. He was getting through to them at last. "Literature is about sentences! Sentences! Make them *beg* on their knees for meaning!" he screamed. He pulled a hair from his hairy neck and twirled it between thumb and forefinger, contemplating the significance of time and place, of pain and meaning, of allusion and reality. And adverbs.

So.

Or was it?

Moral: Intelligence is not interesting.

The Blur, by Felicity Guano

by The Saint

"What do you want to be when you grow up, Felicity?" her father asked, dandling her astride his knee.

"A hack!" she replied.

"My, but that's a very modest ambition, even for a four-year-old," he said.

"Ain't gonna be no fuckin' starvin' artist sittin' in these here drawers!" Felicity said, touching her designer diaper, which she'd forced her father to buy her by threatening to tell the police he was molesting her if he didn't. It wasn't true, but Felicity didn't care. "I'll do anything for money. Anything!" she often said.

"Wouldn't you really rather be an artist, darling?" her father asked.

"Nothing less than a complete hack will do!" Felicity yelled. "I couldn't live with myself if I didn't write for money."

"You don't want to be a hack, baby. Mere money won't make you happy."

"It *won't?*" Felicity thought for a moment. "OK then, I'll be a *pretentious* hack!"

"Don't you think you should finish kindergarten first, read a few books?"

"I already know all I need to know! I'm from New Yawk," Felicity said. "Keep *dandlin'*!"

Suddenly her father sneezed.

"'Gesundheit!' as Heidegger once said. See how educated I am, Daddy?"

Her father touched his chin. "Some people might notice a certain lack of...depth, sweetheart."

"Fuck off, Daddy! What do modern jerks know! I'm gonna be the new Gustave Chekhov. So there!"

The Lord May Barf, by Gordon Meretricious

by The Saint

Charlie and Harry were both uncut, with 37 inches of manhood between them. True, Charlie had only 13, but Harry had 24. In addition, their bodies were young, scrubbed, and rippling with multitudes of muscles. They were also very much in love.

"I adore you, but it's not just your many inches," Charlie said.

"I love you too, Harry, although I wish I had more than 24."

"Beloved, we could send away for that penis elongator we saw advertised. That is, if we had any money. I'm sorry I've got only 13."

"Still, you're so thick it hardly matters!" Harry grabbed Charlie's truncheonlike tool and swallowed it to the hilt. "Doesatfeelgoo?" he asked, his eyes peering up Charlie's perfect body.

"What did you say? Don't talk with your mouth full, darling."

"I said, 'Does that feel good?'"

"Oh, I love you when you go down on me like that, Harry!"

"*I'm* Charlie. You're Harry!" Charlie said.

"Oh, that's right. But what does it matter? We're like one person!"

"I'm afraid there's something that has come up that may spoil our perfect love, darling."

Harry touched the pectoral above his heart. "Oh, no!" His face looked stricken.

"Do you remember that elderly, rich gentleman who asked me to 'visit' him?"

Harry averted his eyes. "Yes, I remember."

"Well, I've consented."

There was a gasp. "But, Charlie, how could you!"

"We both know we need the money. It takes cash for those blood transfusions to keep your 24 inches hard." Charlie hushed Harry before he could answer. "I know we shouldn't speak of it, but one of us must go out and earn some income."

"I just want to stay here with you forever and suck and fuck and measure our inches. Come! I want to measure yours right now. Will you measure mine?" He rushed to the dresser and got the tape.

"I can't measure you now, Harry. I've got to go out and visit that rich, elderly gentleman."

"This could break us up, Charlie. Do you know that?"

Charlie sighed. "I know that."

"The thought of some other man's greasy hands measuring your penis is more than I can bear!"

"I don't want it either. My body yearns only for you—besides, all the germs one can pick up from others nowadays!"

"If you go out that door, Charlie, I don't ever want to see you again! There, I've said it!"

"I'm going, Harry—but it's only because I want you to have those transfusions, my dearest, my only love!"

With that, Charlie was gone. Harry sat on the side of the bed and wept great tears onto his long penis, so much so that by the end of the day it had become wrinkled and sodden. "I've lost the only one with a penis comparable to mine!" he wailed.

Suddenly Charlie appeared at the bedroom door. "Darling, I'm back!"

"But, Charlie, you've been soiled with sex outside our relationship. I can never take you back. You must know that!"

"Harry, listen! It's all come out marvelously!"

"Don't tell me about your orgasms with other men! I won't listen!" Harry slogged his wrinkled, unaroused penis over his shoulder and started to leave.

"But, lover, you don't understand!" Charlie cried out. "That rich, elderly gentleman didn't lay a hand on me. All he wanted was for me to model for him in a McDonald's clerk uniform! He didn't even masturbate!"

"Are you telling me the truth, dear one?"

"I swear it! And you know what else—he wants me to come back every other month and model for him for only 15 minutes at $20,000 per job! And he's already given me a certified check for the first session and a home in Cape Cod!" Charlie waved the check and the deed to the property. "Moreover, he intends to leave me everything in his will when he dies, which shouldn't be too long, since he's well over 100 already. Isn't it all just too wonderful for words?"

"Oh, darling,'" Harry said, "we'll be able to keep getting the blood transfusions for my large member after all!"

"Yes, dearest, yes!" They kissed and Charlie looked down. "But I don't think you're going to need a transfusion this time. It's beginning to get fat and thick and long and rambunctious on its own right this minute!" He embraced Harry.

Harry embraced him. "I knew it could be like this! After all, the Lord won't mind that we're homosexuals, because we're well-hung and beautiful, and the Lord knows and rewards true, true love when He sees it!"

I'm Somebody;
Whom Are You?

by Susie Day

Many of the editors I know harbor fantasies of being writers. I myself harbor fantasies of being an editor. The power! The prestige! The emotional high of enticing writers to "submit" their work, only to say: I Reject You! So I am starting a ground-breaking lesbian literary journal, to be edited by moi, me, me. Here are examples of primo editing in which I improve the work sent in by some kid named "Emily D."

Because I could not stop for Death,
He kindly stopped for me;
The carriage held but just ourselves
And Immortality.

Unclear. Are you not feeling well? You're not dead, are you? If you are not dead, why couldn't you "stop for Death?" If you are dead, how could you be writing this poem? To avoid con-fusing or possibly upsetting your readers, I would suggest a more cause/effect-oriented rhyme scheme at the outset. "As a Lesbian, I can't stop for Death / Because my busy schedule leaves me out of Breath" might clarify.

"But just ourselves" verges on the nongrammatical and is really not very succinct, to boot. "The carriage held *only* ourselves / And Immortality" is more economical, wordwise. Actually, the concept of "Immortality," especially when capitalized, seems a tad grandiose. Perhaps you could work in some grassroots, people's imagery here. Replace "Immortality" with "quilting BEE" or "libertEE" or "live like MEE!"

It's a nice touch to make Death a male, and shows that you are a caring feminist. But do you really think that Death is "kind?" Or do you mean your statement ironically? If so, please rethink how your societal privilege to be ironic could offend a lot of people who are too oppressed to read this. Does Death come "kindly" for the thousands of multicultural lesbians, gay men, bisexuals, and transgendered peasants who fall prey to the machinations of an overweening U.S. capitalist patriarchy? Are these people invited into "carriages" when they die? I think not. Why don't you tell their story? "The carriage held only ourselves and thousands of multicultural lesbians, gay men, bisexuals, and transgendered peasants / All having a quilting bee" is probably closer to what you mean.

On to your next poem:

After great pain, a formal feeling comes—
The Nerves sit ceremonious, like Tombs—

Let me stop you here. Once again, I am forced to blame you for my not being able to understand this. Furthermore, it is not clear from your word choices that you have really suffered. I myself have known great pain. Once, my girlfriend slammed my hand in the door of her Land Rover. We were in the middle of breaking up, so even though she said it was an accident, I never really believed her. From this I learned that after great pain, a throbbing feeling comes. Actually, "throbbing" would be a good woman's adjective to replace "formal," as it denotes a ba-BOOM type sexuality missing here. Try to give your audience the impression that you are the kind of gal who is sensitive enough to have Georgia O'Keeffe wallpaper in her bedroom, yet tough enough to feel at home in a mosh pit.

The soul selects her own society
Then shuts the door;
On her divine majority
Obtrude no more.

This is not a sentence. Are you even trying? Granted, agoraphobia is a big problem in our community, but your imagery is way off. "[D]ivine majority" sounds like a fundamentalist Nixon. Are you a Republican? Also, avoid offending your readers by using big words like "Obtrude" that they have to look up. Big words also wreak havoc with your spell-check. Writer's tip: To attain instant publication in a lesbian periodical, simply replace common, everyday words with references to female genitalia. So, for example, the opening lines of some of your poems might be revised to read: "I heard a Clitoris buzz when I died," or "I felt a Funeral in my Labia."

I regret that my busy, Tina Brown–like schedule allows me only enough time to read the first stanzas of your poems. But if they are any indication, you really need to buckle down and get sensitive before they meet our editorial needs. Good luck. And remember, if you're ever stumped for a topic, dear, just write about what you know!

Cumin the Barbarian

by M.S. "Max" Hunter

"Hey! You ass-lickin' scuzzballs up dere! How 'bout openin' dis fuckin' gate!"

The sudden bellow smote the ears of the Captain of the Guard just as the swollen head of the young sentry's cock smote his tonsils. Startled, he pulled back as the first volley of cannonading come splashed into his eyes and ran down his face—instead of bathing his throat with its hot, sticky wetness.

"Shit!" growled the Captain at this miscarriage of his early morning pleasures. "Some days you just can't win." While the young sentry collapsed onto the floor of the guardhouse, his rigid cock erupting with gob after gob of his copious jism, the Captain leaned over the parapet of the city walls to see what asshole was making such a racket.

Below him, barely visible in the dawn's early light, stood two men. One was a towering giant with broad shoulders above a massive chest. His bulging pecs were barely restrained by a metal-studded harness of shiny leather. Girt round his narrow waist was a brief girdle from which swung a huge broadsword, and below which, between thighs as thick as tree trunks, swung the head of his mighty 13-inch prick.

The man threw back his head revealing a manly but cruel visage beneath his square-cut shock of straight black hair. "Yeah, you dere shitass! You with the come dripping off your chin," he shouted. "Are you gonna open dis goddamn gate or does I hafta knock it down?"

As the man spoke he lifted his heavily muscled arm and shook his huge fist at the Captain. An expanding wave of his Sweaty Underarm Odor assailed the Captain's nostrils, and, in sheer delight, the Captain's quivering prick exploded with a fountain of pent up joy juice. Such a rank, sexy Body Odor could come from only one man! This was Cumin the Barbarian, the Great Unwashed.

Happiness and hero worship swelled in the heart of the Captain of the Guard. Cumin had come at last! Throughout all the lands of Hypertensia, Cumin was known for his superhuman strength, for his reckless daring, for his never-ending battle for the forces of Good over Evil, for his 14-inch cock. None could match him for fucking up whole armies he fought; none could match him for destroying wicked sorcerers and malign monsters; none could match him for leaving whole harems of young boys with come-dripping assholes; none could match him for leaving death, destruction, and pillage in his wake as he rode to the rescue of great kingdoms and beautiful, beardless youths.

The Captain was well aware that King Chi-Chi of Phallacia had summoned his Hero to rid the land of the evil wizard, Kollmi Sur, and to rescue his prisoner, the handsome and noble heir to the throne, young Prince Nai Yves. Surely the kingdom was now saved!

The dark, wiry young man beside Cumin with the frizzy hair and fat ass was, of course, Limerick, Cumin's Faithful Sidekick and our story's Token Black Character. They were inseparable. Limerick adored his Hero in the approved manner for Faithful Sidekicks and Token Black Characters.

Shouting to his guardsmen to lend a hand, the Captain rushed down the stairs to open the gate. "Move your asses, you douche bags," he shouted. "Cumin is comin'! Phallacia is saved!"

Word of the Hero's arrival spread through the city. By the time Cumin and Limerick began their march through the streets to the royal palace, the entire population had turned out to greet them. (Except of course females, who were kept locked decently out of sight as in any well-run and civilized Hypertensian community.) Crowds lined the streets as they passed, yelling, "Cumin is comin'! Cumin is comin'!" Grown men swooned in ecstasy as Cumin's B.O. swept over them. Young boys, spying Cumin's 15-inch whang swinging below his girdle, threw themselves down in his path, legs in the air, shouting, "Fuck me, Great Hero! Oh fuck me, Master!" Others crawled along behind him crying, "Let me be your slave and lick your hairy ass, sir!"

"What a crock!" growled Cumin to his Faithful Sidekick. "Same fuckin' thing every place we go, Lim."

Limerick grinned and licked his lips. Quoth he,

"As through this land we go a' bummin'
While I am with my good friend Cumin,
There's always tricks
With tasty pricks
And sweet young assholes I can come in."

"Yeah, and up yours, too," was Cumin's gracious reply.

They reached the palace and the Captain of the Guard ushered them directly into the throne room where King Chi-Chi

LXIX was posed elegantly on his throne on a raised dais. As our dynamic duo came to a halt before him, he rose, hands on hips, his weight on his right foot, and his head cocked to one side. The king's auburn tresses, delicately coiffed, swirled about his head. His gold and silver bracelets jangled and his fine silk robe of royal lavender trimmed with puce lace swished around his ankles as he descended from the dais to better observe his guests. He walked slowly around Cumin, hips swaying and one long forefinger pressed against his cheek. At last he came to a halt in front of The Barbarian.

"My, you *are* a big one, aren't you?" he lisped. "Just what we need here in Phallacia."

Whereupon Limerick quothed,

"Methinks this Phallacian fool
Is hot for your 16-inch tool.
But we will regret it
If you let him get it
Before we get paid. Play it cool!"

"Gotcha," our Hero whispered back. "OK, Chi-Chi, now cut out the crap and tell me what your problem is."

"Kollmi Sur."

"Like hell I will! I deal with you punk kings all the time. Now get with it."

"Oh, dear me! I meant my problem is the wicked wizard, Kollmi Sur. He has abducted my simply gorgeous nephew, the Crown Prince."

"So what's dat?"

"He's Nai Yves."

"Dat figgers. So is all dese young asshole princes."

"No! No! His name is Prince Nai Yves."

"Oh! Well, where dey got the little cocksucker stashed?"

"At the Monastery of the Odious Order of the Costellos."

"So who runs dat joint?"

"Huzon Furst."

"How da fuck do I know?"

"No! No! Howduff uc Dyno plays short."

"Look, shitass, cut the crap or you'll be playing short. Short a coupla balls!"

"Oh dear me, sweetie, you're no fun at all. I mean the evil Abbott, Huzon Furst. He's Kollmi Sur's asshole buddy."

"No shit! Well, Chi-Chi baby, I'll take care of dem nasties for ya."

Quoth Limerick,

"Hold on, you Fairy King!
Just tell us one more thing.
We gotta know
Before we go
What kinda bread you're offering."

"Oh, yeah," said Cumin, "That's right. What's in it for us?"

"Oh the usual," replied King Chi-Chi. "Half my kingdom and a week to fuck around in my harem."

"Got any talent in dat harem?"

A mischievous grin spread over the king's elegant face. "Just come and see!" He led Cumin to the wall behind his throne, slid back a small panel revealing a peephole, and gestured for Cumin to look through.

Pressing his eye to the hole Cumin observed a large, sumptuously appointed room with water beds and mirrors everywhere. A couple of dozen handsome young men and boys were strolling about buck naked or lounging on the beds playing with themselves or with each other. They came in all varieties.

There were dark ones and light ones, hairy and smooth, very young and not quite so young, heavy hung and not quite so heavy hung.

As Cumin licked his lips over this smorgasbord of male delights, his 17-inch dong rose to the occasion. Unbeknownst to him another panel in the wall slid open right before his crotch. "Eeyow!" he cried as a warm hand reached through the glory hole and hauled his 18-inch peter through, balls and all. "Ooow! Aaahh!" he moaned as a hot mouth engulfed it. His great body shook as he plastered himself against the wall, giving his all to the unseen inhabitant of the harem.

Quoth Limerick,

"Now ain't that just my shitass luck!
Ol' Cumin gets a primo suck,
While I stand here,
Hot ass in gear,
In need of a buck for a fuck!"

"I'll take care of that!" shouted the Captain of the Guard, rushing forward, his rampant rod at the ready. He flipped up Limerick's short girdle exposing those beefy black buns, pushed him down on the floor, and plunged his pulsing prick into Limerick's beckoning bum.

"Oh, my dears!" exclaimed the king from his throne, "Isn't this just dandy fun!"

With a roar like a lion Cumin thrust the full force of his mighty thews against the wall, beat on it until it was like to fall, and finally staggered back with his 19-inch tool still bobbing out before him dripping great gobs of glorious jism.

"OK, Chi-Chi," he cried, still panting for breath, "I admit you got some real talented cocksuckers in that harem of yours.

And the rest of what I saw looks worth a week of my time, too. So we'll take the job." Then turning to Limerick, who was still on his hands and knees in front of the throne getting his ass plowed doggie fashion by the Captain of the Guard, he said, "C'mon Lim, we're off to see the Wizard."

Breathlessly Limerick quothed,

"I'll follow you through a great blizzard
In search of that scurrilous wizard.
But give me a mo.
This guy's gonna blow
His wad all the way to my gizzard."

Cumin shrugged his massive shoulders and turned back to the king. "Say, your Royal Shithole, how am I supposed to get into the joint where they got your nephew?"

"Well," replied the king, laying a bejeweled finger against his cheek, "the monastery is well guarded and you'll be challenged by the guards as soon as you approach. Why don't you tell them that you and Limerick are experts at all sorts of nasty things and so you'd like to join the Odious Order of the Costellos. Then ask them pretty please to take you to see the Abbott so you can enlist. That might do it."

"What!" shouted Cumin so the whole room shook. "Are you suggesting that I tell lies? We say what we mean and mean what we say. Dat's da code. No, you Royal Shitcan, I'll just sneak up behind those guards, cut their throats, rip out their guts, cut off their balls, and then fight my way into the monastery, killing and maiming everyone in my path. Now dat's the heroic and honorable way!"

King Chi-Chi shrugged. "Have it your way, Mary."

The next day, with their broadswords flashing in the sun, with their breath stinking of wine, with their leather harnesses gleaming, with their muscles rippling, and with their hangovers throbbing, Cumin and Limerick approached the Monastery of the Odious Order of Costellos. It had been an exhausting but exhilarating night. They had climbed the walls of the royal harem and passed the night drinking wine, carousing, and fucking, sucking, and rimming with a few dozen of the inmates to be sure the promised rewards of their work would be worthwhile. They were. Now, invigorated by a breakfast of young come and piss cocktails, they advanced on the lair of the Wicked Wizard.

The first line of guards fell in the approved heroic manner, as Cumin had promised. With bloody swords singing through the air they fought their way into the monastery. They were met by ranks of monsters, goblins, ogres, and other icky creatures. Our intrepid heroes disposed of them in the usual way, ripping out throats, spilling blood and guts and gore all over the place, and spreading death and destruction in their path. In short, they kicked the shit out of all the evil and wicked forces in their way. Of course that made quite a mess, but Cumin and Limerick waded on through all the blood and guts until they reached the door of the sinister dungeon where Kollmi Sur and Huzon Furst would make their last stand.

Quoth Limerick,

"Now some may say this is all wrong,
But we slay villains with a song.
And get a big thrill
When we torture and kill,
As it makes our dongs grow hard and long."

"You can say that again," said Cumin, his 20-inch dong pushing its way out from under his girdle.

"Now some may say this is all…"

"Aw, shove it up your gigi, you silly Faithful Sidekick," Cumin growled as he crashed through the door to the dungeon.

Inside our noble pair was greeted by a sight of horror, depravity, and shameful lust. Poor Prince Nai Yves was stretched out bareassed on a table, bound by chains and leather thongs. His ankles were encased in cruel cuffs from which chains attached to the ceiling pulled his legs up and open in a wide "V". A leather thong was tied tightly around the base of his cute little cock and balls, and it extended up to the ceiling also. There it passed through an eye bolt and divided into two strands ending in metal clamps attached to his pretty little brown nipples. Thus, however he moved it yanked cruelly on either his dick and nuts or his tortured tits.

The Wicked Wizard, Kollmi Sur, stood between the lad's legs pushing his fist and his whole forearm in and out of the unfortunate youth's open asshole. At the other end of the table, where the boy's head hung off the edge, the Evil Abbott, Huzon Furst, stood with his long schlong in his hand pouring a steady stream of golden piss into the young man's open mouth. Around this group circled Huzon Furst's short acolyte, the dwarf Howduff uc Dyno, wielding a whip and raining blows on all three of the others.

"Unhand that noble youth!" Cumin roared.

Kollmi Sur pulled his Crisco-covered hand from the princely pussy and turned to the newcomers. "Who the fuck are you?"

Startled, Huzon Furst sprayed his pale yellow offering all over the prince's face and chest. "How dare you interrupt our sacred ritual?" he squealed.

Prince Nai Yves lifted his head, golden nectar spilling from the sides of his mouth. "Why (gulp) don't you mind (gulp) your own business?"

"I'm the Great Hero, Cumin the Barbarian, and I've come at the request of King Chi-Chi to rescue this innocent young heir to the throne."

"Oh! Well, you can tell that faggot that he can have the little shit back when we're through with him," replied the wizard.

"That's right, you big butch thing you," piped the Abbott. "After this initiation the prince will go back and run Phallacia *our* way."

"Never!" Cumin cried. "Stand aside, Forces of Evil! We're going to release that poor boy and carry him back to safety."

So saying Cumin and Limerick waved their trusty swords and attacked. With a cackle of evil laughter Kollmi Sur waved his hand over the table and the prince, and, like a medium at a seance, conjured hordes of evil spirits out of the air to defend him. It did no good. Their mighty swords whistling through the air, their mighty muscles straining against their sexy leather harnesses, their precome oozing from their cocks, Cumin and Limerick slew the specters as fast as they materialized. Kollmi Sur continued to grin and laugh, delighting in his performance and the slaughter, until Cumin, with a mighty rush reached him and drove his mighty weapon (the one in his hand) right through him. With a final howl of wicked glee, the wizard exploded in a shower of brimstone and all sorts of crap.

"Oh really, child! Now look what you've done!" screamed Huzon Furst. "You've killed him and spoiled all his fun. How can you indulge in such immoderate behavior?"

"How can you say dat? I was just tryin' ta strike the happy medium."

Huzon Furst's complaints were cut off abruptly as Limerick heroically sneaked up behind him and lopped off his head with one brave stroke of his sword. In the confusion Howduff uc Dyno, the devilish dwarf, slipped out through a secret door to escape and provide a villain for our next adventure.

There was sudden silence in the dungeon as the battle ended. Cumin turned to Prince Nai Yves. "Now, noble prince, what can we do to help you?"

"Well, for a start, Nosy Parker, how about plugging up this hole you made the wizard abandon?"

Cumin stared at the prince's gaping asshole for a moment, then with a mighty shout he leaped between the lad's long legs. With one ferocious shove the whole 21 inches of his throbbing tool was thrust into the thrilling tunnel.

"Whoopee!" shouted Nai Yves. "That beats Kollmi Sur's fucking fist any day." He turned his head to Limerick. "Now, you lovely Token Black, come over here and take the Abbott's place."

Quothing a babble of incomprehensible limericks, Lim rushed to dump his dark dong in the moist mouth of the pinioned prince. For a few minutes they all shoved and heaved and grunted and groaned loud enough to wake the dead demons around their feet. Cumin drove his wondrous weapon in and out of the proud prince's sexy shithole. Limerick's dusky dong dominated his gaping gullet. Nai Yves tortured tits, and his engorged genitals snapped back and forth at the ends of the taut thong. With a shattering shout, Cumin erupted his molten lava into the boy's body. With poetic passion Limerick poured his gushing jism down the youth's throbbing throat. With a gurgling gulp Nai Yves splashed sperm all over his mighty masters.

With everyone feeling much better, they then released the imprisoned youth and made their way back to the wildly rejoicing capital of Phallacia.

Our final scene finds Cumin sitting on the royal throne of

Phallacia. King Chi-Chi agreed to throw in the other half of his kingdom in return for a chance to eat all the cheese under Cumin's foreskin. This he did with great gusto, but there was so much of it that he couldn't swallow it all. So he took the surplus to the royal chef, Marius von Schlopkuchen.

"See what you can do with this, my culinary genius," the king commanded.

"Oh what a divine aroma!" that worthy man exclaimed. "I'm inspired."

"Yeah, Mary, I knew you'd think of something."

And thus was created the world's first cheesecake, a historical fact that gives our story Redeeming Social Significance.

Now Cumin lolls on the throne with the crown of Phallacia askew on this mop of straight black hair above his coarse but manly features. Kneeling before him, licking the crud from between his toes, is the ex-king. Chi-Chi moans with delight as his long tongue flicks away the wizard blood and the monster crud. Shivers of pleasure course up Cumin's nerves from his filthy toes to his tiny brain.

In Cumin's lap sits the lovely Prince Nai Yves, bouncing up and down on the Barbarian's 22 inch cock, a look of idiotic ecstasy on his handsome face.

"Hey, Lim," shouts Our Hero over his shoulder, "Ain't dis de fuckin' life?"

On his hands and knees behind the throne, Limerick has been tickling his tonsils on a long schlong poking through the glory hole from the harem. He lifts his head off it long enough to quoth softly, so Cumin can't hear,

"The throne of this land holds Our Hero;
Of ruling he knows less than zero.
But happy's the clan

To worship this man;
It might, after all, have been Nero!"

Behind Limerick is the Captain of the Guard, his face buried in Limerick's black butt, his turgid tongue trying to touch Limerick's torrid prostate. Below Limerick lies the Corporal of the Guard gobbling greedily on the Faithful Sidekick's whopping whang.

Around the walls of the chamber, the royal courtiers and a regiment of young Guardsmen, inspired by the example of their betters, are engaging in an orgy of butt fucking and cock sucking. Daisy chains stretch from one side of the room to the other and come flows like wine.

Limerick, licking ropes of juicy white jism from his chin as he waits for another ready rod to pop through the glory hole, quoths,

"Over Sodom Phallacia would win
In a match for the Champion of Sin.
Any king we'd impeach
'less he promised to teach
Us to suck and to fuck and to rim."

Rejection Letter From Bedsheet Books, Publisher of Lesbian Novels

by Shelly Rafferty

Dear Ms. Taittinger:

Bedsheet Books takes pride in bringing only the finest lesbian two-color paperbacks to its loyal readership.

Thank you for giving us the opportunity to review your mystery novel manuscript, *Martyr for Hire.* I am sorry to report that, at this time, we are unable to purchase your work. If you'll take note of the ways in which your submission deviates from our guidelines, perhaps you'll be able to refashion your story into a product that is salable.

Below, I've taken the liberty of pointing out some of the finer distinctions that make a Bedsheet Book a best seller.

1. Lesbian heroines need androgynous, if not downright male sounding first names. (Some of these you'll recognize from our top ten list: Casey, Kat, Mickey, Jess, Max, Jo, Alex, Torrie.) Your monikers of choice—Elizabeth and Hannah—will undoubtedly leave readers confused. How will they answer the question, "Which one is the *man?*"

2. The teaser on the endsheet should be an excerpt from an interior sex scene, not a quote from Sappho.

3. A Bedsheet Books mystery is almost always resolved by the use of a supernatural intervention such as a dream, a Tarot reading, tossed stones and tea leaves, a ghostly visitor, a letter describing a historical event, a premonition, telepathy, ESP, future-casting, witchcraft, chanting, or spells. Your insistence on deductive reasoning and logic is a turnoff.

4. Why doesn't your heroine have a cat?

5. Generally, men in a Bedsheet publication are rapists, kidnappers, idiots, dumb lawmen, wife beaters, pedophiles, sexually abusive fathers, or bumbling sidekicks. Your portrayal of Elizabeth's best friend, Dillon, as a kind, sensitive, and thoughtful working man just doesn't fit the Bedsheet mold.

6. Unfortunately, you've chosen Pocatello, Ida., as your locale. We know from our readership surveys that lesbians like to see themselves in more urbane environs: San Francisco, Washington, D.C., Northampton, Mass., or Provincetown, Mass., work best.

7. The fact that you're writing a "lesbian" novel is something you've failed to signal. Although I read closely, I didn't notice any casual references to our culture. k.d. lang, Ellen, Chastity Bono, Rita Mae Brown, the women's bookstore, a rainbow flag, a lambda bumper sticker, softball, massage therapy school, *The Well of Loneliness,* music festivals, and pink triangles are all ignored. In favor of what? A slowly emerging, deeply felt intoxication of one woman for another? Women who enjoy each other's capacity to discuss issues? *Get real.* Love isn't like that.

8. Metaphor is a poorly understood rhetorical device when used to imply the act of sex. At Bedsheet, we recommend a list of "sex words" we think every author ought to employ. Among these are plunge, surge, moan, secrete, penetrate (obscure), shudder, throb, passion, wave, crest, wet...well, you get the picture. Your tendency toward graphic description—using words such as fuck, vagina, and cunt—is not acceptable.

9. We find it remarkable that you've chosen to write about a lesbian character at all. Other than the fact of Elizabeth's sexuality, which leads her into a relationship with Hannah Boone, you make so little of her sexual preference. Bedsheet never fails to remind its readership that being a lesbian has a price: Losing child custody, alienating a parent, being fired from a job, or simply being harassed by street punks are common occurrences in our product line.

10. Copyediting is no joke at Bedsheet. All manuscripts are subjected to a rigorous PC-based spell-checker. As a consequence, we assume responsibility for any and all errors, which only average eight or nine per book. (Strangely enough, we weren't able to find any in yours.)

We hope you'll consider these comments and suggestions. Standards at Bedsheet Books are an important part of our marketing profile—and our readers have come to enjoy the uniformity and near interchangeability of Bedsheet plots and characters. Never exceeding our "eighth grade reading level rule" has guaranteed us a loyal market share of lesbian customers.

For the future, we recommend that you sample a few Bedsheet titles, such as *Hot Hotel, Love's Prisoner,* or one of the fine *Harvest Moondaughter* mysteries. These books—with their simple storylines and easy-to-identify-with characters—will give you something to shoot for.

We look forward to counting you among our Bedsheet clientele.

In sisterhood,
Megan "Mike" McGraw, Editor

Architectural Digression:
A Unique California Condo
Fantasy

by Robert Carron

The rich, lustrous gleam of polyester in an unimaginable
plethora of subtle hues is the captivatingly dominant theme in
the condominium recently completed in Beverly Dales by in-
ternationally noted interior artists, Lottie Daugh and Hubert de
l'Unctuous.

The owners of the smashing new residence adore polyester,
and in their extensive travels throughout the world they have
collected countless treasured items made of it: bright, multihued
leisure suits; wonderful, specially commissioned native wall
hangings; unbelievable, truly one-of-a-kind blankets; silk-like
pillows; elegant table accessories; and an amazing variety of
bibelots. When they first planned their new home, these international collectors absolutely insisted to their decor engineers that
they be surrounded on all sides by their collection so they might
have the items they love displayed for all to see—to be used and
doted upon daily, to be an integral part of their lives.

Thus, Ms. Daugh and Mr. De l'Unctuous, whose artistic
headquarters are in Flushing, N.Y., decided to repeat the lush

material's distinctive texture all through the home. In the living room, for example, there is a *faux* polyester escritoire in delirious shades of parrot green, yellow, and orange. And in the same room, the original silk brocade of the French chairs was ripped off in favor of an enchanting polyester/spandex blend of shocking pink with chocolate stripes. Walls throughout this lilting home were painstakingly upholstered in gold lamé polyester.

In the master bedroom, the platform, canopy, and drapings of the bed are done in bell-pepper red polyester, and the bed draperies are lined in a Syrian goatherd print in malachite green, fuchsia, salmon pink, turquoise, and burgundy. The designers admitted that ordinarily the Syrian goatherd print would have been accomplished with earth tones, but their clients feel that an earth tone is something most appropriately found and left under a rock.

Seventeen custom-weave matching rugs used engagingly over black, blue, and orange Icelandic tile floors throughout the downstairs pick up the polyester theme, this time in racy shades of lime green, puce, magenta, indigo, russet, and avocado.

It is in the dining room, however, that the designers have used polyester most dramatically. The chrome and Formica dining table is inlaid with a wide band of polyester encased in polyurethane. The console against one wall has a *faux* polyester top over a base of mirror and stainless steel. The service plates used for formal dining are papier-mâché with a wide fringe of polyester. Place mats, napkins, and a number of other interesting accessories are polyester, too.

The interior environment facilitators prefer that color schemes be suitable for year-round use. Hence, they were careful to mix bright colors and some pastels along with somber shades. "If a house is all puce and orange and mint green, then we try to mix in some dark colors, so it doesn't look out of place in the winter," Daugh cheerfully explains. "With this house, now, we simply had to use every color we could imagine and then some. The tacky architecture we're dealing with here is just too terrible. Really pit city, and it needs all the help we can give it. Of course, therein lies not only the heartache, frustration, annoyance, and ulcers, but also the professional satisfaction of overcoming seemingly insurmountable obstacles. And this architecture sure qualifies on that score." De l'Unctuous adds, "In such cases we charge not a flat rate or even by the hour, but by the disagreeability and offensiveness to the sensibilities of the individual project, so the potential for professional financial gain is not insubstantial."

Both interior artistic coordinators believe that, while accessories may follow current trends, basic furnishings should be as nearly classical and timeless as the budget permits. Mr. De l'Unctuous elaborates on this concept. "I have worked with some of my clients for more than 50 years," he proclaims, "and I have done 12 or 13 houses for some of them. In a very few special cases I have done the very same house many, many times. But when clients select really good classic furnishings, we can just use them over and over and over again. Really choice classic pieces can be moved around easily. You can change the color or reupholster them, and you scarcely ever tire of them. Besides, it makes my job a lot easier. Of course, even if we use the old stuff, I still charge the same—sometimes even more if I have it recovered and nobody recognizes it. But never forget, the name of this game is class, and nothing succeeds like classics because, you see, they have intrinsic class. Yes, indeed, I'm all in favor of basic classics, and so I always force ignorant clients who have no taste anyway to see it my way. They usually do, and this saves all of us a lot of trouble, particularly me, and then, like I said, a few years down the line when I have

to revamp the same place, my profit margin increases dramatically. Yes, indeed, I'm definitely in favor of all the classics I can
lay my hands on."

It is thus unsurprising that such dedicated pursuit of quality
should lead this famous team to believe that interior environment specialists must coordinate a home completely, even
down to minute details such as selecting sheets and arranging
closet areas. Only with some difficulty, in fact, are they able to
refrain from a complete restructuring of their clients' personal
lives, including the most intimate aspects thereof.

"Really, a home interior planner is creating the entire environment in which the owner will live," Daugh states. "If the
sheets, towels, and other accessories the owner may already
have are decent, we'll use them. If, however, they are all wrong,
we'll destroy them or give them away and start buying, buying,
buying anew. If a client should object, well, we can deal with
that, too. After all, they must realize they have just shelled out
big, unspecified bucks for the latest, trendiest, totally chic and
classy, really fun designer environment, and so it is *they* who
must fit *it!*"

This relentless attention to detail and pursuit of total effect is
most masterfully evident in the master bedroom. In the 2,000-
square-foot closet used by the owners to house their vast collection of polyester leisure suits, Ms. Daugh lined the shelves
and covered the hooks and rods with the same wood-grained
Naugahyde used in the dressing area. "This momentous choice
of material was certainly difficult to use on those small, hard-
to-get-at nooks and corners, but in the end the clients' pleasure
more than counterbalanced the nervous breakdown I suffered,"
murmured Ms. Daugh.

This Beverly Dales condominium, then, presents a totally
harmonious, if eclectic, look. Gilt Syroco furniture in a late

Baroque style joins an antique Cambodian alligator in the master bedroom, while the living room boasts a perfectly charming mix, including a lovely contemporary couch in periwinkle polyester, antique Louis VIII chairs in black, orange, and canary yellow brocade, a Coromandel screen, and a glass-and-Lucite game table with matching footstools.

The game plan followed by this décor duo has been, very simply, to make life agreeable by providing aggressive, dynamic, yet elegantly luxurious backgrounds for today's lifestyles. After all, virtually every one of their clients is an enthusiastic, involved, fun person on the go. The owners of this condominium, for example, are avid art collectors who yearly scour the world in search of fascinating treasures to add to their unique collection. Their constant searching leaves them absolutely no time to stagnate, since they are always looking to add to their ever-changing collection and enjoy its evolution.

Small chance for stagnation in this household. Their art collection used to consist mostly of names like Picasso, Matisse, van Gogh, Renoir, and Bouguereau. However, under the astute direction provided by Daugh and De l'Unctuous, the old collection was auctioned off and new works were acquired. Their new collection now sparkles with superb pieces by Keene, Buffet, Trova, Nagle, Le Roy Nieman, and Tom of Finland.

The centerpiece of the current collection, and the owners' personal favorite, is a unique sculpture by the noted artist Estévan de Dildaö. This gem is a lifelike rendering of Esther Williams as she appeared in that divine extravaganza *Million Dollar Mermaid*. The completely convincing replica stands guard in the entrance foyer and signals the taste, elegance, and style to be found throughout this lovely home. The sculpture rests, life-size, on a very small pedestal surrounded by an indoor pool. The gold lamé swim apparel perfectly complements the golden tones of the polyester-upholstered walls. Water glistens and streams in a continual mist provided by a small spray duct driven through the base of the sculpture and coming out the head—a vision rivaling the best of Rome's old outdoor fountains. However—and here is a priceless difference—this sculpture goes beyond mere aesthetics: The gold lamé has been specially treated to become luminescent, so this incomparable work of art also serves as a night light.

The interior creators make a final comment on this, their currently most outstanding achievement since they began their long and profitable association. "We sometimes see a home where pieces are still missing—maybe a Coromandel screen or a Lucite table or perhaps a much-needed art masterpiece. This one missing piece can simply destroy the whole effect. What it comes down to is that if a thing is worth doing, no cost or expenditure on our part can be too great. Every small detail must be correct, no matter what the bottom line."

And so it is in this beautiful condominium fantasy home, wherein every last detail is not only important but riveting.

Gigantic

by Jeribee

"I'll see your ten cents and raise a quarter."

I gulped. Twenty-five cents was pretty high stakes for me. In fact, I had only 15 cents in my pocket. Then I had an inspiration. The ticket! I had a ticket on Gigantic, the largest gay cruise ship in the world, owned by Rainbow Star Lines. I'd been trying to get rid of that worthless piece of shit since I found it stuck to chewing gum under my shoe. The ship was sailing that day. It was still good!

"All right," I boasted, "I'll throw in my ticket for a cruise on Gigantic."

"What else?" the gambler asked.

"What else?" I echoed.

"Yeah, what else? You don't expect me to take that worthless piece of garbage and think it's as good as my quarter, do you?"

I knew I had to get rid of that ticket. It was an albatross around my neck; no good could come of it. "All right then, my ticket and 15 cents!"

"Too rich for my blood," one of the gamblers said.

"I'm out," said the other, as he threw down his cards.

"It's just you and me," I said. "What do you have?"

"A pair of deuces! Beat THAT, sucker."

My heart sank. Maybe I could get him to take advantage of me. "All...all I've got is two threes. It looks like you win."

"Aw, shit!" he said and threw down his cards. He shoved the money and ticket over to me and walked away.

I counted the money. Fifty-eight cents. I had never won that much money in one hand in my life. But I still had that cursed ticket!

"You won, Jack Datsun, you won!"

I looked over at my best friend, Breezy, who was practically dancing a jig. "How much money do we have now?" I asked.

He counted my money and then his money. "Well, you and I have, combined, exactly $37.58."

"You want this ticket?" I ventured.

He took it and looked at it. "Look!" Breezy said, "It's a room for two! We can both go on the cruise!"

I thought about it for a minute. I didn't have any other games lined up that night. "Sure," I said. "Let's go."

Breezy and I walked over to the dock. People were already boarding, so we got in line.

"Look at all those gorgeous hunks!" Breezy said.

"What's the big deal about going on a cruise?" I asked.

"Jack Datsun! This isn't just any cruise. It's a cruise on Gigantic, the biggest gay cruise ship in the world run by the biggest gay ship line in the world! This is its maiden voyage...or stud voyage, I should say," said Breezy, getting into the spirit of things. "This is true luxury! And you know what? Some people say Gigantic is unsinkable, that's how well it's made."

"Yadda, yadda, yadda," I said. "Nobody makes a boat to sink; they're all supposed to float."

"See, you just proved my point," rejoined Breezy. Then he turned around, "Look at all those gorgeous bods!"

I looked. One did catch my eye, a tall guy with California-bleached hair and a torso to die for. Two men accompanied him—one was an ugly-looking dude. I continued staring, trying to read his lips at a distance.

"What are you doing?" Breezy asked.

"Reading his lips," I said.

"Really? What's he saying?"

"Nothing. He's just listening to other people talk. His lips aren't moving."

"Wow! You are good," Breezy said.

Eventually our turn came to board the ship. "Tickets please," the steward said. I handed him our ticket.

"Sorry, sir, but you can't come on board here."

"Why not?" I asked.

"Please step over there, sir. You're holding up the real passengers." He pointed to a lower door.

We went down the gangplank and walked to the lower door. "Why do we have to come in this door?" I demanded.

"Because you have gum tickets, sir," the woman replied.

"What's a gum ticket?" Breezy asked.

"These are throwaway tickets," she said. "We put gum on them and throw them around town. People step on them, they get the ticket, and some even come on the cruise."

"But why would you do that?" I asked.

She looked both ways, and then whispered, "Because the man who built this ship, Bruce Dismay, spared no expense for the upper part of the ship, all for moneyed passengers. What extra he spent on top for paying customers, he took away from the bottom. They don't see the bottom, anyway. He figured it would be cheaper to give away tickets and use no-class passengers for ballast."

"Ballast!" I screamed. "We're ballast?"

"Now, now, it's not that bad," she said. "You have the run of the lower part of the ship. Just don't go on the A, B or C decks, don't use the swimming pool, don't play shuffleboard, when the passengers go nude you must at least wear underwear, don't fraternize with the real passengers, don't ask for seconds at dinner, use hot water only on Tuesday and Thursday, and you may only hum at karaoke. Please step in, sirs, you are holding up the other nonpassengers."

Breezy pushed me in. He kept pushing until we got to our rooms.

We climbed onto our bunks. "So this is a gay cruise," I commented.

"Oh, WOW!" shouted Breezy, jumping up and running to the porthole. "Look at all those fish and cups."

I walked over to the porthole, which was about 10 feet below the surface of the ocean, and looked at the trash floating past. "Just don't open it," I said and walked away.

"I can hardly wait," said Breezy. "Can you imagine a five-day orgy as we leave Miami, sail around the Caribbean, visit the Cayman Islands, and return? Anything goes! We have disco night on Monday, nude day on Tuesday—except for us it's 'underwear' day—drag contest on Wednesday, body piercing on Thursday—I just can't believe it's happening to us. And the Island! We get to tour Grand Cayman Island and…and…."

"Come on!" I beckoned. "Let's go walk on the lower decks."

Gigantic left Miami port and the singing began. Breezy and I walked on deck, humming to ourselves. Suddenly I saw the most beautiful sight in the world. There he was, standing on the deck above us, looking out to sea.

"Forget it," a fellow passenger said. "He's too rich for the likes of you."

"Who is he?" I asked.

"That's Ross DeWitt, the most gorgeous, sought-after hunk on board. However, he's already taken. Hal Cockley is his date, and rumor has it that Hal intends to make it permanent."

I turned to my talkative companion. "Hi, my name is Jack Datsun."

"I'm Gloomy Thomas," he said. "We're going to sink, you know."

"Why do you say that?"

"Any accident will send her down," he said. "She can stay afloat with the first four compartments breached. But not five. As she goes down by the head, the water will spill over the tops of the bulkheads…at E deck…from one to the next…back and back. There's no stopping it."

"That's not a pleasant thought," I said. "But we have plenty of lifeboats."

"Sure," Gloomy Thomas said, "If you call *three* plenty."

"THREE! We only have THREE lifeboats? What if we have an emergency?"

"Hel-LO! Are you thinking?" he said, tapping me on my forehead with his knuckles. "This is a *gay* cruise. In case of an emergency, we simply inflate our condoms."

That was a relief. I had completely forgotten about that. "Thanks," I said, and walked away.

I couldn't get Ross DeWitt out of my mind. I walked around the lower part of the ship thinking about him. Thinking and thinking and thinking. Finally I got a headache and decided to go to bed.

Opening the door, I found the lights were off and the room was quite dark. Even the ocean beyond the porthole offered no light. But I could hear two people in the room. Obviously Breezy had brought back a companion. I listened to them for a minute as my eyes adjusted to the darkness. Finally I could see them on the bed. Breezy whispered, "I can see the Statue of Liberty already!

Very small...of course." I turned and walked out.

On the deck again, I saw Ross DeWitt standing on the edge of the ship. He had climbed over the rail, and it looked as if he were about to jump. Quickly I walked over to him.

"Hi," I said. "Whatcha doing?"

"I'm going to jump," he said.

"Why?" I asked.

"Because," he said, "I saw my whole life as if I'd already lived it...an endless parade of parties and cotillions, yachts and polo matches...always the same narrow people, the same mindless chatter. I felt like I was standing at a great precipice, with no one to pull me back, no one who cared...or even noticed."

"Oh, believe me, you've been noticed. I noticed you. And I know Hal Cockley noticed you."

Ross climbed back over. "You really noticed me?" he said.

"Sure. You're gorgeous," I said, helping him back down from the rail.

"Hi," Ross said, "my name is Ross DeWitt."

"I'm Jack Datsun," I returned. "You really wouldn't jump, you know."

"Would too."

"Would not."

"Would too."

"Would not. Would not. Would not. Would not."

"How do you know?" he asked.

"Because you respect yourself too much. You value yourself."

"Can you keep a secret?" Ross asked.

"Sure," I said.

"I wasn't really going to jump. I was taking a pee."

"Oh," I said. "How was it?"

"I should have gone to the stern instead."

I changed the subject. "Aren't you happy with Hal?"

"I should be," Ross said. "Hal has a ton of money, and he's very powerful. He even has his own bodyguard, Spicy Killjoy. I could be rich, secure, and kept."

"Is that bad?" I asked.

"I would have to give up my future, my dreams, my search for a real lover."

"So your dreams are not the same as his?"

"Not at all. But I'm not sure I can break free of him."

"Hey! You! What are you doing up here?" an angry voice called to me.

"Crap! It's Spicy Killjoy!" Ross said.

We turned to face a mean-looking guy with a gun in his hand. Hal Cockley walked up behind him. "What are you doing here?" he said to me.

Ross spoke first. "He's helping me. I fell against the rail. He caught me before I went over. He…he saved my life."

"Oh, that's different," said Hal. "Here's 20 dollars for your trouble." He handed me the money. "Let's go, Ross," Hal said.

"But…don't you think it's worth more than 20 dollars?" Ross asked. He turned back to me, "Jack, will you please join us for nude dinner tomorrow evening? You don't even have to wear clothes…."

"Sure," I said. "I'll be there"

I watched Hal and Ross walk away. Spicy Killjoy stayed behind. After they were gone, Spicy said, "Mr. Cockley and Mr. DeWitt continue to be most appreciative of your assistance. They asked me to give you this in gratitude, and to remind you that you hold a nonclass ticket and your presence here is no longer appropriate." He handed me $20.

"But I already got $20," I said.

"Oh," he said, and took back the money. He turned and walked away.

I walked back downstairs, dreaming about Ross. When I got to my room, the lights were on and Breezy was talking to a guy.

"How'd it go?" he asked.

"Perfect, just perfect. I'm going to dinner tomorrow night with Ross DeWitt. Who's your friend?"

"Jack Datsun, this is Polly Brown. I met him today at lunch."

Polly said, "You're going to dinner with Ross DeWitt?"

"Yes."

"And Hal Cockley?"

"Yes."

"And Spicy Killjoy?"

"Yes, yes, yes. I met them all. Ross is a dreamboat."

"And he's also going to move in with rich and powerful Hal. Son, do you have the slightest comprehension of what you're doing? Well, you're about to go into the snake pit. What are you planning to wear?"

"That's the beauty of it," I said. "I don't have to wear anything. Tuesday night is nude night. I don't even have to wear my underwear. Not up there, I don't."

"Well, at least take a shower," Polly chirped.

The dinner was everything I expected, and more. The posh surroundings were breathtaking. Captain Smeed sat at our table with us. Ross was across from me, flanked by Hal and Spicy. Another guy was there, Bruce Dismay, who built Gigantic. I learned the names of the other people at the table, Ruth Bloodsucker, and Rock Lovesit.

I overheard Rock Lovesit whispering into Ruth's ear, "If your grandma is who she says she is, she was wearing the diamond the day Gigantic sailed. And that makes you my new best friend." That was one conversation I didn't want to get into, so I turned to Bruce Dismay, who was talking to the captain.

"Captain Smeed, I made this ship for great things. It's the

greatest ship in the world. It can launch my career to new heights, and it will be a fitting tribute to you on this your final voyage. This is important for me, for you, for the world. The maiden voyage of Gigantic must make headlines!"

"Tell me, Mr. Datsun," Hal taunted, "how did you get a ticket for Gigantic?"

"I work my way from place to place," I said. "Tramp steamers and such. I won my ticket on Gigantic here in an unlucky hand at poker."

Ross said, "That sounds like an exciting life. Isn't it fun to be free, going any place you want, doing whatever you want, not knowing where your next meal is coming from?"

"Even poverty has its limits of joy," I said. "There's something to be said for having money."

"Well, yes I know," replied Ross. "I do like polo, and water sports, and skiing, and good food, and tropical vacations, and nice clothes, and fine Italian shoes. But there's something special about having nothing."

Hal turned to Ross, "There's nothing I couldn't give you. There's nothing I'd deny you if you would not deny me. Open your heart to me, Ross."

"Oh, Hal," Ross said. "It's not just money I want. It's more. I want poverty too."

"I don't understand you," Ruth Bloodsucker said to Ross. "It's a fine match with Cockley that will insure your survival."

"Ruth, you've seen him. He's sitting right here naked in front of you. His name shouldn't be Cockley—it should be Cock-ette. And he's got a personality to match. Now Jack Datsun—he's different. I don't have to pretend to be happy when I'm with him."

The meal was over and I quietly excused myself and walked outside. In a few minutes Ross joined me. "Aren't you cold out here?" I asked.

"Not when I'm with you. I couldn't stand to be there another minute. Besides, I came out here to warn you."

"Warn me? About what?"

"Well, you still have a nonclass ticket, and Spicy Killjoy is going to have you confined to your room, for continuing to walk around with the real-class passengers after your invitation to dinner. He's looking for you now."

"What is it with Spicy? Is he in love with Hal?"

"Yes, silly. Everybody can see that except Hal. Look! There he is now! Run! Run!"

We took off running…and running…and running. I thought we'd never lose Spicy, but the old fart finally gave up as we ran through the engine room. We hid in a storage room, breathing hard. I collapsed on a pile of ropes covered with canvas. Ross lay down beside me. In a few minutes he rubbed his hand across my chest, and I watched him get closer. Then he gently rolled me over onto my stomach.

"I once thought I'd be getting off in the back of a Ford," he said, "but I never suspected it would be in the rear of a Datsun."

I relaxed and let nature take its course. About 15 minutes later Ross took me up to his room. We sat on his couch and continued talking.

"I would take off your clothes," Ross said, "but you don't seem to have any on."

"I can put some on for you," I said. "What do you have in the closet?"

"Don't bother," he said. "Come on over here and sit beside me. We can think of other ways to entertain ourselves besides playing Dress-Up. What else do you do, besides play poker?" he asked me.

"Pictures. Portraits. I've been traveling around, painting and studying."

"Got any samples?"

"Not with me. I left them at home."

"Then draw me," he said, "so I can see what kind of work you do. First, let me put on some clothes." Ross took something out of his closet. "This is the diamond shirt that Hal gave me," he said, holding up a shirt. It was black with long sleeves and a white diamond pattern going around the chest. Zircons in the collar made it sparkle. "Draw me in this," he said, putting it on, but leaving the rest of his body bare.

I took an ink pen and paper from the desk and started drawing his portrait. In two hours it was finished, so I held it up for his approval.

"Bravo!" Ross shouted. "That will really make Hal furious. I'll leave it out so he will be sure to see it."

It was late, and we both were tired. Ross opened the bedroom door. We took a shower and went to bed.

The next morning brought in the most beautiful day I had ever seen. The sky and ocean were exquisite. Grand Cayman Island seemed like a brilliant green emerald snuggled in a blue velvet setting.

The big drag contest was on for the day. Everyone wore their most gorgeous, revealing, or hideous gowns. Their wigs were blond, green, pink, even rainbow. Some guys had problems walking in high-heeled shoes, but not many. People walking by were practicing their singing, and I tried humming a tune.

I caught a glimpse of Hal and Spicy walking together on the other side of the ship. They were holding hands. Maybe things were going to be all right after all. I took Ross by the hand as we stood by the ship's rail. We talked about going to Cayman Island that day to shop.

"Did you hear that?" Ross asked.

"Hear what?" I asked.

"It was a 'boom,' like thunder."

We heard a splash. "No, I didn't hear a boom," I said.

"Listen! There it goes again! I heard a definite boom."

"Yeah, I think I did, too." We heard a splash again.

"THEY'RE SHOOTING AT US!" somebody screamed.

"Who's shooting at us?" we asked.

"THEM!" he shouted, pointing. "Cayman Island! They're shooting at us!"

BOOM!

"That's nonsense. Why would they...?" We heard a loud crash and the ship heaved and tossed, causing me to stop in mid sentence and grab the rail. "They hit us! They shot at us and they hit us! Smeed! Smeed! Why are the shooting at us?"

Captain Smeed looked down from the higher deck and yelled, "Gay! Because we're gay! They're afraid when people see how wonderful it is, everybody will want to be gay! Families will fall apart, children will be orphaned, divorce courts will be overbooked...."

"But that's ridiculous," I argued. "Besides, we can give them a higher quality of living."

"Doesn't matter," Captain Smeed said. "You don't expect the government to say, 'I'm wrong,' do you?"

Captain Smeed returned to his business and I watched people running back and forth. I heard someone say, "They hit us beneath the water line. We're taking in water! We're going down! We're going down!"

Captain Smeed had come down to lean over the rail and view the damage. Then he left, talking to one of the crewmen. I heard him saying, "That's right. The distress call. CQD. Tell whoever responds that we are going down by the head and need immediate assistance."

Another voice on the ship's loudspeaker said, "Man the

lifeboats! Ladies first!" and everybody on board ran to the lifeboats.

"Inflate the condoms! Inflate the condoms!" Gloomy Thomas began shouting.

People grabbed condoms out of their purses and began blowing them up.

Again we heard a voice from the loudspeaker, "Attention, all nonclass passengers. Please report to your rooms. All nonclass passengers please go to your rooms. You are blocking the real passengers from abandoning ship."

"Well, I guess I better go," I told Ross. "And you need to get off. Do you have enough condoms?"

"Yeah, I think so," he said putting his hand in his purse. "Are 20 enough?"

"That should do it. You can float all the way to Cuba if you want." I turned to go.

"Jack! Wait! I want to go with you!" Ross shouted, taking my arm.

"You're not going anywhere!" shouted Hal from a few feet away. "Jack, you better go downstairs, or I'll report you. They may even revoke your ticket for this. Ross, you and I are getting off this ship."

"I am not," Ross said. "I'm going down on Jack...WITH Jack. I'm going down with Jack."

"Do you think I don't know what is going on between you and Jack? I saw that picture when I searched your room this morning. You're nothing but Jack's whore!"

"Ha! That's all you know. I'll have you know that I'm the top man in this relationship. He's my whore, if anybody's a whore. Besides, I'd rather have Jack as my whore than be your whore. And besides that, I'm going to get Jack off."

"I don't think so," Hal said, snatching my purse out of my

hands and giving it to Spicy. Spicy opened it, put in Ross' diamond shirt and then called the captain. "Captain Smeed! Captain Smeed! Could you come here a minute, please?"

Smeed, always ready to please but nevertheless panicked about his sinking ship, came to see what Hal wanted. "Yes?" he asked.

"I took this purse away from Jack," Hal said. "Open it, Spicy." Spicy opened it and took out the shirt. "You see, Jack stole this shirt from Ross. I want him arrested."

Captain Smeed looked at Hal and Spicy with disbelieving eyes. "We're *sinking*, man. Are you inflating your condoms? Inflate your condoms *now*. Jack, you report to your room with the other nonpassengers."

"Yes, sir," I said, and left. Ross twisted his arm away from Hal and followed me. Looking back, I saw Hal and Spicy blowing up their condoms. Their pink chiffon dresses with powder blue accessories were flapping in the wind.

We struggled against the real passengers to get downstairs. At E deck we could go no farther. "Damn it!" I said. "They have a gate across it!"

"What are we going to do?" Ross asked. "We've got to get downstairs."

I saw a steward hurriedly walking by. "Excuse me, but would you please open this gate for us?" I asked.

"I can't do that," he said, "the real passengers may go down there by mistake. You know how they depend on other people to do their thinking for them. We could be sued if one wandered down there and got hurt. No, I can't do that."

"But I'm a nonpassenger," I said, "and I've got to get below."

The man threw his keys on the floor. "Here! But you didn't get them from me, understand?" He ran away.

I unlocked the gate, we entered, and I closed and locked it

again. Then I threw the keys through the gate to the stairs.

Ross asked, "Is this the floor you sleep on?"

"No," I said, "I'm still three flights down."

"Well, what if one of the other gates are locked?" he asked.

I started calling the steward, "Steward! Hey Steward! I need those keys! Would you get me those keys, please!" However no one replied.

"Great. Now what do we do?" Ross asked.

"Help me! We've got to break down this gate and get those keys!"

Ross ran over and found a fire extinguisher. He came back and began spraying the gate. In a few minutes the extinguisher was empty.

"Why did you do that?" I asked.

"I thought it might help," he said.

I grabbed the extinguisher out of his hand and began beating it against the gate lock. "From…now…on…" I said a word between each hit, "I'm…the…top…man." Finally the gate broke, and I went out and got the keys.

We were wading in knee-deep water when I pushed the door open to my room. Breezy was sitting there naked, hugging a pipe that went through the room. "Breezy! What are you doing handcuffed to the pipes?" I asked.

"Well, you know how it is. Polly and I were having sex, and things started getting kinky."

"Oh, by the way," I said, "Breezy, this is Ross DeWitt. Ross, this is my friend and roommate, Breezy." Ross grasped Breezy's fingers and shook hands. "Where's Polly?" I asked.

"He never came back."

"Oh. Is he a real passenger?"

"Yeah, I think so."

"Did he have condoms?"

"He did last night. But he might not now."

The water was about waist-high now. "Where are the keys?" I asked.

"He took them," Breezy said.

Ross ran and got a fire extinguisher.

"Close your eyes, Breezy!" I shouted. "This ain't gonna be pretty!"

Breezy closed his eyes just as Ross let go with the fire extinguisher, filling the room with a white cloud. In a few minutes it was all over; I took the canister away from him and threw it down. "Did you see a fire ax out there?" I asked.

"Yes!" Ross said, and headed for the door.

"Stop! I'll get it!" I said, and went out. In a few minutes I came back with the ax. "OK, let's break the lock!" Breezy closed his eyes tightly and I hit the chain between the handcuffs hard. They broke. The water was chest-high now.

"Let's go to the other end of Gigantic." I said. Perhaps our weight will cause the bow to raise, maybe even go above water."

"Good idea!" they said, and we all headed out the door.

The ship gave another jar and everything was still.

"What happened?" I asked.

"I think we've stopped sinking," said Breezy.

We began ascending the stairs and eventually found Gloomy. "What happened?" I asked.

"We hit bottom," Gloomy Thomas said. "The water's only 75 feet deep here."

Everybody sighed and relaxed. "Let's go to the deck and see what's happening."

We made our way out again, seeing the beautiful sky and ocean once more. People were excitedly talking and pointing to the ocean. We walked to the side of the ship and saw huge bubbles coming up from the ocean floor.

When they realized they were no longer in danger, the passengers began laughing and singing again. Drag queens resumed prancing, practicing for the contest that night. Some of the men made whistling noises with their condoms as they slowly let out the air.

"Hey, what's that?" somebody asked, pointing to Grand Cayman Island. "It's going down! Isn't it?"

We all stared over the side of the ship. Sure enough, the Island seemed to be getting lower in the water.

"Why?" I asked, "Why?"

"The way I figure it," Gloomy Thomas said, "the Cayman Islands must be sitting on a huge underground air pocket created by a volcano thousands of years ago. When they caused us to sink, the bow of the ship must have pierced the ground and penetrated that air pocket. The islands are deflating like a balloon; they're going down."

It took a day and a night for the Cayman Islands to sink—the most beautiful sight I had ever seen in my life.

Reclaiming the Expletive

by Rik Isensee

I. News Item: WASP Denounces Ironlake

A spokeswoman from the Lesbian Watch Committee of Women Against Smut and Porno (WASP) has charged that Erika Ironlake's poem, "Cunt-Licking Bitch!" is an appalling example of male-identified calumny and abuse: "We denounce this pornographic parody of perfidy, which perpetuates the very subjugation of women that Ironlake ostensibly seeks to challenge."

The group also expressed disdain for Rik Isensee's much-publicized "postmodern" defense of the work, going so far as to suggest he made the whole thing up. "It's total male fantasy," the spokeswoman said. (Ms. Ironlake could not be reached for comment.)

II. Literary Explication: Reclaiming the Expletive in Erika Ironlake's "Cunt-Licking Bitch!": A Poststructuralist, Feminist Deconstruction, by Rik Isensee

In her recent poem, Erika Ironlake counters the pretense of male attempts to define, limit, and subordinate women's bodies by reclaiming the expletive in a provocative and Sapphic ode to cunnilingus. "Cunt-Licking Bitch!" in fact challenges the objectification of women and the negation of female desire by reveling in lesbian oral-genital sexuality.

At the beginning of her poem, we assume a man's voice calls out: "Cunt-licking bitch!" We imagine Erika clenching her fists, ready to do battle. She turns to confront her adversary, when suddenly she lifts her chin, arches her brow, and turns the epithet on its head.

III. The Poem: "CUNT-LICKING BITCH!" by Erika Ironlake

"Cunt-licking bitch!"
Oh, how perceptive.
But why deny it?
Why decry it?
I defy you
to even
try it!

What is a bitch? A female dog in heat—
an uppity, two-fisted broad who can't be beat!

I'm on the hunt,
for a pink and fragrant cunt—
I like my tail,
and I find it without fail—
I'll sniff your box,
and nuzzle it like a fox!
I want your snatch,

'cause I finally met my match!
I love a twat,
So show me what you've got!

They say I'm pushy,
but I always get my pussy!
Meeow-rao-rao-rowwwwr!

I lap her up
from her pink and rosy cup
She pulls my hair,
when I muff-dive way down there
And when she comes, and gushes all her juice
I reach up to kiss her, and slide right in her sluice!

I'm a cunt-licking bitch,
a strong and powerful witch!
A bull dyke and dagger
with a proud and cocky swagger
and a tongue that's quite a wagger!

I'm butch, I'm bold,
I'm terrible to behold!
And yes, I'm vicious—
but, oh! So delicious!

Yum, slurp slurp
yum yum, slurp slurp—
slurp slurp!

Rose: A (Bad) Film for Lesbians

by Anne Seale

Living Room. Late afternoon. FADE IN on CLOSE-UP of a red rose in a vase. Background music swells. EXPAND TO FULL SHOT of Tania and Marlowe sitting on a sofa looking at the rose, displayed on a coffee table in front of them.

TANIA: When did the rose arrive, Marlowe?
MARLOWE: It was in front of my door when I came home from work.
TANIA: How exciting! You have no idea who brought it?
MARLOWE: No. There's no name on the card. All it says is (picks up card from table, reads) "Tonight at 9."
TANIA: "Tonight at 9." How romantic! Maybe it's one of your ex's, wanting to get back together again.
MARLOWE: I don't *think* so.

Marlowe and Tania laugh.

TANIA: Have you met anyone new lately?

MARLOWE: No, just the same old crowd. (beat) Wait! There was this stranger....

TANIA: Where?

MARLOWE: In the elevator. This morning.

TANIA: The elevator in this very building?

MARLOWE: Yes. When I got on, there was only one person there, someone I'd never seen before, a tall woman wearing a motorcycle jacket. She smiled at me, like she was, you know, (sly grin) interested.

TANIA: Wow. Did you talk with her?

MARLOWE: Yes, a little. She said she just moved in, so of course I told her my apartment number in case she needs to use my phone or something. It was only polite.

TANIA: Well, sure. Did she give you her name?

MARLOWE: She did, but I don't remember it. (beat) Wait, I think it started with an R. Let me think. Roxanne? Renee?

TANIA: Ramona? Rhonda?

MARLOWE: Wait, it was a short name, just one syllable. Ruth? Rae? No. (beat) Wait, I've got it! Rose! That's it, Tania. Her name is (beat) Rose.

Tania and Marlowe simultaneously turn to stare at the red rose. Background music swells. FADE OUT.

FADE IN—same living room. That night. Background music swells. Again. CLOSE-UP—clock on the wall as the hands move to exactly 9 o'clock. Marlowe sits on the sofa, leafing through a magazine. The doorbell rings. Marlowe looks at the clock, smiles, opens the door. Rose, wearing a black leather motorcycle jacket and jeans, stands in hall outside.

ROSE: Hello, Marlowe, I believe it's 9 o'clock.

MARLOWE: (voluptuously) So it is, Rose. And Rose, (beat) thanks for the (beat) flower. Would you like to come in?
ROSE: Yes. More than anything.

Rose steps in. They look deeply into each other's eyes, then kiss passionately, mouths open. Background music swells even more than before. Marlowe takes an afghan from the sofa, throws it on the floor, kneels on it, and offers her hand to Rose, who takes it and kneels, facing Marlowe. Rose eases Marlowe's peasant blouse to her waist, kissing each shoulder as it comes into view.

MARLOWE: Ooh. Aah.

Rose sucks Marlowe's left nipple. CLOSE-UP—nipple.

MARLOWE: Ooh. Aah.

DISSOLVE to LONG SHOT of Marlowe's head and upper torso. Marlowe squeezes her own nipples. CLOSE-UP—nipple. EXPAND to FULL SHOT of Marlowe, writhing in climax.

MARLOWE: Ooh. Aah.

Marlowe sits up, pushes Rose flat, and unzips and removes Rose's jeans. She plays with Rose's pubic hair. CLOSE-UP—pubic hair.

ROSE: Ooh. Aah.

Marlowe slips her fingers in and out of Rose's vagina. CLOSE-

UP—fingers in vagina. EXPAND to FULL SHOT of Rose's face as she writhes in climax.

ROSE: Ooh. Aah. Ooh. Aah.

EXPAND to FULL SHOT of both women as they gaze into each other's eyes, smiling secretly. CAMERA PANS, CLOSES IN on red rose on the coffee table. Background music swells one last time. FADE OUT.

Heat the Samovar, Blanche

by Michael Van Duzer

A Russian study during the 1880s. A voice is heard in the darkness.

VOICE: Russia. Eighteen eighty...something or other. A time when the serf report had nothing to do with beaches and a kopeck went a lot farther than it does today. In his quiet Moscow home, Peter Ilich Tchaikovsky, Russia's greatest living composer, is struggling to compose his masterpiece, soon to be hailed throughout the world as *The Nutcracker*.

The lights come up to reveal Tchaikovsky seated at a piano, probably toy. He halfheartedly plunks out a few notes.

TCHAIKOVSKY (near tears): It's gone. Not a note of music in me. I am blocked—buffaloed, as that charming American would have said. A Christmas ballet! I'll never write it. I am empty. Void of talent. Bereft of inspiration. Why is it, that while facing this frustrating, impotent abyss, I find myself thinking of salt water taffy?

The bell rings.

TCHAIKOVSKY: Someone's here. And Dunyasha is not back from the market.

Tchaikovsky moves off and answers the door. He returns a moment later with Alexei St. Petersburg. Alexei carries a portfolio.

TCHAIKOVSKY: Come in, come in.
ALEXEI: Thank you, sir.
TCHAIKOVSKY: How can I help you?
ALEXEI: I am hoping, sir, that I can help you. I recently made the acquaintance of your brother, Modest. He intimated that you were in desperate need of a music copyist, and I might be just the type of person you required.
TCHAIKOVSKY: I see. Dear Modest, always thinking of others. What is your name?
ALEXEI: Alexei, sir. Alexei St. Petersburg. I changed it briefly to Leningrad. But Alexei Leningrad has very little music. So, I changed it back.
TCHAIKOVSKY: Very astute. I don't know what Modest might have told you about me—
ALEXEI: Explanations were not required. I dare to call myself your most fervent admirer. Your music, in performance, has always had the most astounding effect on me. The orchestra strikes directly at my core, and I become a shameless wanton wallowing in a sensual sea of melody.
TCHAIKOVSKY: My, my. I see why Modest insisted on your

visiting. Alexei, you must understand that I am a demanding employer. I am selfish and would require your complete attention. I sometimes get up in the middle of the night to work. Our muses can be stern taskmasters and inspiration is nothing to nap through. You would have to live here.

ALEXEI: That would be no problem, sir.

TCHAIKOVSKY: Your family would have no objection to your moving?

ALEXEI: I have no family. My father died before I was born and my mother outlived him only by two years.

TCHAIKOVSKY: (tearing up) An orphan. I know that feeling of loss. My mother died also (choking up) the cholera.

He bursts into tears. Alexei moves to comfort him.

ALEXEI: Are you all right, sir?

TCHAIKOVSKY: Perfectly. It's just my extraordinary sensitivity coupled with deep melancholia. Hellish personality traits, but they make for magnificent musicianship.

ALEXEI: Is there anything I can do?

TCHAIKOVSKY: Tell me more of your life. After the death of your mother—

ALEXEI: I was raised in the Pimen Orphan Asylum for Young Men.

TCHAIKOVSKY: An institution unknown to me but, no doubt, to be commended in its single-minded attention to young men.

ALEXEI: Might I show you my portfolio?

TCHAIKOVSKY: By all means.

Alexei hands him the portfolio, which Tchaikovsky studies carefully.

TCHAIKOVSKY: Your work is excellent. Clear and bold. Firm strokes. I dislike a shaky hand.

ALEXEI: Thank you, sir.

TCHAIKOVSKY: You appear to be a meticulous worker. I imagine you grasp the stylus with a technique born of long hours of practice.

ALEXEI: I have always given my composers satisfaction.

TCHAIKOVSKY: No doubt. Remove your clothes. I would like to see if the orphanage has had any debilitating effects that might impair you in the performance of your duties.

ALEXEI (taking off his shirt): I think you'll find everything in good order, sir. Father Zossima took particular care to insure my health and well-being with thorough and painstaking physical examinations several times a week.

TCHAIKOVSKY: He sounds like a remarkable man.

ALEXEI: Yes. He prided himself on his fastidious nature.

TCHAIKOVSKY: Where is Father Zossima now?

ALEXEI (removing his trousers): Dead. An unfortunate incident with a deranged parent during his yearly outing with the Pimen altar boys. I believe it to be the work of anarchists, sir.

TCHAIKOVSKY: Call me Peter. I will require all of your attention.

ALEXEI: I have no life or outside interests, sir. (Tchaikovsky cocks an eyebrow at him.) Peter.

TCHAIKOVSKY: You are an inspiring example of mouthwatering, youthful pulchritude. A Slavic Adonis.

ALEXEI (referring to his underwear): Shall I remove the rest?

TCHAIKOVSKY: No. This will suffice for a leisurely afternoon perusal. You will add immensely to my study of advanced physiques.

ALEXEI: Don't you mean physics?

TCHAIKOVSKY: Not at all. I have renounced intellectual pur-

suits and am embarked on a hedonistic exploration of the sole-
ly sensual. My quest for experience is insatiable. You will be a
welcome addition in the laboratory.

ALEXEI: I'm honored.

TCHAIKOVSKY: Your thighs are in superb shape for an orphan. Father Zossima's diddling—sorry, diligence has paid off.

ALEXEI: The good Father was most particular about our legs.
He loved it when I played the Prussian soldier for him.

TCHAIKOVSKY: The Prussian soldier?

ALEXEI: Yes. I'll show you.

Alexei begins a goose-stepping march across the room.
Tchaikovsky is delighted. Alexei halts and salutes.

TCHAIKOVSKY: Wonderful—so brusque, so masculine. It reminds me of something. Please repeat it.

Alexei repeats the march with some further elaboration.
Tchaikovsky sinks to his knees and seriously studies the
movement.

ALEXEI: If you have a riding crop, I could show you Father
Zossima's favorite game.

TCHAIKOVSKY: Not now. An idea is dawning! Something
about the legs. That stiff-kneed march. The scissorlike movement. Eureka! (The march from *The Nutcracker* begins to
play.) Yes, that's it. It's true inspiration!

Tchaikovsky begins to dance to the music only he can hear.

ALEXEI: Peter, are you all right?

TCHAIKOVSKY (stopping his dance and sinking to the floor):

Yes, yes. I'm wonderful now. Alexei, my muse—my idol. You are my inspiration.

ALEXEI: Do you mean it? (moving onto the floor with Tchaikovsky) I have inspired you? It's more than I could dare to dream.

TCHAIKOVSKY: We must start work immediately. (He stops and stares at Alexei for a moment.) Well, perhaps a half hour of further inspiration would be useful.

Blanche enters. She is all in white and speaks with a Southern accent.

BLANCHE: Don't bother to get up, gentlemen, I'm just passing through.

Alexei leaps to his feet in confusion.

TCHAIKOVSKY: Blanche, this is my new music copyist, Alexei St. Petersburg. Alexei, this is my wife, Blanche Tchaikovsky.

BLANCHE: Enchante. That's French for "you are devastating."

TCHAIKOVSKY: My wife has a penchant for the French language.

BLANCHE: Au contraire, it is a deep and abiding conviction that I should have been born French. My name is also French. It means "white." My goodness, what are you men getting up to?

TCHAIKOVSKY: We were working on an idea for the new ballet.

BLANCHE: I thought, perhaps, that you were practicing your Greco-Roman wrestling. I walked into the room and thought only Mr. Lawrence, Mr. D. H. Lawrence, could do justice to this scene.

TCHAIKOVSKY: Why don't you get dressed, Alexei?

BLANCHE: Don't trouble yourself on my account.

ALEXEI: It's no trouble, Madame. In my profession, the minimum qualification is getting in or out of your clothes in 30 seconds.

He slips his clothes on.

BLANCHE: What an impressive achievement.

TCHAIKOVSKY: Now, Blanche, we really need to get to work.

BLANCHE: You will discover, Mr. Alexei, that my husband works all the time. He is voracious about it. He comes into this room and, I swear, he will disappear for weeks on end. I will occasionally get up very early, before the sun rises, slip on a pretty frock and wait patiently at the breakfast table hoping to catch a glimpse of my husband. That is, I suppose, the price of genius.

ALEXEI: You have a lovely accent, Madame Tchaikovsky.

BLANCHE: I am, as you may have divined, from the south of Russia. The Ukraine. My daddy had the most enormous home, and our land was the pride of the county. (The "Tara" theme begins underneath.) My daddy always said "the land was the only thing worth working for, worth fighting for, worth dying for." (She thinks for a moment.) I'm sorry. I'm in the wrong film.

ALEXEI: It must be beautiful there. Is that where you met Peter?

BLANCHE: Yes. My husband was wintering there one year. Under a doctor's orders. There is not much to do after dark in the Ukraine, but there are several resorts along the lake that offer nighttime amusements. The most popular is Moon Lake Casino, and it was there that I met my husband. He was sitting at a piano in the lobby playing the Varsouviana.

A strange little waltz begins, and Blanche dances with the music.

TCHAIKOVSKY: The climate in the south is heavy and oppressive. It makes you think and do… strange things.

He slaps Blanche across the face and the music stops abruptly.

BLANCHE: Thank you. I am sorry, Mr. Alexei. I can't imagine what you must think of me. My only excuse, and a feeble one at that, is that since coming to Moscow, I have been under a terrible strain. Perhaps a tiny glass of vodka would steady my nerves.

Blanche goes to a table and pours herself a drink.

TCHAIKOVSKY: Blanche, it is only 10 in the morning.
BLANCHE: Peter, how you talk! This young, young man will be getting the wrong impression. My lips rarely touch liquor. I use it strictly for medicinal purposes.

She downs the vodka in record time.

ALEXEI: Brother Nicholas used vodka for the same reason. And, I must say, you could always tell when he'd taken his medicine.
BLANCHE: I am not an artist, Mr. Alexei. I am merely an auditor. That is my tragedy.
TCHAIKOVSKY: Don't be melodramatic, Blanche. (The doorbell rings.) Oh, bother! Who is this now?

He goes to the door. Blanche quickly pours another drink. Tchaikovsky comes back with Madame von Meck. She is energetic and carries a large fur muff.

MADAME von MECK: Good morning, good morning, good morning! I'm delighted to see everyone up and facing the day. I have been up since 5 A.M. There is nothing like a brisk morning constitutional to get the breath going. (She demonstrates.) In. Out. In. Out. Breathing is the foundation of a healthy body. Breathe for me, Tchaikovsky. (He breathes while she examines him.) Deeper. Deeper. Breathe from here. (She pats his diaphragm, then looks at Blanche.) Madame Tchaikovsky, you are looking particularly anemic. Don't you ever go outside?

BLANCHE: I'm afraid that the fragile state of my nerves doesn't allow me—

MADAME von MECK: Nonsense! Two hours a day in the sunshine is the perfect prescription for nervous disorders. I think you'll find that the famous Dr. Chebutykin agrees with me entirely.

BLANCHE: I am sure that sunshine is a panacea for most of mankind, but I am cursed with the delicate complexion of an Irish colleen. The sun is a veritable poison to my system.

MADAME von MECK: I have been to Ireland. It is a healthy country where women dig potatoes and cut giant sheets of peat in the fresh air. You would do well to follow their example.

Madame notices Alexei and crosses to examine him. Blanche pours another vodka.

TCHAIKOVSKY: Madame von Meck, this is my new music copyist, Alexei St. Petersburg.

ALEXEI (extending his hand): I am honored to make your acquaintance.

MADAME von MECK: Please, don't touch the muff.

TCHAIKOVSKY: Madame von Meck is my most generous benefactor. When she is in town, she often honors us with a visit.

MADAME von MECK: I like to see where my money's going. This young man looks to be in very good shape, Tchaikovsky. Not at all like that feeble wax work you were employing before.

TCHAIKOVSKY: Yes, I'm afraid Constantine was a mistake.

MADAME von MECK: I told you that the moment I laid eyes on him. He was as moody a man as I ever saw. I am never wrong about such things. The Princess Draguboff wouldn't dream of having one of her famous soirees without my inspecting the guest list. I have a good feeling about you, Mr. St. Petersburg. I believe that you will serve Tchaikovsky well.

ALEXEI: That is my fondest desire.

MADAME von MECK: I expect you to see that he takes some exercise daily. He has an alarming tendency to lock himself up and brood over his music for days.

TCHAIKOVSKY: I am sure that Alexei is a potent tonic for any bout of melancholy.

ALEXEI: I'll do my best.

MADAME von MECK: And I hope that you are not too talkative. Excessive chatter can be extremely distracting.

TCHAIKOVSKY: You may trust me to find alternate employment for his lips.

MADAME von MECK: I approve, Tchaikovsky. This boy will do admirably.

TCHAIKOVSKY: He is a godsend. Not even in the house an hour and he has already given me fresh inspiration.

MADAME von MECK: Tell me.

He signals to Alexei who repeats his goose-stepping display.

TCHAIKOVSKY: It is the idea for my new Christmas ballet. I shall call it "The Nutcracker."

MADAME von MECK: Arresting title. I like it. I hope there will be Cossack dancers. I adore Cossack dancers. The way they leap into the air and stamp their heavy boots into the ground. It's quite thrilling.

TCHAIKOVSKY: Well, I don't know—

MADAME von MECK: I will tell you a secret, Tchaikovsky. Audiences are tired of swans. Give them Cossack dancers and you will have a tremendous success. I, Nadejda von Meck, declare it.

TCHAIKOVSKY: The story is about a young girl who receives a nutcracker on Christmas Eve, I don't see where the Cossack dancers would fit in.

MADAME von MECK: Escort me into the parlor. You will tell me your story and I can determine how best to capitalize on the Cossack dancers. How I love the creative process. (Tchaikovsky takes her arm.) Hands off the muff. How many times must I tell you that it is indelicate to finger a lady's muff.

They move off into the parlor. Alexei turns to Blanche. She holds up the empty vodka bottle.

BLANCHE: Where are my manners? The bottle is empty and I haven't even offered you something to quench your thirst.

ALEXEI: I am not particularly fond of vodka.

BLANCHE: I don't believe we have anything else in the house. I could run down to the corner and get you a nice lemon coke with lots of chipped ice.

ALEXEI: No, thank you.

BLANCHE: Shall I heat the samovar?

ALEXEI: Don't trouble yourself, Madame. I am perfectly fine.

BLANCHE: Don't be so modest. You are more than fine. You are, most certainly, choice. My husband has always had an eye for beauty. For masculine beauty. I often liken him to Mr. Michelangelo Buonaroti. You see, there have been music copyists before.

ALEXEI: I see.

BLANCHE: Music copyists, secretaries, assistants with long, yellow hair and smooth chests—

ALEXEI: Madame, are you all right?

BLANCHE: Perfectly. You see, my husband is an artist. A man who brings culture and elegance into this squalid world of ours. You've heard his music?

ALEXEI: Yes, Madame.

BLANCHE: Well, then you know. When I hear his music, it seems as though I'm seeing all the colors of the spectrum for the first time. Vivid flashes of orange striped with jets of burgundy. And sometimes you can see, very rarely and just for a moment, a delicate sprinkling of fuchsia. I don't need to tell you that I live for these moments. These moments of perfection.

ALEXEI: I understand.

BLANCHE (touching his cheek): I believe you do, Alexei. This is not to say that, as a man, my husband is faultless. He has his failings. There was always something different about him. A softness, a sensitivity that I attributed to his creative soul. But there was more to it than that. Once we were married I noticed him pulling away from me. It started almost imperceptibly but soon he would physically recoil from my touch. I drove myself nearly frantic. What had I done? What was the matter? Then I found out. In the worst of all possible ways. By suddenly coming into a room I thought was empty—which wasn't empty—but had two people in it. And suddenly the colors disappeared completely from my life. Oh, but I am going on. Look at your face, Mr. Alexei. I know that face. That face that says "when will this woman stop boring me?"

ALEXEI: Oh, no, Madame.

BLANCHE: You don't have to lie. Your eyes are wondering about this crazy old woman here.

ALEXEI: Madame, you are not crazy. And you're certainly not old.

BLANCHE: Lord love you for a liar. I know how decrepit I appear, especially this early in the day.

ALEXEI: Madame, you are young and vital.

BLANCHE: Mr. Alexei, I believe you are flirting with me a bit. But I rather like it. I hope you will continue.

MADAME von MECK (off stage): But where are the Cossacks? There must be Cossacks, Tchaikovsky!

BLANCHE: Do you like a Cossack dancer?

ALEXEI: I've never had a Cossack dancer.

BLANCHE: Personally, I find them barbaric. I am not surprised that Madame von Meck relishes their stomping and sweating. She is not a woman to appreciate subtlety. Do you dance, Mr. Alexei?

ALEXEI: I'm afraid not. The good brothers at the orphanage neglected instruction on the social arts, feeling there would be little opportunity for us to practice them.

BLANCHE: When I look at you, I see a natural-born dancer. It is in your blood. I would not be surprised if your parents were gypsies. Come, take my hand.

ALEXEI: I don't think I should—

BLANCHE: Don't think! Listen to the rhythm of your heart. (She pulls him into her and places his arms around her waist.) What a firm grip you have. And such powerful arms. And your chest… I'll bet you were the biggest in your class.

ALEXEI: I grew much faster than the other boys.

BLANCHE (struggling, but making sure he doesn't let go): This is so sudden. I feel compelled to remind you that I am a married woman.

ALEXEI: Madame—

BLANCHE: My, you are just a big Cossack yourself, aren't you? Virile and powerful. You could wrap me up and do anything you like with me.

ALEXEI: I don't want to do anything!

BLANCHE: I am powerless to stop you. I feel your hands searching every inch of my body. Your desire is melting every shred of decency I possess. I am a wanton creature of the night!

ALEXEI: Please, Madame, I—

BLANCHE: Sir, if you do not restrain yourself I shall have to call "fire." Fire!

She cries out and swoons into his arms. He holds her for a moment, puzzled. Big Buster Keaton slapstick routine as he struggles to put her inert body onto a chair. Tchaikovsky and Madame von Meck enter, finding Alexei in a rather compromising position with the still unconscious Blanche.

MADAME von MECK: What is the meaning of this tawdry exhibition?

ALEXEI: I don't...that is I...She....

MADAME von MECK: Stop stammering, lad. My patience is limited.

ALEXEI: Madame Blanche was suddenly overcome during dance instruction. I believe she intended to show me the turkey trot.

MADAME von MECK: Ridiculous woman! These polite society jigs are wasted on one of your natural athletic ability. No ballroom capering for you. You are of the earth, the people, a true Cossack. Isn't that right, Tchaikovsky?

TCHAIKOVSKY: Indeed.

MADAME von MECK: And we have found your place in the new ballet. A stroke of genius. A brilliant idea of mine.

TCHAIKOVSKY: With all due respect, Madame, the idea was mine.

MADAME von MECK: Technically yes, but I agreed with you immediately. (to Alexei) Drop that woman. (He does.) You have work to do. Your place in the pageant of history awaits. If I am pleased with the Cossack dance, I shall finance the entire ballet.

TCHAIKOVSKY (taking her hand): You are too generous, Madame.

MADAME von MECK: Tchaikovsky, the muff!

TCHAIKOVSKY: Sorry, Madame.

MADAME von MECK: Take the young man and prepare yourselves. I shall see to your wife.

TCHAIKOVSKY: I will pray for inspiration before the icon of St. Matthew my (tearing up) sainted mother left me.

Tchaikovsky and Alexei exit. Madame von Meck crosses to the supine Blanche.

MADAME von MECK: Madame Tchaikovsky, rouse yourself.

BLANCHE (fuzzy as she comes back): Shep? Shep, is that you? Oh, you're not who I was expecting at all.

MADAME von MECK: Disappointment is the lot of the Victorian woman. Gather your remaining wits about you. We have work to do. Your husband, with my help, is about to produce a masterpiece. He will need your unconditional support.

BLANCHE: I'm afraid you must think me a tragically unsuitable hostess.

MADAME von MECK: I never think, Madame. If I stopped to think, I might never *do* anything.

BLANCHE: You look at me with such disapproval in your eyes.

MADAME von MECK: My look is neither malicious nor censorious. I am simply anxious for you to fulfill your wifely duties.

BLANCHE: How can I help?

TCHAIKOVSKY (off stage): Heat the samovar, Blanche.

MADAME von MECK: The voice of destiny. (Blanche exits.) Tchaikovsky finished his "Nutcracker." He insisted on that bratty little girl and the rats and the snowflakes and that hideous Sugar Plum Fairy. But there's really only one reason the ballet is revived yearly from the Kirov to Miss Edwina's Des Moines Dance Academy. Cossack dancers!

The Russian Dance from *The Nutcracker* plays. Blanche pushes Tchaikovsky and Alexei out on rolling office chairs. They are wearing big black boots and fur hats. Blanche and Madame von Meck roll them around in a choreographed dance sequence. They remain seated but kick up their legs and move their arms as if they were Cossack dancers squatting and kicking.

The Lost Women's Music Festival Diaries

by Bonnie J. Morris

Women's Music Festivals: Where the Neurotic Meet the
Erotic in Tofu Harmony

DIARY OF BEV, A BUTCH ATTENDING HER FIRST WOMEN'S MUSIC
FESTIVAL

2 A.M.: Arrive in RV and park it at tree line. Remove motorcycle and camping gear and buzz through the woods in search
of the perfect campsite. Set up camp. Decide to change oil in
the Harley before I forget. Take bike apart. Tinker. Solder. Put
bike back in order until whiny women in neighboring campsite
beg for peace and quiet.

3 A.M.: Decide to do my required work shift now—why the
hell not? Get it done the first night; more time to play. Sounds
good. Put on security garb and join other dykes at gate. Tell incoming women where to park. Flirt with incoming women.
Cause traffic jam. Get yelled at. Yell back. Get reassigned to
stage crew.

5 A.M.: Help stage crew rainproof the entire festival; someone felt a drop.

6 A.M.: Help stage crew remove rain gear from stage and sound towers; skies are now clear as can be. Stand in the middle of the stage just to see what it feels like. Sing a really loud imitation of a woman folksinger I hate. Find out her manager is standing next to me. Apologize. Cringe.

7 A.M.: Look for some breakfast chow. Ask for coffee and sausages. Am offered granola and melon instead. Jog through the woods until I smell coffee and sausages. Deliberately befriend the women at this campsite. Gladly help them set up their illegal propane stove. Accidentally blow up a small tree.

8 A.M.: Sleep (fully clothed, right hand firmly on motorcycle.)

11 A.M.: Rugby game. Shirts against skins. Get hit on head while distracted by stunning array of bare breasts and tattoos.

Noon: Lunch. Buzz up to the RV and take packet of emergency hot dogs from cooler. Invite rugby players to a weenie roast at my place. Trade stories about workplace harassment. Trade stories about kicking the boss's ass. Argue about who has the butchest day job. Lie. Boast. Exaggerate. Lick mustard off another woman's wrist.

1 P.M.: Day stage concerts begin. Vigorously applaud raunchy comic. Whistle through fingers and roar approval when she says "pussy." When meaningful folksinger with zither sits down to begin the next set, fall asleep.

3 P.M.: Workshop: "Itemize Your Toolkit."

4 P.M.: Workshop: "Introduction to Vibrators."

6 P.M.: Help two women in wheelchairs set up their space. Offer them rides on the motorcycle so they can see the land at high speed. Buzz around getting yelled at and having a great time. Exchange phone numbers and motor repair parts.

7 P.M.: Dinner. Barbecue up at the RV. Invite the garbage

crew up for chicken enchiladas and corn on the cob. Everyone gets greasy and flirtatious. Party it up. Sing obscenely. Compare interesting scars.

9:30 P.M.: Finally make it to night stage, stopping to buy a coconut Popsicle. Run the Popsicle playfully up and down the nude woman in front of me. Get yelled at by her partner. Do a double take: her partner is Moosie, from my driver's ed class at Belmont High! Big reunion. Pound each other's backs. Roll around noisily in the hay. Ignore the nude woman, who becomes sulky and petulant.

11 P.M.: Night stage needs 300 women to do security. Volunteer, pausing only to change sweatshirts. Sleep under the drum kit, snoring peacefully.

DIARY OF NELL, AN UPTIGHT STAGE PERFORMER

5 A.M.: Awaken in panic. Did I remember to pack extra frets? Fret about frets for an hour.

6 A.M.: Awaken in panic. Large new mosquito bites between fingers of both hands will ruin my rendition of that meaningful love ballad for which I and my guitar are justifiably famous!

6:30 A.M.: Fall back asleep after reciting the Serenity Prayer.

6:45 A.M.: Awaken to sounds of kitchen crew drumming ritually on tofu-bin lids. Give up. Get up.

7 A.M.: Coffee in "performer care" dining area. Note who comes to breakfast with an unexpected new companion. Note who comes to breakfast looking radiant from a night of sexual enhancement. Note who comes to breakfast with the person I had hoped to come to breakfast with. Take partial satisfaction in noting what Perfect Performer X looks like without benefit of blow-dryer.

8 A.M.: Go for quiet walk in woods in secluded area where

no festiegoers will recognize me. Return to tent devastated that no festiegoers recognized me.

9 A.M.: Sound check. Missing guitar frets turn up in toilet kit, but now my lucky guitar pick has vanished! Monitors sound terrible. Voice sounds terrible. Weep. Snarl. Stomp around with abandon. Seek solace in the arms of a burly lighting designer. Get bit by her child. Slurp herbal tea. Try again. Worry about tripping over poorly secured stage wires. Trip over poorly secured stage wires. Argue about which encore would sound better. Argue about being scheduled to perform after my ex-lover, the evil percussionist. Whine. Sing. Sniffle unattractively.

10 A.M.: Attend workshop: "Making Music With Your Own Body Parts."

Noon: Give workshop: "Songwriting For Vegetarians." Meet a hot young festiegoer named Pigeon O'Reilly.

1 P.M.: Lunch. Get into trouble attempting to bring Pigeon into the performers' dining area. Agree to join Pigeon in huge festiegoers' food line. Wait forever, only to be told the kitchen ran out of cheese. Burn breasts to a crisp while standing in line. Decline generous offers from fans volunteering to apply sunburn cream. Suspect that not all of them are really registered nurses.

2 P.M.: Sign albums at record booth. Worry about the drooling fan who wanted her right buttock autographed in indelible ink. Sell a few tapes and T-shirts. Drink a cup of soy milk au lait.

3:30 P.M.: Watch Pigeon dance nude in front of day stage. Get inspiration for new song. Your arms, like wings, o pigeon girl. Your toe marks in the sand.

4 P.M.: Line up to shower while sun is still warm. Worry about having to explain my regrettable tattoo for the 800th time. Borrow toothpaste and Vagisil from someone less famous than myself; pray she doesn't mention it to anyone else.

5 P.M.: Dinner. Cauliflower tahini and rutabaga fritters Florentine. Eavesdrop on conversation between two stage crew technicians who predict a rainstorm during my set. Weep into salad bowl.

6 P.M.: Last-minute rehearsal with other performers I agreed to have as backup singers. Rehearsal piano in bad shape. Tuner cannot be located; she drove into town for beer, cigarettes, red meat, and rolling papers.

7 P.M.: Set up my lawn chair in the field so Pigeon can watch my set from the third row. Get yelled at by a woman who says it's the wrong kind of lawn chair. She has never even heard of my album!

8 P.M.: A 40-minute set of my own on the night stage! A dream come true! Why, then, did my fly have to be open?

9 P.M.: Consoling cuddles with Pigeon in our lawn chair beneath the stars. Pork out on clandestine bag of Twinkies. Hold hands with other wimmin and sing about sisterhood. Feel the joy. Feel the unity. Feel the heavens open unexpectedly and dump torrents of rain on us all. Race to tent.

10 P.M.: Ecstatic, safe sex.

10:15 P.M.: Awkward leg cramp.

10:20 P.M.: Tent collapses.

10:30 P.M.: Bear wanders into campground. Maybe I should have been an English teacher after all.

Scrooge and Marley

by Michael Dubson Sage

When most people think of Ebenezer Scrooge and Jacob Marley, they think of two greedy, grasping, selfish, uncaring, hardened old sinners, men who loved to hear the hard clinking coins in their horny hands while they became the most famous and powerful of moneychangers in all of merry old Victorian London. Lies, lies, all lies.

Scrooge and Marley wanted everyone to believe that. They spent a lot of time working, yes, and more than one Britisher of lesser means would pass by their office on cold, snowy evenings to see the lights flickering behind closed shades. "Those bloody bastards are in there fleecing us out of another three pounds and sixpence," weary travelers would grumble.

They were in there, all right. Scrooge and Marley were a long-term gay couple. The attraction had been quick and immediate when they met at old Fezziwig's accounting firm when they were both hot young British bucks. A fast friendship developed between them, and one night, when most of the staff had gone home and they were working on the ledger sheets,

Marley reached for a new account. His long-fingered hand fell on Scrooge's, and there it remained, the ledger sheets forgotten. Scrooge's dark brown eyes met Marley's blue ones, and their hearts began to pound. Their young, handsome faces began to shine with the knowledge of their love and their desire. They knew what was between them was inevitable.

They were also intelligent, cynical men who knew how to survive in a hostile society. They knew that two men who were openly lovers would have been driven out of business and into social and economic ruin. But two businessmen joined together by ruthless ambition and callous greed would be perfectly acceptable. And so they worked to propel the very values that oppressed them.

"Poor Mr. Scrooge and Mr. Marley," British working-class tongues initially wagged. "They're so involved in their business, they just don't have time to marry."

As they got bigger (their business, that is), the wagging tongues sang a new tune. "Nasty old Scrooge and Marley. Good thing nasty men like that never got married. They're working in there, trying to figure out more ways to screw us."

Actually, Scrooge and Marley were figuring out new ways to screw each other. On the desk, account sheets and ledger books crinkled beneath Ebby's hot, thrusting bottom. On the floor, Jakie's missile hit the target spots in Ebby's promised land. By the door, so that every time it rattled the risk excited them further. In the washing room, hot water cascaded across their trembling, naked bodies.

People thought they were cheap because they wouldn't heat the office, but Scrooge and Marley didn't need to. They generated enough heat on their own on cold winter evenings to last throughout the next day. Of course, much sentimentality has been expended on the way Scrooge treated his principal stooge,

Bob Cratchit. Cratchit, portrayed as a good, gentle soul with a loving family and a true sense of the Christmas spirit, was really a whiny, simpering, unambitious wimp, an irresponsible heterosexual who produced more kids than he could afford, and a duplicitous little twit with a martyr complex. He liked to look like he was cold, with his hands in those finger-worn gloves, while he basked in the leftover heat generated by Ebby and Jake's secret passions, too dumb to ever figure out what really kept the office warm.

They were hated for being coldhearted businessmen. It was a hatred that paled to what they would have received as homosexual lovers in Victorian England. Scrooge and Marley, victims of their era, were frauds nonetheless. Benefiting from their perceived heterosexuality, they became ruthless capitalists, exploiting the poor and the desperate while reinforcing the philosophies of heterosexual corporate capitalism that exists to the greater detriment of all the world today. They failed to take a stand that could have sped up the gay rights movement and led to their business being just as successful, however kinder and gentler it might have been. They refused to risk their lives and safety for the benefit of all who would follow them. They refused to tell the world what the Scroo in Scrooge really stood for!

Their love lasted through both the calendar and fiscal years, and as the ledger pages turned, their hearts continued to beat as one. They grew old together, and those hot bottom nights grew fewer in number, but their love remained strong through the years and more secret than anything Doris Day ever sang about.

When Jacob died, Ebenezer took it very hard. Jacob had been his life and business partner for 50 years. He had to deal with his grief alone because no one had ever learned the truth. So he buried himself in his work for the sake of blocking out his pain, and he became bitter and even more ruthless for reasons no one understood but condemned him for. Had he been open about why he had become more bitter, they would have condemned him for that, too, but the condemnation would have been counterbalanced by real friendships and real support from a genuine, if smaller, percentage of his associates. Yet Ebenezer Scrooge was too much a coward to risk all he could gain for what he might lose. Pathetic fool!

When Ebenezer's vicious, bitter behavior began to endanger his immortal soul, Jacob came back from the dead to warn him, and to show him he needed to change his ways. No heterosexual man would come back to warn his business partner about anything except a mistress-aware wife. Guys like that love to see each other fall. But Jacob's mercy brought a renewed hope and vigor into Ebenezer's life, and bursting forth with life-affirming and loving gay spirit, he went forth into his community, bringing love of life, joy, and economic resources to all those less fortunate than he. Ebenezer went as far as to save differently abled Tiny Tim Cratchit from a premature death. The fact that Tiny Tim became quite a sight to see in his long johns a few years down the road and wanted to spend a lot of time at Uncle Scrooge's was, of course, plenty of motivation for closeted, hypocritical Scrooge.

But did Scrooge ever acknowledge where all that spirit came from? That his renewed lease on life came from his lifelong love of a man? Absolutely not.

Ebenezer Scrooge, benefiting economically from his perceived heterosexuality, and benefiting emotionally and socially from his true homosexuality, never let an inch of the truth out. Jacob Marley, wearing the chains he forged in life, still clanks in his grave today over hot-bottomed Ebby's moral betrayal.

Written on My Body

by Amy Schutzer

The particularness of someone
who mattered enough to grieve
over is not made anodyne
by death.
—*Jeanette Winterson*

For L.K.

Written on my body,
pencil sharp,
words from your teeth and tongue,
left there
for me to find and interpret
without the vocabulary
necessary to translate.

I once had a girlfriend
thin and dipterous,

a gnat that hovered
inches from me,
a constant pest
with tepid skin
and a quick heartbeat
who covered her mirrors
when we made love
so as not to be fooled
by false images.
One Tuesday,
she disappeared as easily
as she appeared,
as if someone had swatted
after a mosquito
and squashed it in their palms,
rubbing,
until all that was left
was a grainy shadow of blood.

When trying to read my skin
for treasonous words or words of love
I roam with fingers
over the hills and dips of the body
like a coracle in a rough sea
navigating by starlight
even when there are no stars.

What I find
are your confessions like spider webs
arcing over my skin,
enduring and dew laden and empty,
a compelling trap for my sepulchral mind.

I once had a girlfriend
muscular but palimpsest,
an easy read
completely changing and erasable,
day to day,
like a popular magazine
with improved dieting tips
and miracle babies
coming in sets of sixes and sevens.
I lived to see
the color of her nails,
her hair,
spiked or curled or swaddled
in strips from the Sunday comics.
The day she left,
I swear,
she looked just like me.

Oxides
are compounds that combine
metals or semi metals with oxygen.
Ice is the most common oxide.
Oh! _____.
Passion has its heat;
it is the moment of forgetting,
of suspending belief,
the jumping off into a humid air,
love burning away all shadows
holding fast to the body,
breathing your breath,
that is what I have taken with me
and frozen inside my bones and heart.

Ice solid as stone.
Fire, you are the fire that dissolves me.

I once had a girlfriend
hard and small,
an asp snaking her way into my life
quoting from the Kama Sutra
and Jeanette Winterson.
When we made love
she was slow as a serpent
coiled in the sun,
whispering in my ear
with her lithe tongue;
"We gamble with the hope of winning
but it is the thought of what we might lose
that excites us."
She wound around me
for hours and hours,
patient and painstaking,
before the strike.
She took up with a troupe
of sword swallowers
and went to South America
where the snakes hang lazily
in wait
from the thick trees.

August. I lean against
the perspex Bob's Big Boy
hoping for a hint of you,
a word to come clear on my skin
or a map leading directly to your heart.

I can smell the french fries,
hamburgers and milkshakes,
the treacle of simple reason,
of putting hand to mouth laden with food.

Food, that secret progenitor of memories
lodged like fat in the veins,
but once shaken and moved,
the eyes will widen
and the tongue will smack heartily
against greasy lips.
Oh! _____.
You are a Valadon still life,
a nude in shades of ochres and blues,
drifting through a field of stout sunflowers,
the rasping of bees,
red dirt and dusk quieting before a waxing moon.
I taste you
instead of food,
my lips know only of your salt
and the moisture on your skin,
the sudden sweetness after sour,
like the first raspberry of summer.
This is what I look for
written on my body,
an anodyne for your absence.

Heather Has a Mommy and a Daddy

by R. E. Neu

Deep in the heart of Dullsville, at the end of a cul-de-sac, be-hind a lawn of scratchy brown grass dotted with giant plastic butterflies, three flaking cement deer, and a philodendron the size of Bob Hoskins, though with fewer decorative parts, lives Heather Thompson.

Heather has a mommy and a daddy. Heather's daddy is an accountant. Her mommy is a homemaker. Before Heather was born they met, fell in love, and got married.

"I love you very much and I'm having your child," Heather's mommy said.

Danitra is Heather's best friend. One of Danitra's daddies is an empowerment facilitator. The other is an aura consultant. Danitra doesn't know what they do at work, except they don't need briefcases. Before Danitra was born her daddies met and fell in love, and after 17 years spent discussing caring and sup-port, handling acceptance, and negotiating intimacy, they had a commitment ceremony.

"I love you very much and I'm designing the rings," Danitra's Daddy Mike said.

One day in school Heather's teacher, Mrs. Weinberg-Lopez, tells the class to draw pictures of their families.

Danitra draws two men, Julio draws two women, and Heather draws a man and a woman.

Keanu points at the woman Heather drew, with squiggly yellow hair, a crude red dress, and simple brown shoes. "This dad here's got some ugly drag going on," he says.

At lunch time Danitra sits on the bench next to Heather and pulls a sandwich out of a brown paper bag.

"Want to trade?" Danitra asks. "I've got grilled eggplant and goat cheese on marjoram foccacia."

"Um, I didn't bring lunch," Heather stammers, kicking her brown paper bag out of sight. "I'm...uh...on a diet."

"*Diet*?" Danitra asks. "Haven't your dads told you not to buy into that patriarchal looks-based chauvinism? And anyway, what's *this* then?" she asks, holding up the bag with HAVE A SUPER DAY! written in sparkle marker on it.

Julio, who was listening nearby, runs up and grabs Heather's lunch. "Yeah, what's this? It's *somebody's* lunch!"

Heather jumps at the bag, but Julio holds it out of reach. "You give that back!" Heather snaps.

"Try and make me!" Julio chides. He pulls Heather's sandwich apart and drops it like it's electrified. He wobbles away, clutching his stomach.

"Oh, my God!" he cries. "There's like *dead* stuff in here!"

Danitra looks at the sandwich lying on the cement. "Is that *meat*? Is that like *Spam*?"

Claudia, sitting quietly at the other end of the bench, bursts into tears. "Heather's eating *Bambi*!"

"It's friggin' Wonder Bread!" Julio scoffs.

Keanu walks toward the bread and peers at it. "And it's got *lube* all over it!"

"You idiot, that's *mayonnaise.*"

"What's mayonnaise?"

"It's like hummus for heterosexuals."

"Heterosexuals?" Keanu asks. "Heather's mommy and daddy are heterosexuals?"

Heather starts to yell. "No! I don't have a mommy and a daddy. I've got two daddies!"

"Hell-o-o-o!" Danitra says, drawing the word out to 12 syllables. "We can see your *clothes!*"

"Um..." Heather stalls, "then I've got two mommies."

"And we've seen you play baseball," Julio answers.

Heather, unable to think of a response, sits on the bench and starts to cry. Danitra pulls a robin's-egg–blue bandanna from her pocket and dabs at Heather's face.

"Maybe your mom's not really a woman," Danitra offers.

"Well," Heather says, sniffing, "she cleans the house, and cooks, and does the laundry."

Danitra fumes. "We're trying to establish that she's *female,* not that she's an *idiot.*"

"Maybe your dad's not really a man," Julio suggests.

"Well," Heather answers, wiping her nose. "He's big and strong and he's got a moustache."

Several of the children wondered what this proved, but nobody said anything.

"So let's say you've got a mom and a dad," Keanu says. "Then where did *you* come from?"

Heather thinks for a minute. "They went to bed together, and then I was born." Some of her friends express further interest, but Heather doesn't have a brochure. "Daddy put his thing in mommy—"

"Oh, man," Keanu interjects. "Is that *legal?*"

"Hell-o-o-o!" sings Danitra, who gets the word up to 18 syllables this time. "We're in Cali*for*nia!"

"And nine months later I came out of my mommy's tummy," Heather adds.

Several of the children wonder why they didn't hire a surrogate with a vagina, but nobody says anything.

One night there is a dance at Heather's school and her parents offer to chaperone. While Heather is dancing with Danitra, she sees out of the corner of her eye her mom and dad—making their way onto the dance floor. She watches in horror as her mom stands there swaying, her gingham granny dress limply hanging to the floor. She grimaces as her dad starts chopping at the air like Jackie Chan being attacked by locusts. Occasionally their movement coincides with the beat.

Heather runs to the bathroom crying.

"Heather, don't feel so bad," Danitra says. "Lots of kids have embarrassing parents." She starts to lead Heather out of the bathroom, then stops. "Um, maybe we should stay in here a while longer," Danitra decides. "They just started doing the Bump."

One day the class projects are due. Heather brings in the model she's made. It's a lump of brown Play-Doh with ketchup poured over it, dotted with marshmallows stuck on with toothpicks. She sets it on the table as her teacher comes over to look.

"Why, Heather! That's...*nice!* Very, very nice!"

"What the hell is it?" Tommy asks.

"Tommy! Heather's parents had me over for dinner once. This is what they call 'Salisbury steak.'"

Heather bursts into tears. "No it's not! It's a volcano! That's lava, and that's steam coming out!"

Mrs. Weinberg-Lopez comforts Heather. Meanwhile, Danitra enters and places her project next to Heather's on the table.

"Why, Danitra—what's this?"

Danitra delicately removes the sheet protecting her project.

"Versailles."

Heather takes a look at the tiny replica of Louis XIV's summer home, constructed by Danitra and her two dads out of 200 cubic yards of teak plank, 30 square feet of gold leaf, 60 pounds of Italian travertine marble from the same quarry Michelangelo used, tiny topiary and functional miniature fountains, and cries even harder.

"Why do I have to have a mom and a dad?" Heather sobs. "Why can't my family be like all the rest?"

Mrs. Weinberg-Lopez pulls Heather close. "Children," she says, "Every family is special, including those conforming to the rigid, stereotypical standard of male domination." She starts to tell the class about her own family, including her hearing-impaired Hispanic mother, her height-challenged Israeli father, her Gypsy recovering-substance-abusing brother-in-law, and her Armenian sex-addict half sister, but stops, realizing the school season is only 4,074 hours long.

"Just because Heather's parents are heterosexual doesn't mean they're slow-witted philistines, though there are strong correlations you don't need a Ph.D. in statistics to understand. But Heather is lucky to have a sweet mom and a wonderful dad and a dog named Molly and a hamster named Samson, and they all live together in a *lovely* house. They've got interesting avocado-colored appliances, carpet as long as your hair, and furniture that's by and large wood and that must have taken them *hours* to assemble. There a big plastic sofa that turns into a bed, and a La-Z-Boy—"

"A *what*?" Keanu asks.

"A La-Z-Boy," Mrs. Weinberg-Lopez repeats. "It's a big vinyl chair that reclines."

"Oh, man!" exclaims Keanu, covering his face with his hands. "And I thought our Herman Miller reproductions were embarrassing."

Mrs. Weinberg-Lopez continues. "But the important thing is, they're a family. They're a group united for a common purpose, where each individual is given a sense of empowerment and their shared bonds are formalized in a ritualistic manner."

"Oh," the students respond in unison.

Everybody hugs.

* * *

If you enjoyed this story about Heather, ask your local bookseller for these titles:

Heather's Mom is Narcoleptic
Heather's Dad Has Epstein-Barr
Heather's Sister's Problem Still Puzzles Specialists
and the latest,
It's No Picnic Being Related to Heather

The Rated-X-Files

by Lou Hill

*"In your own words, Agent Mully, tell us what transpired
during your most recent assignment and, specifically, what
happened to your partner, Agent Dana Sculder."*

*Agent Mully sat across from a panel of three senior adminis-
trators. He pulled the collar of his overcoat tight around him.
Seated next to him was his supervisor, Assistant Director Skinnier.*

*Mully leaned closer to the microphone and began speaking.
"It all began early one morning approximately two weeks ago."*

"Sculder? Wake up, we've got a case."

Dana Sculder's eyes flew open. There on the edge of her bed
sat her partner Fox Mully, wearing a lopsided grin.

"Good morning, Sunshine."

"Mully? How did you get in here?" Sculder grabbed at the
covers, pulling them under her chin. She glanced around the bedroom. The window was wide open, the curtains pushed back.

"Did you climb in through my window?" she asked, perplexed, uncertain she was truly awake.

Mully shrugged.

"Mully, I'm on the third floor."

"You climbed up three floors and entered her apartment through a window?"

"I needed the exercise."

"What if I'd, you know, been with someone?" Sculder asked.

Mully lowered his head and raised one eyebrow. "Oh, puh-le-e-eze. Get real, Sculder."

"It could happen," she protested. "What time is it?"

Mully glanced at his watch. "6:05 A.M. C'mon, we've gotta get going."

"OK, but I'm not getting out of this bed until you leave the room."

Mully stood. "Fine, be that way. I can take a hint." He crossed the room and opened the door. "I'll just go root through your fridge while I'm waiting."

Sculder climbed from the bed and padded into the bathroom.

In the kitchen Mully could hear the shower running. He stood in front of the refrigerator with the door wide open. *Not much of a selection,* he thought. His own refrigerator was normally stocked with several half-eaten boxes of Chinese take-out. He grabbed a carton of orange juice, opened it, and drank deeply, then replaced it on the shelf.

"Mully, I'm ready." Her voice startled him. Sculder stood in the doorway, completely dressed, overcoat in hand.

"Geez, Sculder, you're fast. How do you do that?"

"Practice, Mully. Where are we headed? What's the case? And why do our cases always begin at such godforsaken times?"

"Just outside the city. Possible alien abductions. Because we chase things that go bump in the night. C'mon, let's go. Plenty of time to sleep when you're dead."

Mully reached into the backseat and picked up a manila folder. He handed the folder to Sculder. "Over the past eight months eight women have disappeared from the same home. One of the families has requested our assistance."

"Disappeared?" Sculder opened the folder. It contained photographs and bios of the victims. Sculder flipped through the photographs. Their ages ranged mid 30s to late 40s. All good-looking, she noted. Very good-looking.

"Are you saying all these women were...?"

"Queers. Dykes. Butch babes. Macho mamas. Women-lovin'-women. A little sprinkle of lipstick lesbians for good measure. You got it." His grin widened.

"Perhaps they left of their own accord. What makes you so certain this is a case for the X-Files?"

"Each disappearance occurred in the middle of the night. The women were last seen at dinner and had retired for the evening. The guard reported no one entering or departing the grounds. The next morning when they failed to come down for breakfast, Ms. Dionysus personally checked the room. There was no sign of struggle. No blood. No bodies. Clothes and other possessions were left behind. There have been no ransom notes."

"Does Skinnier know about this?"

"Skinnier is the family requesting our assistance. The last woman to disappear was his niece. She was using the name Artemis. Her picture is the one on top."

Director Skinnier's niece was an attractive woman with blond hair and blue eyes. She appeared to be in her mid 30s. According to the bio, she had graduated from a private women's college with a degree in women's studies and English literature. She was also a published poet.

"Is this true, Director Skinnier? Did you specifically request that Agents Mully and Sculder look into the disappearance of your niece?"

"Yes, sir. I knew if anyone could get to the bottom of it, they could."

Mully pulled into the drive of a large private estate surrounded by a high brick wall. They stopped at a gate manned by a burly guard with a shaved head wearing jungle fatigue trousers and combat boots. The name tag on the jacket identified the guard as 'Tigger.'

"Name?" the guard demanded. Only when the guard spoke did Sculder realize Tigger was a woman.

"I'm Agent Mully. And this is my partner, Agent Sculder." Mully flashed his identification card. "We're with the FBI."

Tigger leaned down to take a closer look at Sculder, her scowl replaced by a salacious grin. "Well, well, well. Good morning, Agent Sculder." She wiggled her eyebrows.

Sculder nodded quietly. When Mully turned toward her, she merely shrugged.

Tigger stepped into the guardhouse and pressed a button on the intercom. She stepped into the doorway and motioned for them to proceed.

"*Tigger?* Mully, who lives here?" Sculder asked. She glanced out the back window. Tigger stood in the driveway, watching the car as it approached the house.

"It's not a who, Sculder. It's a what. The Daughters of Sapphistry. It's an organization dedicated to the study of the poetry and life of Sappho. She's the—"

"I know who she was, Mully. I'm a doctor, for crying out loud."

"You never cease to amaze me, Sculder," Mully chuckled.

"Is this some type of cult?"

"I don't think so. Their leader, Ms. Dionysus, describes them as lesbian poets, writers, and philosophers. They come to the, uh, school on a grant. They study Sappho. And Greek goddesses."

"Wait a minute. You said she was using the name Artemis."

"Yeah, each woman adopts the name of a Greek goddess for the duration of her stay. The idea is to leave the everyday world behind and immerse themselves in their studies."

"And do they wear togas and eat while reclining as well?"

"Who knows, Sculder? Maybe you should ask."

Mully parked the car. As they approached the front door, it opened. A tall, good-looking blond with piercing green eyes, broad shoulders, and perfect teeth stood in the doorway.

"No toga," Mully whispered.

"Agent Mully? I'm Dionysus." She pumped Mully's hand vigorously, then turned to Sculder. Her eyes drank in Dana's light auburn hair, cream-white complexion, and large blue eyes.

"And you are?" she asked softly, extending her hand.

"I'm Agent Sculder. Dana Sculder." Sculder blushed furiously.

They followed Dionysus through the foyer into the main room of the house. True to its intent, the house was decorated with paintings and statues of ancient Greece and Greek goddesses. The furniture consisted of low backless couches, similar to futons, and low tables. Mully and Sculder sat on one of the sofas. Dionysus reclined on another.

"You have questions," she stated simply. "Ask."

"Yes, well, why don't we begin with your version of what's been happening here during the last eight months," Mully said.

Sculder watched the woman as she recounted the events. She

suspected foul play, pure and simple. Those eight women were somewhere in the house, or on the grounds. Or in the ground. And perhaps Dionysus knew more about what had happened to them than she was admitting.

"And when I checked their rooms, they were gone. Just vanished." Dionysus smiled.

"Did they say or do anything in the days prior to their disappearance that would have indicated that perhaps they were upset or despondent? Anything that might indicate a desire to leave?"

Dionysus hesitated for a moment. "No, nothing like that. And if they wished to leave they were free to do so," she said. "But there was something…."

"Yes?" Sculder prompted.

Dionysus leaned toward Sculder. "Several of them mentioned that they had been having vivid dreams. And they were very similar in nature."

"What about the other women? Did they happen to mention any dreams?"

"No, but that doesn't mean it didn't happen."

"What were the dreams about? Do you remember?" Mully asked.

"Yes. They said a mist had appeared at the foot of their bed. Slowly, the mist became a beautiful woman. She spoke to them softly, calling them by their adopted Goddess name. Then she kissed them."

"What was their reaction to the dream?" Sculder asked.

"They were ecstatic." Dionysus looked puzzled by the question. "They felt inspired by the vision. Wouldn't you be?"

Sculder blushed. Was this woman assuming she was a lesbian? "Didn't you find it a bit odd that each of the dreams was so much alike?"

"No, not that I can remember." Dionysus turned to Agent

Sculder. "I didn't really connect it at first. I mean, it happened over a period of several months. But when it happened this last time, to Artemis, I did wonder."

"Has anyone ever seen this vision anywhere else in the house?"

"Mully, are you saying you think the house is haunted?"

"I didn't say that. You said that. Did I say that?"

Dionysus stopped in front of the door. Room 69. "My favorite number," she said with a wink. She turned a key in the lock, opened the door, and flipped on the light.

"Were the windows open or closed?" Sculder asked.

"Closed and locked."

"And the door?"

"Locked from the inside. I used my master key to open it."

"What happened to their personal effects?" Mully asked.

"I boxed them up and moved them to the basement."

"Why weren't they shipped to the next of kin?" Sculder asked.

"Except for Artemis, there was no next of kin. No family, no lover," Dionysus explained. She stared at Sculder as she spoke as though making some pronouncement. "Would you like to see the boxes?"

"Sure," Mully answered. "Sculder, you check out the room. I'll go down and check out the personal effects."

Sculder listened as Mully and Dionysus headed down the hallway to the stairs.

Alone in the room, she looked around.

The room was almost Spartan. A single bed. A chest of drawers. A desk and a chair. A painting reminiscent of hotel art hanging over the bed.

She opened the closet door. On the back of the door hung a full-length mirror. Staring at her reflection in the mirror, she suddenly felt compelled to search for visible signs of aging, a process she was growing increasingly more aware of with each new gray hair and wrinkle. Each seemed to loudly proclaim the passing of time.

Sculder turned slowly, viewing her body with a critical eye. Petite, proportionately built. *Not bad,* she thought. She ran a hand across one breast, cupping it briefly. Her nipple hardened at the touch. She thought of Ethan, a boyfriend of sorts from the distant past. Ethan had never really aroused her, she thought.

"Excuse me, Agent Mully, but how could you possibly know about something which supposedly happened while Agent Sculder was alone in an unoccupied room?"

"Sir, Agent Sculder was an inveterate note taker. I mean, to say that the woman was anal-retentive would be an understatement. I mean, can you say obsessive-compulsive?"

"Yes, well, please continue."

In a corner of the mirror Sculder became aware of some movement. She turned quickly, pulling her service revolver in the same moment. "Who's there?"

There was no one else in the room. Yet Sculder had the feeling she was not alone. She closed the closet door, embarrassed by her unexplained need for self-appraisal in the midst of a crime scene.

She checked inside the drawers. She checked under the drawers and behind the drawers. Nothing. She sat down at the desk and ran her hands along the bottom of the desk. Nothing. She ran her hands along the edges of the painting over the bed. The painting hung from a single nail via a thin wire. She pulled the frame from the wall and was astonished to discover a labrys sketched on the wall behind the painting.

She sat at the end of the bed, staring up at the labrys. It appeared almost three dimensional. Something about it seemed almost hypnotic. Suddenly the lights in the room went out. "Who's there?"

Sculder turned. The movement in the room was now clearly visible. A silver, mistlike cloud floated near the end of the bed. Dana watched carefully as it approached her. She could almost swear a face was visible in the cloud. Then, just as suddenly, the lights came on again.

"Sculder?" It was Mully. "Why are you sitting in the dark?"

"Mully, did you see it?"

"See what?" Mully asked.

"That cloudlike formation. It's gone now. But I swear it was hovering at the end of the bed."

"You saw it?" Dionysus exclaimed. "Damn. I've never seen it."

"I think what we're dealing with here is an E.B.E.," Mully said. "An extraterrestrial biological entity."

"What's he talking about?" Dionysus asked.

"You don't want to know," Sculder answered.

"I think the missing women were abducted by aliens."

Dionysus looked at Sculder. "Is he kidding?"

Sculder raised one eyebrow and shrugged. "Anything in the personal effects?"

"A nice selection of vibrators and dil—Whoa! What's this?" He moved to the wall and ran his hand over the labrys. He turned toward Dionysus.

"It's a labrys. But I've never seen it before. I didn't put it there."

"Maybe we better take a look at the other rooms. Talk to your other guests."

"You can check out the whole house, but I'm afraid there are no other guests. After the last disappearance we thought it best to send everyone home until we figured out what was going on.

And I can guarantee you won't find another one of those in any room in the building."

"Did you, Agent Mully?"
"Did I what, sir?" Mully asked, blinking.
"Did you find another, uh, labrys anywhere in the building?"
"No, sir, we did not. But it's possible that any others were re-moved after the, uh, disappearance."

When they returned to their office, it was late in the afternoon.

"Sculder, it makes perfect sense," Mully continued. "The E.B.E. could take on the guise of a beautiful woman so as not to alarm its victims."

"Mully, I'm certain I saw the mist Dionysus spoke of. But I believe there must be some other explanation. I think we need to do a background check on the school. And Dionysus. Any idea what her real name is?"

"Whoa! A shape-shifting E.B.E."

"Mully, are you listening to me?"

"The touch is probably a way to mark the victim. Maybe it acts as some sort of beacon for the alien craft. Maybe the labrys was a sign. A marker."

Sculder sighed deeply. He's off again, she thought. She moved to her corner of the office, wishing again that she had an actual desk to work from. She sat at the computer terminal and typed in "School of Sapphistry." Seconds later she was reading the school's Web page. It included a list of workshops and an application form for grants. Yadda yadda, Sappho. Yadda yadda, Isle of Lesbos. Yadda yadda, goddess worship. Hmm, nothing unusual. Also on the page was a photo of Dionysus. Sculder studied the photograph carefully. She felt an unusual stirring in her loins. At the bottom of the page she noticed a tiny labrys much like the one she had discovered on the wall of room 69. Next to it was the name Dionysus.

"Mully, I think I'm going to drive back over to the School. I'd like to talk to Dionysus. Want to come with?"

"Uh, no, you go on without me. I'm gonna do a little…uh…research of my own. With some guys I know. Call me if you find anything."

"So you allowed Agent Sculder to return to the scene of the crimes alone?"

"Duh. Yes, I did. I mean, c'mon. We weren't exactly joined at the hip. She's a big girl. She can handle herself. Besides I had important…uh…research to do."

"What kind of research, Agent Mully?"

"Uh…I'm not at liberty to discuss the nature of my research at this time, sir."

Sculder pulled up to the guardhouse. A tall, somber black woman stepped up to her window. "May I help you?"

Sculder smiled and held out her identification. "I need to see Dionysus." Sculder wondered where Tigger was.

The guard nodded and stepped back into the guardhouse. A moment later she waved Sculder through the gate.

Dionysus met her at the door. "Agent Sculder, Dana—do you mind if I call you Dana? Please, come in. I was hoping I'd have some time alone with you."

"You were?" Sculder asked. She allowed Dionysus to take her coat and followed her into the living room. Two glasses, a flask, and a tray of grapes and cheeses sat on one of the low tables. "I'm sorry. Am I interrupting something?"

"No, not at all. Like I said, I was hoping to have some time alone with you. Please join me." Dionysus filled the glasses with an amber-colored liquid. "I think you'll like this. It's Chaucer's Mead, a honey-based wine."

Sculder normally didn't drink, especially not on duty. But it had been a long day and the wine intrigued her, as did her hostess. She sipped the wine and then drank more deeply. The wine tasted like nothing she had ever experienced. Within minutes she began to feel strange, light-headed. A warm sensation ran through her body.

"Agent Sculder? Dana?"

Dana could hear Dionysus. Something kept her from responding. She watched as Dionysus moved toward her. She felt the hands on her face and neck. She felt the warmth of lips against hers. Then she was moving. Dionysus led her up the stairs, down the hallway, and into a bathroom. Dionysus turned on the water in the bathtub. She undressed Dana.

"You are beautiful, Dana. And very special. You shall be called...Dione, for the mother of Aphrodite. Sappho has chosen you. It is most unusual that she would take two in one month. But I knew she would like you the moment I saw you."

Sculder felt as though she were watching from somewhere deep inside herself. She didn't feel afraid, just curious.

Dionysus stood in front of her. She ran her eyes over Dana's naked body. Dionysus turned the water off. She then peeled off her own clothes. Dana watched, admiring Dionysus' body. She found herself longing to touch the blonde woman's breasts. Dionysus took Dana's hand and pulled her toward the tub. They sank together into the warm sudsy water. Dana closed her eyes as Dionysus washed her. She felt so warm and so relaxed.

"Agent Mully, please. I must insist that you report only those facts that you know for a certainty."

"Sir, I know Agent Sculder. And I spoke extensively with Ms.

Dionysus. I am telling you what I believe to be the actual circumstances of the evening in question. Now, please let me continue. Where was I? Oh, yeah."

Dana leaned back against Dionysus. Dionysus caressed her face, her neck, her breasts. Under the influence of the drugged wine Dana felt helpless to resist. In fact, she felt compelled to go along with the obviously deranged Dionysus. In order to discover what had happened to the other victims, the missing women.

Dionysus kissed Dana deeply. It was unlike any other kiss Dana had ever experienced. She felt the now-familiar stirring in her loins. She pressed against Dionysus, who was obviously becoming greatly aroused.

Dionysus stood. She pulled Dana from the tub and dried her body carefully.

The panel of Senior Administrators leaned forward, waiting with bated breath as Mully described how Dionysus had dried Dana Sculder's wet, naked, lithesome body.

Then they made their way down the hallway. Back to room 69.

Inside the room candles were burning. The labrys on the wall had taken on an energy. It cast an eerie glow over the room.

Dana implored Dionysus with her eyes.

"You may speak, Dione," Dionysus answered.

"Why are you doing this?" Dana asked. "I mean, if it's about sex, well—"

"Sex? Is that all you think this is about? Oh, you couldn't be more wrong. You think I'm some sort of sex-crazed lesbian serial killer?"

"Well, the thought had crossed my mind," Dana admitted.

Dionysus wrapped her arms around Dana, pulling her closer.

She covered Dana's mouth with her own and kissed her soulfully.

"Do you think I have a problem getting women?" Dionysus asked softly.

"No, no, no," Dana answered. She pulled Dionysus back for a second, longer, deeper kiss.

"This is really happening, Dione. You have been chosen to join Sappho on the Isle of Lesbos. You shall spend eternity living and studying with Sappho, making love to beautiful women. You will be at peace. I envy you. But I will join you there someday. When Sappho decides it is my time."

"But I've never been with another woman," Dana said. "I've never even thought about it."

"You know that's not true. You know that's why you bury yourself in your work. That's why you and Agent Mully have never so much as kissed. You've never been attracted to men. Admit it."

Dana realized it was true. All of it. And she felt strangely relieved to have it out in the open. But still, she knew Dionysus must be a sex-crazed lesbian serial killer. The alternative was just too strange. Too much like something Fox would believe.

"You know that she believed that, Agent Mully?"

"Yes sir. She told Dionysus exactly that. It really hurt my feelings too."

"Make love to me, Dionysus. If I'm going to die, I don't want to die without experiencing an orgasm at least once in my life."

Dionysus was more than willing to comply with her request. She explored Dana's body with the lust of a sailor six months at sea. She caressed, explored, licked and savaged every inch of Dana's willing flesh. The formerly stiff-backed agent became a wild woman, moaning, scratching, begging for more. She soon wore Dionysus out.

"More!" Sculder cried. "Again!" She straddled the exhausted Dionysus.

"I can't, please," Dionysus pleaded.

This is my chance, Sculder thought. Now she'll tell me the truth about her victims. "Dionysus, please," she cooed. "Before I die, please, won't you tell me what you did with those other women?"

Suddenly the room grew brighter. Sculder turned toward the light. There, moving toward the bed, was the same cloud-like mist....

"Wait a second. Earlier you described it as a mistlike cloud. Now you're saying it was a cloudlike mist. Which is it, Agent Mully?"

"Cloudlike mist. Mistlike cloud. What difference does it make?" Mully demanded.

"Well, none I guess."

"All right then, geez, let me continue."

It moved toward them slowly. It exuded a light which grew more and more brilliant. Sculder lifted her hand to shield her eyes. Dionysus slipped out from under her and lay, prostrate, on the floor.

"What is it?" Sculder cried.

"Praise be to Sappho!" Dionysus called. "She has come for her chosen."

As Sculder watched, the form of a woman became clear. The woman's face was luminescent. Sculder lowered her hand. She was drawn to the woman's beauty.

"Do not be afraid, Dione," a voice commanded. "You have been chosen to join us. Come." The vision stretched out her hand. "You have done well, Dionysus. You shall be rewarded."

Dana glanced down at Dionysus. "Tell Mully I believe," Dana said, her own face radiant. "Tell him to be true to himself." Then she reached out toward the radiant being and disappeared.

The panel of Senior Administrators sat back in their chairs.

"Gentlemen," Director Skinnier said. "The scenario Agent Mully has described for you is the direct result of interviews with Ms Dionysus and his own personal research into the area of alien abductions."

"Director Skinnier, are you and Agent Mully suggesting that this was an alien abduction?"

"Yes!" Agent Mully shouted. "I think what we are dealing with here is a time-traveling, shape-shifting, extraterrestrial biological entity. This alien calling itself Sappho has come to our time to kidnap our lesbian population."

"Agent Mully, why on earth would aliens wish to abduct the earth's lesbians?"

"I don't know, sir. I honestly don't know. Perhaps Sappho herself was an alien. Perhaps she has established a new Isle of Lesbos somewhere in the cosmos. She is kidnapping the best-looking, brightest, most articulate lesbian minds our country has produced."

"Perhaps this is the biggest crock of bull I've ever heard in my life. I would like to interrogate this Dionysus myself, Director Skinnier."

"Well, sir, that isn't possible." Director Skinnier's bald head grew damp with perspiration.

"Why not?" the Administrator demanded.

"Because she disappeared from protective custody three nights ago."

"Let me guess—you found a labrys in the room."

"Yes sir, I did. Good guess, sir."

"That will be all, gentlemen," the Administrator growled. *"You're dismissed. We'll look into this matter further."*

Director Skinnier and Agent Mully walked down the corridor of the J. Edgar Hoover Federal Bureau of Investigations Building. As they approached Skinnier's office, he stopped.

"Mully, why do you suppose this alien took my niece and Agent Sculder?"

"Well sir, I think it's possible that they were lonely here. Perhaps that made them more susceptible. I'd like to think they're happier where ever they are."

"Mully, what did Sculder mean when she said 'be true to yourself?'" Skinnier asked.

"Well," Agent Mully began. He looked down at the floor for a moment. "I think she meant I shouldn't let the bastards get me down. Not you, sir." He began unbuttoning his overcoat. "And that I should be myself."

"I never thought you had a problem with that, Mully," Skinnier said.

"No, sir. But even you've never known the *real* me!" Mully cried, flinging the coat to the ground.

Skinnier shrank back into a doorway. Underneath the heavy overcoat, Mully wore a bright pink tutu and tights. As Agent Mully ran down the hallway, Director Skinnier could hear him singing, "It's raining men! Hallelujah! It's raining men! I'm free! And I'm going to be true to me, myself, and I!"

MEMO FROM THE DESK OF DEPUTY DIRECTOR SKINNIER:

FOLLOWING THE DISAPPEARANCE OF AGENTS SCULDER AND MULLY AND EFFECTIVE IMMEDIATELY, THE OFFICE FORMERLY KNOWN AS THE X-FILES IS CLOSED. FURTHER INVESTIGATION IS PENDING.

About the Contributors

Joanne Ashwell was born in Seattle. The author quickly traded her umbrellas for sandals, venturing to Florida, Hawaii, and California. After postgraduate English studies at the University of Maryland, she joined an intelligence organization and worked for many years in South America and Europe. She recently retired from a second career at the University of California, San Diego, and relaxes in sunny San Diego, proud Gateway to Tijuana.

Dean Backus is a native of the Pacific Northwest, where he has won two awards for his short stories. As a solo playwright he has authored *Thus With A Kiss* (1993 New City Playwrights' Festival Runner-Up for Best Play; 1995 San Francisco Fringe Festival Audience Award), *Is This Seat Taken?* ("Best Of" the 1996 San Francisco Fringe Festival), and *The Vampers* (1997). He has also collaborated on the award-winning *Jumping the Broom* (1993) at San Francisco's Theatre Rhinoceros; in Rhino's *Playwrights' Stew* (1994); and in *Sexy Shorts* (1996) at

San Francisco's New Conservatory theater. Dean has also been an award-winning essayist for *Frontiers* magazine (June 1995), a published poet and lyricist, and is currently hard at work on three scripts and a novel. He resides in Silicon Valley with his partner, Jonathan, occasionally wonders if he should get off of decaf coffee, and *loves* collaborating on projects (hint, hint). He offers special thanks to his friend Christine, who *never* "show(ed) her bosom before 3."

Barry Becker loves the art of storytelling in every medium. In 1991, he cofounded Washington, D.C.'s gay and lesbian film festival, and in 5 years at its helm built it into one of the largest in the U.S. He now manages Lambda Rising Bookstore's Delaware outpost, writes regular columns for Letters from CAMP Rehoboth, and produces Delaware's only Independent Film Festival. He admits he doesn't know anyone who has actually perished at any of Rehoboth Beach's many yummy restaurants or been shot at from a plane, and reminds Patricia Cornwell's lawyers that parody is a fabulous form of flattery.

Caril Behr was born in Cape Town, South Africa. She came to the United Kingdom in 1971, and now lives in North London. She teaches art to adults with special needs at a Further Education College and takes photographs whenever she can. Her short stories have appeared in *New London Writers* and *Queer Words (UK)*. She was awarded the annual Queer Words Short Story Prize in 1996 and 1997.

Shari J. Berman is a teacher, textbook author, freelance journalist, copywriter, publishing consultant, and translator. She and her life partner have a small company with branches in Kona, Hawaii, and Tokyo, Japan, that manages these language services. She has completed three novels and a short story collection. She won first prize in the Lavender Life fifth anniversary short story contest. Her online lesbian serial, *The Selena Stories,* can be found at: http://wowwomen.com/visibilities/fiction_home.html.

Jeff Black lives in Chicago. He is author of the novels *Extra Credit* and *Gardy & Erin. The Flames,* a musical for which he wrote the book, has been performed in New York and Boston. He is currently completing his next novel, *Planting Eli.*

Robert Carron is an artist whose paintings have been in numerous exhibitions and collections. He is the author of *Human Divinity and the Scientific Proof of God*, and has won an Editor's Choice Award from the National Library of Poetry. He lives in Portland, Oregon.

A former college newspaper editor, **Patrick Cather** now writes fiction and poetry, and hopes he has inherited some literary talent from his distant aunt, Willa Cather. He lives in Birmingham, Alabama, where he collects Rookwood Pottery, serves on the board of Birmingham AIDS Outreach, and contributes a column, "Out…Of The Passing Scene," to *The Alabama Forum,* the local gay and lesbian newspaper. He recently completed revisions on a two-act play, *The Last Apollo Ball.*

Susie Day writes political satire for publications such as *Sojourner*, *Z Magazine*, and *LGNY*. She has also written unsatirically for various newspapers and magazines about prison and labor issues. And though she does not think Revolution is a bad idea, she would choose Life over Politics any day.

Caitlin E. Glasson is a 32-year-old professional artist living in Kitchener, Ontario. Turn-ons include her partner, stockings, a bottle of wine, and candlelight (and occasionally power tools). Turnoffs include neoconservatism and spending eternity being preached at by sanctimonious self-righteous zealots with harps.

Originally from Washington, D.C., **Jeffrey M. Hannan** now lives with his lover and their dogs in Berkeley, California, where they are often mistaken for lesbians. A cum laude graduate of the University of California, San Diego, Literature and Writing Program, he recently completed his first novel, *Third Son,* and is currently working on a collection of short fiction. "Chandler Comes Out" is his second appearance in an Alyson publication; the first was "Seeing Red" in the Jack Hart anthology *The Day We Met.*

Trebor Healey's work has appeared in *The James White Review, Evergreen Chronicles, RFD, The Bad Boy Book of Erotic Poetry, Between the Cracks, Sex Spoken Here,* and *Queer Dharma.* In 1994 he was coeditor of *Beyond Definition: New Writing from Gay and Lesbian San Francisco.* He is currently living in Los Angeles and working on a novel.

Lou Hill resides in southeastern Michigan with her partner of six years, their ten-year-old son, and a houseful of pets. Writing has been a lifelong passion, although she didn't actively seek publication until she was in her 40s. She has had several fiction and nonfiction stories published in anthologies and recently signed a book contract.

M.S. "Max" Hunter, a graduate of Andover, Harvard, and B.U. Law School, had careers in law, government, and business before he "retired" and became a writer. Besides several short stories, he has published two novels, *The Buccaneer* (Alyson 1989), which was a Lammy finalist that year, and *The Final Bell* (Alyson 1996), the first gay novel set in the world of professional boxing. His latest novel, *A Killing in Paradise,* is currently seeking a publisher. He lives in Key West, Florida, with a former business partner, two cats, and a young lover.

Jeribee moved to La Crescenta, a Los Angeles suburb, from San Antonio in 1978 with his life companion, Ron. They opened a flower shop, which they ran for nine years. Jeribee's short fiction has appeared in several magazines. He and Ron are now building their own electronic commerce business, but writing stories still plays an important part in Jeribee's life.

Rik Isensee is the author of three self-help books for gay men: *Love Between Men, Reclaiming Your Life,* and *Ready or Not?* (a guide for gay men at midlife). He lives in San Francisco, where he ponders the perplexities of postmodern urban gay culture.

Raymond Luczak is the editor of the anthology *Eyes Of Desire: A Deaf Gay & Lesbian Reader* (Alyson) and the author of *St. Michael's Fall* (Deaf Life Press). A writer of all trades with various published pieces as well as plays produced all over the country, Raymond Luczak resides in New York City and in cyberspace (RayLuczak@aol.com).

Born in West Virginia and now living in Philadelphia, **Kelly McQuain** teaches writing at University of the Arts, Temple University, and Community College of Philadelphia. His short stories have appeared in *The Inquirer Sunday Magazine, Best Gay Erotica 1997, Kansas Quarterly/Arkansas Review, The*

Sycamore Review, Alyson's *Certain Voices* anthology, and three times in *The James White Review*. His nonfiction essays have appeared in Alyson's *Generation Q* and *The Journal of Gay, Lesbian, and Bisexual Identity*. He is a contributing editor to *Art & Understanding* magazine and a prize-winning poet.

Bonnie J. Morris, Ph.D, is a devoted worker-historian in the women's music festival community, and has just written the first full-length book on festival culture (available from Alyson.) She is the author of two other books plus more than 50 articles and essays, and teaches women's studies at George Washington University in Washington, D.C.

R. E. Neu's writing has appeared in numerous publications, including the *New York Times Book Review, Los Angeles* magazine, and the *Los Angeles Times,* as well as several fiction anthologies, including Alyson's *The Ghost of Carmen Miranda and Other Spooky Gay & Lesbian Tales*. He was also a contributing writer for *Spy* magazine, back when it was funny.

Ellen Orleans is the author of four humor books, including *Still Can't Keep A Straight Face* and the Lammy award–winning *The Butches of Madison County* (all Laugh Lines Press). Her essays have appeared in the Women's Glib series, *Creme de la Femme* (Random House), *Funny Times,* and *The Washington Post,* among others. Her first play, "God, Guilt, and Gefilte Fish," was a smashing success at its premiere in Boulder; Ellen is always on the lookout for theater companies interested in producing it. She's currently working on a novel about a family vacation at the Jersey Shore.

Jack Pantaleo received his Master of Arts in Writing from the

University of San Francisco and has taught writing at Vista Community College in Berkeley. His musical, *The Gospel According to the Angel Julius,* was last produced at the Bayfront Theatre at Fort Mason in San Francisco and in Columbus, Ohio, in February, 1997. His articles and stories have appeared in *The Other Side, Second Stone,* and *Silver Quill.* The second edition of his booklet, *Sexuality and Spirituality, An Invitation to Wholeness,* was published by Triam Agency in 1998. He is currently working on his second novel.

Shelly Rafferty is a Lesbian writer, poet, teacher, activist, and parent. Her work has appeared in numerous anthologies including the recent *Hot Ticket* (Alyson), *Hot and Bothered* (Arsenal Pulp Press), and *Close Calls* (St. Martin's Press). Shelly and her young son, Jake, will soon be moving to the mountains.

Michael Dubson Sage has worked in personnel, advertising, and has taught writing and literature at a number of Boston colleges. In addition, he has written regularly for local and regional newspapers and magazines, including *The Curbstone, In Newsweekly,* and *Bay Windows.* He has had stories in the anthologies *Meltdown!* and *The Day We Met,* and he has published erotic fiction under the name Mike McDaniels. In late 1997, his book of humorous, illustrated poetry, *The Odor of Love and Other Aromas,* was published. He has also been a hit at poetry readings and slams and was a member of a now-defunct-because-of-out-of-control-egos Boston improv comedy troupe.

The Saint is a monk who lives in a Cistercian monastery committed to a life of celibacy and devotion to spiritual growth. His work has appeared in *Country Life, Agrarian Reform,* and *Spiricetes: A Journal of Aesthetic Sexuality.*

Amy Schutzer is a poet and fiction writer. She writes about the subtleties and sharpness of landscapes; not just the geological land but the landscape of the body and the emotional/internal ground. Her work has appeared in a variety of literary reviews and magazines, including *Portland Review, Feminist Broadcast Quarterly, Sequoia, Common Lives/Lesbian Lives,* and *Calapooya Collage.* In 1997 she was awarded the Astraea Foundation Grant for fiction.

Anne Seale is a creator of lesbian songs, stories, and plays who has performed on many gay stages, including the Lesbian National Conference, singing tunes from her tape *Sex For Breakfast,* available for $12 from Wildwater Records, POB 56, Webster NY 14580-0056. More of Seale's work can be found in the anthologies *The Ghost of Carmen Miranda and Other Spooky Gay and Lesbian Tales, Love Shook My Heart, Pillow Talk, Hot and Bothered, Ex-lover Weird Shit,* and in issues of *Lesbian Short Fiction.*

A.L. Store is obsessed with Xena. She gets very tingly inside whenever Xena and Gabrielle stare at each other just a bit too long. She has two copies of each episode on tape—one that is worn just before all the good places from rewinding and another that is in pristine condition. As a southern girl, A.L. Store likes to shock the rednecks by kissing her girlfriend in public places.

Michael Van Duzer is a Los Angeles–based playwright/director. His produced plays include: *Mutual Frobnication, The Bottom of the Sea is Cruel, Hopeful Romantic, Cloudburst, Recalled to Life,* and the two included one-acts that were produced together under the umbrella title *Tawdry Tales.* Requests for performance rights should be made through the author. Play history: *Heat the Samovar, Blanche* was originally produced in Los Angeles in 1996 with the following cast: Peter Ilich Tchaikovsky—Dean Howell; Alexei St. Petersburg—Butch Klein; Blanche Tchaikovsky—Mink Stole; Madame von Meck—Michael Dotson. *Posing Strap Pirates* was originally produced in Los Angeles in 1996 with the following cast: Narrator—Jason Moore; Toye Buck—Todd Justice; Miss Marzipan—Mink Stole; Rake Matelot—Dean Howell (later William Rutten); Sabre—Butch Klein; Bilge—Michael Dotson; Beau Ideal—Steve Sobel.

Felicia Von Botchinova is a founding member of BANM (Breasts Are Not Melons)—lesbians against describing breasts as fruit. She also works part-time as a flute-case roadie for LW-PIOTAG—Lesbians Who Play Instruments Other Than Acoustic Guitar. Felicia is currently working on two treatises: "Postgrad dissertations—accessible dialectic suppositions or pansyllabic, helium filled cow dung?" and "Potlucks—the French chef conspiracy to prevent lesbians from learning the culinary arts."

alyson
books

BI ANY OTHER NAME: BISEXUAL PEOPLE SPEAK OUT, *edited by Loraine Hutchins and Lani Kaahumanu.* Women and men from all walks of life describe their lives as bisexuals. These are individuals who have fought prejudice from both the gay and straight segments of society and who have begun only recently to share their experiences.

JOCKS, *by Dan Woog.* Find out what happens when the final closet door—that of men in sports—finally swings open. Is there life after coming out to your teammates? Is there life before coming out? This collection of more than 25 inspiring real-life stories digs deeply into two of America's twin obsessions: sports and sex. Journalist Dan Woog, himself an openly gay soccer coach, interviewed dozens of gay jocks and offers up these inspiring stories of men who are truly champions.

THE GOOD LIFE, *by Gordon Merrick.* In 1943 a high-society murder case drew international attention for its irresistible combination of violent crime, scandalous sex, and enormous wealth. Perry Langham, a dirt-poor Depression-era boy, met and married Bettina Vernon, a rich heiress, and they settled down to live happily ever after. But Perry's eternal attraction to beautiful young men got in the way of the marriage—and Bettina decided to cut him off financially. Gordon Merrick and Charles Hulse put their own fictional stamp on the story, and an entertaining romp through the lives of rich young gay men emerges.

EARLY EMBRACES, *edited by Lindsey Elder.* Tender. Sassy. Loving. Embarrassing. Thrilling. This collection of true, first-person stories by women from around the country describing their first sexual experience with another woman sparkles with laughter, awkward moments, and plenty of hot sex.

CHICKEN, *by Paula Martinac.* Forty-something Lynn is having the proverbial midlife crisis. After being dumped by her longtime lover, she is first pursued by 23-year-old Lexy, then by 25-year-old Jude. Is there any chance Lynn can keep her sanity while dealing with one ex, two demanding new lovers, and three hours of sleep a night? A lesbian tale of love, lust, and the enduringly comic search for Ms. Right in the late '90s.

These books and other Alyson titles are available at your local bookstore.
If you can't find a book listed above or would like more information,
please visit our home page on the World Wide Web at **www.alyson.com**.